The
Turning of the Tide

A. B. Dixon

The Turning of the Tide
Copyright © 2021 by A. B. Dixon

tellwell 🖋

Tellwell Talent
www.tellwell.ca

ISBN
978-0-2288-3867-8 (Paperback)
978-0-2288-3868-5 (eBook)

To
The inspiration for this novel,
My grandfathers and great-grandfathers,
And their volunteer service,
All of whom saw action

Albert Dixon
Infantry Member, Canadian Expeditionary Force, WWI
Regimental number: 2771009

Raymond Dixon
Army Medical Corps Member, Canadian Army Overseas, WWII
Service number: K729

Amil Chornobrywy
Royal Canadian Air Force Member, Canadian Army Overseas, WWII
Service number: 19998   •

Robert Agnew
Navy member, British Expeditionary Force, WWII
Service number: X632

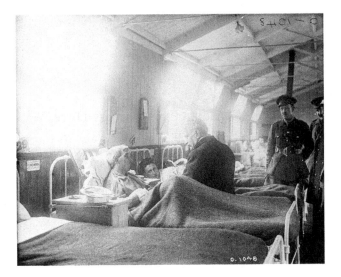

Canadian Prime Minister Sir Robert Borden
speaking to a recovering Canadian soldier in a
military hospital, spring 1917, France. The soldier
sustained his injuries at the battle for Vimy Ridge.

Table of Contents

The Christmas Ball

Lady Aubrey Kingston was, on the surface, everything a lady should be. However, beneath her porcelain skin was a female as conceited and vindictive as she was wealthy. The Kingstons' sprawling estate, Pembina, was located not far from the dominion's capital of Ottawa. Aubrey awoke in her bedroom, where outside, the snow fell lightly that bright December morning of 1913. In her morning frock, Aubrey descended the grand staircase.

Morning prayer was usually in the chapel, but, because it was winter, everyone gathered in the main hall. Her grandfather, Emmett Kingston, was speaking quietly to the butler. The butler was normally addressed by his surname; however, the Kingstons addressed their butler by his Christian name. Llewellyn had been a footman in Emmett's father's manor in England. He then became Emmett's batman. Emmett had been so impressed with his service that he hired Llewellyn to be his butler when Emmett came into his property. Dismissed, the numerous servants made for the green baize door.

Llewellyn was refined and tall. He had toned shoulders and silver-grey hair. He followed a few paces behind in his gentleman's black attire to distinguish himself from the full-liveried footmen.

"Did you sleep well, sweet pea?" said Emmett, the King James Version of the Bible in his hand. The second question was invariably, "What was morning prayer about?"

"God," Aubrey and Emmett said in unison.

Emmett answered his own question, given he was the only one who could. "God only gives his biggest battles to his strongest soldiers." A retired Admiral from His Majesty's Navy, he was forever speaking in terms of warfare. Emmett continued, "The biggest battles usually mean suffering, though one should be honoured Our Lord thinks so much of one's character. These men are mocked, jeered, humiliated, and scorned as the evil one attacks from all sides. Stripped of all integrity, dignity, and pride, their character remains. God's strongest soldiers have the most character — the most courage and resolve. Such traits are needed for the most inordinate battles. And although the most horrid thing the devil has ever done is convince the world he does not exist, and bear in mind he will always encourage a man when acting wrongly, he will never attack more than at two distinct times. The first: when acting righteously. This is why the strongest are given the greatest battles, for only they can survive the full force of the devil, as a gentleman's character is unshakeable and a coward's easily swayed. The second is when a man attempts to abandon the evil one's side, that is to say, by becoming a good or far better person. There is no greater show on earth than this one. This battle is also no greater testimony of how far He will go to bring one back to Him. He will even wage war for one. And at times the force the man is facing is so extensive that He sends His Angels to aid in the struggle. For in a battle against good and evil, character will always prevail, even in warfare."

"How does He choose these people?" Aubrey asked.

"There are two types of males in this world: gentlemen and cowards. And birth, money, titles, or land have nothing to do with either. A man only reveals his integrity, or a country its character, under duress — particularly when he is about to die."

Such a concept was hard for Aubrey to grasp. She knew of only two types of men: masters and servants.

"A gentleman will stand and fight, will go towards a battle and offer his services. A gentleman does not retreat. There is nothing a gentleman abhors more than surrendering."

"What of those who stand in neutrality?"

A great scholar, Emmett recited a passage from one of his favourite novels, *Dante's Inferno.* "'The darkest place in Hell is reserved for those who maintain their neutrality in times of moral crisis.' And these people, sweet pea, are cowards."

"But why are there battles at all?"

"All I can say to that is because the devil exists. However, God has soldiers to triumph over him. It matters not to a gentleman the predicament; he will do what is right until the end. You do not always know who the real gentlemen are, and they are usually the most unsuspecting—"

"And there are so few of them here stuck in the backwaters of the—"

"In this part of the Kingdom, doing the right thing of one's own volition makes all the difference to these colonials, and you ought to commend them for that."

They passed a bowing servant. Their neighbours, the Laurentiens, were hosting their annual and famed Christmas Eve ball the following evening. Because she was seventeen, Aubrey was permitted to attend the dinner but not the ball. A young lady was not permitted to attend balls or dinner parties until she came of age. Aubrey had grown up with the twelve Laurentien children and the two families regarded one another as family. Emmett made the exception for her to attend the greatest of all Edwardian shows: the dinner party.

"Why can't I attend the ball?" said she.

"Violent delights often have violent ends. No balls until you come of age," was her grandfather's stern reply.

"What if an English gentleman, a man like Peter, for instance, is without a partner and I could dance with him?" Since a girl's chief objective in life was to make herself a wife, Aubrey had good reason to attend the ball.

"He might be English, but he is no gentleman."

"But what do you mean?" she cried.

"A gentleman leads solely from the front, for one. Another mark of a gentleman is he will remain serene when he knows the battle is lost. As well, a gentleman will not allow himself to be indebted to another in character."

"But you must want me to marry an aristocrat?"

"Of course, no one else would do for my little girl. But when the time would come to have a proper conversation for Peter's gentleman's agreement to take care of you, I would not have it from him."

"But he is one of the finest gentlemen here!" Aubrey contradicted.

The Edwards were one of the most ancient families in England.

"A man has to be a gentleman to enter into such a contract," Emmett explained. "Bound by personal honour, a gentleman's word is more important than anything else. With his word, he signs the contract that will dictate his actions when no other gentleman is present. It is as well in this absence of other gentlemen that a man reveals himself. A verbal agreement by two gentlemen, or a gentleman's agreement, is not binding legally, and is certainly unnecessarily so, but is far more important than a legal document could be. A gentleman's word is as serious as a law. A gentleman will honour his word until the very end. Besides, you want a man who will go after you, who will be faithful to you, who will fight for you. Peter will not do as such. No more talk of this until you come of age. Besides, why go to the ball if no man will look at you because you are still a child?" Emmett finished, "Sweet pea, be proud you're English and remember, valour comes first." They entered the breakfast room to his newspaper, her lukewarm tea, and to the aromas of their breakfast, of which the third course was her favourite part.

Later in the day, Aubrey was near Emmett's study and heard a conversation through the door that was slightly ajar. Emmett and his fellow Sons of England members were enjoying their brandy.

"Another meeting with the Richardieux," said Sir Westbrook, the father of her dearest friend, Letitia, pet named Lady Bird. "Seraphin, the brilliant businessman he is, was not able to attend the meeting. He stayed in Quebec City. He sent his son instead. The son has a funny name. What was it? No matter. The son's as proud as Lucifer. And, of course, Richardieux is grooming him to take over their family's business. The son is divorced! Can you imagine? I am not aware of a single other family with a divorce to their name. Imagine the shame! I would never let my Letitia near a male like that. And he refuses to learn English, so we had a translator. He gave no apologies for that inconvenience." He said with a snort into his tea, "Typical Frenchman: refuses to be part of our Empire. Honestly," he continued, "If this colony ver goes to war, there'll be conscription because the French will refuse to fight."

The voices of the other gentlemen could be heard as they all laughed softly at the outlandish joke. Aubrey had never heard the term conscription before. A military term to be sure, but what it was exactly she neither knew nor cared. Westbrook helped himself to another of the innumerable dainties placed in and amongst the various coffees and teas.

"Thank God he said he would return to Quebec as soon as the meeting adjourned this morning—"

Emmett stood before Aubrey at the door. "Come in, Aubrey."

The light shone through the bay windows as Emmett, Sir Westbrook, and tall Mr. Lawrence rose to greet her. A lady should not go up to a man smoking; he would be made to do away with the cigar. She stood in the doorway. Emmett explained she was on vacation from Sacred Heart Academy in Regina.

When Aubrey, an only child, was very young, her parents died while abroad on vacation. She had little recollection of her vain father or cold mother. Aubrey became the ward of her paternal grandmother, Gran. Aubrey's maternal grandfather, a widower who became childless with the passing of his daughter, suggested the orphaned grandchild live with him in Ottawa, where he retired. Gran, who did not like girls, was happy to rid herself of her charge. Aubrey adored Emmett for the father figure that he was to her. The pair had a joyful, close bond.

"What are your ambitions after your studies?" inquired Westbrook, a middle-aged, portly man with a kind, fatherly disposition.

To marry was the answer of a proper lady and the one she gave.

"Right," he said and encouraged her on. "You plan to return to Ottawa until you find a suitable husband. Nor do you care to attend University. That shows true intelligence and none of this wanting the right to vote," he stated with an impatient wave of hand. "That is a major problem right now in Parliament. All these suffragettes campaigning for the vote, claiming equal rights for women. You are not a suffragette. You are a lady." After complimenting Aubrey, he turned to Emmett, "You have done a fine job raising her, and practically on your own," he added with a smile.

"Such intelligence, beauty, and charm before us. Any man would be lucky to have her," said Lawrence. His sack suit was the smartest of the three, against his strong, handsome frame, dark, sharp features, and dashing blue eyes. She returned the smile.

Aubrey ascended to her room and rang the maid. Every time she donned gloves, she could hear Gran lecturing, "One can always tell a lady by her hands. The day a lady does not care about her hands or complexion is the day she is positively no longer a lady." Aubrey silently slipped out the back of the manor. She made her way to the stables. Propriety called for a female to be chaperoned by a groom, though two females were permitted to ride with only each other and without a gentleman to accompany them. Aubrey found a stable boy feeding an apple from his own ration to a horse. As mistress, Aubrey reprimanded the servant for breaking a rule by revoking the servant's only day off for the week. The servant envied the heated stall and embossed brass nameplate of the horses' living arrangements.

Pembina faded while Aubrey rode to the outer part of Vauréal, the Laurentiens' estate. Vauréal's property was larger than Pembina, and Aubrey loved it almost as much as her own estate. Riding onto Vauréals property, Aubrey thought of Emmett, who could not understand "certain women of today," as he worded it. The common or derogatory term was "suffragette." Ladies were expected to have polite accomplishments, and jumping was, to be sure, not one. Aubrey went riding with the Laurentien boys, who agreed not to tell of her jumping with them on their property. She adored riding. She loved winter the most of all the seasons and the time of year suited her; her personality was quite cold.

Aubrey rode past the oak grove that was the boys' favourite part of their estate. Aubrey looked in the distance and saw a lone rider. The stranger had stopped at the creek. His back was towards her. Remarkably tall and dressed impeccably, the gentleman was allowing his thoroughbred to drink from the creek. The water was only inches in depth. However, a large tree had fallen across the path. The creek was partially blocked.

Vauréal had several thoroughbreds, but the man was clearly too tall and wide in the shoulders to be a Laurentien. She was unsure whether she should jump the fallen tree, though the tree looked not unlike fences she had jumped before. Her safety skirt was, after all, attached. The lone rider stood up straight. The gentleman seemed so tall he would have to bow to enter a regular doorway. She was keen to stay the course and decided to jump. She thought best not to speak to the stranger, especially if Emmett were to know of her riding alone. The gentleman turned around at the sound of Aubrey's approaching horse.

She had never jumped a felled tree before. If not for her veil, her hard hat would have come undone. After she rode some way with her cape billowing behind her, she turned back to look at the rider. The man was no longer simply standing.

His hands were straight in the air and he wore a large smile. She was perplexed for a moment. A voice called out to her. She did not catch what he said, though it was obvious what he thought of her from his tone of sheer amusement. Not only had she ridden farther than he but she, a lady, had cleared a leap. She had bested a gentleman twice at something only males were supposedly able to do.

Men! Aubrey thought. *Why does everyone think they are superior to us?! What does it matter if I do not act like a lady? No one will know and I will never see this man again. He is clearly no gentleman, to encourage a lady to act disgracefully.*

With anger she could never quite contain, Aubrey forgot herself in the heat of battle. She turned her horse around to face the rider. With a big smile, she lifted her hands, palms up, and shrugged to indicate she was indifferent to what he thought of her. The abhorrent gesture seemed to spur the gentleman. His smile grew wider. He called out again. Still smiling, she turned her hand topsy-turvy to indicate he was merely satisfactory. The man's smile grew larger still. Then, she threw her hands behind her, over her head and let them fall in front as though to say, "never mind." She turned her horse and took off at a gallop down the trail. The stranger was left standing with his arms still in the air and the widest smile. As Aubrey rode down the path she thought, *A shame I shan't see him again, the only man I have ever known who can stand me being myself.*

The following evening, the massive wrought iron doors of the Vauréal manor were opened by footmen. Covering the front room were gentlemen in tailcoats adorned with boutonnieres or silk handkerchiefs and ladies in low bodices and short sleeves decorated with diamonds, pearls, plumes, boas, and full-length white gloves. Footmen took Aubrey's silk and Emmett's satin coats to put amongst the other rich coats, cloaks, and capes. The footmen had only finished laying the thousands of pieces of cutlery, crystal, and glass. The butler deemed the dining room acceptable after taking a ruler to make sure all pieces were laid in correct measurement to their purpose.

All guests, if not from England, were of Upper Canada Gentry. Mr. Michel Laurentien greeted Aubrey and her grandfather with a kiss and a handshake. The Laurentiens had been in Canada these few centuries. Michel was a short though strong man, with dark features and eyes. His children looked very similar to him, far more so than they did their mother. He was a well-known lawyer from a respectable family. Lady Bird was immediately at Aubrey's side. As chirpy as a bird when a little girl and already envious of her mother's title of 'Lady,' and Lady Bird she became. Lady Bird was taller than Aubrey, though not overly so, with high cheekbones, dark hair, and green-blue eyes with flecks of hazel in them. If not for her true nature — she was rather rotten on the inside — she would be considered a very handsome girl. The pair looked in earnest for their other intimate, Peter.

Wreaths and holly lined the four railings of the second floor. In front of the enormous Christmas tree on the main floor were two of the Lawrences, the dashing Edmund and Lindsay. Both were slightly taller than their father, which meant both sons were slightly closer to seven feet than to six. The two could pass for twins if not for a difference of a few inches in height, and Edmund, the eldest, had slightly darker brown hair than Lindsay. *Heir to his father's estate and with his father's handsome features, it is a wonder Edmund has yet to marry,* Aubrey thought. They were with the Harringtons:

Hugh, Harry, Henrietta, Herbert, and Herbert's new bride, Philippa Tomryn. Philippa looked radiant in her wedding gown. Less than six months had passed since her wedding day. Etiquette still permitted the dress to be worn at high-class affairs.

King Edward VII preferred mature, fleshy, and full-figured females. His empire naturally followed suit and continued to do so still, even with the passing of his death in 1910. With Philippa's hourglass figure and coveted chestnut-brown hair, she was a stunning beauty. Aubrey's hourglass frame was not equal to Philippa's. However, Aubrey was still thought to be handsome by most. Aubrey had dark, though rich, brown hair that accented her royal blue eyes to a lovely degree. Henrietta was tall, taller than Aubrey, but thin, and she had unfortunate blond hair. *Ugh, I'm certainly glad I don't look like that,* thought Aubrey in contempt while she looked at Henrietta and Philippa, who stood nearby.

Those females were not truly Ladies, as Aubrey and Lady Bird were, but daughters of merchants or industrialists. Females of "New Money" would never be completely accepted into the sphere of the Edwardian elite, though grudgingly endured as they financed their titled husbands' estates.

Lady Westbrook, a born lady, and Mrs. Lawrence, as stunning and as kind as her husband, were together gossiping about etiquette. Mme. Laurentien was elsewhere, caught up in the complex scheme of introducing one's guests to one another. Mme. Laurentien was a short, plump woman with a sweet disposition and the patience of Job. She was one of Aubrey's favourite women.

Across the room, one of the Laurentien girls, Pierrette, hoping for religious life, was discussing the New Testament with Genevieve Desrosiers.

Pierrette said, "For whosoever makes himself great shall be humbled, and he that humbles himself shall be made great." Then came the harsh and haughty voice of Peter Edwards, who came over to Aubrey and Lady Bird. Malevolence was the thread that held the small band of friends together. Peter was not tall, had plain brown hair, a similar eye colour, and a pompous air about him. Aubrey looked over to Emmett while Peter and Lady Bird launched into conversation of their invitations to skate at Rideau Hall. Emmett was endeared by all and possessed the rare attribute of speaking to master and servant in the same tone. He was always one of the tallest men in the room and, Aubrey thought, one of the most handsome. Her grandfather was an imposing man who had wide shoulders, even in old age, elegant features, and bright green eyes. He looked over at her and returned her smile. She could just hear his conversation with Michel. Emmett and Michel were at a distance. Though one was Protestant and the other Roman Catholic, their love of theology was a mainstay in their decades-long friendship. Aubrey heard Emmett say, "Every Kingdom divided against itself is brought to desolation."

Michel finished, "And a House divided against itself cannot stand."

Lawrence and Mr. Harrington were next to the trio, speaking of the gentleman's agreement between America and Japan a few years prior. The Lawrences were British aristocrats. The Harringtons were Canadian industrialists. The Harringtons were a small family of four children, all blond-haired and taller than average. Mrs. Harrington had long since died in childbirth, delivering a stillborn. By Providence, the baby had only been a girl.

The trio moved to the main room. Lady Bird snickered about Philippa's transformation even though the article entirely matched Philippa's hair colour.

Étienne, the eldest of the Laurentiens, came to Aubrey's side. He stood just taller than Aubrey with dark green eyes. The rest of his features he inherited from his father. Étienne said, "There is someone I want you to meet. Our fathers are cousins. Very peculiar he is here at all, considering we have not seen him since we were children. He is so busy with work; he will not even play a game of hockey with us. He extended his stay in Ottawa. Father says this is, to be sure, his first vacation! He has never been to a family reunion. But he wanted to be here tonight, and no one can seem to understand why. He wanted to stay for the ball — father said he did not dance at his own wedding."

They looked to the entryway as the butler, Thierry, a small, older, and kindly man, announced, "Mr. Aurelien Richardieux."

The moment Richardieux bowed in order to enter the doorway, all jollities came to an end. One could tell a gentleman by his walk, and this one harboured arrogance most unbecoming to his class. The slicked, chestnut-brown hair, thick eyebrows, and mustache complimented his strong jawline and cheekbones. The crisp white bow tie and black tails against his powerful frame soon had more than just Aubrey, though grudgingly, admiring him.

Étienne said, "Lady Kingston, permit me to present to you Mr. Richardieux."

A frigid bow, by way of greeting, came from her. A kiss on either cheek, too long to be considered gentlemanly, was indulged in by him. The man had nearly the most handsome French accent she had ever heard. Later, even Peter could not make fun of this man's accent; his voice was dashing. His steel-grey eyes seemed to find her amusing, though he did not smile. After conversing a short while with Aubrey, Étienne and Richardieux excused themselves. They were obliged to obtain the name card from Thierry that told them which lady to escort into dinner.

Lady Bird whispered to Aubrey, "Apparently Richardieux is as notorious a womanizer as his father. Richardieux's divorce was the scandal of Quebec City the whole year and all over the front pages of the papers. Naturally, both parties had to leave the dominion for a year. She went to France. He went to Switzerland, I think so, given he was thrown quite upon his honour by her father — branded a cad for life."

Aubrey looked up at Richardieux, who looked over to her. She flushed and turned back to Lady Bird. She had never been introduced to someone who was divorced.

The dinner gong sounded in a low tone so as the females would not take fright. Each male found his partner according to rank. Michel led Philippa, as new bride and guest of honour, ever to his right and also when they were seated at dinner. The next highest-ranking lady followed behind the host and on the arm of the male of her equal. Mme. Laurentien did not wish to offend anyone with Richardieux present, being that he was divorced, and since Aubrey was the youngest lady, she was paired to be escorted by and seated with Richardieux at dinner.

The shaded candles cast an intimate glow the length of the elaborate dining room. Lady Bird had recently been to a dinner party that had electricity. She said she positively looked a hundred years old. The measureless conversation of comportment, weather, and familiar prattle that encompassed the Edwardian dinner party soon began. While Aubrey and her rival made their way to the end of the dining table, Rev. Mrs. Tomryn, a plain, devout Protestant, and Mme. Desrosiers, a petite devout Roman Catholic, their families both Canadian-born, were at odds with each other over the appropriate time to remove one's gloves once seated. Next to these matrons was Emmett, who sat opposite Francis Lawrence. He looked similar to his brothers, except for he had inherited his father's eyes while his brothers had brown eyes. Francis had recently taken the bar. His aim was to enter politics, much like his father.

Emmett said gravely to Francis, "England's influence and dominance have remained steadfast these centuries. When I first came here, Canada was a mere colony. Now, she is a self-governing dominion. Perhaps you shall lead this dominion into nationhood."

"I should do my best, Sir," came the modest reply.

Fitzwilliam Kellynch and Mr. Desrosiers, a silver-haired, blue-eyed, short, and very successful businessman, discussed a sensitive matter. They conversed quietly so as not to alarm the ladies.

"Is there no decency?!" muttered an unwed Kellynch in response to Desrosiers's narrative. Kellynch was to inherit a vast fortune and the title Earl when his father passed. He had pale blue eyes and a decided look about him. He stood at regular height, was toned, and had excellent intelligence and character.

Mme. Laurentien was the last to enter, as hostess, and always with the highest-ranking man. Michel's guests sat, and he signalled the dinner should commence.

Aubrey sat poorly, forgetting that one can tell a lady by the way she seats herself. The stewed trout was served.

Across the flower arrangements, Richardieux paralleled the seriousness of the footman behind each chair. She would soon learn he rarely moved from this position. Étienne was to be Richardieux's translator for the evening. The eldest Laurentiens were fluent in both languages and had the barest trace of a French accent. Though Aubrey had a working knowledge of the modern languages, she did not excel in French. She wondered if Richardieux would tell Emmett of the previous day's outrageous afternoon.

The footmen cleared the poached salmon with mousseline sauce and cucumbers so they could serve the roast duckling. Peter laughed loudly at his own joke. The ladies surrounding him replied in kind, though they laughed gently in a way that did not affront those around them. A lady was also known by the charm of her voice. For the first time in the evening, Richardieux spoke. He inquired after Peter.

Étienne asked Richardieux in French, "The one with the pale, smooth complexion?" Richardieux replied in the affirmative and asked Étienne a question about his dinner partner. Étienne laughed and said to Aubrey, "My cousin says that comes from avoiding manual labour your whole life. In English, you call him a Remittance Man. And my cousin would like to know your hobbies aside from, that is to say, show jumping?" Étienne finished uncertainly, his brow furrowing quizzically while Aubrey's did in detest.

Aubrey answered, "I am rather fond of Shakespeare, *Hamlet* being a favourite."

Richardieux replied quietly in French, "Une femme qui lire (French for 'A bookish female')."

Impatience got the better of Aubrey. She understood the slight against her. A lady should be pleasant enough to

16

be knowledgeable of the world, though not academically inclined.

Over the sixth course, which saw a separate dish served for each of the trio, Étienne asked Aubrey, "My cousin would like to know what music you fancy."

Aubrey replied, "Beethoven."

Richardieux's eyebrows raised, "Une femme intelligente (An intelligent woman)."

The elaborate ice sculptures began to melt. Étienne told Aubrey that Beethoven was also one of his cousin's favourite composers. The next wine was served to pair with the next course. Aubrey found herself goaded by Richardieux time and again. She could hardly retain composure. She faltered at every turn with the man. She wanted to tell him to go to the devil sooner than any man she had known. She would rather storm from the hall than remain with this person, though that would shock the other guests. A lady was judged by the way she left a room. Besides, she could not leave before the older gentlemen and ladies because that would be the height of rudeness in a young person. The ninth through eleventh courses were eaten in silence.

Étienne attempted conversation and tried for a lively debate, "Father said women may soon obtain the vote."

Quite under his breath, Richardieux retorted, "Si l'enfer devrait geler (If hell were to freeze)."

Aubrey understood what was said and had had enough of her dinner partner. To loathe him for eternity was the silent agreement made by her.

She blurted, "You mean I am not already in Hell seated here with you?"

She sat astonished at such callous disregard for the gentleman's code. The etiquette of a lady was equal to the education of a gentleman. Étienne nearly spat out his glass of wine laughing. He called for more, as was expected over the duration, alcohol being as common as tea. Richardieux was a teetotaller. As a lady, Aubrey's champagne lay appropriately full. Before she could possibly recover to tell Étienne not to, translate he did. When Richardieux was told what Aubrey had said, he lost all pretences. He made the great faux pas of resting on the back of his chair. Then he hung his head and laughed. Though the most wretched man was seated before her, she was loath to admit in his smile a more handsome man could not be found.

The fifteenth and final course of absurdly moulded peaches in Chartreuse jelly and French ice cream was set before them. The footmen were now relieved to stand in the hall for an idle evening. They would find repose subsequent to walking a few tens of miles inside the manor throughout the very day.

The dinner concluded with the new acquaintances staring at one another across the way: she, with a look of one informed the groundhog had not seen his shadow and winter was to last much longer; he, with the look of Canadians in the first days of spring when the snow has assented to melt, the sun has strength to be of warmth, and the birds commence their songs after too harsh a winter.

Regina

Aubrey loved to titivate her appearance with powders and liquids. On a cold January day, she left the sole store in Regina that sold make-up, through the backdoor and veiled, lest another recognize her. For all that times were changing abroad, all was still extremely conservative on the prairies.

"Lady Kingzdon."

A gentleman should refrain from acknowledging a lady in thought and action until she takes the initiative. But, there Richardieux stood. He was at the bonnet of a Rolls Royce Silver Ghost. His horseless carriage model was certainly one of the only ones in Saskatchewan, if not in western Canada. Aubrey could hear the voice of every mother she knew exclaim, "The automobile is the house of prostitution on wheels." No lady entered one unaccompanied by a chaperone, the sole exception being an earthquake. The prairies did not have earthquakes, but she would think of an excuse later. She looked to either side to ensure the coast was clear.

She sat up in her seat and away from him, lest he kiss and therefore impregnate her. Like any young aristocratic female, Aubrey was left unaware of the process of procreation. Once the pair was inside the convent, Mother Augusta immediately asked for an explanation as to the whereabouts of one of her youngest charges. Augusta was an aged, salt-and-pepper-haired, short, sharp as a whip "North of Scotland woman and hard to get along with." Aubrey stood in the entryway, growing hotter. However, a lady did not remove an article of clothing in the presence of a gentleman. Richardieux excused himself for not having called earlier. In his best, if not quite broken, English, he introduced himself as her chaperone and a friend of the Kingstons from Ottawa, though he was in Regina to become a Mountie in the Royal North-West Mounted Police Force. It appeared, after more than thirty years, this man had finally unbent and was learning English. Aubrey played the fool. Richardieux never would have garnered the approval of Emmett.

Aubrey had few female companions in Regina, though she did share a room with two other young females, Christine McKercher and Hortence Gallaher. Christine was sweet and clever, with dark blond hair, green eyes, and porcelain skin. A Roman Catholic, she had the ill fortune of falling in love with a Protestant in Calgary, where her family lived. Her parents forbade the match, given the two lovers were of opposing religious denominations. Instead, when Christine was eighteen, the McKerchers had sent her to Sacred Heart to become a nun. At times, Aubrey heard Christine crying at night over the loss of the love of her life.

In contrast, "Good men are hard to find" was the invariable reply Hortence gave when asked why she had yet to marry. Hortence was average height, with mousy brown hair that Aubrey always associated with rats and the eye colour to match. Her face was too plump, and her glasses were too large for her features. She was average in intelligence, kindness, and just about everything else in life. Her parents had sent her to Sacred Heart, too, though for the opposite reason. Hortence had lived all her nineteen years in Saskatoon, north of Regina.

Apart from Regina, Saskatoon was one of the biggest cities in the province and therefore had a large selection of possible suitors. However, she had yet to make herself a match. Her parents hoped that a wider resource of connections would help her find a suitable marriage partner. It was not quite her plain features that caused Aubrey to think, "Beggars can't be choosers." Irritation always became Aubrey around Hortence, although Aubrey could not quite put her finger on the exact reason why.

At Sacred Heart, history class was in the morning. Aubrey's final exams would be about England's conquers across Europe and India, the triumph over Napoleon and the Spanish Armadas, as well as accomplishments on the Drake Sea. Canadian history had yet to be taught in the dominion. After dinner was religious studies. The bright spring afternoon had Mother Augusta lecture on "Forgiveness reigns supreme."

"When you stand before The Lord, He will have those who wronged you apologize. More importantly, He will ask if you forgave those who wronged you and this — MISS AUBREY — will be the true judge of your character. Forgiveness is not about whether what the person did was right or wrong or if they should be punished." Augusta went on.

Aubrey was not paying mind. She was looking at the pictures of Queen Victoria and the second picture of Victoria's husband, Albert, that hung above the chalkboard. Aubrey often thought of their titanic love story. One thing Aubrey hoped for the most was to have a love affair for the ages.

Augusta continued, "In the eyes of Our Lord, spite is wrong. If you had the power to change someone for the better, through forgiveness, would you? What if you could cause that person's one pivotal moment that enabled them to become a better person? As well, if you do not forgive your transgressor for how they treated you, they are the victor. But if you forgive your transgressor, you put them at your mercy, no matter the crime."

After class was dismissed, Aubrey left the academy front doors. Across the courtyard and on the street, Richardieux sat astride his steed. Beside him and against the nearby tree was the infamous bicycle. The bicycle was thought to be a significant contributor to the fall of ethical behaviour among the youngest generation. Matrons and chaperones had a hard time keeping pace with the bicycle, and the newfangled invention was deemed an undeviating agent to immorality. Aubrey did not know how to ride a bicycle and would have to learn. She would also have to buy the almost equally infamous bloomers: a certain skirt designed for cycling that fell modestly at the back.

No lady should accept presents from a gentleman caller, not even her fiancé. However, Richardieux did not seem to care for her in a romantic way by any means. Edwardian couples were considered reputable if they appeared no different than any other pair in public. Physical affection beyond a handshake was out of the question, and he had always been respectful of physical boundaries. Richardieux retained the required eighteen inches of distance from her when they sat in a church pew. One did not move one's head in church, and he never wavered from that rule either, even to look at her. A very serious man, he frequented church daily and confession weekly: not even the sisters confessed that often. He had not joined singing carols during sleigh rides down Wanuskeiwin Drive in winter. Any activity more amusing than church was not allowed on the Sabbath, but numerous times weekly he would escort her to non-existent knitting clubs, church events, and charitable fundraisers, always under the false pretence of "Mr. Kingston's orders." Females were raised to volunteer in all ways for the greater good of their Empire, so the plausible lies were believed by the sisters who thought it ever thoughtful of Richardieux to escort her, given so many young ladies were led astray by the decline of the chaperone. He routinely took Aubrey to picture shows, but spoke to no one, and to card games, though he did not play himself. At forbidden tango teas (Gran had almost fainted the first time she saw the polka), he sat and watched and did not converse with anyone.

While they went down the street, Aubrey proved rather fair at riding a bicycle. The lecture on forgiveness was related by Aubrey.

Richardieux concurred, "The old bird iz right. If you want to get back at someone, give them eh taste of their own medicine. But, if you want eh person to understand you, attack the conscience. Your conscience might not prevent you from doing zomething, but it will prevent you from getting away with it."

"In class, Mother Augusta spoke endlessly that remorse is the worst form of all punishment. That the very definition of Hell is knowing what you did was wrong, but you cannot receive forgiveness and are made to live with that all-consuming remorse for eternity."

"And be careful with 'om you associate, Lady Kingzdon. Denial 'as the power to quite simply end your life. Ladies are ze only creatures on earth who will sense danger and carry on. In fairness, you 'ave been conditioned, as females, to be zis way, but you must be aware of zis."

"How can one even know if one is in danger?"

"When something bad happenz, the first thing that went wrong iz that you did not listen to your intuition. What you feel is intuition. What you think is merely logic. Regarding dangerous others, the first thing you will not like about ze person is 'is voice. The devil sounds harsh. Intuition, however, iz unmistakable, always right, and the 'oly Spirit sounds far more beautiful than your intuition. Above all, always heed your intuition."

A few of the only friends Aubrey had in Regina were the mettlesome Agnew cousins. Briarch and Rupert were just older than her and born only months apart. Their mannerisms were exactly like the other from so much time spent together. They stood at almost the same height, had deep set shoulders, dark auburn hair, and merry grey and hazel eyes, respectively. The two could nearly pass for twins. The difference in their brogues set them apart. They moved from Ireland with their families when they were young. Their fathers had adjoining farms near Moose Jaw. The perpetually cheery Briarch and Rupert always had everyone in stitches, except their parents, who found them so very vexing.

Briarch said, "After our last ruse on the farms, father said we should be locked up!"

Rupert added, "Pa wanted for Kingston Military College. But Ma—"

Briarch continued, "—Nor mother would hear of us being so far away. So, we were shipped off to Depot," the pair laughed while they told Aubrey why they were sent to Regina when the three met.

In 1873, Sir John A. MacDonald commissioned a police force. His objective was to aid the colony's unsettled and freshly attained north-west territories. The name "North-West

Mounted Police" was slowly accepted. The temporary police force, one hundred and fifty members, was ordered to Manitoba. In 1874, the force consisted of three hundred members. This group of Mounties was commanded to the territories. The march west would remain the only time in history in which the force in its entirety would march together. Fort Macleod, Alberta, would host the principal permanent post of the force, to the extent that half its members were stationed there. By the mid 1880's, the force faced disbandment from the newly elected Prime Minister, Sir Wilfrid Laurier. Although, as providence would have it, the Klondike gold rush ensured the force's future, if for a short time. In 1904, King Edward VII granted the Force the prefix "Royal." Over the years to follow, contracts were signed between the Mounted police and the new provinces of Alberta and Saskatchewan. In Regina, the sole training academy for new members was called "Depot" and was pronounced the French way.

Richardieux could not be in Regina to find a wife because Mounties were not allowed to marry until they had served a minimum of five years on the force. Others found it rather odd. What was a gentleman from such an aristocratic family doing in the role of a Mountie? Mounties did not earn an aristocratic living. Richardieux was at first thought of as simply the strong and silent type, another "Forbidden Mountie," by females in the city. But Regina was happy to have a French Canadian join the Force, since there were so few. However, after a paltry short time, Richardieux showed to be recalcitrant towards authority and the least fit to be a Mountie. He quickly became a renegade, Regina's bête noir. How he passed the "morally upright" part of the examination before being accepted into the academy was beyond any matron. Before long, scrolls were passed throughout

Regina to see him hanged, or at the very least, dismissed from Depot. Ahead of the trial, he was counted little above murderer. *Maybe they will hang him. Then grandfather would never know about the tango teas or any of the other things I have done here that a lady should not,* Aubrey thought. Aubrey knew not all offenses stacked against his character, numerous though they were. Not only was he not hanged, Richardieux was exonerated of all charges rightly laid against him. However, not a thing could dampen her spirits. She was shortly to return to Ottawa to stay, given her schooling had finished.

The Royal North-West Mounted Police Ball took place on a clear and charming June evening. Aubrey and Richardieux began waltzing in a sea of scarlet serges and elaborate ball gowns. For some time, Aubrey and her strong lead danced in silence. Richardieux looked positively dashing in his serge.

Because he arrived at the eleventh hour, to the point where she worried he would not come at all, she mocked him, "And where, pray tell, were you? Let me venture a wild guess: at the office?"

Richardieux answered, "Yes, I was working. Why iz that so funny, Mizz Aubrey? What iz more important to eh man than 'is work and what he 'as to show for 'imself as eh result of 'is work?"

"Love, family, or the pleasures of life are not more important than earning a living? Love is life, and if you miss love you miss life."

He asked, "To be clear, 'ow can eh man enjoy such thingz without first 'aving the means to acquire them? Zis is why work should be number one in eh man'z life, except, of course, eh man'z religion."

"Though one is never entirely certain when the dance will end, and I do not mean waltzing, Mr. Richardieux. Priorities must be in place in the meantime, or so they say. Anyhow, am I correct to presume you were not playing hockey?"

He replied with barely suppressed sarcasm, "If you will agree with me, when you stop acting like a lady and like one of those suffragettez, I will join eh 'ockey team."

He always did make her laugh. "If that will make you see things clearly."

"May I have the word of her Ladyship?"

"I always get my man," Aubrey teased one of the Mounted Force's most famous, though unofficial, mottos in entering into the agreement with Richardieux. "Why did you come tonight? Was it for a lady?"

There was a pause from her partner. "I am only interested in women, not ladiez. There iz eh difference, to be sure. That term, 'lady,' means different things to different people. The term 'lady,' by conventional standards, is what females are supposed to aspire to. But, the terms 'lady,' 'woman,' and 'man' for that matter, are all earned and deserved.

She added, "And the difference between a lady and a suffragette is a lady does not fight and gentlemen respect her because of that."

"And what of Mrs. Nellie McClung? Publicly laughed at and mocked by members of Parliament for wanting the vote. Will she not be remembered in 'istory? Iz that not rezpect worthy? Or those four other suffragettez. The five of them are becoming quite famous, no?"

Aubrey answered indifferently, "Well, if you ask me, it doesn't make one button of difference if those suffragettes are extended the vote or if they're not."

"The government and general populace argue that eh wife might openly defy 'er husband."

27

The Dominion Elections Act decried, "No woman, idiot, lunatic or criminal shall vote."

"'owever, you 'ave reason and are perfectly correct. Ladies take fright easily, whereas women do not take fright. They also fight. They act like themselves — not what society tells them to be — and they are not afraid to do so. Most ladiez do not realize zis, but zis is 'ow you truly garner eh man'z respect. And males 'o think otherwise, you do not want that sort of respect any'ow."

Aubrey wanted to know why he had come to the ball in the first place and asked, "You mean to say you did not leave work early to come here?"

For once, Richardieux lost all pretences. This time, however, his tone changed to that of impossibility as he replied, "Ma chere (my dear), the day I leave ze office early you will know I care more for eh woman than anything else in my entire life."

Pembina

The house was a great house. Pembina's expansive landscape had, without equal, beauty, optimism, and charm, like the Edwardian era it belonged to. The "Skivvy" woke in the early morning hours. She was the lowest of the lower five, though the number of servants who made up the lower five was considerably more than the term implied. Her simple uniform of black and white dress and apron was bought herself and took a few years of savings before the material could be purchased. Female servants slept in the attic away from the males, who resided in the basement. The unheated attic housed multiple hard, aged, iron bedspreads in an open area, walls that had patches of whitewash fallen off, and meagre pieces of furniture too old to be seen in the main part of the manor. Going about the sparsely furnished basement halls, the skivvy made ready for the day. A portrait of Queen Victoria and stitch work that read *Humility is a servant's true calling* hung in the hallway.

The next to arise was the hall boy, who slept on a straw pull-out in the hall. The two would wake their respective superiors: the kitchen and scullery maids along with the footmen. A footman's livery was given to the lad by his masters and cost more than the earnings he made in a year. By this hour, the maids-of-all-work, laundry maids and the outdoors servants — the gardener, coachman, and stable master — would be at work. The housemaid and footmen would take tea, toast, and jam to the upper five: the housekeeper, lady's maid, chef, butler, and valet.

Rickety, steep, narrow, and dimly lit staircases, involving tens of steps from basement to attic, were climbed numerous times daily. The lack of natural light would end for servants at the green baize door that opened onto the main floor of the manor. On the other side of this door was marble flooring and towering windows under ornate frescos. Edwardians fancied natural light and sunshine, at distinct variance to Victorians, who nearly lauded darkness with small windows, dark furniture, and bric-a-brac everywhere. The butler and lady's maid would greet their master and mistress with a morning tray each and draw their baths to start their leisured day. There were tens of fires to light and tend to, shutters to be thrown wide, and shoes to polish.

One's rank was of the utmost importance upstairs as well as below stairs. The housemaid would refuse to acknowledge any girl who worked in the kitchen, and the skivvy was ignored by everyone below stairs. All basic cleaning had to be completed ahead of the family's breakfast and before the servants were allowed to have their first meal. The lowest orders were not permitted to dine with the upper five but dined in the Steward's dining room. In smaller estates, they ate under complete silence and the watchful eye of the butler, who had absolute authority. The lower five were given cold meat and tea while their betters ate roast chicken and dessert.

In the mid-morning, the chef would meet with the mistress to set the day's meal plan. Preserves, cold meats, and cakes were freely given to the youngest servants, most around the age of twelve, to take to their families. Male chefs were a status symbol for Edwardians and they could ask for greater than double the butler's salary. They were the highest paid servants. Mid-morning found the master and butler going over the day's plans, the estate, and the finances.

In church, servants sat before their masters so they could be monitored.

Away from those dreadful Roman Catholic Latin masses in Regina, Aubrey could better understand the Rev. Tomryn as he droned in English, "You are a chosen generation, God's special possession, that you may proclaim the praises of Him who called you out of darkness and into His wonderful light."

The carriage, with the servants walking behind, passed Lansdowne, the Westbrooks' residence. Lansdowne was the estate to the west of the Kingstons', whereas Vauréal was situated to the east. Of those in the area, Pembina was the most distant manor from Ottawa. The Kingstons had returned from Muskoka the day before. At the resort, Aubrey and Lady Bird began a rumour about Genevieve Desrosiers on account of neither being invited to Genevieve's debut. They spread word that she was a fallen girl. Their ruse worked so well that Genevieve was sent to Quebec to stay with relatives until the storm blew past.

There was news of Austria's Archduke, heir to the Austro-Hungarian Empire, Franz Ferdinand, who had been assassinated by the Serbian terrorist group, the Black Hand. The death brought little interest to the dominion. The gentlemen agreed that the small European matter would come to naught. Great Britain would not honour a trifle and forgotten piece of parchment, anyhow. Emmett usually played a round of golf with the Prime Minister at Muskoka. But he was unable to this summer due to Sir Robert Laird Borden's early return to Ottawa to attend to this very matter. The gentlemen did agree the most pressing distress Parliament needed to consider in autumn would be senate reform.

The summer months involved countless balls, dinner parties, ballets, operas, races, and tournaments of cards and sports. Masters rang for service at any hour of the day or night, and servants were to be in complete compliance with their masters' wishes. Servants were fortunate to be allowed one afternoon a week and one day a month without work as respite from their habitually sixteen-hour workdays.

The main job of the hall boy was to light, trim, and put out the numerous lamps in the manor and candles in the chapel. The majority of this servant's waking hours were spent fulfilling this one chore. The last flame at Pembina was extinguished. The final great house fell to darkness.

Summer 1914

Aubrey's carriage could go no further through Wellington Street the bright, sunny morning of August 4th, 1914. One could not see the ground because there were so many people. Thousands had converged onto Ottawa's streets. The first story of all buildings could not be viewed because the Union Jack, Tricolor, and Red Ensign waved furiously. Bagpipers, a dozen rows deep, passed by her carriage. Gabriel Westbrook, Lady Bird's brother, recognized her footmen and came near. She well-nigh had to bang the glass to let the driver know to open the door. The sound outside was near deafening. Gabriel helped Aubrey alight as she was assaulted with the words, "SEND HIM VICTORIOUS!"

Aubrey said, positively astounded, "What in God's name? Has the Queen had another baby?"

"LONG TO REIGN OVER US!"

Gabriel responded, "It is better than that! The most glorious news!"

They had to speak quietly in order to hear one another; the crowd was so boisterous.

"HAPPY AND GLORIOUS!"

Gabriel practically shouted with jubilation, "The King has declared war! England is at war! The Empire is headed for the battlefield! We're going to fight the Germans!"

Aubrey's reply was lost on Gabriel for the crowd finished with the last line of the official anthem so loudly he could not hear her. He pulled her into the mass of people and they started to waltz alongside a dozen other couples. "Rule Britannia" was the next song roared down the street. Then, "La Merseillaise" was sung until voices were shouted into hoarseness.

With a regular army of three thousand males, a Navy built on two ships purchased second hand from Britain, only one of which could sail, and an Air Force yet to be founded, the dominion was unqualified for battle. But, at being called upon by the mother country, and with great pride and enthusiasm, Canada entered into warfare.

On August 24th, the Belgium city of Mons was captured by Germany in the principal engagement of the war. The day of Aubrey's debut, and three weeks since George V had declared war, was as glorious as all the summer days preceding it. In Pembina's pristine garden, a single lazy peacock walked through the lot.

"Mother Britain will not fight alone!" Kellynch cried almost viciously.

"We won't stand for 'ome to be insulted!" said Gabriel, equally distraught.

"And it is a jolly good idea we send a division to show our devotion to the Empire!" added a smiling Lindsay.

"Here! Here!" came the chorus of reply from all dignified gentlemen.

Every corner of the Empire, the foundation of morality on earth, was euphoric with battle fever. Canadians, like all Empire patriots, valiant defenders of freedom, were eager to do their bit for England.

"Britain has asked for our aid and the Prime Minister has accepted the call," said Hugh elatedly.

Laurier, now the leader of the Liberal Party, represented quite possibly all of Canada in stating, "It is our duty to let Great Britain know, and to let the friends and foes of Great Britain know, that in Canada there is but one heart and one mind and that all Canadians are behind the mother country."

When the war would be explained to future generations, their elders would invariably say only those present could possibly comprehend what that glorious summer was like. Canada was simply mad with delight! Canada did not dictate its international relations and was therefore naturally at war alongside England, although Canada would decide its own level of involvement in the war. The War Measures Act was passed, giving the dominion's government the ability to ensure the "Security, defence, peace, order, and welfare of Canada."

Ottawa quickly became the focal point of all affairs for the coming battle. Newspapers published daily articles, politicians gave speeches, and chaplains preached what was the cherished right of all Englishmen: to uphold the honour of the Empire. Rudyard Kipling and other authors wrote novels, essays, and poetry to raise awareness and encourage support for England's plight.

Posters were at first deemed unnecessary. They had never been needed before in wartime. But soon they were in every location imaginable. Signs read, *Last, Best, West*. Others were of King Lion with a crown atop his head, with his little but loyal subject, the beaver, at his side with sword in hand. The caption read *Let's Go!* in bright red, big, friendly lettering. More posters boasted the British bulldog with his four pups behind him. On every street was a poster of a British soldier who stood before the Union Jack in his dashing kilt. The words stated, *This is your flag! Fight for it!* Railway cars were gay with banners and chalk phrases encouraging chaps to go. The impending scrap was all anyone could discuss.

Fearing the worst, that battle would end before Canada could raise a proper army, a regiment was formed of almost exclusively former British reservists and university chaps. Of the regiment, three out of four lads had military decorations or medals to their name. Princess Patricia, the daughter of the Governor General, the Duke of Connaught, gave her name to the regiment. Montreal's Andrew Hamilton Gault founded the regiment with a private donation of one hundred thousand dollars. The Princess Patricia's Canadian Light Infantry was created in the first days after war was declared. The Governor General, his wife, Princess Louise-Marguerite, their daughter, Princess Patricia, along with the Prime Minister, Laurier, and the Minister of Defence, Sam Hughes, said goodbye to the regiment privately at Lansdowne Park. Also, at the farewell was the Edmonton Caledonian Pipe Band. When the band arrived, they agreed to "Pipe the Regiment to France and back." The Princess Pat's were piped to "All Blue Bonnets Are Over the Border" during a marvellous send-off. Thousands lined the sidewalks to cheer them. The regiment was sent home, on the double, to represent the colony ahead of the first convoy of troops.

"This is a war for civilization!" Kellynch cried.

"And Canada will not stand idle while a barbaric foe attempts to take Britain's God-given rights away!" added Lindsay.

This war was not a war between nations but a crusade for righteousness, abstinence, peace, and democracy from a tyrannical, oppressive, and monstrous rival.

"Outside the armouries, the street or either sidewalk could not be seen; there were so many fellows in their Sunday best. The entire area was positively covered in bowler hats. Guards were posted at the doors with bayonets to keep the lads at bay!" Lindsay recalled, laughing. Raised in the strict Victorian perspective, this lot had been taught that the older generations had defeated the Yankees in 1812, stopped the Fenian raids during the time of Confederation, settled the 1885 Northwest Rebellion, and had garnered glory in the Boer War. Considered to be the last great war, the Old Home's call was being answered by the thousands from sea to sea. Lindsay joined the cavalry and was going with the Royal Canadian Dragoons. "However," he continued proudly, "I was able to join the first day." British born were given first rights to spots for the sole division needed for the war.

For Aubrey's chums, an officer's commission was simply adhering to the gentleman's code. Signing up was a simple process; sergeants sat at folding tables and wrote down height, weight, religion, and apparent age. At the armouries, no information could be given on uniforms, pay, or allowances. At the same time, medical requirements were stringent.

Harry, who stood next to Pierre Laurentien, had joined the army on the second day.

"I told the sergeant my age," Pierre said to the group at large. He had managed to sign up the third day. Those younger than eighteen who wanted to go along had to have parental consent. "He informed me only adults, not boys, were allowed to go. He then asked my age. I excused myself and told the sergeant I was eighteen and he let me get on board."

Many underage fibbed about their age and because passports (the Canadian passport had yet to come into existence), birth certificates, and high school diplomas were uncommon, officers generally filled out the paperwork that the eager lad was eighteen. Boys wore short pants and stockings until about eighteen. Donning trousers was then permitted as they entered manhood. Many young lads found the wearing of military slacks too enticing to withstand. Older males, frightened they too would be turned away due to age, put black polish in their hair and on their chest hair. Males lied about their marital status but not to disregard their families. Those with wives and children were the last allowed to go.

"Mother told me it was all stuff and nonsense; however, every gentleman has to have his priorities!" Pierre said with determination.

"She should not be so hard on you, a plucky young lad ready to do his duty for King and country dear," Kellynch said in Pierre's defence. "For my country[1]," of course, meant England.

"Father gave his word to mother that Pierre's older brothers would stay on either side of him," Étienne said, speaking for Jean-Baptiste as well.

Neither of the elder two Laurentiens saw reason in going, but because Pierre was to go, Michel had his two eldest go in order to look after him. The Laurentiens would remain some of the only French Canadians Aubrey would know who would even try to sign up, their ties to their mother country broken three centuries before.

To English Canada, "Patriotism" meant love of England and Empire. To French Canada, solely the dominion was thought of. Many French Canadians were quiet about the war England was presently engaged in.

All British families Aubrey knew had at least one relative who had joined, and all were proud to say so. Of those who

---

[1]   A Canadian World War I epitaph

were mortifyingly rejected, some choked back their tears. Kellynch had fifteen cousins in England who were already in uniform and waiting to mobilize. A loving son, fond brother, true friend[2], Gabriel and his entire cricket team, excepting one, signed up after their last practice. Harry's militia's officer, before their last drill exercise, wanted to know who was going. Every one of them signed their name to the role call. Males signed up as they walked home from work, on their way to daily service or after cards with mates on the weekend.

Many of Aubrey's friends cut their last school term for the King's service.

"Mother said I should finish university first, then do the grand tour. But Europe will always be there, and the war will not. I told her, 'My country before even you, mother dear[3].' Besides, this circumstance needs our most earnest attention," said Harry.

After a month of impatience, everyone was worried that the boys would not even get the chance to sail before the war ended. Universities were giving a "Year in full" to students in their final year who were responding to the Old Country's call. Students who were in other levels of their degrees, who were going as well, were granted different levels of credit. Female university students, as second-class citizens resentfully tolerated on campus, did their patriotic duty, unaccompanied by acknowledgement from the same universities, as selflessness was simply expected of females. Officer Training Corps had been temporarily set up at every university.

---

[2]   A Canadian World War I epitaph
[3]   A Canadian World War I epitaph

Most males left splendid incomes behind and the workforce also experienced huge voids. Employers let their workers go off to the war with encouragement, agreed to provide workers their income while they were away at the war, and agreed to give them their jobs when they returned. Conflicts in the 1900's went on for mere weeks.

Affectionate only son[4], Gabriel also joined the cavalry, though he signed up with Lord Strathcona's Horse. One of Westbrook's footmen would accompany Gabriel as batman to lay his master's sleeping bag and polish his master's boots and family sabre on loan. The thoroughbred that Westbrook recently gifted Gabriel, upon his coming of age, would also need to be currycombed.

"Strike me pink! I told the officer I was Belgium born and wanted to avenge my people. He tried hard not to smile for he knows father, but he let me in!" explained a laughing Gabriel.

Others falsely said they had served in the Imperial Regular Army or British Navy or claimed they had served in the Boer War. Those with military service were among the first chosen for the limited places.

"The Prime Minister asked for twenty-five thousand, and thirty thousand stood forth in two weeks. Action is eloquence," Edmund said. A dearly beloved and honoured son[5], he was trying to be the gentleman he feared he could no longer be. While it was tradition for middle class and aristocratic fathers to volunteer their sons for war, it was also customary for the eldest son in a family not to fight. Fellows had to ask their father's permission to sign up, even if they were married with children of their own. Edmund, like

---

[4]   A Canadian World War I epitaph
[5]   A Canadian World War I epitaph

Herbert and Ernest Tomryn, each the eldest in their families, had been told by his father he was not allowed to go.

"But who will dance with us if all of you go off?" Aubrey spoke to the group.

"Awe, we'll be back by Christmas," reassured Lindsay.

"That's what everyone is saying; you boys will be back by Christmas. You can't possibly return sooner?" she asked rhetorically.

Volunteers gave their consent to assist the military for minimum a twelvemonth. At most, volunteers would consent to fight until the end of the war plus an additional six-month period. But the war would never last so long. Therefore, no one was concerned.

"Old Kaiser Bill said his boys will be back by the time the leaves fall," said Gabriel in response to Lindsay.

"They won't come back! We'll pink them every time!" replied Hugh.

"'ow will zis war end quickly wid machine gunz?" Richardieux spoke for the first time that afternoon.

The young Canadian army had only a few machine guns and little artillery at their disposal. Richardieux continued. He said that the lads were off to confront the Kaiser's trained professionals. No empire was superior to Germany's might.

All gentlemen turned to stare at Richardieux after his remark. The Royal North-West Mounted Force had never or would experience again the patriotic vigor that characterized this period in its history. Mounties were made to pay fifty dollars to be discharged. Others were simply free to go. Richardieux, too, had left the force and by the worst means possible: desertion. It was common knowledge that there was a legal warrant out for his arrest. His punishment could include a few hundred hours of hard labour and possible jail time. The males were restraining themselves at such callous disregard for the gentleman's code.

While twirling her parasol, Lady Bird unknowingly gave to the group a welcome reprieve from the tense moment and said, "And what of that invention, by those Yankee cattlemen?"

"Do you mean to say barbed wire, dear?" Lindsay teased, but his eyes were kind. He explained in simple terms, given the feminine mind did not comprehend far, "Those tools have no place in warfare where England and her gentlemen are concerned."

Englishmen believed such weapons were not gentlemanly and therefore simply did not belong in any war in which the Empire was concerned.

"The British army always goes into battle on horseback. And pluck, discipline, and the spirit of the bayonet will always carry the day!" Lindsay finished.

"The British Lee-Enfield rifles, with their 'mad-minute,' can fire fifteen rounds a minute and are known the world over for this," concluded Kellynch, in further explanation to Lady Bird.

"England has the most powerful Navy in history," added Gabriel.

"—Who commands all the oceans, and only the King himself determines who can sail on them!" said Hugh.

"Germany won't come out to sea to attack our ships before you get to France?" questioned Lady Bird.

"The Germans would be too frightened to! Because the Union Jack will be flying on our ships and we will wage battle after battle for our beloved Empire until all the foes are wrested from the world for good!" answered Hugh.

"Germany 'as built ze largest Navy in the world, second only to England," Richardieux said in fairness.

"And she'll protect us!" finished Lindsay, pretending that Richardieux had not spoken.

The lot at large carried on, "There is a chore at hand!... The old rag needs our assistance!... The loveliest flag in the world!... Our dominion's guiding star!... What Britons are fighting for!"

A man who was straight in all things and beloved and respected by all[6], Emmett and the other patriarchs were conversing quietly away from the group.

"At Rideau Hall, I heard it said by the Governor General himself that Hughes is a 'conceited lunatic,'" said Lawrence.

"Borden is unsure if Hughes is 'entirely sane.' The liberals call him a 'martial madman,'" Harrington concurred.

The new army, desperately untried in leadership, discipline, preparation, uniformity, and action, would have benefited enormously from a trained military. Canada had only one permanent Regiment, the Royal Canadian Regiment. Sam Hughes, a teetotaller, publicly referred to the small permanent force as "Barroom loafers." Hughes did not hold them competent in any regard and seemed to detest them for personal reasons. He had sent them off to Bermuda for "Garrison duty." Hughes was certain "the boys" would accept the call of the Empire more than what was even needed. Only one week prior, Hughes stated, "I call for volunteers — volunteers, mark you. I have insisted that it shall be a purely volunteer contingent. Not a man will be accepted or leave Canada on this service but of his own free will and, if I know it, not a married man shall go without the consent of his wife and family."

---

6   A Canadian World War I epitaph

"The Minister of Finance, Sir William Thomas White, said this will be the 'suicide of civilization,' and with Hughes at the front of it all White will be jolly right," Tomryn trailed off, grumbling.

Most of the gentlemen at the table, intimates to the highest politicians, asked for acts of goodwill and to forewarn that the conflict would cause the crumbling of the Empire and the Edwardian way of life.

"But the coming battle will improve business," Westbrook responded in good cheer.

"A nation spoke to a nation[7]," Emmett referenced one of Kipling's poems. "But what with the Schlieffen plan, to bump France in six weeks, I wonder how much our economy will really benefit in so short a time?" he asked.

"Well, what could be worse than the Boer War? That war was the most gruesome fighting the dominion has ever seen," Westbrook said to no one in particular.

The sole war Canada had been involved in was the South African War, mainly called the Boer War. Canada had served with honour, for all that her troops were known for their disregard towards discipline.

"At any rate, it should be a jolly good show," said Westbrook, who heaved a sigh. He turned to Emmett and the pair began discussing reparation matters.

Archibald Tomryn and his new wife were sitting together not far from everyone else. He had joined the Royal Canadian Navy as a Lieutenant. For a militia male to marry before authorization meant barrack life and discontinuation of pay. Militia council had to grant a Lieutenant the right to marry, a right that was just extended to Archibald. Aubrey knew of a few acquaintences in the Navy. The dominion's Navy had

---

[7]   A Canadian World War I epitaph

only a third of sailors needed to crew the sole ship of the "Tin-pot" Navy. Borden said Canada would not see action on any ocean. The objective was not to create an entire fleet or Armada, because that would be absurd. Government was doing everything in its power to ensure the boys would get there before it was all over too soon.

"Those who do not fight are cowards," Kellynch said seriously while he looked at Richardieux. Britishers believed in the justness of the Empire's resolution. All young males were expected to sign up to prove that the honour of the Union Jack was at the heart of every Englishman. Besides, France was Germany's arch rival.

"Eh male 'o does not fight 'iz own battles is eh coward, isn't that right, Mr. Edwards?" Richardiuex replied in his usual calm demeanor and turned to look at Peter.

The lively conversation turned dour. A momentary pause came from all gentlemen once more.

"The recruitment drive has been suspended. No more troops are needed," Peter replied confidently, although he avoided Richardieux's eye as well as Kellynch's.

Everyone concurred that this was true. If anyone detested Peter more than Richardieux, it was Kellynch. Fitzwilliam and Peter were the two wealthiest of Aubrey's acquaintances. However, Kellynch did not care to associate with Peter under any circumstances.

"Two of my brothers are in uniform and are awaiting to cross the Channel. Like so many others in his position, Father has offered up the country estate as a convalescent hospital," continued Peter.

Aubrey looked about her. The sun was high in the sky. The little boys, hoping against all hope the war would last long enough for them to join their big brothers, had stopped playing. England had obviously won their jolly game. They were now looking to catch mice to throw onto the dance floor later that evening. The ladies continued to chat while the gentlemen were uncharacteristically still. Aubrey could not quite put her finger on what was the matter. She looked to the gentlemen for some sort of explanation, but all were too polite to discuss the apparent tension in front of the ladies. The whole matter of war was temporary, besides. So, Aubrey turned to Lady Bird, and the pair discussed what was equally important to Ladies: presentation at court. The previous year at her presentation, Lady Bird had been horror-stricken about stumbling over her train in front of Her Majesty.

The long summer carried on. Seemingly, time was at a standstill for these Edwardians. English Canadians were exceptionally merry over Borden's recent knighthood, the romance of Great Britain at war, and a summer that never seemed to end. "What more could anyone ask for?" was the rhetorical question asked endlessly.

Valcartier

"Why don't they close the gate?"

Richardieux turned back to stare. He was attempting to explain to a female England's agreement to protect "Brave Little Belgium," the Race to the Sea, and the Iron Gate to Paris. Aubrey could hardly bear the boredom.

Ottawa was in its autumn glory. Belgium saw its women raped and its men ineffectual against the Germans as their army enclosed on Paris by not more than fifty kilometers.

The birds were cooing loudly in their cages. Thierry was loading Auré's rifle, as a gentleman considered doing so beneath one's dignity.

Richardieux took the gun from Thierry and, breaking the cardinal rule of not treating a servant as an equal, looked Thierry in the eye while he rolled his eyes in response to Aubrey's question. Richardieux turned and took aim.

"You are eh real lady," he said quietly to himself.

"Pardon me?"

"Yez, my daughter of ze Empire, that would be eh start," he said in a louder manner.

On the back lawn of Vauréal, Mme. Laurentien and Emmett were sipping lemonade and indulging in chocolate mints. Nicolas was tossing Richardieux's Stetson, gifted to him after Richardieux left the force, while chanting, "Ready, aye, ready[8]." Nico, who was called so by all but Richardieux — he did not believe in jollities — received the name because he was the smallest of the Laurentien boys. Nico despised his size and his pet name more so. *Chevalier sans peur et sans reproche*[9] (A knight without fear and without reproach) was what Nico thought of Richardieux. With dreams of becoming a Mountie, in Nico's eyes his uncle could do no wrong. Michel was watching Auré shoot.

Emmett had had trouble pulling the trigger at times over the course of the early afternoon. The unusual behaviour prompted Richardieux to ask "Sir?" more than once. Emmett had left the shooting to the young people.

The Imperial Order of the Daughters of the Empire, Red Cross, St. Johns Ambulance, and the YMCA erupted as soon as war was declared from regular numbers across the dominion. Females felt the need to take care of males as much as males wanted to be the guardians of the Empire's security. Aside from their normal Empire and local work, females were expected to assist doing "pretty work," such as selling flowers and collecting the hundreds of canned goods, parcels, bedding, and blankets for the cause.

London had asked its colonies to help Belgium, who struggled with starvation. The Ottawa Women's Club responded with the formation of the Belgium Relief Fund Committee. To raise funds, bridge tournaments, luncheons, bake-sales, bazaars, and plays where held at local theatres. Patriotic calendars and souvenir regimental badges were sold as well.

The dominion's largest fund was the Patriotic Fund. Kellynch was president of the Ottawa branch.

---

8 A Canadian World War I epitaph
9 A Canadian World War I epitaph

Newspapers printed the names of males who had taken the King's shilling and were now in uniform. On every corner, a recruiter called out, "Do you feel happy walking down the street and seeing other lads wearing the King's uniform?" Universities ended classes early in the day to allow males to drill and females to do cheerful war work, such as sewing bandages and knitting the endless comforts of scarves, caps, wristlets, leggings, and socks. Children graciously bestowed their pennies to the Empire's plight.

Parades, rallies, and church events helped the drive. Public cutting for the plain clothed was supported, too. Failure to enlist meant cowardice, and such was symbolized in the handing out of white feathers to males who had not yet signed up. Originating in England, talcum powder from turkey feather dusters was poured over those not in uniform. Chaps received several feathers daily. Fellows who stayed behind were asked by all why they had not yet gone.

"What have you done for the crusade?" asked Mme. Laurentien to Aubrey.

Daughters of England were to contribute "Support, substitution, and supplication" to the country "In her hour of need."

"She iz going to join ze Cavalry," Richardieux replied seriously, mocking her.

Aubrey fumed. She replied she had handed out numerous white feathers. Her and her friends had badgered any number of lads solely to see their names in the paper for volunteer work.

"'as my feather girl given one to Edwards? Our ladz ought to rezeive eh medal simply for taking 'is place," commented Richardieux serenely.

"You are not a gentleman of the company," she corrected him with a Shakespearean reference. "Étienne wrote that the three of them are some of the only Francophones at Valcartier. Do you not want to be there with them?" she inquired.

"Our two familiez 'ave alwayz been at odds over this Lady Kingzton," explained Richardieux. He added, "Ze mother countries are ze root of the problemz and the problemz can be traced back through the centuries. There will be no peace between our families az long az thiz lastz." He took aim and shot the bird clear in the head. The dove fell to the ground and was no more.

Michel, wishing to prevent a more heated conversation, interrupted, "What is unmistakable about the photos from Valcartier is the joy that emanates from the photos. In a few of the shots, the trains are literally still there while all the fellows disembark. The lads are mulling about in front of the trains. They're so gay in their finest kilts or civvies. Uniforms have yet to be delivered. It is as though they can hardly believe their luck that they are the ones chosen to go. To look at them, one would think a wedding was taking place because they are so genuinely happy." Michel finished, "Auré, do you know of any one in uniform?" Michel meant French Canadians. "C'est La Guerre" or "Pour La Patrie" were the smart sayings in France. In French Canada and at this point, the feeling towards the war was mainly of indifference. Francophones did not care to identify themselves with France, a country they saw as riddled with atheistic and immoral issues. Quebec was largely a farming province and, with machinery unavailable to much of its citizens, males of working age were necessary to provide for families. Auré replied in dissidence.

The three Laurentiens had recently left for basic training. At train stations, the lads faced innumerable females kissing them before the lads were allowed to embark. Once on board, they were given packages containing handkerchiefs, buttons, needle and thread, two pairs of socks, and a medallion of the patron saint of soldiers: Michael. Train after train proceeded past cheering throngs, through all provinces, excepting the host province, Quebec.

Aubrey added that Mother Augusta had written. Both Agnews were going. Crowned with the sunshine of eternal youth[10], after their last joke at Depot had them court martialled, their fathers ordered them to sign up. Parents could tell even their adult sons to enlist and they had to obey them, though most wanted to go.

Mother Augusta wrote, *The two were so jolly over their "further discipline" they practically skipped to the registrar's office. May God have mercy on the Germans should Briarch and Rupert be captured. But they are young and impressionable, so let them have their fun. As well, Rupert was gifted a handsome new set of bagpipes to take along with him.*

None of the other members of the large Agnew clan were going because they were needed to stay in order to feed the Empire.

Mme. Laurentien had received her first letter from Étienne. The boys had made it to Valcartier.

Hughes looked over the thorough warfare outline for Canada and with perfect ease did away with the document and created his own mobilization plan. His plan did function but was very chaotic. Dismissing the dominion's sole training facility at Petawawa, Hughes chose what was a campground of desolate sand-filled fields twenty-five kilometers north of Quebec City. Hughes superintended the construction

---

[10] A Canadian World War I epitaph

and made the layout of the area reflect his personal tastes. Carpenters and labourers built and assembled well into the night. The water system and latrines would later have to be relocated due to being set up alongside the tents, parade routes, and electrical lighting. The campground became one of the dominion's largest cities very quickly. It also boasted the longest rifle range in any country. The range was one and a half kilometers long and had one thousand, seven hundred targets.

Richardieux said, "'ow ironic training iz located at Valcartier. I am zurprized Quebec 'as not spat them back out."

Mme. Laurentien explained, "Their little trip is turning out quite splendidly. It's been mainly sunny and training has been gay." she finished with a smile. Mothers were supposed to give their children willingly, along with anything else deemed necessary for the effort. Opposition to going was not acceptable.

Étienne's letter opened with, *If Hughes was shot it would astound no one. He is by far the most contemptible person at Valcartier. He sits with his feet on his desk in his tent, china tossed all over his office, blustering orders I'm not sure anyone actually hears. When he walks about camp, he points hither tither to males nearly out of earshot and either concedes or reduces their rank on the spot. He cancelled training three times alone in September for parades for journalists and politicians. "Skunk it" was what he publicly professed the English would do and stated that the Canadians would best the German army by ourselves. His discrepancies are endless. With his dark, sharp features and hawk-like stare, he even looks mad.*

In his early sixties, the manic Hughes said the impending battle was "A call to arms, like the fiery cross passing through the highlands of Scotland or the mountains of Ireland in former days." A former member of the army, having seen action in the Boer War, Hughes had been a grand soldier but expelled from South Africa after audacious insubordination. In one instance, he vehemently insisted to be bestowed, not solely one, but two Victoria Crosses, the British Empire's highest award for gallantry. Though he was of the high opinion he could continue to be Minister of Defence and command the Canadian army, Hughes was asked by Borden to choose a single role.

For the indisputable reason that no Canadian was accomplished enough and that Borden would not permit Hughes to lead, Englishman Lieutenant General E.A.H Alderson was chosen by Lord Kitchener to Command the Canadian Contingent. A long-standing veteran of the British Army, and at fifty-five years of age, Alderson had served with distinction and led units of the colony in the Boer War. British High Command was of the opinion their "Rough colonials" would take to Alderson, given his past affinity with them and because he had earned the Canadians' trust in the Boer War.

Étienne's letter continued, *Meals, clothing, and lodgings are all provided for. Ruses on each other are committed by everyone. A favourite is to pull the pegs of other tents or to cause the waterway or latrines to flow into our mate's tents.*

In the evening, films are viewed in the barn-turned-makeshift theatre. Also, the first allowance was just given. Like everything else at Valcartier, pay was devised on the fly. No official record of the money was recorded. The chaps simply lined up in rows. The money was handed out over tables in the open. Some went from line to line collecting numerous allowances. We didn't realize money was going to play a role. The only factor was to serve for the greater good. The most basic of instruction is given from dated textbooks and manuals. We are taught how to spank the enemy with bayonets into bales of hay. Long marches with wood in place of the yet-to-arrive rifle and drilling make the bulk of our days. At times we do practice shooting. The officers don't have the desire to use large guns that can strike unseen targets at a great distance. In essence, artillery is not a factor. More pointedly, officers do not have the time to figure how to incorporate such contraptions into a battle against a smartly-equipped foe. Discipline is rudimentary as well. Mates who joined together are to cease speaking if of different ranks. Such rarely happens. If a private and an officer get into a squabble, a fistfight usually ensues. Others have already been made to leave for failing to be English born.

Emmett suggested to Aubrey they retire, although early, for their next meal. He was keen for a toddy and his cool library after continual shortness of breath. After Emmett's last remark, Richardieux asked to walk with them to Pembina. He wanted to show Michel a fallen tree along the property line by the oak grove, even though they had a head gardener and four servants underneath the gardener to attend to such matters.

The end of September saw the Prime Minister give his much-awaited consent. Hughes broke down and cried. The entire training site erupted in applause. In the evening, the boys had a dance and were each other's partners. Pen could hardly be put to paper to tell families of the most exciting news.

The quartet was almost at the grand stairs of the back of Pembina. Geese were flying overhead. Their wings beat valiantly in departure of nature's impending show. Michel explained to his nephew that his sons were in the regular part of the army. They were not able to join the sole French speaking company (150 troops) because it had already filled its numbers. Hughes disallowed French Units.

Thirty-one thousand, from a colony of seven million, set off for the coast, a remarkable feat given the allotted schedule. The muddled and rabbled 1st Canadian Contingent marched along the St. Lawrence, singing gaily. Bagpipers and drummers played the boys past the Citadel, where the Royal Navy escort and the dominion's finest ocean liners, quickly repainted in gay war-inspiring grey, could be seen. The convoy sat waiting in the harbour of Gaspé.

Emmett had been lagging for a bit of time. Aubrey, walking ahead of the rest, turned to speak to Emmett. But as she looked to Emmett, she noticed he was standing stationary. His right hand was above his heart. She choked on her words as she watched one of Emmett's knees fall to the ground. The tips of his fingers of his left hand barely touched the grass. His right hand then went to his collarbone as though gasping for breath.

The lads were repeatedly marched onto the destroyers and off again. No one quite knew how to fit so many, along with seven thousand horses and hundreds of pieces of equipment. Also rang the question was how to load more than one hundred thousand flour bags to be given to England, in His Majesty's name, as a gift from Canada.

Awaiting to set sail, too, was a contingent from the small colony of Newfoundland. The island did not have a military or a militia, though hundreds volunteered in the initial days after war was declared. Their chosen training camp was a cricket field in Pleasantville, St. John's. The "First Five Hundred" agreed to "serve abroad for the duration of the war, but not exceeding one year." They would also be called the Blue Puttees for the remainder of the effort, due to their illegal military leg wear from the lack of khaki fabric in the colony. Experienced officers, along with machine guns, binoculars, and well-nigh all matter of warfare accessories, were not to be found on the island either. Their uniforms had yet to arrive. Other items that needed be delivered from Canada, as well, were their rifles, along with revolvers from England.

Richardieux was already looking at Aubrey while Michel continued to explain matters further. Richardieux turned backwards to see what dismayed her. He then hurriedly yelled at Michel to go for aid. Michel turned to look behind him and became torn between fetching the now-obsolete doctor and remaining with one of his oldest friends in his final moments. Aubrey ran towards Emmett at the same time Richardieux hindered her pathway. While Richardieux's arms wrapped around Aubrey, her last view of Emmett was of his second knee falling to the ground. Richardieux half carried, half dragged her back into the manor, walloping and screaming to no consequence of her sympathizer.

Present at Gaspé were all dignitaries and tens of thousands of citizens, who came to cheer the troops. The three flags waved in nearly as many numbers as those present. Bands and buglers played endlessly. Both anthems were sung any number of times. Tens upon tens of hymns were shouted to the Heavens. Hughes boarded a ship to say goodbye in person.

The ships ventured from the harbour. The largest armada to cross the Atlantic in history set sail. Given nearly seven out of ten on board were British born, as the boys sailed for home, they penned in their newly issued military diaries, *Every soul on these ships will remember this day, even if we lived for centuries.*

The Proposal

Her period of mourning was to last nine months. Aubrey now had organdie at her collar and cuffs instead of full black, given it had been a few weeks since Emmett's death. His name was dear to the memory of his friends[11]: however, she had not attended the funeral because females were still largely considered incapable of maintaining composure at such an event.

A man[12] who was unexpected was shown into the manor by Llewellyn. Llewellyn was in mourning dress, given by his mistress to wear for the same length of time as his master's family. He refused to bow from the room. Richardieux would never have dared call upon Aubrey in his late master's presence.

Richardieux offered his condolences in regard to her grandfather.

"His life was gentle that nature might say to all the world, this was a man[13]," Aubrey replied meekly.

"I know what a lover of Shakespeare Mr. Kingston was, being an intelligent and elegant man," he conceded.

---

[11]   A Canadian World War I epitaph
[12]   A Canadian World War I epitaph
[13]   A Canadian World War I epitaph

In my life will his remembrance ever linger[14], she thought in response. She asked Richardieux where he had been that morning. Since confession was his answer, she knew what was to ensue. Because he was divorced, and she was a daughter of a gentleman, both families refused to announce their engagement. An engaged couple could address one another by their Christian names, Aubrey started to call him Auré, as he was called for short. Auré had set the wedding for one month to the day after the proposal. His gift[15] to her upon their engagement was a stunning sapphire, yellow gold ring, the epitome of Edwardian chic. Her court dress was turned into her wedding dress. The Laurentiens were the only family from the groom's side, and there were no relatives at all from the bride's side at St. Patrick Cathedral for the ceremony or at Chateau Laurier for the reception. Because neither of their families would greet them, the scandalous and imprudent match began in Niagra Falls for its honeymoon.

---

[14] A Canadian World War I epitaph
[15] A Canadian World War I epitaph

Salisbury

At the Christmas ball, Michel added in his prayer that the boys might bring glory to the Empire. He ended the prayer with, "Thanks be to God who giveth us the victory[16]." The Empire was not cared for at all at Vauréal. Michel was nevertheless considerate of his guests.

The Prime Minister sent the contingent a Christmas message. Troops received cards from George and the Queen. Princess Mary gave each lad a small gift box. Every gold-embossed tin held a few items from the princess. Smokers were given a packet of tobacco, a carton of cigarettes, and a tinder lighter. Other boxes were of a packet of acid tablets, a khaki writing case, as well as a lead "bullet" pencil. All boxes contained a card and a picture of the lovely princess.

Because the boys overseas were sacrificing, so would Michel out of gratitude. He served[17] a mere single figure course meal at Vauréal's Christmas ball, out of respect. In Salisbury, the boys were given a bill of fine fare for Christmas dinner: roast turkey, boiled ham, cabbage, potatoes, buttered beans, cornstarch pudding and jelly, mince pie, apples, oranges, nuts, and plum pudding.

---

[16] A Canadian World War I epitaph
[17] A Canadian World War I epitaph

Westbrook asked Michel how his sons were doing at Salisbury. The reply was they were having a swimmingly jolly time. Everyone chuckled along the length of the dining table.

After a dull fortnight at sea, the Armada arrived in Plymouth Hoe, southern England. The contingent was greeted by cheering Britons who had come to welcome their colonials home. While rain poured down, the contingent drove or marched three hours to their temporary training facility at Salisbury Plain. Newfoundland trained at Salisbury for seven weeks. The regiment was given their primary glance at the momentousness of the battle, given they were now surrounded by thousands of their anxious brothers-in-arms.

Aubrey thought of the photos sent with the letters from all her acquaintances. During the crossing, kodaks were taken of them on the decks of ships with guardrails in the background. They looked so dashing with their broad shoulders and smiles as they piggy-backed one another.

While his glass of Madiera, the Edwardian drink of choice, was being filled, Westbrook turned to Auré, "Mr. Richardieux, you have not given us your opinion yet, and it would be entertaining to the ladies to hear some talk of war."

The only thing the ladies wanted to know was why the boys had not yet returned. The big breakthrough should have already happened.

"His Majesty said 'e will abstain from alcohol az long as ze war lasts," Auré replied.

"Quite rightly so, and a fine man to do so in his position. A capitol idea!" answered Lawrence.

"I will drink 'is share," Auré continued.

"Come now, see reason!"

"Why in the King's name!"

Michel smiled but caught himself before anyone could see his grin.

"But what do you mean?" cried Sir Westbrook. "I mean to zay if England'z troops were made to train at Zalizbury in ze conditions ourz are going through, they would mutiny."

Give credit where credit was due, thought all grudgingly, though not a soul would dare say so aloud.

The contingent's hosted training site was nothing short of ghastly. In Salisbury, the rain would pour down relentlessly three out of four days, or eighty-nine out of one hundred and twenty days, during the whole of their stay in one of the most woebegone winters in British history. Gales brought down lecture tents where they gathered for instruction. Uniforms were hastily made. The seams unravelled on their too snug tunics. The cotton and wool sewn to make greatcoats did not a thing to protect against the wet or cold. Boots simply fell apart in the muck. Chums remarked that cardboard was used to make the soles of the boots, and Hughes was pet named "Sham Shoes." Laddies queued in downpour for tea and porridge breakfast, fat bacon, and Irish stew for dinner, and supper consisted of bread, jam, and tea. Troops said it was as though a village was being evacuated from a flood, given how one had to wade through the wallow and water so much of the time. The training area had been lessened to a muck-like bog. The English were caught off guard that the colonials from the Empire's coldest outpost even noticed the weather.

Auré continued, "You zay every Englizhmen 'as eh patriotic duty to the Empire at thiz moment. This iz the dominion's capitol. How many Englishmen speak French? Very few indeed. European students are taught eh 'andful of languages and that iz considered normal to them. Ze foremost European countries mainly 'ave one official language, though Europeans learn so many of ze other languages of the continent. Our official languages are French and English, though nowhere near 'alf the dominion is bilingual. It is remarkable how ignorant we are of one another."

Tension was felt by all, because of his nephew's inexplicable rudeness, so Michel interrupted by stating, "What my nephew means is that when one learns another language, by default one learns that culture and therefore that culture's perspective. One axiomatically become more accepting, or at least tolerant, of that perspective because one understands that culture. It is said no culture is better nor worse than another, solely different. If worse came to worst, that is to say if Quebec ever tried to leave or if the dominion went to civil war, it would not be the fault of any given political party or one sole province, but the failure of all of Canada. If the majority of Canadians were bilingual, neither catastrophe could happen because so many dynamics would change in the dominion that would prevent either measure from happening. Those two distresses could not come close to transpiring if the majority of the dominion was bilingual. And my nephew is correct to say that at the most basic level of patriotism, every Canadian has a duty to be bilingual."

Much to Michel's chagrin, his nephew added, "And in fairness, it iz almost alwayz French Canada who learnz ze other's language."

Aubrey added, "Also in fairness, on the prairies, outside of cities in Saskatchewan, in towns and villages, few teachers speak French, which I suppose is a problem in itself — meaning our perspective needs to change. And in my experience, when you ask an English Canadian if he speaks French and he answers 'no,' you can hear the guilt in his voice. It is not that Western Canada is necessarily ignorant; it is that the resources are simply not available to learn the other language. And vice versa in French Canada."

In hopes that the conversation would come to an end, Michel finished by saying, "Lest we forget[18], if we are to understand the other figuratively, we must first understand the other literally. And yes, there are flaws in the system."

The awaiting full orchestra could be heard by Vauréal's hushed guests from across the grand hall. "Silent Night," in both English and German, drifted across the opposing trenches the other side of the Atlantic.

Michel tried to defuse the situation by stating, "Let us agree to disagree." He mentioned the boy's training to dissuade the present conversation from continuing.

Lady Westbrook added, "Well, there will always be disagreements with so many brash young lads in one area. Our youngest born[19], Gabriel, wrote they are behaving in a most bombastic manner." This included, but was certainly not limited to, fights amongst the kilted units over which colour tartan each should be granted. Alcohol was always available in the villages not far from camp, but if one was well-raised, one did not surrender to the wicked desire.

Oblivious to his wife's intention to aid Michel in a change of subject, Westbrook carried on, "But, by jove, you cannot mean you want independence from England? And be isolationists, like the Yanks?! Surely not!" If the two families could agree upon one subject, it was to be un-American.

Michel asked that Auré aid him in bringing cigars to the table once supper had finished, however scandalous it was to ask a master in place of a servant for anything at all. As the two left the hall, the ladies raised their eyebrows at one another over their

---

[18]   A Canadian World War I epitaph
[19]   A Canadian World War I epitaph

teacups. Richardieux knew where his loyalties lay. "Proud," "Rabble-rouser," "Blooming liar," and "Un-British" were labels given to Richardieux the moment he was out of the hall.

Gentleman's agreements broke out all along the newly formed Western Front. The two rival armies gifted each other chocolates and cigarettes, partook in football matches together, and extended the compliments of the season to one another in the barren terrain. Interpreters aided Chaplains in giving service and mass.

Westbrook said, smiling to no one in particular, "That Richardieux seems to have quite the bee in his bonnet over these matters."

Kellynch, who sat next to Westbrook, replied under his breath, though more to himself, "Indeed, I do believe he is a war profiteer."

"In the name of Saint George (England's Patron Saint)*!* That is a terrible thing to say!" said a Westbrook astonished.

Aubrey and Lady Bird slandered those who looked skinny in their wedding dresses the last season. The gentlemen would eventually remove to the smoking room to discuss the contingent. They would then turn to the important matter of where England was presently engaged. The landing of the Princess Pat's in France earlier in the month under a British Division, the 27th, and that England had declared war on Turkey would also be scrutinized. Then the conversation would turn to Borden's sacred agreement for the New Year. Fifty thousand was many indeed for so small a colony. Nevertheless, as long as Christianity, truth, and justice were being wrested from a barbarous foe, no number could eclipse the patriotic fever that was Canada. "For the Empire!" the dominion cheered.

Dinner Party

Auré was surprisingly tolerable company, even in his perpetually dour state. At times, Aubrey was really quite smitten with him. Aubrey knew she was fortunate to have him for a husband. Legally, a husband could beat his wife with an object no wider than his thumb but Aubrey had always felt completely safe with him. Embarrassed, mothers would write their daughters letters explaining the process of what would happen on their wedding night. Matrons said that the bedroom would be disgusting and embarrassing, but it would all be worth it for the sake of the children. Though when Aubrey was with Auré at night it was not like what she had been forewarned of at all. There seemed to be a hunger in her husband's arms, something language could not transcend. But she would always wake up alone in the mornings, instead of him at her side, proof that he did not want her. Auré would invariably return to his room or, most likely, wake up in the early morning hours to work. Whether she wanted to or not, he was fully respectful towards her in regard to the bedroom. The bedroom was not an obligation on her part in any way; that was how she knew her husband was already having affairs. However, he had not so much as raised his voice to her. Auré had told her it was cowardly for a man to raise his voice to his wife or daughters. In fact, she had trifle to complain about of married life at all. Auré was considerate towards her in every way. If only she could find another gentleman with whom to fall in love.

Pembina's new master proved to be strict but fair towards his servants. In traditional manors, males and females spent their days apart, and Auré had the servants do likewise. The male servants were even ordered to use separate staircases from the females. Not even Emmett had such antiquated rules for the servants. When a servant broke an item, the cost was not garnished from their wages, as was customary. A servant was never reproofed by any means but by their master speaking sternly to them. As determined by sex and position held, daily meat, sugar, beer, and tea allowances were afforded to servants. Bread was the sole exception, though the unwritten rule was only day-old bread could be eaten freely. Auré increased the servants' portions so they were more plentiful.

He saw no point in frivolities, and Aubrey always went to the endless circuit of Edwardian functions without him. He preferred solitude in order to work. He did enjoy the outdoors, although he went alone. Of course, he was expected to be present at her dinner parties, which he said was more than enough.

Outdoors, the wind made the snow beat against the windows, the sort of weather that made it hard to breathe. It was six in the evening, the usual time for dinner parties to start.

"Is the peacock coming?" Auré asked. A black tie could be exchanged for white, and a dinner jacket could replace the coat if a master entertained in the company of dear acquaintances. However, it appeared Auré had no intimates.

Auré looked strikingly handsome in his full evening attire. Aubrey did not bother to compliment him. One of the most serious men she had ever known, she thought he would not care for such a superficial remark. They were certainly not in love, though momentarily she wished he would be romantic with her.

"Yes, Peter will be in attendance," his wife answered him. Extremely busy since her wedding, Aubrey had little time for herself. Given she was now accepted into society, teas, card clubs, balls, and dinner parties took up so much of her days. It was customary for an aristocratic wife to throw a few dinner parties a week; however, Auré had been so busy with work, and with his refusal to throw a party during Lent, this was the first time she had been able to give a party since their wedding. The seating plan had been akin to a bomb waiting to explode. No one was found suitable to sit beside her husband without being affronted. The figuring of who would do well seated next to whom and how her husband's business could profit from future contacts and contracts had taken hours of Aubrey's time. The planning of the eighteen-course meal for the intimate dinner party took time as well.

A society hostess' main role was to further her family's fortune. A charming and witty wife could immensely further her husband's career and could prove more valuable than a wife whose highest claim of social standing was beauty. Acquainted with every aristocrat in the city and he not, Aubrey reasoned their union was the opening wedge into Ottawa society for the expansive Richardieux trade business to develop further throughout English Canada.

Goose was a must-have centrepiece to an Edwardian dinner party. The prosperity of an aristocratic surname could be greatly affected by hosted dinner parties. As such,

Aubrey carefully ensured her guests' dinner would be a luxuriant affair not to be forgotten. For the main course, she had planned the epitome of Edwardian suppers: the lush and ostentatious plate of pâté de foie gras set interiorly of a truffle, set interiorly of an ortolan, set interiorly of a quail.

"Well, I'm sort of apprehensive, I do like to be prim. But it is the first time we, an esemble of women, will leave Canada with a clear direction," said Henrietta, in response to her host's questions of her near departure.

For the cause, London asked Ottawa for seventy-five nursing sisters in January of the new year. The Canadian military, employing five nurses, asked citizens to fill the new positions. A few thousand applied in the first fortnight. The standard age of an English-Canadian nursing sister was twenty-four. All were, quite respectably, single. A large number had immediate male relatives in uniform. Nursing sisters were to be paid two dollars plus an additional sixty cents field allowance per day. Margaret Macdonald was in command of the nurses and the sole woman of the Empire in the position of a major. Thought of by few as lucky to be going, Henrietta had been accepted in the role of a nurse. Auré listened intently with shining eyes. He was in the minority of those who had a high opinion of her. Improper to the point of being sinful, to allow females near an operation of warfare, the most common response to women fighting was, "But why?" Parents feared seeing action may harden their daughters to the point of becoming questionable companions and caretakers to their future families. Besides, before wedlock, ladies should be left entirely unaware of the male frame and its workings.

"And Hughie joined the Flying Corps," Aubrey said, teasing.

Hugh nodded, relief flooding over him, given he was not able to join soon enough to go with the 1st Contingent the previous summer. London asked the dominion for "six expert aeronauts." However, no pilots at all could be found. Hugh had joined the Royal Flying Corps, though his father, like most, wished his son would make something of himself and join the Cavalry or the Navy, instead of trying his hand with those flying machines.

One of the gentlemen remarked casually to the group at large, "So, they are staying over there a bit longer than expected? Well, the contingent won't bring out the Northern Lights, but we are privileged to serve England."

Peter added, with barely suppressed laughter, "Hughes simply does not stop! Never mind that he continually grants his own chums senior ranks. He took a ship to London himself and strode around the city in uniform. He barked to the English press that Canada would send hundreds of thousands of lads. Borden was cross, incredulous at Hughes' statements. The Canadian cabinet wanted Hughes to be brought back — like a caged bear. At any rate, a British NCO who was instructing the Canadians was quoted as saying to them, 'Gentlemen, when I see you handle your rifles, I feel like falling on my knees and thanking God that we've got a navy.' At least England's guidance is considerably more pragmatic. I'm told bayoneting is a favourite with our colonials. At least the officers are being given a separate form of instruction than the regulars now. The legalities of militarism, technical and tactical competency, prudent military strategies, signalling, trench framework, and guiding the lads in battle are all explained at the officer training schools. Am I right to say they have chapel service right at Stonehenge?"

One of the gentlemen at the table answered in the affirmative. Peter went on, "They regularly practice in view of the structure."

Aubrey did not pay much attention while the gentleman spoke of the war. The Canadian contingent would never amount to a thing, besides. She and Lady Bird gossiped quietly of their married acquaintances, of who was sleeping with whom and why and how they would let the wives of unfaithful husbands know without coming across as wrongdoers themselves.

Kellynch shook his head and added crossly, "And the ones who have bought those untidy contracts from Hughes."

Munitions contracts that Hughes was in charge of were often allotted to his intimates and chums. Ottawans condemned these males of war profiteering.

Auré, for once, spoke, "It iz bad form to insult one'z 'ost."

The dinner party became entirely still. Kellynch's eyes narrowed in distaste. One of the gentlemen cried, "Do you mean to say, Sir, you are hand in glove with Hughes and his cronies?"

Pembina's master replied, "Pleaze, I will not allow further discussion of zis war under my roof."

The party in its entirety turned to stare, bewildered, at their host's strange utterance. The mistress of Pembina was told by the master ahead of time to sit to his left, so that his sword arm would be free, and that Peter was to sit directly across from Auré. This indicated to Peter that Auré did not trust him and his host would welcome a duel. The signal was not lost on anyone at the table, but their host's comment proved to be too much.

Peter said condescendingly, "Let's say, hypothetically, another contingent was raised, won't you defend your Mother Country, and if not, to be certain, the Imperial Mother?"

Humiliation at being turned away from the military was so great in England that rejectees were ending their lives. Government responded with badges attesting to the honourable attempt to join, and they were widely distributed. Auré was in the pink of condition and everyone knew he had not tried to sign up. Auré seemed immune to all pressure to enlist. His disapprobation towards the effort was his shield.

Auré ventured, "Why should I defend eh mother country that doez not defend our dominion? And Quebec 'as no mother country. After France deserted uz centuries ago, we 'ave flourished culturally, passionately, and on our own. Az an azide, England ought to be viewed az eh distant cousin to us."

Those at the table were shocked at their host's unapologetic position.

Once dessert was finished, the lady of the house would bow or smile to the lady of the highest rank to signal the females should withdraw from the dining room in the same sequence that they entered. They would then enter the drawing room to chat for an idle hour with coffee. Gentlemen would stay seated in the drawing room or, if not, would remove to the smoking room or library. Gentlemen's conversations deemed inappropriate for ladies, such as politics or business, were accompanied by smoking and nightcaps of port and brandy. Afterwards, gentlemen would join the ladies in the drawing room for modest dancing or cards. However, out of protest and incredulity, Pembina's guests left before coffee and brandy could be served. Auré excused himself from the dining room, but as did so, he forbade Peter from Pembina's grounds henceforth. Aubrey was left flabbergasted and in dismay at the irrevocable catastrophe that was her first dinner party in society.

After four months of training, the King, mounted, assessed his English Canadian sons. In a downpour, the lads stood at attention, then marched in front of him for the last grand training exercise. George gave his blessing for them to embark for France. Excitement was nearly beyond articulation. The boys shouted, wild with delight, "After all, nothing could be worse than Salisbury!"

Ypres

Late February hosted the contingent's arrival in France. The lads marched or were packed into cattle cars to be taken to the front. The troops in the cattle cars could not sit for as long as forty-eight hours. The contingent's property would be the Armentières section of the Ypres Salient and close to the Belgium French border. Such was the most perilous region of the Western Front. On march, the contingent sang, "We'll Never Let the Old Flag Fall."

> "We'll never let the old flag fall
> For we love it the best of all
> In peace and war, you'll hear us sing
> God save the flag, God save our King
> To the ends of the world
> The flags unfurled
> And we'll never let the old flag fall"

The English Canadians were brought under the charge of the British. One Tommy was paired with one English Canadian to teach the basics of warfare. Systemic problems were pervasive throughout the entire Canadian military. British superiors acting as Commanding and Staff Officers proved absolutely vital. The contingent was given two full days to be taught the rudiments of battle. In the trenches, the first lesson learned was, "Fear God and keep your head down." The lads were shocked upon being informed that the fighting continued on the Sabbath day. They were equally taken aback at the language where they were. From quiet Christian townships and aristocratic households, the lads were not used to hearing foul words. Shouting to the opposing army was a constant. Their first evening, Germans jeered across the way, "Come out, you Canadians! Come out and fight!" The foe met replies that newspapers refused to print. Shells landed uncomfortably close, which would spill the boys' tea. They would get to their feet, denounce the foe as ill-mannered, and holler, "Have to do a little better than that, Fritzie!" On the other side, trenches were properly equipped with running water and electrical lights. The mother countries knew Belgium would soon become free and, therefore, trenches that were beyond basic proved unnecessary. Officers were given dugouts for sleeping quarters. The regular private used waterproof sheets and slept outside in the muck and rain, as the opinion of their officers was that privates would otherwise grow soft. As they drilled and learned to build exactly ninety-degree angled trenches, they sang,

"We are Sam Hughes' army
No bloody good are we
We cannot march
We cannot shoot
No bloody good are we"

Along with temptations of Demon Rum and electric pianos, the boys at large wrote to their families about their time at the front.

England captured victories at—... After supper the general asked to hear "God save the King," "Rule Britannia," and end the evening with a hymn that we simply adored. Much of the time violins, mouth organs, and fiddles are present... Am certainly thankful we were able to reach the front before the war ended... We get along splendidly... Football is indulged in... It seems the effort has taken a turn because kodaks are no longer permitted at the front... I'm glad socks were sent along in your care bundle because muck is at times in our ditches. The ones in my unit are grateful for the fine sweets sent too... A tall lass needs to duck down continuously given the ditches are not high enough to cover him, although the ditches do have a few strands of wire to protect you from brother boche... There seems to be a different atmostphere in the trenches than in civilian life... Jolly Fritz is listened to so many tens of yards over the way while a bewitching secondary trench is taking shape, although I'm not sure how much use it will be... News from Old Keiser Bill, who is constantly observed by the airships, is that all of this will be over in a few months, so I fancy being in Gay & Gallant France for the moment.

The contingent saw its first battle engagement on March 10th. The village of Neuve-Chapelle was being defended by the English and its Indian army, which were to the right of the

English Canadians. The lads would not venture into No Man's Land but were to offer firearm support to prevent the foe's reinforcements from going into battle. Three days later, the fray ended with 100 English-Canadian casualties. The lads most likely did not kill any foe at all, though they staved off the Germans from counterattacking. As well, they prevented additional enemy soldiers being brought forth to engage the British.

In early April, the order was given to depart from the contingent's tranquil locale, and the boys were mandated to the infamous Ypres Salient. The trenches that greeted them had corpses to walk on with limbs and bare white bones sticking out from the walls. The sides of trenches were partially made with the deceased, although, after the first year of the English Canadians being on the western front, this practice stopped. What lay beyond their new trenches and sandbags, which enemy snipers could fire through, was terrain covered with corpses. Also, in front of them, and before the historic city of Ypres, the Allied and German lines met in a concave bend. The Allied trenches were fired upon from the north, south, as well as the east. The lads were confined to the lower area of the region. The sole key town in Belgium that the Allies still possessed, Ypres prevented the foe from taking over the English Channel and, with her, the French ports. To control Ypres, or "Wipers" as British troops nicknamed the area, was of the utmost importance.

So young, so far from home[20] in England, with news of the coming battle, the contingent sent excited word.

Father, it appears we are frightfully unfit to
see action... It can be argued the countless

---

[20]   A Canadian World War I epitaph

times we spent preparing with sword and lance might come to naught... In France, their officers do take their sabres with them, although I gave mine to a civilian couple... However, "patience, pluck, and cheerfulness" will conquer all... Our moment has come to protect Great Britain... I hope to see home shortly and then cross the Atlantic and back to our lovely residence of the maple leaf... All my love, your Canadian Tommy boy.

Bag pipers and their brass and pipe band mates were ordered to act as stretcher-bearers should the need arise. The lads crouched in the ditches, wearing felt hats to protect against the rain.

Thirteen thousand of the 1st Canadian Division were made to stay in England in the role of supplementary troops. The army that landed in France consisted of twelve thousand regular troops and nearly five thousand horses. A further six thousand made up the artillery, engineering, medical, and service sections of the contingent. Eighteen thousand comprised the 1st Canadian Division. The Canadian military was the most insignificant, self-contained army at the front. The Canadians were the laughingstock of the Allies for any number of reasons. Pet named the "Comedian Contingent" of the Empire, if not the whole of the Allied Forces, starting in Valcartier, the Canadian disregard towards discipline and rules was legendary. Officers were openly called by their Christian names, an unpardonable offense in British militarism. They did as much with British officers present, shocking these officers to their very souls. Salutes were casually disregarded and given solely to superiors who had garnered the approbation of one. Defective equipment was grossly and endlessly an embarrassing matter. Every level of command had scant knowledge of leading in peacetime or in warfare. The entire military seemed to be headed by a mentally unbalanced Minister of Defense. The wild Canucks were sent in for their first mission.

The servant handed Aubrey the day's mail on a silver platter. Servants were so lowly that they could not come into physical contact with their betters. On the platter was a stack of letters from the front. The evening of April 22nd 1915, the division was ordered to the delightful occasion of warfare. At the same time, Germany used "Disinfection," or what they secretly called poison gas, on their enemy. Aubrey opened Étienne's letter first.

Dearest Aubrey,

Our commanding officer was perhaps overly joyful when he gave the order to stand to. A massive artillery bombardment ensued. An hour later, what came next, before our very eyes, was a gargantuan green-yellow cloud, six kilometers in length and almost a kilometer in depth, holding one hundred and sixty tons of gas. The mass came forward by a light wind from Fritz' cylinders dug in before their trenches, shocking the contingent.

To the right, the English Canadians were safeguarded by two British divisions. To the left of the contingent, the next colony received the main part of the gas attack and retreated. Bedlam instantly ensued. Thus, there was a six-and-a-half-kilometer break in the Allied line. The enemy came into position of possibly surrounding fifty thousand Allies. The whole of the Salient that the Allies commanded would fall if the gap was left in disrepair. The English Canadians were to close the breach. Taught from childhood that "Good Englishmen do not run" and with innocence almost beyond comparison, the lads, ordinary citizens months prior, left the safety of the trenches to spar with the foe in what would be one of the most selfless feats of the war in its entirety.

Étienne's letter further read, *The order was given by the officers, "No British soldier crawls into battle on their belly." After this, our lot, and a number of us Ottawans, started to make our way across what were famers' fields. A rifle bullet flew quite near to my batman.*

By jolly chance, Germany had not anticipated such a break. Their reinforcements could not take advantage of their ground gained and were equally not equipped to deal with the gas. A total of three kilometers of ground was gained by the foe. Then they dug in. "He rushed into the field and foremost fighting fell[21]," Étienne quoted Byron in how he explained his brother's death. Pierre was gone in the first quarter hour of battle. *Only a boy, but he did his best, not forgotten[22], Pierre*

---

[21] A Canadian World War I epitaph
[22] A Canadian World War I epitaph

held on for a handful of minutes or so. His
last words were, "I'm in the pink!" He died
cheerfully in my arms. And there went out
that day to the god of battles the soul of a man
who loved battles[23]. Sa mort a laissé une plaie
profonde dans nos coeurs[24] (His death has left
a deep sorrow in our hearts).

Pierre died in Étienne's arms, to be sure, though in perfect torment. Hydrochloric acid came from the gas and water blending together. Pierre slowly suffocated in his own, though scorching, fluids after his skin turned black from lack of oxygen. Others turned the shade of mahogany or grass green. Any number were violently sick. They literally coughed their lungs out in a sticky substance as they writhed on the ground, their faces spotted with their blood and froth. The ramification of gas would perpetually stay with the chlorine-lessened lifetimes of the doctors, sisters, and troops who would survive the duration.

The gas felt as though it could strangle you
and smelled very strong. One knew when one
was in its presence as the eyes, nose, and
throat became instantly vexed. As there was
no sort of protection from the gas, say, a mask
or respirator of sorts, officers rushed through
the lot of us, calling out to urinate on our
handkerchiefs to neutralize the effects, then
to wrap it around our mouths. The officers
doubtlessly prevented innumerable deaths.

---

[23] A Canadian World War I epitaph
[24] A Canadian World War I epitaph

The entire night was used to try to secure the breach. As well, an oak plantation called Kitchener's Wood, situated near St. Julien, saw a counterattack to push Fritz away. The higher section was controlled by Germany and if the contingent did not capture it, the lads would be massacred come daylight. Eventually, we took over the elevated ground. Daybreak saw two additional, truly devastating, assaults attempted on the foe. Dear time was bought, though at the cost of excessive chaps wounded and a small amount of land claimed.

The Ross Rifle was a pitiful match to Germany's machine guns. Hughes stated the Ross, Mark III, was, "The most perfect military rifle in the world today." *The bolt does not always seal. The steel is not tempered properly. While it fires quickly, the Ross jams. The bayonet simply falls to the ground and the barrel constantly needs to be cleaned. I used mine for the first dozen or so times, then I turned it into a bat. We threw away the long and weighty Ross and, during battle, recovered the Lee-Enfields that the British had left behind. Other chaps used the discarded Mausers they took off the German cadavers.*

The battle for St. Julien came second. Another fierce bombardment accompanied by gas, much like the first time, befell the Allied lines. The enemy picked a new target this time

around — our contingent. By the 24th, we were
outnumbered by two to one.

After four days of fighting and on April 25th, the poor bloody infantry was relieved. Outnumbered, outgunned, and outflanked, frequently attacked from two to three sides at once, and without sleep for the smash in its entirety and nearly the same length of time without food or water, the English Canadians defended Allied territory from fully three chlorine attacks. The Princess Pat's fought alongside the mother country as well. The division assisted in valuable measure to England for her soldiers to be brought forth to take control.

Commanding Officers of the contingent gave fine compliments, "The boys take to danger so splendidly."

When led behind British lines, captured German generals commented, truly unconventionally, that the English Canadians were of higher calibre than their own troops.

The first letters, post-inaugural battle, were sent to Canada.

Oh, to be blunt, this madness cannot be called
"war" but pure bloody murder... My unit and
those surrounding mine were really rather
marvellous in battle... Our Brother Boche,
who we took prisoner, exclaimed that we
fought like the devil was in us... I would fight
for England forever... A splendid mate who
did all he could... It was absolute confusion...
Gratitude towards the laddie who perished for
Great Britain... he is laid to rest in a foreign
field, forever England.

The Laurentiens would shortly receive an official war office telegram.

Dear Mr. and Mrs. Laurentien,

Will you kindly accept my sincere sympathy and condolence in the decease of that worthy citizen and heroic soldier, your son, Private Pierre Laurentien. While one cannot too deeply mourn the loss of such a brave comrade, there is a consolation in knowing that he did his duty fearlessly and well, and gave his life for the cause of Liberty and the upbuilding of the Empire.

Again, extending to you my heartfelt sympathy.

Faithfully,
Sam Hughes
Major General,
Minister of Militia and Defence,
For Canada

Post-battle, there were 6,500 English Canadian casualties, of which more than 2,000 were deaths, a ghastly high ratio for the effort. Along with those casualties, the lads also received the difficult-to-obtain esteem of the enemy. The foe took 1,410 of the division as prisoners. The division then set about burying their fallen themselves and would routinely do so in the future. An English-Canadian physician was on sight and penned a poem one morning, soon after the division was relieved, and then tossed the poem aside. His mates retrieved the poem that would be published by the end of the year. A cobbled-together hospital was later overtaken by the Germans. Every English Canadian not able to walk from the hospital was bayoneted. On route to the next fray, Aubers Ridge, the contingent sang,

"You say that the First Contingent
Are dolts, and rotters, and snydes
The dregs of the nation's manhood
And a whole lot besides
We ruined your reputation
But you must admit we're men
We held the line for the Empire
We fought at St. Julien."

Muskoka

News of the conflict made way to Britain and dribbled through the country in due course to the dominion. Canada's sons justified themselves to be an exemplary military in their principal engagement in a European war. The dominion was stunned at the atrocity of the battle. Newspapers on Sparks Street posted the casualties. The romantic conviction of warfare departed in perpetuity, though there was splendid reason to rejoice. First Canadian Contingent[25] was the only colony to maintain the line. Thus, the unassailable region of Ypres was so gallantly held by Canada. British Field Marshal Sir John French expressed the Canadian Contingent "saved the situation." Cabled congratulatory messages were sent to Borden about his boys. In downtown Ottawa, all citizens had purchased an edition of the *English Press. The guns were recaptured by a deed of the Canadian troops, which will fill the heart of the Motherland with love and pride. The Canadians advanced with magnificent steadiness... No words can express the gratitude of the nation to the great Dominion for this valour of her sons... One topic has this week absorbed all our thoughts and conversation, the magnificent effort of the Canadian Division in Flanders, which saved Ypres from capture, and the Allies from possibly an overwhelming defeat.*

---

[25]   A Canadian World War I epitaph

The Canadians held on with grim courage under terrible shellfire and a dense cloud of poison gas … The Empire unites in sorrow for their dead and shares the pride in Canadian gallantry.

Aubrey found herself in the family way soon after her wedding. Females who were expecting hid from the public eye. Soon-to-be mothers had servants or relatives to do things for them in order to stay in their house and were not made to venture out. However, respectability did permit expectant wives to take promenades in the evening time, accompanied by their bashful yet prideful husbands.

North of Ottawa, steamships brought guests to Muskoka, the handsomest cottage country of the Empire. Overlooking lake Rousseau was the most stunning resort Muskoka could boast, the grand and elegant Royal Muskoka Hotel. During the evening meal and in the grand hall of the hotel, Harrington discussed Ypres with other gentlemen from Ottawa.

"'Ypres' has been spoken of endlessly these past weeks. They did indeed hold true until reinforcements were brought in. England should be proud of our boys; they're a dependable little troop," Harrington said with such pride in his eyes it would seem he had led the division himself. Harrington continued, "Government thought it better to be safe than sorry and had another division brought about. Which reminds me, the contingent was renamed the 'Canadian Division.' The 2nd Canadian Division landed on British soil just ahead of the 1st reaching French soil. And training in England has been mainly moved to Shorncliffe, though there are camps spread out in the southeast of home. It is well suited and equipped to prepare the lads for action. The new main training site is less than a handful of miles from the ocean with many sheep grazing nearby. As well, that suffrage campaign has been suspended momentarily, because more females are necessary to aid with the cause. We must have our priorities right. The Princess Pat's saw action at Frezenberg in May and were almost entirely devastated in the southern area of Ypres. The division's last smash was the village of Festubert, a part of the La Bassée front, from the 15th to the 27th of May. Companies from our division went into action on the 18th across clear fields during daytime with scarcely any artillery to aid them, I might add. Their start time was five o'clock in the afternoon. They were relieved two or three days later."

The division suffered 2,605 stupendously massacred casualties in frontal charges against the smartly entrenched foe at Festubert. The Orchard was one of the main objectives for the division, along with numerous trenches. Maps given to the English-Canadian officers were catastrophically printed in reverse as well as upside down. They proved unreadable. They were also inaccurate by hundreds of yards. Also, intense firing had annihilated any number of critical points shown on the maps.

Harrington explained further, "At precisely their start time, the artillery was still firing over top of the poor bloody infantry. The lads were forced to wait until the shelling from their lines halted some twenty-five minutes after the scheduled hour. The error came from miscommunication between the back and front lines, as well as between the gunners and the lads they were supporting. British Tommies, who were north of the division, had gone into battle at their expected time. The division's officers in the front lines were forced to make a hasty decision of whether to remain safely behind and leave the British on their own or to go after the British in aid and into near annihilation. Moments after artillery ceased, our officers and troops went over the top and after the British.

The division's Highlanders captured what is called 'The Orchard' and it proved the smash's furthest British-obtained position. It was renamed the 'Canadian Orchard.'"

Festubert would be counted among the worst battles for the Canadian military over the duration. After the fray, the lads took to the weariness and humdrum society of frontline fighting. The division would not see another substantial smash for the rest of 1915, except at Givenchy in June, when a further 400 casualties from the division were claimed.

Rifles were the topmost weapons before the war started. But rifles proved difficult to operate in trenches. By and by, hand grenades were thought to be smart weapons. Nails and gunpowder were crammed into jam tins, then a light was set to the fuse. The thrower would toss the bomb towards the opposing trenches. Numerous fellows lost hands from the bombs setting off unseasonably. A few short months would have the mother country produce the Mills No. 5 grenade to achieve a higher degree of safety than self-made bombs. The Mills could even be sent across the way by a rifle with a range of up to two hundred yards. Slightly over a fortnight was the average lifetime of a bombing officer.

In reply to Harrington, Edmund said, "As of late I've received letters from a few chums in France. They seem to be having a jolly time over there."

"Ze first casualty of war iz truth," a solo Auré spoke for the first time in the evening. A splendid son for whom no praise is adequate[26], René Philippe Richardieux was born prematurely, though healthy, to proud parents at his family's cottage estate. "René" was thought a handsome name by both parents. "Philippe" was after Auré's only brother. Aubrey

---

[26] A Canadian World War I epitaph

picked for her son's christening the scripture "Chosen of God and precious[27]."

"That is neither here nor there," Edmund replied, a touch cross.

In an attempt to make Auré see reason, Kellynch asked, "If you will not defend home or France, will you not defend Canada?"

Kellynch's question was met by another question.

"Why zhould I defend eh dominion that does not defend Quebec?" Another cross response was given, "To be fair, French Canada 'as alwayz been treated worse than British Canada by England and by our other zo called 'motherland.'"

Auré excused himself and left the grand hall in mute protest.

The look of pain registered in Harrington's eyes at what seemed to be his sons and daughter in uniform taken lightly.

In disgust, Kellynch dashed his napkin upon the table. He muttered to Edmund, "The gall of that man."

Equally dismayed, Edmund whispered, "At the risk of sounding bold, what can one expect from a Frenchman."

---

[27]   A Canadian World War I epitaph

Corps Generalities

Dear Aubrey,

Dinna forget[28] you, never could. I hope this letter finds you in good cheer. I can solely take a few letters at a time due to the large amount we carry in "our all's" — or our kits. It's horrors if muck envelops our all's when it's inspection time.

While the homefront is seeing recruitment slowing down, Canada is still seeing soaring numbers. Big news: the 2nd Division, commanded by Boer War Victoria Cross recipient hero, Major-General R.E.W. Turner, arrived on September 13th. This means the "Canadian Division" has ceased to exist. The Canadian Expeditionary Force, or the Corps, has been created. However, English units are still attached to the 1st Division for guidance.

---

[28]   A Canadian World War I epitaph

The commanders are quite stringent about regulations and authority. Slowly but surely, army discipline is improving up and down the lines.

Duty requires a Tommy to be at the front for four-six days, then rotate to support trenches for another four-six days. In the support area, we are made to take ammunition, supplies, and the like to the very front lines. After this, one is away from the front for four days or so for drill and instruction, work, and leisure in abandoned areas a few miles behind the lines. We usually co-habit with livestock in the barns. Horses fare better care than us chaps because horses are harder to come by. Switching companies of chaps in the front trenches and in the rear is done during nighttime for safety. This is one of the uttermost dangerous tasks of the effort.

Where we reside is called the trenches, but that is a formidable overstatement. Ditches without a rubbish or a sewage removal sytem is a more accurate description. Putrid is not a strong enough word for the odor that eminates in these areas. One can, at times, hardly bear to be in the trenches for this reason, and I write with certainty that every mate who has been in these areas will remember the smell of the front for the rest of his days. Personal cleanliness is so poor I won't go into much detail about it, Aubrey. A bath happens once every so many weeks, and I have a feeling this will worsen as time goes on. Numerous fellows have gangrene or cholera. The trenches are now deeper, at about two metres, and are still quite narrow, although they are narrow for a purpose: to minimize eruptions overhead from impacting those in the trenches.

The evening brings all home[29] to the trenches, but during a smash, casualties will crawl back to the safety of our trenches and will be injured further by the lads who are yet attacking. The cries of these boys never seem to leave you. In the trenches, clean air is positively non-existant, given chaps are beneath the earth. Come wintertime, the British have already informed us it will always be frigid at the front. I will, of course, refuse to wear trousers in wintertime, too. Those trousered units! The kilted units make fun of them. An inordinate amount of time is spent filling proper sandbags, which we now have atop the trenches, and maintenance on parapets; every able-bodied chap is required to do eight hours of labour per day. Behind the lead trench, three to four backup trenches are taking form. While digging the new trenches, we've been singing "Miles and Miles Behind the Lines."

*"We've got a sergeant-major
Who's never seen a gun*

---

[29]   A Newfoundland World War I epitaph

He's mentioned in dispatches
For drinking privates' rum
And when he sees old Jerry
You should see the begger run
Miles and miles and miles behind the lines"

Leather boots disintegrate all the time in the wallow. This grievance simply doesn't stop. Chatts multiply beyond belief and all over kilts and trousers, though they make jolly bunk mates. Every infantry lad in warfare history has had chatts, and now I understand this.

I would say daily portions are sufficient; we usually have biscuits with honey and jam, corn-beef and bread, tea, evaporated vegetables, cheese, and bacon. However, others say rations are too small and those mates are consistently famished. But bread, milk, coffee, and butter can be purchased from the farm people. Cigarettes are given out weekly. At least at breakfast time, there are agreements, by each army all down the lines, of a ceasefire during the serving and eating of the meal. This includes the wagons that bring the food. However, if a senior officer becomes aware of the agreement, he attempts to have it stopped.

At daybreak, and right before dusk too, there is often times a chance of an assault because the opposing army would have to counterattack in broad daytime, though at least both sides are always on guard this way, and there is rarely an assault at dawn. Once this is over, inspection happens, then breakfast, and the daily rum portion is given out. All the lads are given a daily two-ounce tot of rum. Rules are a Tommy has to have an officer for company in order to be allowed Rum; however, some officers are teetotallers and do not permit their troops to drink at all. These troops receive lime juice and pea soup instead. Rupert tried his first shot of rum. He fainted and was taken away on a stretcher. I tried my first tot, met the same fate, and was carried away as well. We both missed the next stand to and were given latrine duty again. If our fathers knew we had been drinking, they would be glad to have us shot at.

Playing jolly baseball games, reciting poetry, and performing musicals above all are the most fancied hobbies of the Corps. That our officers partake in baseball games with us regulars, and partake in the name-calling too, has the English standing aside the playing fields looking on in bafflement. They do not understand how officers and privates chum around with each other, go on leave, or take meals together.

Because the recently published Anne of Green Gables is so favoured in Canada, it has been distributed in the trenches to read.

Brother clasp the hand of brother stepping fearlessly through the night[30]. This line reminds me of the other evening, when Rupert was leaving the front for rotation. He saw brother boche from across No Man's Land and threw over a sweet from his last care package. Brother boche, jolly with his gun, thanked him with a smile and a small nod. A Lieutenant-Colonel watched the whole thing, became frightfully cross towards Rupert, and cursed him with latrine duty.

"Jack Johnsons," after the Yankee boxer or high explosives, are endless. So too are "Whiz-bangs." These are shrapnel shells. You can tell which one is flying towards you by their sound. A chap either bobs his head down or holes up against the side of a trench, depending.

After any given scrap, there is usually a flag raised in agreement, and both sides help with burying the other's deceased. When not our prisoners, Germans can be trusted as stretcher-bearers.

News is that Newfoundland suffered the first death in their ranks this September, a twenty-one-year-old Pte. Hugh McWhirther. He was shelled by the Turks shortly after they landed in Sulva Bay, in the Gallipoli Peninsula. The

---

[30] A Canadian World War I epitaph

first of our lads, four of them, were killed off the Chilean coast in the battle of Coronel, back in November of last year. They were the first English Canadians to die in battle in this war.

As of to-day, troops cannot obtain permission to pay for a discharge, and wives can no longer prevent their husbands from joining future divisions. As you most likely know, troops can now be granted harvest leave, though neither Rupert nor I will be going back this fall. But don't take fright, it can't be long before we return.

There is not a lot else going on at the moment so I will write my goodbye,

Briarch.

Lansdowne

A late yet hot summer day greeted the Westbrooks' guests the afternoon of the cricket tournament. Huge white clouds hung in the sky. A lark was heard singing nearby. René was left with his nanny at Pembina. Near the end of the party, Auré made an appearance, presumably to fetch his wife. He seated himself at the same table as Michel, who was speaking to Desrosiers. Jean-Pierre, Desrosiers' son, was with them. In between sets, Kellynch was taking a brief rest. He sat alone at a table opposite the other four. Ladies were gossiping pleasantly at nearby tables. Auré spoke in French to his uncle, "Hopefully this war ends soon so business can resume as normal. It is certainly hard to sign contracts with those overseas. The process of agreement on any given subject has slowed down a sight too much."

Overhearing and noting the hypocrisy of Auré's words, Kellynch ventured in French, "Perhaps if more gentlemen were overseas, Germany's army could be overtaken sooner. The coward is, after all, the first to speak and the gentleman the first to act."

A jolly call was heard from the cricket field, "Jean-Pierre, it is surely your turn to bat next."

"No, thank you. I will sit out," was the polite response, even though Jean-Pierre, who looked similar to his father, was a star player and his team was down so many points. The conversation between Kellynch and Auré continued in French. Noting the bold, unjustifiable slight against him, Auré replied only loudly enough for those immediately near him to hear, "The irony of the coward is he does not realize he is a hypocrite. More Englishmen are needed over there. This does not pertain to all gentlemen of the dominion. There is a difference in the two terms, *Sir*."

The game ended. Frédéric Laurentien, Edmund, Herbert, Harry, Jean-Marie, and Jean-Luc Desrosiers came off the field, laughing along with a few daring ladies who took part in the game. The players that had just come from the game took lemonade from the servants. Michel and Desrosiers motioned to their sons that the chaises near them were empty. Frédéric, Jean-Marie, and Jean-Luc turned to the conversation their silent fathers were intent upon listening to.

Kellynch corrected his falsely-labeled farsightedness and continued, "If a gentleman does not understand his most important duty is to his empire, his vision is severely impacted — impacted, I'm afraid, to the point where he can no longer see himself as a man."

"You forget yourself. I'm afraid it is well known that it is you who does not see things clearly," Auré responded in a calm tone, but also one that welcomed a confrontation. It was common knowledge Kellynch was rejected from enlisting on account of defective eyesight. He had Scarlet fever as a child, and it had partially blinded him in one eye.

The guests made their way to Lansdowne's terraced balcony for refreshments. The matrons were the first to head for the grand staircase. Next were some of the gentlemen who discussed the cricket game. Lady Bird linked arms with Aubrey, and they were the last ladies to make their way up the grand staircase. The pair laughed about some servant Peter turned dollywop. "How could he have wanted that freckly thing?" they cried. Lady Bird's numerous Corgis toddled up the steps behind them. Aubrey wondered where her husband was and turned around in search of him. The sight Aubrey saw made her freeze. Auré remained seated opposite an immobile Kellynch. Every Francophone at the party was either stationary beside Auré or behind him. Not an individual on the patio moved, not one spoke, though it was obvious not a Frenchman would leave Auré. Aubrey knew how strongly Auré disapproved of the war. However, Aubrey felt a tinge of sympathy towards Kellynch. It took character to stare down seven men on one's own. His manhood axed, Kellynch turned scarlet. Though his jaw was set, his eyes locked with Auré's.

Auré's Letter

A letter, written in Auré's penmanship, was published in the main newspapers in Ottawa. The open letter stated,

To whom it may concern,

Canada is expected to fight for a King and country that has revoked its most basic rights. Canada has always been and is as yet treated as a backwater colony, despite its massive war effort. There is an inexcusable and utter disregard for Canada shown by either mother country, as well as for Francophones by the Canadian government, and such is proven by the following facts.

Montreal is, by far, the British Empire's largest French city. The city's first social club was founded in 1913. The club does not permit Francophone members.

In 1912, the Ontario Conservative government banned the teaching of the French language in all schools, public and separate, across the province. The law, called Regulation 17, came into effect due to fear that Canada's other official language, taught to the youngest generation, would inflict harm on the honour of the Protestant Anglophone province. The ministerial order states teaching French is not allowed past the first two years of grade school. The consequence of the new law is all Catholic French-language schools have been obliged to close down. Quebec, in recent years, has seen employment shortages that have forced many to move to Ontario to provide for their families. In Ontario, Francophone children are prohibited from learning their mother tongue and culture, and they are forced to assimilate. The sole exception to the law is that French is allowed to be instructed only if the child does not know English and as a short-term step before being taught English. This law has not only stupendously ostracized the Franco-Ontario population but Francophones across the Dominion.

English Canada's agreement that French Canada join the effort to fight for their rights is first and foremost hypocritical, as well as inauspicious and deeply insulting. To quote Nationaliste Armand Lavergne, "Give us back our schools first."

In regard to the effort, Valcartier was run by Anglophones. Throughout the Corps itself, a French Division does not exist. Francophones are rarely given permission to switch to

French units. Seldom are Francophone Officers given important positions and none are allotted senior positions.

England is treating Canada at naught. London does not consult the Canadian Prime Minister on Canadian military policies. England's war orders are placed in America, a neutral country, instead of in Canada.

More Canadian sons are fighting per capita than England's sons are in the war. Certainly, this is a mark of gentlemen.

By law, Canada was ordered to join the war by England; therefore, the mother country should defend Canada from the enemy's horrific treatment of our colony. Germany, due to the country's low opinion of colonials, chose Canada, among additional colonies, to unleash upon the most heinous weapon invented in warfare history at Ypres: poison gas. This was inexcusable in every sense of the word. Neither motherland did nor will do anything as restitution on behalf of Canada, regarding the nature of Ypres. As well, in regard to the battle of Ypres, the French army unquestionably deserted the Canadian Division during the battle.

England has continually sent its colonies into terrible circumstances, instead of leading

from the front, as character should demand
of the ruler of all the Dominions.

The Allied and Central Armies together gave the formidable title of the war's worst posting in its entirety to the Mediterranean. Britain refused to send its proper military to these islands until the locales were deemed safe, instead sending its colonial armies ahead of time to ascertain the situation. Troops wrote, *White women should never be posted to the Mediterranean.* English Canadian nurses would struggle from near death by dehydration, starvation, and unhygienic living conditions the whole of their duration in the Mediterranean.

> *The Canadian Army Medical Corps, including the nursing sisters, was ordered by England to the Mediterranean. Two English-Canadian nurses, a matron and a sister, have fallen while serving on Lemnos due to living conditions. Our nurses were sent there to die at England's hands, for which there will be no pardon given by the Monarchy or British High Command who sent them there. The conditions in the Mediterranean are so appalling, Canada should be granted a Royal pardon as recourse. But this will not transpire because we are colonials. The Canadian Medical Corps being mandated to the Mediterranean, too, is inexcusable in every sense of the word.*

> *Over the course of this war our Dominion has continually come to the aid of both mother countries, while England and France treat*

Canada in considerably less than gallant ways.
This speaks endlessly to Canadian integrity.

In this war, French Canada is largely regarded to be cowardly in its apparent neutral stance. This perspective, however, is entirely inaccurate. Silence is complicity, as English Canada has proven itself to be of mute resignation towards the treatment of our Dominion the whole of this war. The "superior" countries continually demonstrate deplorable treatment of Canadians, on top of always insulting and laughing at our citizens in uniform, who supposedly cannot even speak English or French properly, for being colonial "inferiors." Our military defends these countries too. All of this is an irrevocable insult to our fallen, our Expeditionary Force, and the memory of Canadian veterans who will come out of this war. Our military matters too.

The letter was signed, *In response to how Germany, France, and mainly England are treating Canada as a colony in this war, Quebec replies; a gentleman does not retreat in the face of distress. Quebec en a assez de L'Union Jack* (Quebec has had enough of the Union Jack).

Monsieur Aurelien S. Richardieux.

The letter was printed in the *Ottawa Journal* and *Ottawa Citizen*. The story then ran in the *Mail and Empire*, the *Toronto's Daily Star*, and the *Manitoba Free Press*, the most prominent one in Western Canada. The article was also published in *Le Devoir* and consequently in *La Presse*, *La Patrie*, and the *Montreal Star*, all uncompromisingly in favour of French Canada.

Auré was now openly a speculator, a zealot, and a traitor to the cause. He was denounced as a possible enemy spy. Loafing and treason were also marks struck against his name. British born were absolutely outraged. Canadian born were frightfully cross as well — not to the same degree, but they still saw themselves as British. Ladies drew their skirts aside when they passed Auré on the street. Gentlemen glared at him with glances as frosty as the late fall days. The premier of Ontario was so insulted he urged the Prime Minister to have Richardieux disenfranchised. A second circular to see him hanged was brought about, but this time the petition was given to the Minister of Militia and Defence. Now considered more dangerous than a German Prisoner of War, Auré was the vermin of Ontario, quite possibly the whole of English Canada.

Christmas 1915

The Laurentiens' grand hall was severely toned down as a reflection of the current times. Harrington and Tomryn were discussing the Fokker E.III: the most frightful plane of the war. Tomryn's son, Kelly, had gone away with the 2nd Division. Clarence Tomryn had signed up with the 3rd Division. At the Laurentien ball, a toast was given to the 3rd Division to be formed on Christmas day. The Corps and the Princess Pat's, who had returned to fight with the Corps, would find rest until spring.

Ottawans knew Britain's effort would fortify the Empire and that she would emerge after the duration stronger than ever before. By the tens of thousands, volunteers donned uniforms across the dominion. One of the finest officers of the Corps, Arthur Currie, had detailed the rubbish instruction that was being taught to new troops and sent the report to London. In answer to Currie's documentation, training extended to fourteen weeks and included all forms of waging this different war. New troops were taught that they apprehended but did not execute the captured enemy. At the same time, a briefing was given that any Tommy who attempted to remake the gentleman's agreement of the previous Christmas would be shot.

Both Harrington and Tomryn knew Borden's agreement concerning recruits would be lifted to five hundred thousand as of New Year's Day. They silently wondered if the crown colony could support such a number.

In response to condolences regarding Pierre, Michel spoke to those he stood with, saying Pierre was "A prompt volunteer[31]. His commanding officer's tribute was, 'Though a boy, he played a man's game to the finish'[32]. He gave his life for others, was kind, loving, and dearly beloved[33]. As well, a German found Pierre's war diary on the battlefield and mailed it to Vauréal, and the diary has given Mme. Laurentien a bit of comfort." Michel then excused himself and left the hall momentarily to attend to a servant matter concerning the dinner.

"The first telephone call across the dominion went through in 1915," said a thoughtful Desrosiers to his lady. At the same table, Aubrey and Peter snickered over Philippa being cut from society when Auré sat down. Aubrey had always been jealous of Philippa's beauty and had wanted to sleep with her husband. At the last Saturday-to-Monday party, Aubrey had taken care of Philippa. Name cards designated which bedroom belonged to which couple. The true purpose was to indicate where a man could find his lover at nighttime and his wife come morning. The task befell the garden boy to ring a bell at six in the morning so maids who brought morning tea to guests would happen on the rightful couple in each bedroom. A single name card had been changed by Aubrey late at night. Cast out of Edwardian society, because it was the wife who was ostracized no matter who was unfaithful,

---

[31]   A Canadian World War I epitaph
[32]   A Canadian World War I epitaph
[33]   A Canadian World War I epitaph

Philippa was no longer a nuisance to Aubrey. As more and more returned maimed, not an English rose would dance with Auré. The sole reason he was present was Mme. Laurentien felt comforted by male relations in her home after Pierre's death.

"Currie, a teacher of all things by trade turned Victoria realtor, has solely a high school education, unlike our British officers, and the only knowledge of warfare he has he taught himself from books. Oh! I still say we ought to return to one of our own leading colonials! What was High Command thinking, employing a male who is not a gentleman nor a proper officer to position of Brigadier-General!" Peter laughed.

"Eh high school education means he is amongst the most educated in Canada and makez him very qualified to be an officer. And eh woman is spear'eading ze campaign in England. I did not know eh woman could lead men into battle. Az an aside, what sort of man allows eh woman to fight for 'im? Self-respecting men do not permit women to die before them in warfare," Auré replied calmly, though he was tired and rather frustrated.

British Nurse Edith Cavell had been stationed in Belgium. She aided hundreds of soldiers, from both sides, in making their way to neutral Switzerland. Once Cavell was captured, international pressure was placed on Germany to set Cavell free. The enemy carried on with orders to execute. A soldier in the firing squad refused to execute her. He was shot and buried next to her. Her body was exhumed and returned to England, where thousands lined London's streets for her funeral procession. In the handful of weeks since her death, Britain's enlistment, which had come to a standstill, saw augmentation by tens of thousands.

"Everyone can see incomparably more Britishers have left than Frenchmen," Peter replied pompously, while he tried not to laugh outright at Auré's hypocrisy.

"Excuze me," Auré said quickly and removed himself from the table. He went to fetch Michel a drink.

"The king has a high opinion of Canadians ever since Ypres, despite the fellow who shirks his duty," said Kellynch to the Lady as he led his dance partner from the floor, seeing Auré pass by with a rum in hand.

Alcohol was not to be consumed until the war ended, out of decency to the boys. Christmas presents, too, were not to be purchased this year, as the various patriotic funds needed to be fully funded. Romance was thought to be abstained from as well because frivolous endeavors were an insult to the sacrifices shown at the front.

Auré stopped cold at the insult directed at him, turned about, and faced Kellynch. While deliberately looking Kellynch in the eye, Auré slowly consumed the beverage meant for Michel. Auré did not even drink to the toasts at either of his weddings. Still staring at Kellynch, he serenely returned the glass to his side and walked away.

"Don't you want your son to be proud when he asks what you did in the war?" Kellynch hissed, frustrated from months of his chums being deserted in death by neutrality.

"I'll tell my son I rezisted!" Auré roared. His anger was now coming to the surface, after more than a year of his and his family's gallantry being questioned due to their not volunteering for the war.

Instantly, the ballroom fell deathly silent. The glass Auré held sailed inches from Kellynch's temple. Kellynch did not even flinch. "I will tell 'im I fought for those who were publicly 'arassed and ostracized by your white featherz!

Propaganda! And insults 'urled across Parliament for not enlisting in eh war that had nothing to do with them!"

As Canadians were British subjects, Kellynch replied, his jaw clenched, "This is every Englishman's war."

The flag unfurled. Auré took one wild look at Kellynch. Then, Auré advanced. Screams and shrieks came from ladies. Gentlemen removed themselves from their places of seating in a call to arms. Westbrook, Lawrence, Harrington, and Tomryn surrounded Kellynch. Edmund, Herbert, Ernest, and Gavin gathered behind their fathers. Frédéric Laurentien stood to one side of Auré and Desrosiers the other. Jean-Pierre, Jean-Luc, Jean-Ives, and Jean-Marie took their places behind the trio.

"This iz ze war of those European generals 'o will not fight their own battlez, so they call on ze Empire's men and let uz call our men what they really are: mere boyz 'o are ordered to walk shoulder to shoulder acrozz No Man'z Land to be mowed down by the Germans with their machine gunz!" Auré yelled.

"It takes character to traverse No Man's Land," stated Kellynch, his eyes angry slits of fury at his friends' characters being assaulted.

"It takez character for one province to take eh stand against the 'ole Empire!" shouted an irate Auré.

"We are waging war on the very earth of and are brothers-in-arms with your ancestors—," cried Harrrington.

"—Who deserted us on the Plains of Abraham!" spat Desrosiers.

"With double duty to the two mother countries, you ought to be offering more sons than we!" Lawrence stated, pointing his finger down on an imaginary desk, bent over between Kellynch and Westbrook, though still taller than either.

Two of Lawrence's sons of military age were at the front. All Desrosiers' sons of military age stood behind their father.

"A just crusade is being led by Hughes—," said Tomryn while he glared at Auré.

"—Orangeman!" shouted Desrosiers.

"The last time our leader fought for our rights, you 'anged him! Give us our rights back and we will aid you in attaining yours!" retorted Frédéric.

"—And you're doing everything in your might to lead our sons astray!" A livid Tomryn finished.

"Duty called and he answered promptly[34]!" Desrosiers practically snarled in retort at Tomryn.

"I will be equal to any duty required of me no matter what it costs[35]!" Auré shouted in response to Tomryn.

"Gentlemen unfraid[36]! We are proud to have him fight for us!" said Frédéric with one hand on Auré's arm.

"Equally ready at the call of country and at the call of God[37]!" Desrosiers yelled as he cut off Frédéric, yet again in defense of Auré.

"Be ashamed to die until you have gained some victory for humanity[38]!" Kellynch answered furiously.

"We will not stand idle when England's freedom needs to be defended!" interjected Lawrence.

"Defend your kinsmen before mother countries who treat us both as savages!" roared Desrosiers.

"If Germany is to be defeated, British honour demands—," commanded Kellynch.

---

[34] A Canadian World War I epitaph
[35] A Canadian World War I epitaph
[36] A Canadian World War I epitaph
[37] A Canadian World War I epitaph
[38] A Newfoundland World War I epitaph

"—*French Canada has sacrificed enough of*—," hurled Auré.

"—And upon my honour—,"

"—Her citizenz—,"

"—Before the crown—,"

"—Her 'eart and her soul—,"

"—And on my word as an Englishman I will safeguard my people—,"

"—For England!" both cried in unison.

"*GENTLEMEN!*"

The hall fell into a muted hush. Michel had been retrieved. He came striding towards them, positively shaking with fury. "Make firm, O God, the peace our dead have won[39]!" he ridiculed them. "And there are ladies present!" he spat. A few ladies had fainted. He stood in between the two parties. "I will thank you to remember yourselves!" he shouted, beside himself.

Auré looked as though he would strike Kellynch.

"Remember your cousins on the front lines," Michel said quietly to his nephew, speaking in French. For one horrid moment, it appeared Michel might break down at the memory of Pierre. "They do not understand us, what we are fighting for. I will thank you to leave."

Though Auré towered over Michel, he was given a command by an elder of the family and had to obey. Auré blinked, and the expressionless mask adopted since the commencement of the effort fell over him once more.

The room was reduced to all sorts of undress. The servants, too shocked to move, were told to clean the shattered glassware and reset the strewn tables and chairs. A violinist, their bow still in midair, was instructed by the conductor to

---

[39] A Canadian World War I epitaph

lead a waltz, at Michel's insistence. Smelling salts and brandy were given to ladies who had been overcome with fright. Peter explained repeatedly that he stayed seated to calm the ladies.

Westbrook wanted to challenge Richardieux to a duel on The Hill with the Governor General presiding. "If only duels were not disallowed here! They only recently became illegal at home, after all!" he said, nearly shouting. "We have lost our way, criminals are allowed to go too far to-day, I say! And that vermin would not have the decency to present himself in tails!" sneered Westbrook.

Herbert and Edmund muttered Field Punishment No.1 was too good for Richardieux. "Crucifixion" was the pet name the Corps gave this castigation, which involved the regular publicly having his hands and feet tied to a post or a wheel and being left to demeaningly serve his punishment for a two-hour period daily.

"No, he has forgotten where he comes from. He is a traitor to his countrymen. I petition a vote! Right here, right now, my dear gentlemen! Out of respect to our boys who are fighting for the Empire at this very moment—" Kellynch protested.

"Here! Here!"

"In haste, do we enter into a gentleman's agreement," stated Kellynch.

"—I second this!"

"—Disgraced the Mounted Force—"

"Cast him out," Kellynch said quietly, and turned to the entryway that Auré and, consequently, Aubrey were headed towards.

Vauréal

After the infamous Christmas row, Auré was cut by Ottawan high society. If an aristocrat, especially a female, comported themselves at variance to the rigid Edwardian rules of etiquette, they quickly found themselves cast out from polite society, and often times irrevocably. A tarnished name was swiftly struck from guest lists and the aristocrat was left out in the cold. Aubrey wished her husband had not ostracized himself so much. Affairs were now certainly harder to have. Auré did not seem to mind being cut, but in the new year, he had grown silent on the topic of war and no longer defended his not being in uniform.

In the afternoon of a late February day, the sky was a dull grey. It had recently snowed, and the powder lay fresh across the landscape. Given the elder sons were gone, Vauréal was rather quiet. Aubrey was with Mme. Laurentien in one of the parlours. Mme. Laurentien gave a small brick to Aubrey. It was purchased from the Ottawa Women's Canadian Club that sold pieces of debris from The Hill fire as a fundraiser for the Prisoners of War drive.

On the evening of February 3rd, a fire broke out in the reading room in the centre block of Parliament. The blaze soon engulfed the lumbered room. Roofs fell through, which sent innumerable sparks flying. Within a short time, the whole of the centre block was in flames. Borden and his secretary managed to exit the building almost by crawling. The Victory tower still stood intact, but before the clock could reach midnight, the grand bell plunged from the tall spire. The Prime Minister looked on as the Victoria Tower crashed down into rubble. The House of Commons roof caved in. Members of Parliament and employees escaped by crawling, lowering ropes and ladders made from towels, and jumping from windows as high as forty feet above ground. Seven people perished. An inquiry found that the blaze was started by papers that caught fire from a lit cigar on a table. Scepticism about German treason would not entirely diminish the length of the effort. The neo-gothic style of Parliament was a matchless structure in terms of architecture, in England as well. A temporary locale for the House of Commons was found at the Victoria Memorial Museum, a mile south from The Hill. The museum showcased the oldest fossils in the dominion.

Objective gained[40], Nico and Joseph were sneaking chocolate chip cookies to the nursery. On the main floor and when Nico, sweets in hand, was precisely before a side glass door, their father was found to be on the other side. Last words to his comrade "Go on, I'll manage,"[41] whispered Nico to Joseph, in front, who slipped around the corner to the back staircase, unnoticed.

Michel and his nephew came in from out of doors. They had just visited Pierre's tombstone. Michel handed his coat to Thierry.

Michel related to Auré about the fire on The Hill, "Hundreds of books of immeasurable value would have

---

[40]   A Canadian World War I epitaph
[41]   A Canadian World War I epitaph

perished that night but for one of the librarians. The bright, dear lad was able to close the library's giant steel doors before managing to get out. But the Victory tower was reduced to ruin; it will need to be reconstructed."

Nico piped, "The new tower's name ought to have the word 'peace' in it."

Deciding to overlook the baking, his father asked, "Whatever for?"

"After the lads, Sir."

Michel turned to Auré and said, "Parliament should have a lasting tribute to our boys. Nicolas is right. They left us to defend the empire and have been gone far too long, indeed."

"It is well done, dad[42]," Nico ended the conversation, speaking out of turn.

While Auré walked up the staircase, he heard the little boys' conversation in the upstairs nursery, since the door was ajar. Auré listened while the little ones carried on. The boys had yet to learn English. Albert Desrosiers spoke in French, "Our dear daddy and our hero[43] said more chaps are needed over there so wives can continue to spend all their husbands' money in freedom." Auré rolled his eyes in agreement. "Mother got cross and father laughed. Father says it's only a matter of time before conscription passes. Maybe they will conscript us. Then our fathers would have to let us go! I would capture all the Hun I cared to and France's Croix de Guerre."

Joseph Laurentien then declared that any man not in uniform was a shirker. Valiant in battle[44], Nico defended their uncle Auré; he was not a coward, even though he was

---

42   A Canadian World War I epitaph
43   A Canadian World War I epitaph
44   A Canadian World War I epitaph

not fighting. The boys went on to say that perhaps the war would last long enough for René to fight, as there should be a uniformed male in every family. Auré stood in the nursery entryway and took a long look at his son. René was being used as one of Bijou's dolls for tea. Bijou was one of the younger Laurentien girls and was petnamed "Bijou" for her love of jewellery. The best air was being served at her tea party. Once Nico saw his uncle, he ran up to Auré and gave him a bear hug. For once, Auré did not turn away from physical affection but took Nico in his arms for an embrace and then put him down. Auré then met Michel in the study for coffee and a discussion of the protest on The Hill about Francophone rights in the province. On February 24th, five thousand Franco-Ontarians denounced Regulation 17 and demanded the law be annulled.

Aubrey actually returned to Pembina before Auré did. When he came in the door, she asked where he had been.

"Michel said you walked home. That was a long walk in the snow."

In lieu of a response, her husband came up to her and gently brushed the side of her jawline. He seemed distracted. He went to inform Llwelleyn that instead of a customary five-course supper, the chef was to lessen the meal to a four-course one. *How very peculiar of him,* thought Aubrey.

Suffrage

On March 1ˢᵗ 1916, the Suffrage bill passed, though it failed to become law in Ontario. But in the west, on January 28ᵗʰ, Manitoba's Parliament abounded with politicians and civilians. Following third reading and royal assent, Manitoba's government, and for the first time in dominion history, extended the provincial vote to women and the right to hold office. Cheers overwhelmed the gathered assembly, desks were thumped up and down, and all took part in the singing of "For They Are Jolly Good Fellows." The eldest politicians proclaimed they thought they would never see this day in their lifetimes. Ontario women took great delight in the event. On March 14ᵗʰ, women in Saskatchewan were granted the right to vote. On April 19ᵗʰ, Alberta extended the vote to women as well.

With a newspaper in hand, one cold, overcast day at Pembina, Auré related to his wife, "I understand your sisters on ze prairies received the vote. They say the 'ole dominion iz to follow the uncivilized west."

Over her brawn, Aubrey retorted, "They ought to give us the legal rights to our bodies first."

Auré agreed. "What will be next, women being allowed to serve on ze front linez?"

Aubrey said, incredulous at such a notion, "But that would be absurd! That is simply not realistic!"

Auré asked, "What about the fairer sex fighting iz not realistic?"

Aubrey could name any number of reasons. "For goodness sakes! The very weight of the packs the fellows are made to carry every day, to start."

"'ow much do young children weigh that you, or rather, your nannies, carry about all day? Children weigh about ze same az the packs the troopz carry."

"The living conditions are said to be terrible at the front."

"What were, and still remainz in zo many areas, the conditions of pioneers 'o broke the land to grow the colony into the modernized dominion it iz today? It involved back-breaking work. At timez ze work was so exhausting that the pioneers were worked to death, especially the women. I can't imagine being in the family way and delivering in a sod house with no one around but your 'usband and maybe eh female who lives so many miles away to help you. But more to the point, pioneers saw what women were capable of because their wivez 'elped break the land as much as they did themselves. Males on the prairies were the first in the dominion to say women need to be granted the vote."

"Being wounded or going through surgery... females could not handle that sort of pain."

"What about ze pain of childbirth? You're tougher than you think you are."

"Well, I never! What about the near certainty of going to one's death? Females could not handle such an extreme situation. We are far too sensitive for such stress or anxiety."

"The childbirth mortality rate being what it iz, there iz no one braver than an expectant mother. Reality is only what society focuses on, ma chere. Due to the fact that all of these matters are women'z work, it iz surely invisible.

What is greatly to your credit az women, though no one will ever credit you for this, is *how* you 'ave accomplished what you have, concerning improving your quality of life and that of your children, and obtaining ze franchise. And that'z something men generally don't believe in — that iz to say, resolving oppression peacefully. For instance, with males, one man was shot and the whole of Europe went to war az consequence. All their empirez dragged their colonies into the conflict, and before anyone knew it, the world was literally at war. One thinks of ze few tens of millionz of civilians 'o will be killed or wounded in this war in comparison to women who 'ave done an extraordinary amount in recent years to change laws to simply be given basic 'uman rights, without killing or harming at all. And you 'ave been deemed for centuries not intelligent enough to vote. As well, I'm afraid it takes time to change eh perspective."

St. Eloi

Rupert wrote to Aubrey.

We are in the Messines Ridge area, roughly five kilometers south of Ypres. The 3ʳᵈ Division just came, a battalion and a brigade at a time, from January to March. The Prime Minister has asked for half a million lads, though he gave his word only volunteers would go. Until recently, the Corps was using the Colt, which is a fine gun but inclined to catch after numerous firings. Now in use is the Vickers machine gun; it is weightier and more durable. It fires as much as ten rounds a second. Targets as far as two kilometers away, but normally considerably less, can be hit, so that will aid advancing infantry assaults. Fritz has the MG-08 Maxim that they man with five mates and is comparable to the Vickers. Flamethrowers and liquid fire are now a part of our battles, though as far as can be discerned, neither tool has done much to change the attritional state of things.

Dear knows, we needed the Vickers for St. Eloi, Aubrey.

Before we came to the St. Eloi sector, we were told there would be seven craters to inhabit because the British and English Canadians had detonated underground mines beneath enemy lines. A number of residences could fit into each crater. The most frightful one measured 60 yards from one end to the other and 21 yards in depth. More than 30 craters were soon accounted for, many smaller in size than the main 7. No one quite knew what crater belonged to the Allies or not. We did not even know where the enemy was. Reports were practically endless, between the front lines and High Command, of which crater was occupied by the Germans or the Corps. Basically all reports proved false, anyhow.

The St. Eloi scrap was intended for a purpose even the officers had a difficult time understanding. The officers' maps were useless, given the terrain had altered so much due to recent fighting. And aeroplanes could not deliver proper photographs because the weather did not permit them to. We were left unsure of where our lines were — and the foe's too. We went into battle at 0415 hours, March 27th, on a slender field about 650 yards wide, perpetually devastated by rain and shellfire, like all battle locales out here. Fritz could hit us on three sides, due to the layout of the region. One of the officers said our area was

123

on a forward slope, in full view of the enemy. Which reminds me, since St. Eloi is over, every one of the officers have been killed, excepting the Lieutenant. The officers who saw the front lines wanted to clear out of the area, because nearly all stated it was pointless to hold any part of St. Eloi. The poor bloody infantry was basically deserted because no one in back of the lines knew where we were or how to aid us, including the artillery, along with the British and our High Command refusing to give up an inch of the "sanctity of ground." In the end, Germany took over our section after aerial photographs proved we were in a dreadful predicament. The frightful smash ended April 16th.

The battle for Messines took place from April 6th to the 19th. In March, the English gained control of a certain section of the region and the Corps' task was to maintain these British lines. Our front lines were found opposite the Messines Ridge. The 3rd Division of the BEF was battered while the 2nd Canadian Division was sent numerous days ahead of schedule to relieve the British. A few days after getting into the trenches, a grand German counterattack swept over our lines, including the raw 2nd Division. Fritz knew untried fellows were their enemy. After a fortnight, we were ploddingly moved from the area by the battle-tried foe. The lack of artillery arms and poor aerial reconnaissance were factors in defeat as well. It was a difficult-to-swallow setback after hard-won British gains.

On a lighter note, the British Expeditionary Force has now put into practice steel hats, or helmets, I should write. Not all British soldiers are permitted to wear them by their generals, for fear their men will grow soft, but our generals allow us to wear ours.

Rupert.

The Canadians sustained hefty casualties, some 1,373 killed and wounded at St. Eloi. Hughes thought he would do a grand job of the role, but British High Command determined Sir Julian Byng would take command of the Canadian Corps and did so on May 28th, 1916. Alderson's successor was a slight, middle-aged Viscount, a professional Cavalryman and educated, British-born aristocrat. He came from a military family, his record in the Boer War was fancied, and he arranged the marvelous withdrawal of Allied soldiers from Gallipoli. Upon being told he was made commander of the Corps, Byng replied, "Why am I sent to the Canadians? I don't know a Canadian. I am ordered to these people and will do my best, but I don't know that there is any congratulations in it." However, the lads quickly became fond of their new commander for his regular presence among his troops and because he withstood political mucking about from London and Ottawa regarding the Corps. Hughes' power throughout the Corps lessened because of Byng, as well. The Corps' new commander said the Canadian military was "too good to be led by politicians and dollar magnates." As well, he was part of ordering the Ross Rifle out of the front lines.

The Corps was particularly jolly over this decision. Byng wanted the Corps' direction to improve. He told his newly-met officers, "What I want is the discipline of a well-trained pack of hounds." The Corps' discipline steadily improved under Byng's guidance.

Briarch's Letter

Letters from Briarch and Rupert were delivered to Pembina at the same time, per usual, though by normal post this time. Their letters were so similar, they could have just written one to Aubrey. Briarch's letter started with,

> *Our unit is presently situated near* ____ *(censored). Don't mind the lead, Aubrey, it is just ink has become reserved solely for addressing letters as well as for grave front line messages. Church parade only ended, so I have the time to write now.*
>
> *Newfoundland was ordered out of Gallipoli, where the regiment fought with distinction and was sent to the Western Front. So, the regiment's here with us this spring, although will stay with the Old Home's Division under which she fights. The Australians have come from Gallipoli, as well, and intentionally came to us to teach them of trench raiding.*

'A jollie good booke whereon to looke was better to me than gold [45],' was what our mate said after he took part in a raid and was given a furlough. If one volunteers for a successful raid, one can be granted leave by the officers. However, Rupert and I were allotted our first furlough. After about a year here, a regular is allowed ten to fourteen days of leave per year, while officers are granted four furloughs a year. Among the rank and file, there is continual stress over this matter.

Canadian Tommies, when granted leave, habitually took to England, Ireland, Scotland, and Wales to visit relatives. For the Tommy Canuck on furlough who did not have family in the British Isles, they would visit Bath, Picadilly, and Shorncliffe, though the biggest draw was incomparibly London. Since Vancouver, Toronto, and Quebec City were the sole cities to claim over one hundred thousand people, and Montreal the only city with one million citizens, the boys often wrote to their families about the large and bustling city of London, including females who drank and smoked in public and who wore trousers.

Patriotic citizens, ever concerned for "their boys" and the integrity of the Corps throughout the Empire, created The King George and Queen Mary Maple Leaf Club. The Maple Leaf Club was ever welcoming of her sons in the motherland's capitol. The establishments allowed for inexpensive room and board, reading, billiards, and common rooms where fellow English Canadians could socialize with one another. The Canadian lads' only social club allotted for a place where the

---

[45]   A Canadian World War I epitaph

chaps could be "cared for and mothered a bit," and it proved tremendously popular. The Beaver Hut was established by the YMCA, found on the Strand, and was another alternative for Canucks to relax, instead of them possibly succumbing to the darker temptations of a big city.

We went to London, you see, and stayed at the Maple Leaf Club. We had a grand old time. We met a few VAD's. It takes time to train nurses, and since time is not on our side, women who want to serve who are not nurses can do so with the Voluntary Aid Detachment. All the fellows call them "Very Adorable Darlings." They work as partially trained nurses assisting nurses, they drive ambulances, and they are employed as clerical staff in convalescent hospitals.

However, after we returned the Major did away with our bear. One of our mates took the bear cub that he found near his residence before he embarked to England for basic training. Our mate was living in Burnaby. The bear was christened "Burnaby" and "Bernie" for short. Poor little Bernie had been court-martialed a while back for eating the Major's supper then trying to take down the officer's tent. The major was of the opinion that because Bernie was no longer a cub, but a medium-sized bear, he had to go. I sent mother a picture of myself bottle-feeding Bernie a little while ago. She wrote back she nearly fainted when she saw the kodak. She thought the bear was still a cub when I initially explained Bernie to her.

Mascots were well-favoured in the Corps. Dogs, cats, and especially goats were the most sought-after animals. Bears proved the biggest delight for mascots. They were either brought from Canada or found in abandoned towns or in the countryside near the front. Newfoundland fancied Labradors they took with them from their island. The pets were like family to the troops, and affection towards mascots was shown in granting the animals ranks.

Bernie outranked the major, so we did the only thing to do when loyalty is split. We went after Bernie. Our unit (50 troops) scoured the area. We came upon a battalion of Jerry's. One of them was taken hostage, bribed, then released. Bernie was found outside a small village. The major was livid over the derring-do. He yelled at us, loud enough for the Germans to hear, that should our "asinine behaviour that shamed the King" happen again, he would take his riding crop to each of us.

North of Ploegsteert Wood in Belgium, the Corps executed its principal trench raid. The raid began near La Petite Douve farm the evening of November 16th, 1915. The 5th and 7th Battalions took nearly a fortnight to prepare. Ahead of time, gunners fired relentlessly to ensure the path would be void of barbed wire. Ten officers and one hundred and seventy troops set out for German lines during nighttime. The groups of raiders were given certain roles, from wire-cutters, shovel mates, and bombers, to grenadiers, along with rifle and reserve rifle lots to aid in the triumph of the raid or against return fire.

Prior surveillance found that crossways throughout the terrain were partially underwater. Ladders and mats to cover barbed wire were brought along. The two battalions left the safety of their lines without kits or identification tags, which were left behind. However, they did have black camouflage. Wire along the way was still intact and, on that account, the ones who guided the groups held wire cutters at the ready. The 5th Battalion started from the south and worked their way north towards the farm. Along the way, the noise made from crossing a wire-filled ditch gave away the battalion as they made mad dash to cross the obstacle. The battalion quickly faced enemy fire and were made to retire, though not a casualty was claimed.

Under harsh rains and with more than three hundred yards west to go, the 7th carried on from north to east. The German guards who stood watch, caught unawares by the rain and the hour, fell at the hands of Captain J. L. Thomas and his troops. In silence, the party went about in enemy trenches. The troops hurled bombs into enemy dugouts, and as the confused Germans came out, English-Canadian rifle lads and grenadiers fired and bayoneted away. Instantly, close to thirty foe fell or became wounded.

Twenty minutes after the fighting commenced, the troops left, along with twelve Boche prisoners and a newfangled gas respirator made of rubber, to be promptly given to the intelligence sector. Enemy reinforcements then appeared to slice the Allies back. They found their front trenches entirely clear of any persons, friend or foe.

Enemies who remained in the trenches or who tried to go after the Canadian Tommies into No Man's Land soon met with English-Canadian fire, as per rehearsal. A number of Germans succumbed to their wounds from the fire. The

Canadian Tommies endured no casualties, aside from a sole mate who fell after an English-Canadian rifle was mistakenly discharged from a fumble made in the dark, as well as a casualty by random German fire. La Petite Douve would prove one of the most esteemed raids of the duration in its entirety. Canada would make quite the name for herself as aggressive and efficient in trench raid warfare.

A few weeks later, Pembina received just one letter from the Agnews. It was penned by Briarch. His letter began with, *He sleeps an iron sleep, slain fighting for his country*[46].

---

[46] A Canadian World War I epitaph

The Battle for Mount Sorrel

"That's what Rupert's life was for?!" An exasperated Aubrey said over supper.

Rupert died at Mount Sorrel in the valiant effort for the British flag.

"Heaven gives its favorites early death[47]," her husband tried to console her.

"More than eleven hundred of the Corps gave their lives and two thousand went missing for a single hill?! And I'm told this hill is thirty meters high and can be fully walked in a few hours' time?!" she continued.

"The battle for Mount Sorrel began at 0830 hours on June 2nd and lasted until June 13th," Auré answered. "Eight thousand, four 'undred and thirty Tommy Canucks fell, were wounded, or went missing at Mount Sorrel. Over five hundred Canucks became POWs in one day during ze smash. Nonetheless, Sanctuary Wood will remain one of Canada's most spectacular frays. And that'z something females do not understand about malez. Why would one ever start eh war? Why would you lay down your life for eh single mound of dirt? But the British will always answer the call to King and Empire. It's in their roots. Their blood. Always will be. They say, 'Generals are always fighting the last war.' High Command naturally scrutinized the past, for instance ze Boer

---

[47]   A Canadian World War I epitaph

War, to calculate 'ow to do battle in this current war. At the same time, this show is proving to be unlike anything seen before."

Allied High Command ordered massive shelling as a precursor to the main assault. The onslaught was hoped to shatter the foe's first lines. Therefore, Allied troops would be able to simply stride into enemy trenches. After eight days, three thousand guns, and more than one and a half million shells fired, the Allies attacked. What High Command did not consider was that the foe was cautioned beforehand about the shelling. The Germans bid time in the safety of their fortifications. Actual ruin of enemy lines did not come to pass, given numerous British shells were defective or failed to detonate at all. English troops were bold and crude in stating the probability of the Corps maintaining the area would come to naught.

The 3rd Division went into action for the initial time. The Corps met with an impressive enemy artillery barrage and decimation in the battle's first days. Afterwards, the 1st Division hurriedly counterstriked, though to poor results that failed to recover Mount Sorrel, Hill 61, or Hill 62, also called Sanctuary Wood. On the last day, the 1st Division attacked again. A perilous night assault was ordered by Currie to enemy stupefaction, which would aid in attaining success. Following cautious strategizing and the figuring of how to maintain the area once taken, the poor bloody infantry attacked again. They did so with exact precision behind the barrage. The three positions were retaken. The second barrage brought brilliant results, due to a thorough and competent counter barrage. Currie and Brigadier Harry Burstall, aided by Byng, fashioned what was the first "set-piece" assault of the war. The set-piece's main purpose was to strategically take planned strongpoints. This was unlike the usual big pushes that were suppose to eradicate enemy lines once and for all. This style of fighting also reduced the amount of deaths and casualties in frontal assaults. The Mount Sorrel triumph began what would be considered an English-Canadian manner of fighting. During one of the first days of the battle, the British Expeditionary Force attempted to halt enemy reinforcements with an artillery barrage. Because he broke his leg and lost his hearing from an enormous enemy artillery barrage, General Mercer endeavored to make way to a more secure area. British shrapnel hit and proved fatal to the general. He fell at the base of the Mount the morning of June 3rd. A corporal was tasked with finding and burying troops who fell in the vicinity. The corporal found Mercer's cadaver, which would have otherwise been lost to the wallow. The general was given a full military funeral, overseen by every battalion of his division. British General Haig mentioned Mercer posthumously in dispatches for gallant conduct. Mercer was, in total, honoured three times by such a distinction. Major-General Malcolm Smith Mercer, commander of the Corps 3rd Division, was Canadian born and the highest-ranking English Canadian to fall in action over the course of the duration.

Enemy bombardment also wounded Canadian-born Brigadier General Victor Williams. He was commander of the 3rd Division's 8th Brigade and was with Mercer at the time. The pair was part of a reconnaissance mission. Williams was captured and was the highest-ranking officer of the Canadian military to be made prisoner of war throughout the effort.

Of the Canadian Tommies in the front trenches, a paltry amount survived. Of the 4th Canadian Mounted Rifles' seven hundred and two lads, 635 were killed or wounded by battle's end. One of the Corps' trenches had blood in its base that measured a handful of inches in depth. Though a great deal of the forward lines were taken by Germany, minor groups left did not relinquish and fought to maintain their area. A German officer penned of the Princess Pat's, *The resistance of the officer, and some men who remained to the last in a portion of an almost obliterated trench, was magnificent.* With ill will, though veneration, Germans acknowledged that the English Canadians refused to quit and fought until every lad fell trying to defend their severely damaged fortifications.

"Mont Sorrel was Canada's first deliberately planned attack in any force and resulted in an unqualified success," documented the British Official History of the war.

The letter detailing Rupert's death ended with, *A general, but who stayed mounted, informed us we will be moving to the Somme River in between Arras and Albert, mainly Albert. Fritz is trying to bleed France white in the Verdun area. France's army is being annihilated and pressure there needs to be relieved. The Allies will bombard Germany all along the Somme to aid the French, for if the French crumble, so will all other Allied armies. By this I know, thou favourest me, that mine enemy doth not triumph against me*[48]. *It is rather lonely here, to be sure, without Rupert; however, gwell angeu na chywilydd*[49] (Gaelic for "better death than shame").

The Newfoundland Regiment was ordered into action the opening day of the Somme. The Regiment's objective was to gain control of the Somme's valley, towards the village of Beaumont-Hamel. Post-battle, initial cables sent to Newfoundland brought news of magnificent triumph in the face of the enemy. Further, accurate telegrams reached the island, and consequently, Newfoundland fell into the darkest abyss she would ever know.

---

[48] A Canadian World War I epitaph
[49] A Canadian World War I epitaph

Beaumont-Hamel

Near the end of June, in the Beaumont-Hamel area, the Allies bombarded the foe. For eight days, Allied shelling did not pause as nearly two million shells, the most in any battle to date in military history, rained down endlessly on the Germans. British High Command believed artillery did its duty thoroughly, though a large number of shells did not detonate, and an untold length of barbed wire lay uncut. Ahead of the initial attack, scouts were dispatched to ascertain the condition of the enemy-held region. Reviews sent back to General Head Quarters expressed that a favourable outcome for the Allies would be simply preposterous. Reports strongly encouraged delay in order for more damage to be done to enemy lines, though questioning senior officers went astoundingly against British protocol, and not a general would petition reorganization of the battle. What High Command failed to contemplate, too, was that Germany had been forewarned of the plan, had expected an assault long ere this summer, and sought cover in well-fortified bunkers.

Allied officers were of the opinion that tumultuous damage had been done to enemy lines. Thus, Tommies were ordered to carry extra supplies and ammunition on their kits in the total amount of about half their body weight. Tommies were not able to move at faster than a slow walking pace, due to their hefty kit, when the command was given to walk across No Man's Land in neat, orderly lines.

The opening day at 0700, comrades, British and Dominion, went over the parapets. Given that the majority escaped the shelling without serious wounds, the Germans came out as well with torrential machine gun fire and artillery support. The Beaumont-Hamel area was quickly overwhelmed with fallen and soon-to-become fatally wounded Allies. Even in the face of grave casualties, British High Command instructed further advancement.

At 0915, commanded by Lieutenant-Colonel Arthur Hadow, the Newfoundland Regiment advanced from its position. They left their support trench, pet-named St. John's Road, for Newfoundland's capitol. St. John's Road was, in effect, two hundred yards in back of the front lines. The entire time fighting to reach British front lines was spent stepping over Allied dead and wounded who congested the area. The Regiment then came within reach of the fire trenches. Snarls of barbed wire lay so densely around the front trenches that the scant number of holes troops could forge through were clearly seen by enemy machine gunners.

The slope that the Regiment traversed had a gnarled tree that the Newfoundlanders called the "danger tree." It was the target of heavy shellfire. Scarcely a smattering of the Regiment made it to the tree. Dozens of corpses of Newfoundlanders would be identified at similar thoroughfares after battle. The sprinkling who moved past the tree were cut to ribbons. The Regiment's vision of sight then became greater than five hundred yards of open fields. Beyond the fields, there was elevated ground and therefore the unrestricted visibility of the foe. It was recorded, of the Newfoundlanders, "many of them tucked their chins in, almost like they were walking into the teeth of a blizzard back home. But this time it was not snow flying all around them."

The opening day of the Somme proved the most horrid day history would write for England's military. Of the 57,000 casualties, 20,000 deaths were accounted for. All these were the glory of their time[50], Newfoundland's Regiment's fallen comprised of fourteen pairs of brothers. Four lieutenants were killed, two of whom were brothers and two cousins, all belonging to the Ayre family from St. John's. The Regiment fought under the 29th British Division, commanded by General Aylmer Hunter-Weston. He stated, of his Newfoundland soldiers, "There were no waverers, no stragglers, not a man looked back. It was a magnificent display of trained and disciplined valour, and its assault only failed of success because dead men can advance no further."

Epitaphs for fallen Newfoundlanders included, *This sacred dust is Newfoundland, not France, and held in trust... The only son of his mother and she was a widow... In your charity pray for a faithful soldier from Newfoundland... O France, be kind and keep green for me my soldier's grave, Mother... Loved we our country much, he loved it more... Sacrificed... An obedient son. A loving brother. A lover of King and Newfoundland... Tell Newfoundland that we who died fighting for her rest here content.*

---

[50]   A Canadian World War I epitaph

Summer 1916

Above Metclaff and Wellington Streets, large white clouds drifted in the blue sky on a crisp summer afternoon. Auré and his wife walked to their automobile after a day in the city. While they made their way from Rideau Club, where they had taken their afternoon meal, posters urged masters to have their servants join the effort. *Have you a Butler, Groom, Chauffeur, Gardener, or Gamekeeper serving you, who at this moment should be serving King and Country? Have you a man serving at your table who should be serving a gun? Have you a man digging your garden who should be digging trenches? Ask your men to enlist today!* Other posters aimed at mistresses read, *The boys at the front need socks. Can you knit a pair?* The University of Ottawa halted theater nights until the effort ended, as universities were doing from coast to coast. Regular documentation of casualties was posted on chalk boards in telegraph offices and in the windows of post offices.

Practically every factory had been turned into a munition's factory. Aubrey commented on women being encouraged to take up munition jobs. Auré explained that was only to free males to fight. This new industry brought new employment for thousands, and the pay was far higher than what serving afforded. Aubrey and Lady Bird had widely slandered the servant girls who left Pembina and Lansdowne to work in munitions factories. The two could hardly accept that their servants voluntarily left their positions. In munitions factories, the harsh chemicals made the women workers' skin turn yellow. Munitionettes were dubbed, Empire wide, "Canary girls." Aubrey and Lady Bird laughed endlessly at those girls. Aubrey said, "I would be too frightened to do that job."

Her husband responded, "You would 'ave eh right to be frightened, and I would not want you to do that job, anyhow."

The dominion tried to create regulations to protect the safety of the carriers of its future sons. The Imperial Munitions Board took into consideration the timeframe of shifts and the offering of healthy foods in canteens, as well as restroom accommodations and factory rearrangement, to obtain a greater level of safety for some of the dominion's first females to enter the workforce. All the same, the Federal Government, and labour unions too, usually called the performance of female workers in munitions factories "diluted." Both parties were vocal about the fact that skillful and proficient workmanship was becoming weakened because of female workers. The new "common factory girl" was also thought to be the fault of venereal disease among middle-class males whose wives could contract the condition from the "disintegrating social force."

However, women proved excellent at their temporary jobs, though they were thought not to have the ability to maintain such effort or skill over time. A large number of females took to working in banks. Banks expressed the hiring of female clerks as "a courageous experiment," and females quickly garnered the unforeseen esteem of management. Women were rarely given promotions, as the banking industry was of the opinion that transferring females was not right, out of a sense of propriety. Other areas of employment were not as encouraging to female employees. Conductorettes faced adversity and strikes in response to their being hired. Male railway employees said they would prefer to have fare boxes before female co-workers. At certain automobile companies, though, equal pay was much vouched for and women labourers who were let go without just cause were returned to their former positions.

Women were often times viewed initially as "pets" or "ruses," but after some time in the workforce, managers found themselves saying to their female employee, "If you were a man I would promote you." A man earned twice as much, if not more, as a woman worker did for the same position.

Auré then went on to state the empire had set a new low with suffragism and that the woman in question was English Canadian too. But, on July 1st, the British Empire agreed to its first female magistrate, from Edmonton, judge Emily Murphy.

Harrington and Kellynch passed Auré and his wife as they walked towards Rideau Club. "Good afternoon" was said by all. The two gentlemen were both board members of the Ottawa branch of the Patriotic Fund; Harrington was the treasurer and Kellynch was still the president. They excused themselves because they needed to be on time for their meeting. The matter being discussed that day was the shirker problem, while one of them nodded to Richardieux's Rolls Royce behind the lot, as if to indicate the board members did not care to socialize with a slacker.

Auré corrected them politely, "Three of my nephews were in uniform. One of them waz killed at Ypres. He was a 1914 volunteer[51]. He hesitated not when duty called[52]. To him it was the call of duty[53]. Excuse my lack of 'umility, gentlemen."

"Blessed are the peace makers, for they shall see their God[54]," Harrington mustered in response to his wrongful accusation of Richardieux.

Both gentlemen offered their condolences at the slacker's unexpected graciousness, while Aubrey turned to stare at her husband's patriotic remarks.

Later the same week, a char-a-banc passed by before an unexpected vehicle came to a stop outside Chateau Laurier. Aubrey had finished playing bridge with Lady Bird. One of the carriages, and not one of Pembina's automobiles, had come to collect her. Auré ascended the step to help her alight. In the carriage, Auré explained he had given the Rolls Royce for the effort. It was donated to the Red Cross. She was taken aback at the generous donation because the automobile made affairs far easier. *How callous of him! Instead of being discreet about his infidelities, he will be more open about them without any automobiles on the grounds,* Aubrey thought. She felt jealous and hurt by his apparent indifference to subjecting his wife to such blunt behaviour.

He had been acting so strangely as of late, too. Alcohol was no longer permitted at Pembina. Emmett's cigarettes were donated to the front. Auré had given a fine amount of money to the Patriotic Fund; the majority of the sum went to the Widows and Orphans fund section of the branch. Llewellyn had been given an order for the gunsmith recently.

---

[51]   A Canadian World War I epitaph
[52]   A Canadian World War I epitaph
[53]   A Canadian World War I epitaph
[54]   A Canadian World War I epitaph

Aubrey had found that odd, too. It was not yet hunting season and, besides, the guns ordered to be cleaned were not rifles but his Colt pistols. A while ago, she had overheard him discussing with Llewellyn that he relinquished his contracts with Hughes. *He could not be thinking of — no! That would be preposterous*, thought Aubrey. She could not press him even if she wanted to, given a wife questioning her husband's actions would be an insult to his intelligence. The carriage departed and, per usual, a lady was on the sidewalk selling flowers, this time forget-me-nots, as a fundraiser for the cause. Auré asked after Aubrey's card game. Aubrey absently related how Lady Bird let her nanny go and did so through a letter. Most often, the sole instances where a servant would encounter the mistress were the days they were hired and fired.

Auré said, "That's cowardly. Firing eh servant ought to always be done in person. There's a term for mistresses who fire their servants that way, and the term iz not 'Lady,' it's 'Bitch.' If you want to know if a female is a coward, pay attention to this rule — it never fails. Likewise, if you want to know if eh man is eh coward, that can be ascertained by how he treats the women in 'is life, particularly his wife and when no one else is about. Take Peter for instance. His wife had eh terminal disease and he cheated on her for months until she died. Around the same time, the Edwards dealt with one of ze other brothers who beat 'is wife. In regard to the other brother assaulting 'is wife, Peter told their father 'we should leave this alone' — gutless son-of-a-bitch. That is surely the boys' club. Instead of protecting the female, 'e protected the male. Until the day I die, I will not understand such eh dastardly position.

Apparently, that was ze last straw for Duke Edwards. He banished the elder son to India and Peter here with orders not to return to England until they 'ad become gentlemen. The father iz to be applauded. When eh relative does something immoral and another family member defends them, that is surely a way of causing extreme problems in eh family. One has to do the right thing, even if that means siding against your family. And in fairness to their family, the female should not 'ave gotten involved with that so called 'man.' One can tell 'o those males are a mile away. I will never understand why any female would enter into that sort of a relationship. That being said, no female deserves to be treated in such eh manner. And only a coward would accost a lady. But the family agreed not to confront the brother and act az though they did not have any knowledge of the abuse. One reason why this problem iz so pervasive is because the families of these males often timez do nothing about the abuse. Especially when children are involved, I cannot understand 'ow anyone can be so cowardly. The Edwards are cowards, the lot of them. They act like scum.

The Picnic

Human nature is at variance with rules. Picnicking was all the rage to Edwardians. The summer months usually found lunch taken out of doors. A picnic called for a fully laid dining table complete with white tablecloths, silver service, and servants. On the front lines, each and every dignified regiment would afford its officers the same commodities.

Aubrey hosted a picnic for her numerous companions. The item must have fallen off at the picnic quite by accident, given its expense. By wicked fortune, one of Pembina's servants found the piece of jewellery and not the owner. After the picnic, one of Aubrey's lady's maids handed her mistress an elegant gold necklace with a locket. Unsure who the necklace belonged to, Aubrey opened the locket to see if a photo was on the inside. To the left was a picture of Edmund. The picture on the right was one of the Lawrence's very servants, a lady's maid, Emma. The servant had in fact been at the picnic and had served Edmund and the whole group.

Aubrey turned the locket over and read the outside inscription. The lovely engraved words were, *All my love.* Carved underneath were the initials *E & E.* Aubrey burst out in incredulous laughter. *This can't be true! Edmund, in love with a servant?!* thought Aubrey in mad glee. *But how could this be? Say, if this girl loved Edmund from afar and wanted to pretend a master could ever love her, a servant could never afford such an article. She couldn't have purchased it herself. The necklace had to have been bought by Edmund. The proof of the pudding, as it was said, was in the eating.* Masters did not permit their lowers to have followers. Masters were of the opinion that servants could not discern proper from improper matches. If a female servant was found to have a romantic partner, she could be fired immediately: her leaving with a reference would be based on the judgement of her mistress. A male servant could stay on with his master's family, provided he let his partner go. Withal, in the eyes of masters, the only acceptable cause for a servant to terminate their employment was marriage — a double standard of morality. Immediately, Aubrey thought to tell Lady Bird, who would be fit to be tied of Edmund's humiliation if his secret were made known. Aubrey knew Mother Augusta would say that *gossip is the most damaging force on earth. The repercussions would be tumultuous for Edmund if another found out,* thought Aubrey. A better idea came to mind than to tell Lady Bird. Aubrey would tell Lawrence of his son being in love with a servant.

A boudoir was the embodiment of Edwardian chic. Pembina was not an exception to the rule. A mistress' bedroom or boudoir usually had an adjoined parlour for guests. The "Handed," or afternoon tea, was usually between the hours of three to six. Masters took tea outside their residences. Their wives stayed home and entertained guests with tea and dainties, if they were hosting other mistresses. When entertaining mistresses' husbands, romance and dalliances were quite often the order of the day. An unspoken agreement between spouses of respective lovers was in place in many Edwardian marriages.

As soon as the discreet servant bowed from the room, Lawrence was always shown into the boudoir after being shown into the parlour. Aubrey still did not know who Auré's official mistress was. She could not bring herself to ask the servants where he went in the afternoons. One never questioned servants about family matters, and lady's maids, as well as butlers, were expected to keep their master's secrets. One afternoon at Pembina, while Auré was presumably with his lover, Lawrence's chief mistress said goodbye to him on the second-floor landing. Lawrence had only just left the manor when the sound of gravel being driven over was heard in the drive. For a moment, Aubrey was perplexed. The sound heard could not be Lawrence because he had already departed. *Could he have returned for something? Could it be Auré? But who else could it be at this hour? He must have returned early from wherever he had been!* Aubrey thought in despair. In haste, she went to one of the front windows. Whoever the person in question was could not be seen from the first-floor balcony. She could not discern who had only come into the manor. With great hurry, she ran to her bedroom. She would make it seem as though she had just awoken from a lie-down, given that only a wrap covered her frame. Before the bed could be reached, the mistress' bedroom door was thrown open. Pembina's master stood in the doorway, stationary. The look Aubrey saw she could not quite discern. Ladies were not privy to frankness such as brawls. Had Aubrey ever witnessed a physical confrontation, she would have understood the stunned expression before her. Her husband's eyes were nearly shut, as if swollen from a fight, though bruises had yet to become apparent. A bit of time proved necessary for discoloration to appear after a man took an open-faced hit.

Fall 1916

It was one of the last summer evenings before fall set in. The wind did not reach the terraced guests, who were treated to a panoramic view of the stars. Peter was speaking to a British Naval Officer, Rear Admiral Sir—. The Admiral was a gentleman by circumstance of birth and, later, of chosen character. Dignified and excellently mannered, he stood close in height to Peter. Because the royals had gone from the Duke's position of Governor General, Peter only associated with pilots — as they were the "smartest" of all soldiers — Victoria Cross recipients, or the highest-ranking officers, and he would not lower himself to attend a party without such military personnel present. When his country called he came[55], and upon being wounded at Jutland, the Rear Admiral was sent to Ottawa to convalesce due to British hospitals being at near capacity. Peter was vehemently discussing the servant problem with his polite, though disinterested, listener. If Peter looked down on one group of people more than colonials, it was servants.

Wanting a change of subject, the Rear Admiral said, "Old Neptune fought hard for our King. That naval show transpired on May 31st, right? Both sides claimed victory; Germany did so because she sunk more of our ships than we did hers. Be that as it may, we staved off the invasion from their taking

---

[55]   A Canadian World War I epitaph

control of the ports, and that was Germany's intention, so we rightfully take the glory. Who will surely be the youngest Victoria Cross recipient of the war garnered his medal in that scrap. Jack Cornwell, an English boy, one of ours, by George," with unmistakable pride in the Admiral's even tone. "His shipmates were dead about him. He was manning a gun when he was gravely hit and kept fighting. Evacuated and died later in hospital — of his multiple injuries, the stomach wound was what got him. Sixteen years old. A dark week for the Empire, to be sure, the battle of Jutland along with Kitchener dying. There was not a figurehead the empire turned to more than him. His death was incomparable. When he died, Britain stood still out of respect for their army hero and minister of war. Canada suffered, as well, when Kitchener drowned while headed for Russia on The *HMS Hampshire*."

Rejected four times, accepted the fifth[56], the last of Peter's remaining brothers paid the price of admiralty at Jutland, the grandest naval battle of the war. One of Peter's brothers fell in the initial fighting of 1914; the other was slaughtered in the Somme. Peter, though the youngest, was the only son left of Duke Edward's. Aubrey had never seen him so jolly as in recent times, given that he was now the rightful heir of his family's fortune. Auré said that, if not for being his father's sole heir, Peter would become the first male of the empire to be financially dependent on a woman, that is to say his wife, when he would eventually remarry solely to secure financial security. This made Llewellyn laugh out loud, as the very idea that a male could be financially dependent on a woman was incredulous.

"Father wrote to me, which he has not done in quite some time. I am to return home if I enlist." Redemption was seen in

---

[56]   A Canadian World War I epitaph

the look of the sailor. "Unfortunately, I replied to father that the war will end soon and, considering the time it takes to go over there and whatnot, it would not make sense to enlist. Weeks or months are necessary to complete basic training before embarking to the front," a cavalier Peter explained. The light went from the Admiral's eyes as he stood serenely listening. Peter carried on of a light affair, "Father has not replied to me, what with how busy he is, naturally." The Admiral smiled at Peter's oblivious and mistaken reason why the Duke was ignoring his only remaining child.

Aubrey was seated at a table with friends near the dance floor. Lindsay had returned. After a few attempts with a knife, his left foot and ankle were amputated from trench foot in a frontline hospital. *Such a pity, one of the most fun leads for dancing I knew*, thought Aubrey in response to Lindsay's, "Twas my cheerful duty[57]."

Cavalry squadrons were by and by broken up and sent to fight in the poor bloody infantry. Trenches were usually quite water-filled, although they were dry in summer months. Tommies would stand in trenches for days at a time. Often times frigid, wet feet would become blistered and inflamed, would lose circulation, become entirely deadened, balloon to several times their normal size, and turn red, blue, or a more disagreeable colour. A bayonet could be stuck through an infected foot and not a thing felt. The agony would commence when the swelling subsided. Troops would scream themselves into delirium or unconsciousness until surgery removed the foot. Trench foot was an all-pervasive and remarkable problem the first two years of the effort, specifically during winter. As time went on, British High Command tried to eradicate the extraordinary pandemic across its Forces by revoking leave

---

[57]   A Canadian World War I epitaph

privileges of a Tommy's whole battalion if a lad was found to have the condition. Mates took care to ask after one another for this reason. Duckboards were eventually put at the base of trenches in order for troops to be out of the water and muck. Basic devices to do away with the water were installed at the bottom of trenches as well. Eventually, boots reaching past the knee were distributed to the poor bloody infantry.

Aubrey glanced to the entryway to see if Auré had come to collect her. He was present indeed and stood at the top of the dance floor, head and shoulders taller than any given male. So shocked was Aubrey by the sight of her husband that she dropped her champagne flute. A servant turned to stare at a lady who caused a scene before he removed the shattered pieces.

Gentlemen and ladies at surrounding tables quitted their conversations in astonishment. Kellynch, who was dancing, actually stopped waltzing altogether. His partner was made to look around at what the commotion was. Hatred, coupled with astonishment, registered in Fitzwilliam's eyes, as the most wretched male in Ottawa made his way across the dance floor. Ladies stared too, for most could not resist a man booted to the knee in those signature black puttees over brown boots, wearing khaki trousers and the tight-fitting seven brass-button serge, completed by the peaked cap which housed the iconic gold maple leaf emblem of the Canadian Expeditionary Force uniform.

He enlisted?! It cannot be so, was all Aubrey's mind could absorb. Auré walked up to their table. A seated Desrosiers said to him, "Come now, see reason," and said it with a smile, though he refused to shake Auré's hand upon greeting. *How astutely rude,* thought Aubrey, at the blatant disregard of etiquette on Desrosiers' part. Her husband, however, seemed unsurprised by the slight. But Aubrey was too flabbergasted, too shocked to consider the tension Desrosiers tried in vain to conceal. The English ladies at the table asked why he enlisted. The reply was a resounding, "Ze war iz now personal."

"A crusade for Christian soldiers? To fight for the King? Gallantry to the Empire?" were all suggested.

Auré corrected them, "Government iz now telling women to deny their husbands ze bedroom if not in uniform. It'z time this war endz."

The statement was true, although the effect the latest enlistment gimmick had on civilians had been almost naught. Desrosiers roared with laughter and spat out his drink quite unintentionally, so much so that others turned to stare. Lindsay looked as though he wanted to hang his now brother-in-arms.

At Pembina, later the same evening, the maid was dismissed by her master once he walked into her mistress' room. Auré sat and watched Aubrey undress by herself. The question of why he enlisted was asked. A long silence ensued. The reply given was, "Conscience doth makes cowards of us all." She dare not contradict him, as a lady doubting her husband was akin to her striking him, but she knew Auré's Shakespearean answer was a lie. To congratulate him was quite certainly thought of. If a Frenchman wanted to volunteer, his kinsmen emphasized the abandonment of their heritage by their motherland. From long experience, she knew better than to discuss such issues with him. Mainly, she was shocked into silence. The Somme was still raging: Auré was headed to the worst bloodbath in history. Aubrey did not have further time to ponder his enlistment at his words "come here."

Auré Leaves

Richardieux was now an officer of the King. The French could scarcely believe their leader had defected. Britishers were baffled; something was afoot. Although he was an undesirable, Auré was silently thought of by others as doing the right thing. After all, a man fighting for the King was the only man who mattered now-a-days. Nevertheless, in the ensuing weeks, rumours abounded and Auré was accused of them all. Because he was taken on strength with the Van Doos, it was said no other battalion would endear him. The 22nd Battalion was the dominion's most acclaimed French battalion. The pet name Britishers assigned the battalion was the "Van Doos," a knock-off of the French word "twenty-second" or "vingt-deuxieme." The 22nd was so called across all of English Canada. Cashiering would, in all likelihood, be ordered once his true identity was revealed. Many were of the opinion he should be shot before further damage could be done to the prestige of the Corps within the Empire. He deserted the Mounted Force and joined the Expeditionary Force. At least if he deserted this force he would be executed, English Canadians said triumphantly.

Returned troops like Lindsay or Kellynch, who disliked Auré intensely, tried to make others understand that the accusations were unjust and to see reason. In fairness, that year saw almost all who were inclined to go enlist, and Richardieux could claim greater gallantry than just about any other Franco-Ottawan. Furthermore, after summer 1916, conviction in the big breakthrough receded, numbers of recruits dwindled, and the sentiment of pushing fell in the light of smashes seen in recent times. England's Canadian sons joined their brothers-in-arms by the few thousand each month; however, most wanted to be part of the Artillery, Engineer, or Medical Corps. During the previous year, the government let down rules to allow a good deal more enlistees into the military. Citizens or municipalities could organize battalions themselves. Sportsmen, Teetotaller, and Highland, among other battalions, were raised privately. Unbeknownst at the time to these new enlistees, once overseas, the same battalions would often be disbanded, and each lad was scattered to a different section of the Corps. Medical restrictions, which prevented those in the early years from going, were amended. Bantam units were created for males who were five foot, three inches tall or less. The Forestry Corps recruited those with poor eyesight and who were hard of hearing, if experience had already been fielded. Initially told the duration was a "White man's war," some coloured males were accepted with prudence and, eventually, hundreds of Chinese and Japanese Canadians would enlist. An entire Black labour battalion was formed. The Corps' buried or returned sons, in the amount of 80,000 a year, were not able to see replacement at anywhere near full volume. Numerous battalions were not in positions to retain numbers and, in turn, these battalions were broken up to become railway chums, sent to the Forestry Corps, or acted as reinforcements to the fighting units at the front. With spotty statistics, and Hughes spearheading the faulty good cheer of lads in uniform far and wide, few Ottawans realized voluntary agreement to go was coming to a close.

Because alcohol had become an enemy of the war, posters downtown read, *He who is for alcohol is against England!* as well as, *In the great tug of war, help Britain by abstaining from drink!* Days before Auré departed, he ordered Pembina's liquor to join the ranks of all patriotic Ottawans. The sole exception was Emmett's fine rum. Auré had the rum given to the front. One suggestion made in the dominion was that the boys should be disallowed their daily rum, though the most widely accepted opinion was that they should be allotted one of the only respites in their horrid days. In mid-September, prohibition was declared in Ontario, as well as in British Columbia. The summer months saw the other western provinces officially abstain from drink. King Alcohol was publicly poured down city drains and into ditches and lakes from coast to coast. One by one, each province went dry, except for slacker Quebec. At the same time, vacations to "Historic old Quebec" exploded. It was agreed that alcohol was an insult to front lines sacrifices and that troops should return to a dominion superior to the one they left to defend. Wheat, fruit, and the like proved necessary for the effort. Wine was the sole alcohol of any kind that could be consumed, though bars, clubs, and stores were prevented from selling all forms of alcohol. Citizens were permitted, however, to drink in their own residences. Distilleries, too, could manufacture liquor and send the substance to other provinces.

Auré had enlisted "for the duration." But, now, no one knew quite what the "duration" meant. Citizens wondered if troops would return. Such a thought never occurred in the first few years; at train stations, solely cheers and well wishes were given. In 1916, tears were surely in the eyes of those on platforms bidding farewell. Recruits were telling their families, "I couldn't die in a better cause[58]... One crowded hour of glorious life is worth an age without name[59]... Adieu, parents, je meurs pour Dieu, Le Roi et ma Patrie[60] (Farewell, parents, I die for God, the King and my country)... I have only once to die[61]... Mon âme à dieu, mon coeur à ma mère, à ma patrie mon sang et ma vie[62] (My soul to God, my heart to my mother, and to my native land my blood and my life)... A glorious death is a living memory[63]... If I fall, I shall have done something with my life worth doing[64]... It is sweet and glorious to die for one's country[65]... I count my life well lost to serve my country best[66]."

Floods cannot quench the love of a parent[67], and the evening prior to his leave, Auré found himself in the nursery. "You cannot pass beyond our boundless love[68]. Sleep on, beloved, and take thy rest[69]," he said while he ran his hand over his sleeping son's hair. A badge that read, *My father is at the Front*, which all young boys took extraordinary pride in, was laid on the nightstand. Auré took a last look at René, then the little one was left to his dreams.

The morning of his departure, Pembina's master and Llewellyn were deep in discussion. Leaving a lonely wife

---

58   A Canadian World War I epitaph
59   A Canadian World War I epitaph
60   A Canadian World War I epitaph
61   A Newfoundland World War I epitaph
62   A Canadian World War I epitaph
63   A Canadian World War I epitaph
64   A Canadian World War I epitaph
65   A Canadian World War I epitaph
66   A Canadian World War I epitaph
67   A Canadian World War I epitaph
68   A Canadian World War I epitaph
69   A Newfoundland World War I epitaph

and child[70], Auré looked resplendent in his officer's uniform complete with a collar and necktie. Officers bought their proper uniforms of tailored, refined, rich material, often times complete with sword, pistol, and binoculars. Llewellyn gave his solemn word he would see to the immaculate running of the estate as long as its master was absent.

The Laurentiens came to bid their farewells. Only at Michel's command did Nico finally let Auré be. All remaining Laurentiens were present, except Frédéric, who had gone as a regular with the 4th Division. Edmund would soon join the 4th Division. Edmund refused to forsake his partner once Lawrence found out about the lovers. Consequently, Lawrence disinherited Edmund and then ordered him to enlist, which was done not so much for honour as it was to have Edmund leave Ottawa before a scandal could break. Regardless, for the first time since the war started, Edmund stopped drinking daily, as the endless humiliation of remaining behind finally ended.

Put together in Bramshott, England, in April, the division crossed the channel on August 12th. Hughes and his colleagues were obstinate in not authorizing French regiments or raising new ones. Let brotherly love continue[71], Frédéric cared not at all for the Empire that caused his brother's death; however, he was delighted to avenge his brother, as males did so per the gentleman's code from coast to coast. The military gave Frédéric his uniform, including a rough serge with a button-up tunic collar.

Mme. Laurentien gifted her nephew a uniquely Canadian wartime food: a Trench cake. The dessert was made of lard, molasses, flour, baking soda, raisins, spices, and brown sugar

---

[70] A Canadian World War I epitaph
[71] A Canadian World War I epitaph

rather than white, to keep with the changing times. It was a simple, though delightful, light spice cake. She regularly sent the sweet to her sons. Since only items that could keep for a lengthy time were sent overseas, fruitcakes, maple sugar, cigarettes, chocolate, and tea were the most common foods, parceled in spectacular numbers.

Because an officer was entitled to a batman, James, a footman, stood awaiting at the carriage in the morning. The sergeant who did James' paperwork knew the servant was underage, but chaps were needed overseas, and a male willing to go was harder and harder to come by. On the attestation papers, James was eighteen. He was to go to shine his master's shoes, do his room, prepare the morning bath, burnish belts, and wake his master.

The double row of servants curtsied and bowed to the master as he walked by them. René was in a dress and would remain so until the age of about four. "My best boy[72]," whispered the nanny, a sweet, fair, Welsh girl, as she held René in her arms. Auré asked René for a gentleman's agreement to take care of his mother until his father's return. En lieu of shaking hands, Auré momentarily enclosed his son's plump fist in his own hand.

Llewellyn and Mrs.—, the head housekeeper, stood side-by-side at the opposite end of the rows. The pair kept a watchful eye on the lower orders. Trepidation radiated from the main housemaid in the eyes of the servants. Her large key ring, a staple sound on the estate, lay still out of deference to the master's parting. Llewellyn turned slightly to her, borrowed a line from *Hamlet*, and whispered, "Something is rotten in the state of Denmark."

---

[72] A Canadian World War I epitaph

The master of Pembina then walked up to the mistress. Momentarily, the sabre dangling at Auré's side was all that was heard in the lovely, brisk fall day. Aubrey pulled her shawl a bit closer in uncertainty. She tried to block out the thought of all the infedelities in their marriage. Gently, he put the leathered glove of his gentleman's uniform to the side of her cheek. He bent down and kissed her on the side of her temple. "Dilectus (Latin for "Beloved")," Auré whispered simply at her side.

Though she feared their final moment together, he displayed graciousness after all that had transpired in recent months. It was as though she was struck by lightning. The changing of the guards that kept her heart passed from Emmett to Auré. She fell in love with him. *No! He can't possibly leave! He must stay! This can't be happening!* she thought in great despair. Auré seated himself in the carriage. Aubrey watched her husband go down the drive and off to war.

Mother Augusta's Letter

Mother Augusta had written to Pembina.

*We shall not look upon his like again[73];
Briarch bombed his way out of an enemy's
holding area where he was being detained
and worked his way back behind Allied
lines, apparently unscathed. As I write this,
I wonder how Rupert knew and Briarch
knows so much about the war in detail. The
average lass at the front rarely knows most
information pertaining to the battle they are
involved in. Regulars usually only know what
they can see before them on the battlefield.
But Briarch always seems to know specific
information that is usually reserved for
officers or even generals. How does he have
access to maps, and who are these generals
who are giving him this information? I think
of the trouble that those generals would
face if they were found out, but perhaps our
lovely Agnew boys had or have other means
of recovering this knowledge. Also, how do*

---

[73]   A Canadian World War I epitaph

Briarch's detailed letters pass the censory review board? He must have someone, or some sort of mcguffin, who carries his letters from the front to regular avenues of mail. The repurcussions Rupert would have faced and Briarch continues to brazingly defy would be considerable if his commanding officer were to know of his understandings of battles. I choose not to think about these matters.

A generous boy, God bless him[74], Briarch has been released on harvest leave. The poor thing has not been as lively since the loss of his dearest friend. 'Tis hard to plant in spring and never reap the autumn yield[75], and how good it was that Rupert died for the mother country that his ancestors cared so much for. At the battle of the Somme in his eighteenth year[76] and shortly before he left the front, Briarch was commissioned as a Lieutenant. Additionally, he moved to the newly arrived 46th Battalion to be closer to mates from his own region after losing Rupert. The military is using strategies to see chaps from the same areas stay together when they go overseas. While historical battalions have kept their traditional names, battalions created for this war have instead been given numbers for a greater sense of uniformity throughout

---

[74]   A Canadian World War I epitaph
[75]   A Canadian World War I epitaph
[76]   A Canadian World War I epitaph

the Corps. Rightly so, British-born made up almost exclusively the ranks in 1914 and 1915, given their birthright. Fortunately, with the war lasting so long, this is surely the year when the largest numbers of Canadian-born lasses are going in answer to England's call.

Since war started, farmers have been urged to produce greater quantities of grain, wheat, hogs, and cattle for food. The venture has proved easy due to farmers receiving the nicest yields in decades this summer. "And I will restore to you the years the locusts have eaten[77]", to quote Joel. Because so many fellows are over there now, more hands are required to bring in the harvest. There is a startling trend about. "College Maidens" turned "Farmerettes" are taking the place of males to help bring in the yields. These females call themselves "Women warriors." Naturally, farmers didn't know what to make of them when summer started but were forced to accept aid. Farmerettes wear dark bloomers and khaki blouses. And they wear their trousers with pride! Priests, as well as ministers and reverends, for that matter, are highly concerned that permitting females to wear pants will lead to immodesty and promiscuity. Females will no longer act ladylike and will soon act feral and fancy free instead of shy and humble. Many fear

---

[77]   A Canadian World War I epitaph

that these farmerettes will never go on to marry because no self-respecting male will marry them. I wonder what is to become of them? Editorials argue that females dressing like males will lead to male authority being doubted. The family unit as we know it could become shattered. Unmanly qualities would show in males, and they would become powerless. Articles also state women wearing trousers has the power to create "social and moral chaos" and the distinction of "the sexes would be obliterated." Now that harvest is almost complete, I have heard from a number of farmers that their female labourers' work is simply outstanding.

Have you noticed, Aubrey, the longer the effort continues the less the lads talk of it? When they write back, they ask about their families more than they give details of being overseas. They want to know how harvest is going or if frost will come soon, and they describe battles in less and less detail. Briarch does not discuss the front lines very much, only when provoked by his younger siblings. Reconnaissance Balloons were explained to them and they were most intrigued. Briarch also explained a new battle invention called "Landships." They are monstrosities of steel that lasses maneuver from within the contraption itself over No Man's Land. Initially, the English tried to conceal these weapons as water tanks. The

nickname given for these machines is "Tank."
It was first used at the battle of Courcelette. So
far, he says, they have proven useless and do
little but startle Fritz. They greatly bewildered
the Allies, too, when first introduced. Some
Germans surrendered when they first saw
the tanks in battle. Due to the fact that tanks
cannot handle corpses, a lass is positioned at
either front side of a tank and is made to walk
alongside the tank as it rolls over the territory
to clear the way of bodies. Given that tanks, or
"Monsters" as some call them over there, can
move at no more than a walking pace, all the
lasses say this task is the most selfless role on
the Western Front. A flying pig, or a mortar
bomb, is surely the most frightful mechanism
of warfare, aside from gas. Rubble from a
mortar can fly upwards in the hundreds of
yards. Concerning gas, chemical gas has been
created, which means the substance changing
direction from wind and moving backwards to
attack its proprietors is no longer a concern.

Our one & only[78] Briarch has brought back a
few trinkets from No Man's Land. All troops
collect souvenirs from the war, although the
Corps does so to a near obsessive level.

The Corps admittedly hoarded possessions found in battle
to a point where one could not call the English Canadians
in their hobby exactly normal — or, to be uncharitable, one

---

[78] A Canadian World War I epitaph

might deem them slightly mad. They hoarded so much that the German army declared, "The English fight for freedom, the French fight for freedom, and the Canadians fight for souvenirs."

> *British High Command did not have the Corps see action at the Somme until the first week of September, unlike poor Newfoundland, oh my gosh. However, British Newfoundland troops have recovered from Beaumont-Hamel, reinforced with more lasses from their island. Their troops did marvelously at Gueudecourt, on October the 12th, where they fought with distinction. They pushed five miles from their front lines at Beaumont-Hamel. Newfoundland's resiliency is simply astounding.*

The territory taken by Newfoundland would remain the largest territorial gain made by the Allies at the Somme. The Regiment took six hundred yards more of German territory than the Allies who attacked with the Regiment, killed two hundred and fifty enemies, and turned seventy-five enemies into Prisoners of War. 120 Newfoundlanders were killed in action.

> *At Pozière, the Anzacs were replaced by the Corps. Before, our lasses were in Ypres and marched 140 kilometers to their sector at the Somme. The feat of this procedure proves our staff officers are maturing in competency.*

Our English Canadian lasses were easy targets, given their trenches consisted of white chalk that easily stood out to the Germans. A death was recorded in the Corps almost every minute, once the Corps' got into the trenches at the Somme. In response, they shovelled their way to safety further underground. While they dug, corpse upon corpse was found underneath them. As well, I'm afraid English Canadian barrages hit and bombed our own attacking poor bloody infantry.

During the Corps' respite over summer, Lieutenant-General Byng and his ever more trusted officer, Currie, reviewed frays that took place over the course of this year. They found that the battles we won were mainly due to those attacking with the bayonet being safeguarded as much as possible by artillery. Aubrey, did you know "artillery" means "great big guns? Guns so big they can only be used in warfare?" I was not aware of the fact until the war started. At any rate, Fleurs-Courcelette was the first battle for the Corps at the Somme. They attacked, on a 2,000 metre section, west of the Courcelette village. They went into action with the Corps first use of the "Creeping Barrage" on the Western Front. Briarch related this most peculiar method of attacking. Essentially, it is a massive array of artillery firing together to produce a colossal wave of shells, so many at once that a literal barrage or wall of steel is created. Artillery works together in as perfect unison as possible so the barrage traverses in an arch-like frame across No Man's Land. The main role of the creeping barrage is to prevent the enemy from firing on our lasses as they advance across No Man's Land, for the troops literally advance underneath it. Can you imagine! It must be the most marvellous thing to see.

From what I gathered from Briarch's explanation, instead of the lasses crossing No Man's Land in a sole perpetual march per usual, they proceed after the barrage does, in large waves, while the barrage "rakes" its way across ahead of them, acting as a shield of sorts. The whole assault is timed so every few minutes the artillery knows to, as they say, "lift" the hail of shells, or the barrage. A planned number of yards then sees the barrage advance farther towards enemy lines. By the time the barrage reaches enemy trenches, the Germans have already naturally taken cover in their dugouts and are not able to be in their front trenches to fire upon the Allies. Our lasses are able to reach enemy lines before the foe can come out of their dugouts and attack them. The opposing trenches are not meant to be decimated by the barrage, but at times that does indeed occur. The main objective is to force the foe to hide in the safety of their bunkers. By the time they come out of their bunkers, our lasses are literally on top of them and are awaiting them. The barrage is thought to be a brilliant tactic by English officers.

Naturally, with a procedure so large, there are downfalls. A barrage is remarkably perilous. Some troops move along without keeping time, as anxiety can get the better of one. The ones at the back can move too quickly and, in doing so, make those leading hit shells from friendly fire. Gunners can mistake readings on charts and fire too closely to the primary advancing waves. It is very difficult for the Artillery and poor bloody infantry to communicate, and, therefore, it can move too quickly and leave at least some of the lasses exposed. A Tommy can also be wounded from behind by stray bullets. I dare say there are more downfalls.

P.S.

Before I forget, the first waves to attack, which are closest to the barrage itself, do so in a manner called "Leaning on the barrage."

Yours in Christ,
Mother Augusta

Hugh's Letter

Dear Aubrey,

It sure is a lovely fall day. I've come from flying atop the trees as close as I can without touching them. Pilots are permitted to fly for jollities when not working. I went to England for a brief respite, where Henrietta met me during her leave, too. We mainly stayed in London, with family. We met some of the 66th Battery. They've just landed in England and will be sent to France next year in August. What a jolly lot they are. My squadron has been singing "Call of the Motherland," "Fall in Canada!" and "Hats off to the Flag and the King." But the 66th have original songs.

*"The best artillery battery
That came to France this year
Was the 66th from Montreal
With fourteen kegs of beer
They marched right up to Windsor Station
And got aboard the train*

They said good-bye to ten thousand Janes
When the train pulled out
They were heard to shout
Hurrah, hurrah, hurrah..."

I'm leaning against my Sopwith Pup in the hanger. She's a single-seater biplane. Her maximum speed is one hundred and eleven miles per hour, though with a pleasing wind, it can go quicker. It takes only fourteen minutes to reach three thousand meters, which is as high as we can fly out here.

When I return, I ought to give you my white scarf. But its use is functional. The jackets worn are of rough leather. Necks are rubbed crudely because one turns constantly looking for Old Fritz. The iconic scarf prevents friction from occurring. Goggles are worn since the cockpits are open, and it is quite chilly way up in the clouds.

A Halberstadt, not sure what model, flew over the aerodrome just now. As is customary, shots are not taken at airplanes that fly quite low over aerodromes; however, this one did not. Enemy pilots drop messages stating Allied hospitals will soon be bombed or if one of ours has been taken prisoner. If one of our noteworthy boys goes down, a Heinie will drop a wreath of condolence or a message stating so over our airfield. As well, if a pilot goes down, traditionally, the other side flies beside the chap and adopts a somber expression as a salute of sorts. However, the one that flew past just now did not drop a thing. My mates' anti-aircraft guns have gone after it.

The first day of instruction, you are taught the right way to swing a propeller. In flight school, officers instruct that if an aim can be hit, to "give it a go." After ten hours or so of on-ground instruction, I was given my first plane to pilot. I cannot put into words how careful one has to be in piloting. More boys fall during one of their first take-offs than from enemy action. The average life expectancy for a British pilot is about a fortnight. One mainly becomes knowledgeable about flying by trial and error. The first year of the effort, pilots gave dirty looks and shook their fists at the enemy. They also brought darts and pistols from their households. Then the army gave hand bombs to drop as they flew by the enemy. But in spring 1915, a Frenchman put a machine gun on his aircraft. He was captured by the Germans, who made the Frenchman show them how he did so. The Germans copied the idea. Now, machine guns on aeroplanes are quite common on both sides. We mainly use the Lewis gun.

In the beginning, we were the "Eyes of the army" or "Cavalry of the clouds." The Royal Flying Corps' main role was to keep enemy reconnaissance planes at bay so they could not obtain information about English readiness on the ground. At Aubers Ridge, wireless radios were given to the two-seater planes for artillery observation. The devices can send but cannot accept messages. This method of communication has made a huge impact on how business is done. Because confidentiality on the ground is not relevant anymore, their main job is to help the artillery see enemy guns and soldiers. Flying my Pup, my job is to protect the planes observing the artillery. In doing so, more Allies are safeguarded now. However, I just received a promotion and will be flying a different plane shortly.

I'm certainly glad chutes are not required, at least they haven't been up 'til now. At any rate, you can't be entirely certain that a sheet of silk can prevent you from dying. British pilots are not allowed to wear chutes, as what we fly are very costly pieces of machinery and are made of the finest wood, wire, and canvas. Generals are of the opinion that not carrying chutes will force a lad to save his plane or at least work harder to save it. If enemy guns jam mid-fight, the other pilot often times will disengage and salute, then fly off to do battle another day. And, Aubrey, we have the most splendid air duels. I will tell you all about them when I see you next.

Sincerely yours,
Flight Commander in the Royal Naval Air Force,
Hughie H.

Late 1916

Due to Auré being bound for the front, Aubrey found herself wanting greatly to know of the war. She read newspapers daily.

Given that Canadian troops were deemed Imperial ones, the Corps was made to completely follow the British Expeditionary Force's regulations. When the duration started, Hughes spoke to the House, "We have nothing whatever to say as to the destination of the troops once they cross the water." No one was truly concerned as to who would govern the Canadian military. However, in November 1916, Borden determined the military would cease to be "The Canadian Division" of the British Forces but would be given a new name, the Canadian military, under the recently formed Ministry of Overseas Military Forces of Canada. After two years of scandal, incessant drama, and embarrassment in the ministry of defense, Borden asked for Sir Hughes' resignation, which Borden received.

Aubrey read pamphlets pertaining to war as well. From London, the government acquired posters, brochures, booklets, and pamphlets in the thousands to distribute across the dominion throughout the effort. Kellynch lent Aubrey British doctrinal pamphlets that educated the reader, *An attacking force often lost half its strength simply by leaving the trenches and then by crossing No Man's Land. It may be taken for granted that in attacking the front system of the enemy's trenches, the first three lines will be wiped out. The fourth may reach the enemy's second line. The fifth may capture it.*

I see thee not, I hear thee not, yet though art oft with me[79], Aubrey thought, as she had hoped to hear from Auré before long. Thus far, she had not received a single letter from him all of September. Auré had made it to basic training without so much as a telegram to his wife. How her heart yearned for him! Her fretfulness at him being gone was considerable. Her acquaintances at the front had sent her lovely embroidered postcards made of splendid cotton or silk material with ornate details of patriotic emblems or their regimental insignias. She had not even received a Field Service card that the lads referred to as "Whizbangs." These postcards functioned as a way for the front lines to communicate faster with their families, so that censoring was not necessary. Lads merely circled one of the numerous already-printed choices on the postcard, such as, *I am quite well.* Not even a piddling, standard *Somewhere in England* letter had been sent to let her know he so much as landed in England.

Dear.........

Safe at port of disembarkation.

Nothing unusual to relate, and daily drill, physical exercise, games, and music all add to the pleasures of the journey.

---

[79]   A Canadian World War I epitaph

Will send letter on arrival at headquarters.

Address (name and rank)

CEF
C/O army post office, London

Instead, Aubrey sat woefully reading Étienne's correspondence.

> *As boys come trooping from the war, our sky*
> *has many a new gold star[80]. "At evening time*
> *it shall be light"[81], to quote Zechariah. The*
> *eruptions from the guns and star shells emit*
> *enough light for me to write to you to-night.*
> *Seemingly, shells can reach Heaven. Snipers*
> *still fancy the Ross, though throughout the*
> *Corps it was replaced almost entirely by the*
> *classic Lee-Enfields, which has been in use*
> *Empire wide for fifty or so years. The Somme*
> *is still raging: the battles for Thiepval and*
> *then for Le Transloy just ended. I can hardly*
> *articulate what a shell explosion is like.*
> *However, a battle can be heard across the*
> *Channel on a calm day. A team and wagon*
> *can go through a gap in a structure. If a shell*
> *reverberates against a dugout, sometimes*
> *discerning torsos from respective legs cannot*
> *be done. Skulls, femurs, and the like become*
> *missiles. One can shatter eardrums 3 meters*
> *off. All of a mate's teeth can be torn from their*

---

[80] A Canadian World War I epitaph
[81] A Canadian World War I epitaph

177

roots in one go. Slight concussions are endless. A shell can actually lengthen bone — a body can be recovered at over a foot longer than when the chap was alive. The force of one can send a mate more than 100 yards distant. A shell that erupts near can cause no damage whatsoever; however, those hundreds of yards behind the explosion will feel the force of it. A clean shot will leave the fellow cut to bloody ribbons. The figures are monstrously high — the Boer War in its entirety cost less than any one battle out here.

As for your husband, Aubrey, he does not really fancy chumming with other officers or mates — I'm unsure if he has any mates here — but he uses his liberal time to review maps and read the Bible, or he spends time outdoors in the fields not far from the front. I wonder what it's like for French civilians who reside just a few miles from all of this. It's like a different world there. You must know, my cousin's worth as an officer can be proven by those whom Auré commands would garner greater approval from the King than the King's own gaurds for how disciplined they are.

Fold up the tent, a voice is calling me to rest, to rest[82]; it must be the Colonel. I will pen another letter again and shortly. Give my love to those in Old Ottawa for me.

---

[82] A Canadian World War I epitaph

Étienne wrote "mum's the word" at the bottom, code for he was not able to divulge any further information. The letter was ripped apart in frustration. Aubrey wondered why her husband had not written her as of yet. Consequently, Aubrey did not bother to correspond with Auré thus far; she saw no point. Besides, a letter from her would not be kept, as rules were that a letter was to be read and then spoiled, so that the enemy could not obtain information from front-line troops.

Brief, brave, and glorious was his young career[83], Francis was accorded the coveted Victoria Cross, posthumously. When strongly pressed by Aubrey, Lawrence spoke resignedly.

He sighed and said, "'Even so, father, for it seemed good in thy sight[84],' were Francis' last words to me before leaving for Valcartier." He served his generation[85] in the Boer War; however, Lawrence felt he was too aged to fight in the current war. Inasmuch, he permitted his sons to enlist. "Francis' epitaph will be, 'He took my place. Father[86].' We gave our son, he gave his all[87]. We miss our boy, but it helps to know that he fell facing Britain's foe[88]."

The Victoria Cross was established in 1856 during the Crimean war by Queen Victoria, whose husband suggested the medal be named for her. Only soldiers could be awarded the Victoria Cross because the medal was solely earned for excellent bravery in the face of the enemy. Canada had been bestowed eight Victoria Crosses before the present war. Obviously, there was no Canadian honours system.

---

[83] A Canadian World War I epitaph

[84] A Canadian World War I epitaph

[85] A Canadian World War I epitaph

[86] A Canadian World War I epitaph

[87] A Newfoundland World War I epitaph

[88] A Canadian World War I epitaph

During the first week of October, the Corps' 16th Battalion was stationed north of Courcelette. They that take the sword shall perish with the sword[89]; their objective was to take a section of Regina Trench. The over three-thousand-yard network zig-zagged atop Thiepval Ridge. A piper often times went with units in the trenches. The noble army of martyrs praise thee[90], Piper Private James Cleland Richardson pleaded with his commander to go with their battalion into the front trenches, as he was not scheduled to. The commander conceded and was killed before Richardson's unit left their trench. Richardson piped his mates over the parapet. The unit went to advance on their target: to reach the top of a slope in plain sight of the enemy, unable to out-flank the opposition, and in a narrow locale. However, the 16th soon came against a wall of enemy fire and wire that artillery had not succeeded in cutting. The number of the battalion's dead and wounded grew considerably. With no one to lead them, the unit's hope floundered. To fall back to Allied lines under heavy fire was decided on by the majority. "Wull I gie them wund (wind)?" asked the Scotsman, who lived in Chilliwack after immigrating with his parents to Canada at a younger age. The company's Sergeant-Major agreed. Richardson stood outside their trench's wire, in full aim of the Germans, and played his bagpipes up and down the line for roughly ten minutes. He remained unhurt while bullets stupendously sliced the air around him. His unit became inspired and drew courage from his *splendid example* and *greatest coolness*, the Victoria Cross commendation later stated. Richardson piped one hundred mates onward. Still under heavy fire, the Highlanders rallied, their bayonets cut the wire, and they

---

89 A Canadian World War I epitaph
90 A Canadian World War I epitaph

charged up the slope. The notation concerning Richardson's involvement with the Highlanders assault on Thiepval ridge read, *The effect was instantaneous... the company rushed the wire with such fury and determination that the obstacle was overcome and the position captured.*

After aiding with bombing operations on the very same day, Richardson was tasked with leading an injured mate and captured Germans behind Allied lines. Richardson began his errand but he went back to claim his bagpipes left in a barn. His body would not be located until the duration ended. At first thought to be missing in action, the military officially declared his day of death to be October 9th. His parents were called to Buckingham Palace to accept the medal in their unwed son's stead. He was killed in action a month after he turned twenty years of age. Richardson would remain one of three bagpipers in Empire history to be awarded the Victoria Cross. His bagpipes would be recovered in Scotland and returned to Canada almost a century later.

Francis' mates detailed the capture of his Victoria Cross in various letters to the Lawrences.

Our unit was about to be annihilated by the foe... Deo Legi Regi Gregi[91] (Latin for "For God, The Law, The king, And the People"), *Francis, acting solo... dashed at the trench... fully manned... brought down —Germans & —machine gun nests... In sacrificing himself, Francis enabled our unit to push our objective: a ridge spanning fully four metres.*

---

[91]   A Canadian World War I epitaph

The War Office Telegram

Late one evening, Aubrey sat and tended to the Christmas presents for the servants. Material for a new uniform was gifted annually to maids at Christmas time by their mistress. Most servant girls had trouble affording the money or time to fashion their begrudgingly-received present. At this time, Pembina's servants had been difficult to control and the manor had fallen into callous disarray. Aubrey could not even get them to bow, but they faced the wall in the other method of acknowledging a master when she entered a room. The regular workload was not being maintained, though it always had been with Emmett. As a result, more servants were hired for the same amount of duties. In an attempt to restore order, maids were made to display to Aubrey exactly how much dirt they collected per day. Aubrey had fired two girls for laughing while they cleaned a room no one else was in. Daily portions had come to a halt. Curfew moved to a few hours ahead of the normal previous time. Servants were now forbidden to socialize at all. Aubrey did not allow the annual Christmas party to happen altogether. There was no invitation to the Laurentiens' Christmas party. It was cancelled, like practically all parties of any fashion.

Unexpectedly, Llewellyn walked into the room. Duties faithfully fulfilled[92], the customary bow to leave was not made, though his unreadable countenance gave nothing away. Before she could ask, "Whatever is the matter?" his reason for staying in the room was made ghastly clear. Before her, placed on the silver platter, was a telegram. *How very odd, the mail coming at such an hour — No!* thought Aubrey in inarticulate despair. Every female lived in hourly dread of the much-feared war telegram. The missive informed a family their loved one was dead. The telegram usually came in the evenings. Simply to see the telegraph boy as he walked by downtown proved ever a fright. To look over the post was a daily torment for wives of males in uniform. In households that could claim a telephone, the ringtone of a call as it waited to be accepted was an endless strain to the owner if a relative was over there. Every "next-of-kin" female had dreadful anxiety over such matters.

The delivery boy's departure was faintly heard while his bicycle went over the gravel. Aubrey could scarcely speak for fright to ask Llewellyn the rhetorical question the missive implied. *Killed in action on duty*[93], read the telegram. Auré was gone. She knew a Lady whose husband died on the battlefield. His last words were his wife's name. Aubrey wondered, almost absurdly, whether they would find a last letter on Auré's person, though he was the least sentimental or romantic of people.

"They never fail who die in a great cause[94]," Llewellyn spoke without being spoken to, but out of attempt to

---

92   A Canadian World War I epitaph

93   A Canadian World War I epitaph

94   A Newfoundland World War I epitaph

comfort his mistress and deference towards his late master. *Farewell in hope, in love, in faith, in peace, in prayer*[95] Aubrey thought, dazed. Then she laid down on the floor and wept.

---

[95]   A Canadian World War I epitaph

Michel's News

Days had passed since the news that brought the joy in Aubrey's life crashing down about her. All Aubrey could think of, about her fallen husband, was *He did but do his duty simply, bravely, and in the doing died[96]*. The official letter from the Palace had just been received. *The King commands me to assure you of the true sympathy of His Majesty and The Queen in your time of sorrow.*

Secretary of State for War.

And there will be joy in the morning[97] as right before breakfast, Michel was heard by Aubrey while he rushed through the halls of Pembina. He was an "extra." He had unforeseen war news that was just delivered. *What in God's name?!* thought Aubrey at the commotion. Unaccompanied by a footman or Llewellyn, he had burst into the room.

"Aubrey! Aubrey! The day of sorrow and of doubt is gone, thy love remembered and thy haven won[98]! He's alive!" said Michel, with a telegram from Étienne in hand.

As her mind raced to whom Michel could be referring, Aubrey violently exclaimed, "Who?! Jean-Baptiste? If not, then—"

---

[96] A Canadian World War I epitaph

[97] A Canadian World War I epitaph

[98] A Canadian World War I epitaph

"No more sorrow, no more weeping, no more pain[99]! It's surely Auré!" interrupted Michel, still recovering from disbelief.

For a moment, the shock was so great that Aubrey could not comprehend the situation. The pair nearly succumbed to tears, the former from inexplicable felicity, the latter from pain refreshed anew at the reminder of his sons' deaths. Étienne's message read, *Please do not be alarmed, given this is a sealed cable, but I write joyful news. I hope the official government letter has not arrived at Pembina yet.*

Mix-ups were fairly commonplace. Harry, wanting to get away from the mud and rats of the trenches, joined the Royal Naval Air Service like his big brother Hugh. Not long after the transfer had taken place, the Harringtons received an Official War Office letter explaining their son had fallen. The document solely stated H. Harrington had been killed in action. Government did not consider that both brothers serving had the same first initial. The Harringtons did not know to whom the letter referred. The family waited for a number of horrid weeks until the organizational muddle was corrected and a second letter was sent, notifying that "Hugh Lancelot Harrington" had been killed upholding the honour of the British name. Aubrey wondered how Mr. Harrington had even slept during that time.

Hugh died by fire in his Sopwith Pup. It was obvious he was burnt alive, the type of death pilots feared the most, unable to reach his gun, still in front of him, once his plane was discovered. But his mates penned a polished version of his death in letters to his family. Aubrey had heard of a maritime family, she thought, whose son was serving at the front. One day, the son was ordered with a mate to drive to

---

[99]   A Canadian World War I epitaph

another location in a vehicle. After a bomb landed nearby, the pair was killed. Government Official letters were sent to the son's family, stating he had fallen. The entire community of the son's family went to the funeral to pay their respects. A few weeks after the funeral, the brother of the lad, who was also serving, quite simply saw his brother from afar while on furlough in London. The brother who was thought deceased was in London on leave as well. After the pair embraced, the brother found to be alive explained that the last moment saw a verbal instruction given by an officer for the brother to switch places with another regular. The switch went undocumented. Aubrey wondered how quickly the pair must have gone to a telegraph office to cable their mother.

To be sure, a few days later, Aubrey received acknowledgment from her husband's commander. The crisp letter was clearly written in a tent, one of the few luxuries officers were entitled to. The black-bordered mourning stationary was at variance to the content, and the letter was written in a gentleman's penmanship. The letter read that Auré was thought to be killed after a raid, but proved to be a Prisoner of War in a German camp. *He is in Hunland!* thought Aubrey. Over the course of the next week, more letters were delivered, explaining the most current updates of her husband's predicament.

James had written on stationary from a captive Hun. Aubrey had not realized James was literate. The parchment was dirt-smudged and scrawled on for lack of a hard surface to write. James wrote that civilians fled around their regiment as the Corps marched into the town. A night raid was staged. Being an officer who spoke all languages involved, Auré was made to be in charge. They came upon an enemy platoon with whom Auré had seen hand-to-hand combat. After crawling under wire, he and James were separated. James ensured, however, that Auré was unconscious at the time of surrender. Aubrey breathed a sigh of relief. Surrender was akin to cowardice. Being incapacitated at the time of capture was the only option deemed honourable.

The letter was signed, *He was always kind and generous*[100]. *Am honoured to have fought for a master such as mine. I'm also acquainted with some blokes who would do well to not think solely of themselves.* James would not leave his master until released and would send further word as soon as possible. Because his mistress did not know how to, it was Llewellyn who cabled money to James, along with a message to return: he need not stay because Auré was prisoner.

Prisoners asked for many of the same articles; sugar was hard to get, along with cigarettes and writing materials, but her husband did not eat sweets, and he was certainly one of the only males she knew who did not smoke and did not keep a diary. Briarch had informed her that strawberry jam had become very fancied at the front. She had heard from all the boys that nothing raised their spirits more than a letter from family or friends. The post was delivered at the front near daily. Before he fell, Jean-Baptiste wrote to Aubrey how he would cringe when he looked at his mates who did not regularly receive letters and that when they returned to their dugouts, they would often wipe away tears. If there was ever a time to tell one's husband one's true feelings, it was when he was a Prisoner of War. Tender thoughts from a distance[101]: to pen such a disclosure, to simply write *we are thinking of you every minute*[102], was at the forefront of Aubrey's desires.

---

[100]   A Canadian World War I epitaph

[101]   A Canadian World War I epitaph

[102]   A Canadian World War I epitaph

Still, since his departure, not one letter had come from him. Perhaps he penned letters to another, one of his mistresses whom he was in love with. At this probability, Aubrey put aside the very idea of composing a letter fit for her husband. The letter she wrote solely described details concerning Pembina. The one endearing part was the letter closing, *We miss you*[103].

Auré loved Aubrey's hair down at night and in soft ringlets. She had cut a lock of her curls to enclose in the package. However, because he was probably sleeping with other ladies, Aubrey could not bring herself to convince her husband to want her instead. The curls were put away in the top drawer of her stationary. Candles were placed in the care package instead.

Aubrey thought, *What if he does not come back? He could be shot. Or made to be an enemy bearer and be killed in a crossfire. He could be in Hunland for the remainder of the war — even longer. There could be any number of possibilities. René might never be acquainted with his father. What was the name of Auré's commanding officer? Harvey, was it? What an ugly name. Thank God my mother had class.* No, Aubrey specifically remembered his commander had a handsome name. *Mr.— was quite the gentleman Auré had referred to before his departure.* Perhaps further news of her husband could be ascertained from his commander. The thought of whether the officer was still alive came to mind. She was used to the question by now. She had long ere grown accustomed to officers being killed at alarming rates and knew better than to address the letter with the name of the most recent officer, as one could not hope he was still living. The letter was simply addressed with "Dear, Sir."

---

[103] A Canadian World War I epitaph

The enquiry was answered in prompt fashion and, by Aubrey's correct presumption, was from another officer who had replaced the late one.

At present, I have nothing else to report, Madam, but by British High Command the boys are ordered out of the Somme area. A splendid show was fought by the 4th Division, north of Courcelette in October. The 4th Division alleviated the 1st through 3rd Divisions, who were terribly thrashed, attempting to take Regina Trench since the middle of September. This trench is known to the boys as "ditch of evil memory." The 4th successfully took Regina Trench on the 11th of November. Desire Trench was then taken by our lads as well, a week after Regina Trench. The Desire Trench was the last campaign of the Somme. The calmer region of Artois will be where the Corps will spend Christmas. The boys will find exceptionally toiled for repose after endless attacks and counterattacks, always under heavy shellfire, for soil that never seemed to change hands. Here, the Corps will have its numbers heightened to exemplary capacity and aided with the arrival of the 4th Division. I hasten to add that Major Richardieux deeply regrets not being able to be with the boys as we prepare for the next assault in springtime. Nevertheless, the approaching campaign will be, rest assured Madam, of no great importance, a mere side-show for our glorious superiors. I ask to remain your obedient servant,

C.O. Sir—.

The Somme ended with torrents of rain in the middle of November. Smashes were literally unable to persist due to weather. One centimeter of mud was gained for every Allied life laid down. In areas, one thousand shells pulverized one square metre of earth. Casualties between the Allies and Germany numbered over one million since the campaign began, with not a thing done to bring about changing Germany's position, including positions that were supposed to be taken the principal day of the campaign. Canada suffered a stupendous 24,029 casualties, of which one third were deaths, in the most perpetuated campaign history would write for British warfare. Withal, the Somme solidified the Corps as an elite fighting force. David Lloyd George, who recently became the British Prime Minister, gave the highest commendation and adulation to the Canadians for the success at Courcelette because taking this village was one of the sole clear Allied successes of the Somme. He penned, *The Canadians played a part of such distinction that thenceforward they were marked out as storm troops; for the remainder of the war, they were brought along to head the assault in one great battle after another.*

Far in the outer reaches of St. John's, a massive herd of caribou was charging the plains. The numerous hooves were the sole articles to displace the damp snow unseen by man. Leading the herd, the bull bowed his head, then ferociously hit the horns of the mammal next to him. In response to the command, hundreds of antlers clashed in unison, veering to one side. The herd assaulted the steep assent of the cliff[104].

---

[104] The opening day of the Somme, July 1st, 1916, remains Newfoundland's most horrific battle. The caribou is Newfoundland's military emblem. There are five statues in France and Belgium, each of a caribou atop a cliff, to commemorate Newfoundland soldiers who served in the First World War

Preparing for the Vimy Show

Byng petitioned High Command against taking one of the greatest protected areas of the Western Front. Byng's plea rescinded, the Corps was ordered to march to an area situated near a small northern French coastal town, at Pas-de-Calais. The battle was for the Vimy Ridge. As they went along, they sang, "Where Do We Go From Here?"

"Oh, where do we go from here, boys?
Where do we go from here?
We've been from Ypres to the Somme
And haven't found good beer
We're sick as hell of shot and shell
And generals at the rear
We've got no rum and we're feeling bum
Where do we go from here?"

After three weeks, the English Canadians were in the ridge area. Germany had taken hold of the area in October in the first year of the war. In December of the same year, France, with six divisions, attempted to recover her rightful land, though the attempt proved unsuccessful. Known as the "Shield of Arras" or "Valley of Sorrows," the Ridge was fifteen kilometers in length. Ice, snow, and black frost covered all in the hardest winter in decades. The Corps' objective had been strenghthened over three years with a terrific and complex system of security. The Corps found kilometers of trenches, three rows deep. The trenches were fortified by hundreds of machine guns in concrete bunkers and pillboxes. The barbed wire laid was untold in length. The entire ridge was reinforced by numerous communication trenches and concrete tunnels. The enemy was able to take shelter in underground chambers when barrages attacked. The ridge housed German soldiers who belonged to the 1st Bavarian Reserve Division, the 79th Reserve Division, and the 16th Infantry Bavarian Division. A complete field of sight was afforded to the enemy, as she looked down on the unhurried descent to where the English Canadians were. The Corps encampment was found near the base of the Ridge. As the boys looked out across the immense graveyard, they agreed "at least we could try."

The west side of the ridge hosted England's armies. To the east was the Douai plain held by Germany. The Ridge held a commanding range of vision of the plain and Allied lines. To capture the terrain would be to give the Allies a superb advantage.

On the other side lay Paris, one hundred and fifty kilometres away. The Ridge was the focal point of protection to Germany. The mother country would journey with Canada on both sides.

Every detail was to be observed to aid His Majesty's promising Corps. Byng employed perhaps his most consummate officer, Currie, to aid him. At forty-one years of age, Currie was the youngest Major-General of the British Forces. He stood six foot three and had broad shoulders and blond-silver hair. He proved shy and unable to build a strong rapport with his troops. Even so, his officers respected and held him in high esteem.

Currie was a brilliant tactitican, who had a marvellous capacity for detail. He recommended reviews of the Somme be given by the regulars to figure how the Corps could improve in future battles. Summaries from France's and England's armies were also conducted and discussed. A number of the findings were that communication was almost always severed between privates and officers. Unclipped barbed wire, bum fellowship between the regulars and artillery, and beggarly time to organize battle plans all led to failure on the battlefield. Troops also suggested poor amounts of grenades and ammunition on each individual and lack of preparation were large factors that left them unable to conquer in a battle. The poor bloody infantry was normally left brutally exhausted from their daily labour tasks. Currie changed their work load as much as possible. Going forward, front line troops would be somewhat more rested before battles.

The Byng boys, a petname the lads gave themselves in laudation of their cherished commander, set about preparing to take Vimy Ridge. Byng was called "Bungo" by his intimates, including the King. Advancing in waves was rehearsed continually over the winter months, as directed by Byng. The fray would see the four divisions attack side by side opposite the ridge.

All four divisions were to leave their start line at the same time. They would simultaneously traverse forward across the terrain to meet the first objective: the black line. Twenty battalions, along with secondary waves, would advance in the first wave. After the first objective was taken, a number of battalions were to reach the secondary objective: the Red line. An additional small third wave of battalions would move onwards to take the third objective: the Blue line. A smaller-still number of battalions would progress past the third wave to meet the fourth objective: the Brown line. Each section had proper supplementary troops who followed behind, and one of their roles was to take care of the remaining enemy. This would allow for less confusion, and the troops would more easily be able to secure newly attained ground.

Each division had its proper curriculum to ready itself for the assault. The 1st Division created a grand duplicate of enemy lines made clear by white tape and fashioned in the fields behind the Corps' base. All stages of the coming fray were outlined. As they walked through their real-life syllabus, machine gun nests and concentrations of barbed wire were made clear by flags. Posts designated trenches. Stop-watches were used to replicate the timing of the creeping barrage. The chaps exercised the map on a daily basis. If the highest ranking officer became a casualty, the troops were to look to the next level of command for leadership. One by one, the highest ranking officers would leave the exercise, stand on the edges, and observe the lads. The remaining were left to ascertain how to continue on with only one another.

Commanders taught, "Should your officer be knocked out, it is up to you to improvise and fight your way forward." The ideas of "do not stop" and maintaining communication with the companies near one's own were greatly instilled.

Enemy machine gunners could possibly live through the first stages of the artillery bombardment. Should such prove true, the lads were to outflank the gunners with grenades. Then, they were to use bayonets. Platoons were to be in contact with the ones on either side of them at all times. Every unit was given a specific aim and knew the aims of surrounding units, so that a unit could take command of an additional objective should a unit be wiped out. Junior officers and non-commissioned officers knew the roles of commanders set over them should the position need to be replaced during battle.

Officers reinforced the idea that when the show started, everyone was "to be his own general." Privates and officers would work nearer to one another, making change-of-course and direct orders more probable. Also, artillery would work more in accordance with the poor bloody infantry than in previous battles.

Fifty thousand horses were brought to the Vimy area to transport stock. In the muck, horses would sink to the base of their necks pulling supplies. After being worked to death, they were left by the wayside. A whole side field contained one hundred carcasses of horses that the lads had not yet been able to bury. One veterinarian Officer journaled, *They were mercifully killed; after such exhaustion, they were beyond taking their oats.*

Nearly infinite shells were brought forth. Especially important, the most advanced shell fuse, Number 106, brought en masse, erupted on contact, instead of the usual enfoldment into the ground. Poison gas and shrapnel were to be used as well.

Tunnels, dug mainly by New Zealand, were left at the Corps' disposal. The lads, in gruelling fatigue, shovelled to make trenches deeper by up to three yards. Twenty kilometers of underground passageways, dimly-lit, were excavated for casualties, command posts, ammunition stocking, medical facilities, and telephones that would allow the rear to communicate with frontline troops, and they enabled the lads to work in safety away from enemy weapons.

Mobile charges and ammonal tubes were used to ruin mines under the ridge. After months of favourable outcome, the mines and counter-mining enterprises of the foe were overturned. The Corps became in control of the battle beneath the ridge.

Flash spotting, triangulation, and trigonometry were used to chart enemy artillery and machine gun nests that enabled the targeting and demolishing of these sanctions. Lieutenant-Colonel Brutinel's "indirect firing" exactly settled shells on the foe's structures. Before the day of battle, the vast majority of these batteries were to be annihilated. In charge of such operations was Lieutenant-Colonel Andrew McNaughton: one of the Allies' most brilliant artillery officers. Before the duration, he was a professor of engineering at McGill University.

At his headquarters, McNaughton played host to English scientists, some of whom were recipients of the Nobel Prize, and expert meteorologists, to gain further knowledge of how science could improve the accuracy of and create superior methods of attack for the artillery. McNaughton made sure they felt welcome and acted with greater integrity than officers in the regular part of the British Expeditionary Force did. In turn, the scientists shared with the English-Canadian officer, in considerable detail, the ways that artillery could benefit from new tactics.

An escaped lion cub, Tony, had been adopted by McNaughton, who lived in one of the engineering officer's tents. As McNaughton pored over maps, he would pet the cub who was continuously found at the officer's feet. Tony was ever protective of his adopted master and would scarcely permit a soul near McNaughton. British Generals, upon entering English Canadian officers' tents to conduct meetings, were utterly incredulous to discover such comportment from their colonials.

The Train Station

Sharp has your frost of winter been but bright shall be your spring[105]; the silver tray was placed before Aubrey. The post had come. Not one but two official letters from the front were delivered, Aubrey was elated to find. The shock was almost too much for her. The Red Cross had found and released Auré. All in mere months! Given her husband was an officer, special attempts had been made to have him released.

The first envelope was the typical letter from the Palace to a returning dominion troop. In haste, she did not realize the letter was addressed to Auré and not her.

The Queen and I wish you God-speed, and a safe return to your homes and dear ones. A grateful Mother Country is proud of your splendid services, characterized by unsurpassed devotion and courage.

George.

The next letter addressed to *Mrs. Aurelien Richardieux* had the impossible return address, *Somewhere in France.* Penned by Auré's Commanding Officer, it expressed: *Upon being released from the Prisoner of War Camp, Major Richardieux attempted to finish the mission he had begun in fall before capture found him—*

---

[105] A Canadian World War I epitaph

Astonished at her husband's infrangible work ethic, she gasped increduously, "In Heaven's name, he attempted what?! Does he not want to return to me? To René?"

Hurriedly, Aubrey read on, *However, was rendered unfit for action. Forever done with sword and conflict where all is calm and bright*[106], *Major Richardieux has been discharged from the front, dear Madam I am pleased to inform you, with honours.* Dishonour went hand in hand with a regular discharge. So distracted was she by her husband's survival, only pieces of the rest of the letter were taken into account *...has been invalided home for medical attention and he will be on the next available ship to Canada in about a fortnight's time.*

Auré was marked for Blighty (Soldier slang for London)! If an officer was in need of medical aid, particular attempts were made to see to his recovery. Wounded officers were cared for in their own wards. On trains, officers were given personal quarters. In case of death, the name was printed in casualty documents, whereas a regular's death was marked by a number.

She would go to England for the remainder of the duration if he wanted her to. But he had not given indication thus far of wishing to see her overseas, even while he was on leave. Her husband never took leave of any sort, still and all.

Voyages to England were commonplace to visit relatives in uniform on furlough. Hundreds of thousands of English Canadians serving were over there, and relatives flocked to England to visit them. Chance meetings in London between relatives, friends, and neighbours of English Canadians were of regular occurance and were often noted in war diaries and letters. Aristocratic wives usually stayed in England to

---

[106]   A Newfoundland World War I epitaph

see their husbands when time permitted. The lower classes were fortunate to go to England for short affairs to see their uniformed relative, if at all.

Aubrey desparately wanted to see her husband, but any plans had been thwarted. In the new year, the goverment disallowed crossing the Atlantic, due to Germany's declaration of unrestricted submarine warfare. English-Canadian females were greatly pressed to venture to Britain only for serious volunteer positions or for grave purposes.

Mail usually required a fortnight to arrive either way. Perhaps an update on Auré's status could be obtained. As expressed by the current officer, at present time, no further information could be discerned regarding Major Richardieux. Aubrey steeled herself to confront the truth. He most likely would not write her to begin with. If he did, his letters would not be censored, that is, they would be void of any sentiment anyways.

Cutting out or blackening words with lead pencil or black paint were the common censoring methods. Every letter sent from the front was begrudgingly looked over by an officer before being delivered to the Official censor review board and then onwards. Perhaps he was too injured to write. Because the mail would reach her almost as soon as he was to return, he might not see the point in writing her.

Although the truth of the matter was he could not possibly love her. After all, he would rather be at the front than with her. Aubrey could not explain how she felt about him because he clearly did not feel the same way towards her. The decision made was to pen trifle lines of how René eagerly awaited his return. Guarded though her letter was, at minimum, a correspondence of sorts could be struck up.

A harsh thought came to her mind while she sat before the parchment. What if he laughed at her letter? Or worse, did not respond at all? She wondered if he slept with those prostitutes at the front. Many soldiers did. Aristocrats seldom married for love. Aubrey had certainly not married for love. The speculation of why he married her remained unanswered. Since their wedding, his demeanour towards her had changed little from in Regina. Thus far, the words "I love you" had not been spoken by the husband or wife, their wedding day included. Given that he was not in love with her, why would he be faithful, especially since he was so far from her for such a length of time? Yet she was ever and ever in love with him! How could such a cruel position find her? Life was so unjust! The parchment remained blank; the quill was returned to the jar. She was left mentally counting down the days until he returned.

At the train station, Nico stood and pined with enormous difficulty. He never faltered[107] in his nightly prayers for his uncle. Nico had begged his father to let him come along. Other little boys proudly puffed out their chests to display badges, buttons, or pins proclaiming their brothers and or fathers were serving. Males out of uniform looked a bit weary, though such common expression from these fellows no longer registered to Aubrey.

On the platform, despairing propoganda surrounded Michel, Aubrey, and Nicolas. Demands that males prove their devotion to the King and insults to their masculinity if not enlisted were commonplace. Posters of trees split in half analogized shell explosions to the populace. Females were also heavily pressed to have their male relatives fight. Such

---

[107] A Canadian World War I epitaph

posters read, *To the women of Canada, Do you realize that the one word "Go" from you may send another man to fight for King and country?* among other points. The three stood before a poster that read, *The boys who wear the khaki: Go or be sent for.*

Aubrey had a new outfit and an ivory sapphire slide in her hair. Other females nodded their disapproval towards her frivolities during such trying times.

At last, Auré's train pulled into the station. Convalescents and sisters on board sang "Tipperary," and the gathered crowd on the platform joined them. The ditty was wholly insufficient so far into the war, though it still made those present tear up.

Aubrey could have blushed to see him. However, she did not see him first. As Auré stood before the disembarking train, she saw his kilt before she could see him entirely. *He transferred to an English battalion?!* was all her mind could absorb. The officer who penned the letter of his release did write that Auré was transferred. Aubrey assumed her husband was simply sent to another Francophone company.

Commended veteraned officers of the Van Doos were sent to other French battalions to potentially improve numbers. French Canada brought about thirteen of the (eventual) two hundred and fifty-eight battalions pertaining to the army. From 1915 henceforth, Francophone units regularly dissolved in order to assist the 22nd Battalion and units wanting for larger figures. The Van Doos aside, every French-speaking battalion would grapple to raise and hold sufficient numbers the whole of the effort.

Of his own free will and accord[108], Auré had *asked* to be transferred to an English battalion. He had joined the most common one of her acquaintances: The Royal Ottawas.

---

[108] A Canadian World War I epitaph

He was now their commanding officer. The battalion was associated with the Duke of Edinburgh's Own.

Troops could convalesce as near to their place of residence as viable. The Imperial Order of the Daughters of the Empire provided a "little bit of motherly touch" in their private residences-turned-convalescent hospitals. Convalescents returning to the dominion were trained to Ottawa, then onwards to their final destination.

Auré would convalesce at Pembina. Aubrey was to take on a husband who was injured. He sprang to duty's call and paid the price[109]; supposed to be in a wheelchair, Auré was on crutches, which almost always accompanied a uniform.

"'ow lovely it is to see you." Auré's accent had lessened considerably. She was crestfallen, though really much worse than that; she was humiliated. No move to embrace or kiss her was made by him. He could have struck her, for all that would have hurt to the same extent. Auré was noticeably darker, slighter, and considerably scarred. His hands were terribly calloused from the labour he did at the front. The 18-pounder was England's daring. The gun was named for the exact pounds the artillery piece fired. The Howitzer was the heaviest gun the Empire could claim. Dozens of troops pulling multiple ropes were required to move such great guns. While the lot descended the staircase, a graffitied wall decried, *Slackers beware of the green-eyed monster.*

The days were becoming longer. In the automobile, returning Canadian geese were heard high above. Because a light blanket of snow still lay on the ground, Aubrey was of the opinion geese always returned too soon. Auré asked after his cousins at the front. Michel replied Étienne was the

---

[109]   A Canadian World War I epitaph

only one left of his unit after the Somme. During the Somme, complete units were annihilated. No further questions were made. At the news that one of his relatives in uniform was yet alive, Auré was pleased enough.

Aubrey could claim quite possibly what no other wife in England could: war had softened her husband. Nico played with shrapnel that Auré brought back in unwonted fashion. Children relentlessly badgered relatives in uniform for like items, however illegal it was for troops to leave the front with anything pertaining to battle. As an officer and a gentleman, Auré would not have been searched. Before bedtime, and at the behest of nannies, little ones refused to remove caps or relinquish haversacks given by their fathers and brothers on leave. World-renowned Belgium chocolate, which Auré purchased while a prisoner near the Belgium border, was gifted to Aubrey.

At certain camps, captured Allied officers were allowed to leave their prison to visit local villages or surrounding countryside unescorted for day visits. Before leaving the camp, an officer's written word as a gentleman was surely given to the extent of, *I will not escape nor attempt to make an escape, nor will I make any preparation to do so, nor will I attempt to commit any action during this time to the prejudice of the German Empire.*

Except to attend Mass and buy cigarettes for his troops, Auré rarely left the camp where he was detained.

Michel relayed that in Quebec, a splendid fundraiser was held in February for patriots to give a day's earnings to the Patriotic Fund. The outcome was very favourable. The servants waited outside the manor in anticipation of their master's homecoming. Beloved by all[110] the servants,

---

[110]   A Canadian World War I epitaph

René was adorable in a white and blue trim sailor's suit. The nanny held his hand. Numerous rehearsals to greet his father had taken place. The nanny whispered to René, then gently nudged him. René took a small step forward and saluted his father.

Dr. Musgrove came in the next few days to look over Auré's abdominal shell wound, the cause of his being invalided back. An abdominal shell wound would cause death to the rate of three times more than an abdominal gunshot wound. Wounds became grossly infected because the missile oftentimes passed through the manured fertilized fields before being lodged in a troop's frame. Officers from the Canadian Medical Corps noted shell wounds by *holes that you could put your clenched fist into, filled with dirt, mud, bits of equipment and clothing, until it all becomes a hideous nightmare.* For once, Musgrove seemed jolly to see Auré. There is a calm beyond life's fitful fever[111], and after the assessment, Musgrove gratefully declared that apart from trench fever, which all front lines troops contracted from time to time, Auré now suffered no great ill. Middle-aged, average height, and with a strict Victorian soul, Musgrove bid farewell with a cheery "til the morrow." Once outside the manor, Musgrove said a silent prayer, thanking God for another of the brave ones brought back. He went jauntily to his horse. The only non-aristocratic man Aubrey knew who owned an automobile, even he had given his Studebaker for the effort.

Instead of a usual cluster, a few ladies from the Imperial Order of the Daughters of the Empire came to welcome Auré. Aubrey's invitation to sit was scandalously declined by her guests. The usual care package left included a discharge button

---

[111] A Canadian World War I epitaph

from the Patriotic Fund. Those turned away from service due to medical or age restrictions could obtain specific pins or badges, lest they be deemed a slacker, physically impaired returned troops included.

Vimy Eve

The sole important information about the fray, withheld from the regular private, was on what day the attack would commence. At the end of March, Currie communicated to the Corps that the impending battle would begin in mere days' time.

> *Under the orders of your devoted Officers, in the coming battle, you will either advance or fall where you stand facing the enemy. To those who will fall, I say: You will not die, but step into immortality. Your mothers will not lament your fate, but will be proud to have born such sons. Your names will be revered forever by your grateful country, and God will take you unto Himself.*

The Corps protested, for they were to begin the attack on the Sabbath day. The week preceding battle, artillery from England and Canada pulverized the Ridge by way of more than one million shells. The remaining days, as darkness fell, shelling stopped to prevent the troop's location from being made known to the enemy. Machine guns took over, firing innumerably. Shells flowed over top of the chaps in countless numbers daily. The bombardment prevented the foe from mending the blasted trenches and dugouts that Allied artillery had created during daytime. Consequently, the enemy could not obtain food, water, rest, or reinforcements. The bombardment was so grand that German High Command would state the seven days prior to the show would be remembered in German history as "The Week of Suffering." The triumph of the artillery garnered great spirit among the lads.

Nighttime saw the Corps dispatch parties to inspect barbed wire. Telecommunication lines were cut. Bold, mud-covered officers crawled outwards during the day to collect additional information. Spies as well as raids, involving hundreds of chaps, gathered further knowledge of enemy lines. A captured German officer laughed, "We know all about your plans. You might get to the top of the Vimy Ridge but I'll tell you this, you'll be able to take all the Canadians (who reach the Ridge's peak) back to Canada in a row-boat."

At the beginning of March, the 4th Division saw numerous killed, including veteran officers, from a trench raid that ended in disaster with an almost fifty percent casualty rate. The gas attack backfired on the four battalions that assaulted during nighttime and did nearly no damage at all to the Germans. The morning afterwards, an enemy officer waved a white flag before going into No Man's Land himself to assess the dead and wounded. He permitted the Corps to bury the fallen and transport their casualties behind Allied lines. Nonetheless, all battalions had more troops than required. Every division was privy to a thirteenth battalion. The foe would be greatly outnumbered by ten thousand to thirty-five thousand. Greater than double the number of guns would be used than at the Somme. Twelve thousand troops were held back: in case so many fell, new battalions could be brought into battle.

While the lads worked, they watched high in the sky splendid air duels, which they adored. Pilots routinely gave their lives to provide their army mates greater luck of advancement. British pilot Canadian Billy Bishop became an Ace, with five kills, in early April. Bishop claimed twelve enemy aircrafts the month of Bloody April alone, the most downhearted month for Allied pilots over the course of the duration. At times throughout the war, the average airman's service at the front could be measured in days. Bishop received the Military Cross and a promotion to Captain.

In the few days beforehand, the gathered, half of whom were Canadian-born sons, looked out at the landscape they had come to know as well as at the Germans. The locales of all strongpoints, machine guns, and bunkers were known by memory. The terrain was considerably more noxious than the Corps had ever witnessed. The wallow was sufficiently extensive to consume a chap.

The barrage would advance three hundred yards ahead of them. Leaders gave brisk edict that if one proceeded too swiftly, one's artillery would pink them. If one proceeded too leisurely, Fritz would have a chance to shoot.

Byng gave what would be his final great command, "Chaps, you shall go over exactly like a railroad train, on the exact time, or you shall be annihilated."

The evening prior, the chefs set protocol aside; a fancy dinner was laid of coffee, bacon, and oranges, given many of the Corps members were scheduled to perish.

Jumping-off trenches were made to underground. In the tunnels, while battalions progressed passed one another, in the many accents from across Canada that were by and by taking the places of British ones, calls rang out of, "God Bless Vancouver! There goes Moncton! Good luck Charlottetown!"

Perpetually wettish in wool trousers and kilts, the lads attended mass and service. Nerves, mixed with anticipation of the impending battle, were so profound that sleep found few a lad.

As daybreak drew near, shells gradually rescinded to hoodwink the enemy to think that reprieve was soon to follow. Silence was uncommon, which new recruits found more unsettling than guns firing.

Following standard practice, unwed lads replaced the wedded, and the fatherless replaced the ones with children, as should they perish, it would be to less consequence. The last words of the underage were often, "Ask mother that she forgive me." The final requests of fathers were that their daughters' teddy bears, given to them lest their daughters be forgotten, should be returned. Concluding agreements between officers and their troops were to carry on no matter the predicament. All asked for their last letter to be sent back.

On bended knee in the trenches, of which numerous had wallow and ice a foot high, the lads withstood a frigid morning, their breath apparent in the air. Rain, sleet, and snow started to appear and would not cease over the battle. Dawn found startling quietude. At precisely two minutes to the commencement of the show, the last order was whispered down all lines, "fix bayonet." As the sun rose, a colony rose from the trenches with orders to capture what the Entente and Central Forces agreed was the impenetrable fortress.

The Vimy Ball

Aubrey made her way to the master's bedroom the evening of the ball. Dressing for the fundraiser, Auré explained to Llewellyn, "Officers have held their place for eh long time throughout the Corps. And we have very experienced 'igh Command because our officers have risen through the ranks and understand their positions." Llewellyn was doing Auré's tie when Aubrey came to the door. "Purposely sank two of his ships. Wilson is furious, so are his people. So the Yanks are joining the fray. They will bring 'undreds of thousands of soldiers, horses, mules, and tonnes of food to restore ze Allies' depleted resources. At least they will bolster hope throughout the Corps for this task — it'z madness."

His back towards the door, he added in a louder manner, "I am quite at leisure, my English roze." She walked in. He gave her the once over, "I had almost forgotten green thingz grew." She positively glowed at the compliment.

At the Red Cross ball held at Chateau Laurier, forced acknowledgement of Auré came from both sides. Neither party seemed to know quite what to make of him. In the presence of civilians, proper troops were to preserve formal quietude on impolite particulars of the front. Auré found solace in a fellow officer. Henrietta had recently returned from the Mediterranean. English Canadian nursing sisters were the first women of all militaries in the world to be made Officers, and the rank conceded was that of Lieutenant. The Royal Red Cross, first class, was awarded to her.

Aside from England and France, the Canadian Army Medical Corps was stationed in the eastern Mediterranean at Gallipoli, Alexandria, Salonika, and small islands as well. Aubrey was always, always surprised at the change in a returned troop. Henrietta's frame now supported less than seven stone. Any length of poisoning was a casualty suffered by all the Corps' members who served on Lemnos. Henrietta's poisoning showed by her rough complexion. Though she was in her early twenties, her hair had turned almost as silver as blond.

"England's Medical Corps disallows their Bluebirds to dance, although ours are fine with our nurses dancing. The motherland's nurses thought we would be a rough and tumble lot. I suppose we were," Henrietta laughed.

For a considerable time, Britain's medical doctors had asserted that if they were rendered sick or injured, the worst place they could possibly find themselves to receive care would be Canadian Army Medical Corps. "Common Canadian" was the nickname British medical persons had for their Canuck Bluebirds. British sisters were held to a higher level of integrity and professionalism than their Imperial nurses. Therefore, English-Canadian nurses were superintended by matrons with far greater regularity than British ones. English Canadian Bluebirds were expected to behold the British in greater esteem than themselves.

Henrietta continued in a low voice, "But we wanted to prove to England that we could do it. We were most likely the first white females that Lemnos ever hosted. From lack of rain, the island seemed void of any living thing. The region did not have of any plant life but was made of earth, rocks, dust and no colour of any kind to brighten our days. The first several weeks, everyone was absolutely downtrodden. Proper hygiene was basically non-existent. Water had to be carried from quite far off. We were not able to clean the faces of the initial ones we tended to for a full day. The flies were grotesque. You could positively not consume any food or water without taking them in. The number of insects was frightful. Our diet was deplorable the whole time. It always surprised me the troops were able to improve with what they were given to eat. A pity that no activities were to be found for our boys to take their minds off their days, like in France and Belgium where there are furloughs to cities, games, and physical activities or the chance to chum with other allied troops. They say the most frightful form of torture is boredom. Malta fever, enteric fever, extreme dysentery, and bugs bitterly plagued our wounded. The medical staff were sick too, the doctors, orderlies, everyone. Dysentery escaped no one. Maggots and discharge from injuries were incessant and would not go away for anything. Because of the extreme heat, it was about one hundred degrees, we did away with the sleeves of our uniforms. Insects bit us until the day we left, and months afterwards the blemishes of those insects were still on us. The medical persons hardly had access to washing sites for personal use. Was it ever the Crimea there! But, I'm glad we, and not another branch of England's Medical Corps, were able to look after Newfoundland's Naval members. A beautiful moment between our two colonies, no? And isn't that the way you would have wanted it to have been, the Canadians tending to the Newfoundlanders where we were? Thrown into the Meditteranean, at least we had each other. In fall, once the dominion was more aware of our situation, things did get better for us. We were given floors for our living areas subsequent to that. But then, rain and severe winds followed. Orders were given then countermanded almost daily. Lack of certainty was never ending. We could not get messages through to Headquarters. Cargo always seemed to miss us from the ships that passed us by and the harbour that was nearest to our location. Thousands of military men's and women's lives counted on those shipments that contained food and medical supplies.

Pet named "Bluebirds," given their blue dresses, white headdresses, and long white veils, troops would refer to the nurses the remainder of their lives as "Sisters or Angels of mercy."

"The boys did so hate to see their Bluebirds suffer any sort of hardship. The military police, all of them, would have laid down their lives before letting harm come to us. Oh, they say 'it's the little things' — Naval personnel brought us hampers consisting of cocoa, oatmeal, butter, and bread every day. Those hampers surely got us through our time out there."

Auré granted her a rare smile. Henrietta finished saying that after they were evacuated from Lemnos, they were ordered to Cairo. A Commanding Medical Officer, set over the English-Canadian Bluebirds in the Meditteranean, expressed, "Of such soldiering material were they constituted that complaint was rare."

Gabriel was seated not far from the pair and was noticeably thinner, too. He had been wounded in a charge near the village of Guyencourt on Marcy 27th. His charger had been shot.

Nine of every ten British warhorse would fall in battle over the cause. Cavalry units were plentiful on the front lines but were routinely disbanded ahead of seeing action. Many a Cavalryman turned field telephone operator or dispatch runner.

No longer able to hold a sabre, pistol, or the constant shovel, Gabriel had been invalided from the front in an unheard-of timeframe of mere days. Congratulated on receiving the Cavalry Victory medal, he responded, weak in smile, "For King and country[112]."

As the evening progressed, Aubrey and Auré were found together. A scandalous Viennese waltz had barely finished. *Arma aptissima virtus*[113] (Latin for "Courage is the most useful weapon"), Aubrey steeled herself reassuringly.

With a fine amount of dash, Aubrey started, "For quite some time I have wanted to declare, that is to say, how much I—" she faltered. In a stammer, she finished, "Adore such evenings and to ask with whom you will dance the next set. So many pretty females; it is hard for a man to choose which one he wants." She flushed, *That was such a gammy excuse. One of the best*[114]*dancers I know, but he does not dance besides.*

"Not in all of England, Aubrey," was the serious, though rather quiet, reply. Married couples addressed one another as Mr.— and Mrs.— in public. Christian names were reserved solely for private use. She felt positively unclothed by his candour.

Steadfast and undaunted[115], conviction revived at his encouragement, she dared to carry on, "I—"

"We've taken her! We've taken her!" Gabriel was heard shouting to the hall at large.

---

112   A Canadian World War I epitaph
113   A Canadian World War I epitaph
114   A Canadian World War I epitaph
115   A Canadian World War I epitaph

Auré quizzically and easily looked above her head and over at Gabriel, who was running to the center of the stage. The music came to a ceasefire. Everyone turned to stare at the commotion. The moment was lost to tell him she loved him!

Oh, they must have reached their fundraising goal, excited as Gabriel is, thought Aubrey, ever downtrodden. Auré had gifted a handsome donation.

Gabriel was incredulous and elated. The entire ballroom listened with rapt attention as Gabriel proclaimed, "THE CANADIANS HAVE CAPTURED VIMY RIDGE!"

The hall fell into absolute silence. Even the gentlemen were shocked into speechlessness. No one knew quite what to say or quite what to do. After a bit of time, the conductor went on stage. A few words were whispered to Gabriel, and a smile came to him as he nodded in agreement. Gabriel turned to face the crowd, "The — the conductor's right — we should toast to our men on the front lines!"

The conductor readied his sentinels. Auré's baritone voice was wonderful for the song. Henrietta, standing nearby, was a clear soprano. Aubrey's alto voice was only fair. The dance floor crashed with the orchestra into the liveliest and loudest rendition of the unofficial anthem that Aubrey had ever laid witnessed to, "Oh, Canada."

Vimy

Canada has sent across the sea an army greater than Napoleon ever commanded! blared the *New York Tribune. No greater army in world history than the daring and glorious Canadian Army Corps*, read other newspapers. Canadian headlines stated, *The Canadian Forces accomplished in mere days what the British and French failed to achieve in two years and with 150,000 casualties.* In all, three hundred thousand German, English, and French had become casualties in the battle for the Ridge. Newspapers across the world congratulated Canada on her performance. The King sent a congratulatory telegram to Field Marshal and Commander-in-Chief of the British Expeditionary Forces, Sir Douglas Haig. *The whole Empire will rejoice at the news of yesterday's successful operation. Canada may well be proud that the taking of the coveted Vimy Ridge has fallen to the lot of her troops. I heartily congratulate you and all who have taken part in this splendid achievement.* France exclaimed the capture of Vimy Ridge was Canada's Easter gift to the Allies. France and England conceded the victory to be a Canadian accomplishment. Vimy was the furthest penetration into enemy lines by the Allies as well as the Canadians took more guns and prisoners than any previous British assault. Therefore, the battle was the grandest Allied success of the Western Front to date. 3,598 Canadian sons fell at Vimy Ridge. A further 7,004 Canadians were casualties. These numbers were yet significantly lower than all previous Allied attempts to recapture the ridge. An estimated twenty thousand casualties were sustained by the Germans. The Corps took over four thousand prisoners.

England's armies attacking alongside the Canadians were vanquished; however, the battle could not have been conquered without England's aid. The Corps was the sole victor. Canada became world-renowned for being outstanding in offensive fighting. Enthusiasm in the Corps and among the Allied armies surged exponentially. The capture of the Ridge would enable the English to gain further ground over the Germans in later battles.

After refusing on two occasions to depart as leader of the Corps, Byng was ordered by Haig to lead the British Third Army. Byng said farewell to his cherished Corps with tear-stained cheeks. Byng would return to lead Canada with distinction once more, although in the position of Governor General after the war. Currie was made Commander-in-Chief of the most exemplary Force on the Western Front. For the initial time in Canada's history, her military was brought under the command of a proper son.

For weeks afterward, letters poured across the Atlantic, in staggering numbers, of the taking of the Ridge. Any number of letters were published in newspapers and read aloud at functions.

> *In the early morning hours of April 9th, at exactly 0530 hours, the largest artillery eruption of the war started. All firearms the Western Front could claim appeared to fire.*

With strict precision, mines exploded, gas shells fell on targeted locations & transport ways and artillery fired. 425 field guns or 18 pounders and 225 heavier guns and howitzers were aimed at the Ridge, including 4 English companies, all 16 machine gun corps, and the 1ˢᵗ Canadian Motor Machine Gun Brigade. The majority of the shells were focused on artillery locations. How it sounded was nearly indescribable, given 1.6 million shells hit the Ridge. To make out anything at all above the noise, one had to place one's hands around the ear of another fellow and yell at the top of one's lungs.

The most marvellous creeping barrage, consisting of almost 1,000 heavy guns, started to rake over No Man's Land and towards the ridge... Beneath her were 20,000 of us, loaded weightily with 32 kilograms of kit and roughly an additional equal amount in wallow... As the start lines were departed, many of us bowed our heads, while the barrage jibber-jabbered like mad, like an unstoppable blizzard of evil shells... Our 1ˢᵗ Division had the longest to go, roughly five kilometers to Farbus Wood... The 1ˢᵗ Division was commanded by Major-General Arthur William Currie from Strathroy, Ontario ... Pertaining to the 1ˢᵗ Division, Western Cavalry's 5ᵗʰ or the "Tuxford's Dandy's" (Saskatoon), *7ᵗʰ* (Vancouver), *and the Fighting 10ᵗʰ* (Edmonton, Calgary, Lethbridge)

Battalions' start line was situated to the furthest righthand side, or the most eastern side, of the Ridge... The 15ᵗʰ (Toronto), *14ᵗʰ* (Royal Montreal Regiment), *and 16ᵗʰ* (Canadian Scottish) *were to the left, or to the west, of the 5ᵗʰ, 7ᵗʰ, and 10ᵗʰ... Shoulder to shoulder we marched in the Vimy glide, which meant, dear wife, one hundred yards per three minutes... The wallow made some of my mates' boots come undone. They continued in socks towards the stirring campaign... The mud sizzled from falling shrapnel... More than a dozen times, we came to a standstill to allow the barrage to go another ninety meters... One in thirteen of the chaps fell to the barrage... Twenty-four-year-old Private William. J. Milne of the 16ᵗʰ was thwarted, comrades were dead about him. He crawled then tossed grenades into a machine-gun nest, and all the crew were killed. He captured the machine gun. His battalion was then able to progress. He then knocked out a second nest and its crew. He would die later in the day, being awarded the Corps' first Victoria Cross for Vimy Ridge, posthumously... We followed the marked stakes, which were painted, across the horrid terrain... Over the landscape, there were grand craters, dozens of them, everywhere, some as deep as 15 metres. Craters were so big they often touched the sides of the other craters and we snaked around the edges of them... At the ridge's base... The 5ᵗʰ, 7ᵗʰ, 10ᵗʰ, 15ᵗʰ, 14ᵗʰ, and 16ᵗʰ reached enemy front trenches, called*

"Zwolfer Stellung," and then the second trench line named "Zwishchen Stellung" that was situated behind the first trench or the Corps' black line at 0600 hours. This line spanned the entire length of the ridge's base... The 1ˢᵗ (Western Ontario) *and the "Dirty Third" 3ʳᵈ* (Toronto) *marched through our 5ᵗʰ, 7ᵗʰ, and 10ᵗʰ Battalions. We gave encouragement and they took over... To the left of the 16ᵗʰ, the Fighting 18ᵗʰ* (Western Ontario) *and 19ᵗʰ* (Central Ontario) *harrowed in at the base for three quarters of an hour while artillery ceased for stray troops to rejoin the crew... Fritz was stunned to see British troops in their front trenches because they were accustomed to timely delays from barrage to laddie... Balloon trench was passed by the 19ᵗʰ. They were to the left of the 18ᵗʰ... The 21ˢᵗ* (Kingston) *marched through our 18ᵗʰ Battalion and the 19ᵗʰ at 0645 hours... Twenty-two-year-old Lieutenant J.E. Johnson, a rifle lot with him, happened on a cave. After Mills bombs were thrown in, Johnson went in solo with his gun raised. He came upon 105 armed Germans. He gave false statement that an Empire assembly was awaiting them. He disarmed and led them all, in small parties, up to his wee group of mates... By this time all manner of surprise had perished. They began machine-gunning us with everything they had... Thélus hamlet, Turko-Graben trench, and the red line were taken twenty minutes from the interlude. They fell to the 21ˢᵗ. The 25ᵗʰ and 21ˢᵗ*

*also took 400 prisoners and 8 machine guns...
Signalling flags were waved to air cavalry...
The 2nd Division* (Canadian born Major-General
Sir Henry Burstall), *to our left, went into
action... The poor chaps in the 1st Division
suffered tremendously, practically all mine
craters passed were blood red with mangled
corpses tangled on wire, beggaring
description... Though the first line fell swiftly...
Our 2nd Division had less ground to traverse
than the 1st... At times, we leaned on the barrage
no less than fifty metres from it... Byng gave our
division all eight tanks; each was unemployable
and quickly abandoned... Our division saw the
heftiest action... A big shell crater was passed.
In it was a chap* (a Canadian). *The mate in there
continually yelled, "Water. Water." The
complete top of his skull was gone. His brain
was entirely visible. He would be gone shortly.
The agreement was to carry on no matter what.
Halting for any reason was not allowed, even to
comfort a chum in his final moments. But the
bearers could get to one, provided he held on
long enough... The grand discipline instilled in
the lads proved infrangible, as they were to
continue no matter what befell the fellow next to
them, whom they had trained with from the
start... Lance Sergeant Ellis Sifton and others
of the Fighting 18th were completely hampered
by machine-gun fire. He rushed the trench and
took down all the Germans in it with his rifle.
He continued on. Once his gun was empty, he*

used his bayonet on every German he encountered until the others were able to meet him, and they took the trench. An enemy, nearing death, shot Sifton, who succumbed to his wounds but would be accorded the second Victoria Cross for Canada at Vimy, also posthumously... One unit, belonging to the 18th, lost their officer to a shell, and as dreadful consequence, the officer had their rum as well. They forged ahead broken-hearted. They were lamenting about him being killed. After some time, their officer appeared from behind the lot. The shell that landed near in actuality did not hurt him, and the rum was unscathed as well! They gave three cheers, for they had their beloved officer & rum back again!... The 24th (Montreal) *and the Fighting 26th* (St. John's, New Brunswick, and one of the most acclaimed battalions of the Corps) *reinforced by the 105th* (Charlottetown) *reached the red line... The 25th* (Halifax) *was piped over the parapet. Their officer gave agreement, "Even if one man is left alive, the objective must be taken and held." They leap-frogged through the 24th and 26th to attain the red line... The 22nd, part of the 5th Brigade, was initially in the following up waves that cleared the trenches and dugouts. This job was, at times, easy enough, but other times it was hard because some Fritzies fought to the bitter end. A number of ones in the 22nd thought their role was overly simple and went ahead and joined the attacking waves. Those in the*

Van Doos greatly aided the 25th in reaching the Red Line and in occupying Turko Graben Trench... The next immense barrage exploded at 1226 hours... To the left of the 3rd was the "Mad Fourth" 4th (Aurora, Brampton, Brantford, Hamilton, Niagara Falls)*, who advanced through the 15th & 14th. The 4th was piped over to their purpose by the 16th in a display of Corps unity... In the 4th Battalion, a shell tore past a fellow, who hardly avoided it, but the shell decapitated a gunner* (a Canadian) *a few yards from him. The gunner continued to walk, blood spewing furiously from his open neck. The shell also tore one leg from the chap who came after the gunner... The 31st* (Alberta) *made their way through the 21st... Not a scratch of earth escaped the damage done by our artillery... The blue line started to the very righthand side of the ridge from our lines and worked its way to the centre of the 2nd and 3rd Division start lines. This line consisted of Hill 135, the heavily defended village of Thelus and the wooded areas outside the town of Vimy. It was demanding; our units fought by bayonet after ammo and grenades were spent... much of the battalions whose objective it was to take the blue line, the 1st, 3rd, 4th, 21st, 28th, 29th, and the British 13th Brigade, who led the dominion troops for this stage of the operation, affirmed the line was theirs by 1300 hours... We traversed ever-escalating treacherous country... Vickers and Lewis machine guns and rifles along with* *"wooden crosses" were posted into the mud for body-snatchers, or bearers, to find their charges amid the steaming crimson snow... The Sergeant-Major that we took captive told us, "Camerads, you take Vimy Ridge, you win the war"... Fatal gas was everywhere... The 21ˢᵗ, to the left of them, the 28ᵗʰ* (Moose Jaw, Regina, Saskatoon, Port Arthur, Fort Williams) *and to the left of the 28ᵗʰ, the 29ᵗʰ* (Vancouver), *who marched through the 19ᵗʰ, reached the blue line... The majority of the Ridge was under our control at twelve noon... A Canadian hero*[116]*... The Brown line, or the strongly defended Farbus Wood, spanned from the furthest righthand side of the ridge and ended after Farbus Wood: the very left of the line was directly in the centre of the 1ˢᵗ and 2ⁿᵈ Division start lines. The line was reached by two fifteen in the afternoon by the 2ⁿᵈ* (King's Own Scottish Borderers from Eastern Ontario), *the 1ˢᵗ* (Royal West Kent Regiment from Western Ontario and Alberta) *accompanied by the 27ᵗʰ* (Winnipeg) *and the 29ᵗʰ who went through all previous 2ⁿᵈ Division Battalions to reach their aim... Three white rockets were spent in acknowledgement to headquarters... In the end, the 2ⁿᵈ Division was aided by the British 13ᵗʰ Brigade... After they went through the 25ᵗʰ and to the left of the 29ᵗʰ, the Iron Sixth* (Western Canada) *carried the last phase in the Bois de la Ville area... There were*

---

[116]   A Canadian World War I epitaph for a soldier who died at the battle for Vimy Ridge

seemingly countless casualties. The bearers were overwhelmed, going this way and that, attempting to do what they could for those who were screaming bloody murder in delirium, and for others who could no longer speak due to their wounds. The bearers assessed who was most likely to live and would take that one with them, leaving the others beside that casualty to their fate... The 3rd Division (British Major-General Louis Lipsett) *went over the top... By war's end, the 3rd Division would be counted as one of the British Force's most exemplary fighting units... The Princess Pat's were stationed centerfold in the Corps' lines. Their band rose alongside them and piped them 'til battle's end... It looked like, dreadfully near, was the prince of darkness in the flesh... From our division's start lines, directly on the other side of the ridge, was the town of Vimy... Our path was shorter in distance; however, it was steeper than the divisions before us, and they gave our 3rd Division, as well as the 4th Division, strictly the Black Line, at the ridge's crest, and Red Line, on the very left side of the ridge, to capture... To the right of the Princess Pat's were the Royal Canadian Rifles* (London). *To the right of the C.M.R was the 4th Canadian Mounted Rifles* (Toronto). *To the right of 4th was the 2nd C.M.R.* (Victoria), *and to right of the 2nd C.M.R was the 1st C.M.R.* (Brandon)... *A part of the 2nd C.M.R, a high explosive shell wheeled its way into the mud right jolly in front of a chap.*

He was shot tens of yards into the air. Once he landed on the ground, he looked himself over to assess any injuries. He suffered none at all. After he took up his helmet and rifle, he carried on... To the left of the Princess Pat's, our 42nd (Montreal's Royal Highlanders) *Battalion advanced on the red line... The enemy's conversations could be listened to, since our unit was that near to where they were... The majority of the Corps had reached the red line, which included La Folie Farm, the toughest stronghold that was now in our hands. The Farm was taken 90 minutes after the battle started.... The 49th* (Edmonton) *captured the Folie Wood... The 4th Division* (Canadian born Major-General Sir David Watson) *had the bleakest task of all, which was capturing Hill 145 and, to the northwest of the Hill, the Pimple: the two highest and therefore strongest held points of Vimy... To the left of the 3rd Division, we were being slaughtered... The 38th* (Ottawa) *rushed the southwest part of Givenchy-en-Gohelle, the far-left side of the brow of the ridge, and reached the black line. The 78th* (Winnipeg Grenadiers) *moved past them to take their goal, the red line... Seven hundred metres of the steepest ascent was the next task... We were being annihilated from above, machine guns were firing down on us from the Pimple... amidst the almost blizzard of snow and waist-deep mud in places... Captain Thain MacDowell (38th) happened on a dug-out. He fooled*

*seventy-seven Prussians, two of them officers,
into thinking his battalion was with him; all
surrendered, and MacDowell was awarded
Canada's third Victoria Cross for Vimy*
(MacDowell would be the sole Victoria Cross
recipient awarded the medal from his actions at
the battle for Vimy Ridge who would live to see
the end of the war)... *Hill 145 required
proceeding through four lines of resistance...
Distressingly, the Hill and the Pimple were still
very much intact from the failure of the
onslaught, in the days beforehand, to perform
adequate harm... Added to the dismay, the
barrage and the 4th Division were at variance
with one another, which prevented their lads
from reaching the Ridge in a secure fashion...
Their primary assemblies were cut to ribbons...
Of the un-afflicted, numerous were constrained
to shell-holes or mere crevices, sheltering them
from death by inches... Junior officers
accounted for many of the casualties in the
initial wave... Communication from our
Division to Commanders behind our lines was
greatly thwarted as a result... Confusion set
in... The 102nd* (Comox-Atlin) *was followed by
the 54th* (Kootenay) *and 75th* (Mississauga,
Hamilton, London), *who attacked rear of a
stone's throw... As we advanced up the Hill,
bodies torn open from head to foot, our push fell
to bedlam... Pre-battle, the artillery was told by
brigade headquarters to retire from one trench,
so to give us a safe haven from the torrential*

fire and to act as an instruction-like post. However, this trench was not empty, as was supposed. Within the first handful of minutes, more than half the 87th (Montreal's Grenadier Guards) *were gone... We were panicking, given that once evening came, enemy replacements would come en masse... We did not have enough troops to conquer her... Hopelessly, the Commanders turned to the 85th* (Nova Scotia's labour unit of no combat experience). *The Scotians were flabbergasted. Their badges have their saying embossed on them, which reads, "Siol na Fear Fearail"* (Gaelic for "Breed of Manly Men"). *One of their company's captains avowed, "We will take it or never come back." However, the commanding officer cancelled the barrage for the 85th. The C.O. was afraid his troops would perish from inaccuracy; however, the runners carrying this message were not to be seen again. Runners often times do not make it to their destination. Thrown into the front lines the afternoon of April 9th, the 85th was left unawares that they no longer had any protection. In place of a formidable barrage, those Highlanders met with silence and absence of direction. Essentially, they were left by themselves. Any officer will tell you the definition of insanity is to charge No Man's Land without a barrage in front of your unit. With unparalleled courage, they went over the top alone. The Germans were at an utter loss. Covering hundreds of metres, the 85th made mad dash* with bullets flying every which way. They captured three machine guns and more than one hundred enemy. After an hour's battle, most of the Hill, aside from sections of the eastern part, had fallen to the incredulous 85th. Mother, the Germans and Allies are calling Nova Scotia's act one of the most daring feats of the war in its entirety. Their motto is "Do your bit and a bit more." I dare say they did... Stationed to the left of where the 85th fought, the 72nd (Vancouver Seaforth Highlanders) reached the end of the black line on the other side of the Ridge to where the 1st Division's black line started. This line spanned the entire length of the ridge, excepting the area where the Pimple was located. To the left of the 72nd was the 73rd (Montreal Royal Highlanders), who reached the end of the red line to the very left-hand side from our lines. The red line spanned the entire length of the ridge, as well, and extended just further to the left of the black line... The first evening, the thought was that an enemy counterattack would happen, but it did not transpire... The following afternoon, April 10th, the Corps attacked again... The Pimple was the last objective to be rushed and found at the very far left of the Ridge from the Corps side. A section of the 44th (Manitoba) seized their goal: the Blue line, after going through the 54th. They were to take the very left of the Hill... But machine guns were pulverising the 50th (Calgary), who were supposed to take the

Pimple. The other section of the 44th were to the right of the 50th ... "On we go!" & "Never stop!" were chanted the entire battle. If this isn't an endearing part of Canadian history... Private John Pattison, who belonged to the 50th, charged a machine-gun post alone by jumping a number of shell-holes. He threw 3 grenades into a trench, then killed all 5 surviving gunners with his bayonet in the shattered trench before the rest of the 50th's troops materialized. His battalion was then able to take the remainder of the ridge. (Pattison would fall in the Douai plain weeks later, knowing only commendation for the fourth and final Victoria Cross the Corps would be bestowed at the battle for Vimy Ridge. The medal would be presented to his family in his name)*... On April 11th, the command was given to assault the last part of the battle... Every where one looked there were corpses wearing German green or Canadian khaki... With mud-jammed guns, Canadians attacked in a bayonet charge against German machine guns at point blank range, often resulting in hand-to-hand bitter combat, and the Canadian Tommies won... Hill 145 was completely under our control at 1945 hours ... April 12th ... at 0200 the 44th, 50th, and the 46th* (Southern Saskatchewan) *were awoken and given soup, biscuits, and rum. These three battalions, as well as the 73rd, were the only ones whose objective was outside of the Black line. Their start lines were to the very left-hand side of the*

Ridge and where the Black line stopped. The 73rd went forward towards Givenchy-en-Gohelle. To the left of them was the 44th, then the 50th, and the 46th respectively... They were tasked with seizing the Pimple, originally a part of the red line, and one hundred and thirty-five metres from the ridge's base. It fell mainly to the 50th and 46th to take her. The surface of this German stronghold was a maze of trenches and, beneath the ground, there were deep dugouts and covered ways and every form of defense the ingenuity of those brilliant German Engineers could devise... At 0500, the 46th were rained down on by Mausers, and 100 of their lads became casualties, merely doggedly crossing N.M.L in the wee hours... The E Battery (Yukon Motor Machine Gun), *stationed near Givenchy, between the Pimple and the Hill, gave us cover with their machine guns to aid in the capture of the Pimple. They also provided support for Hill 145... The blizzard that came in caused laddies to go beyond their targeted position by dozens and dozens of yards given it was difficult to discern nearly a thing... Taking the Pimple fell to continually a smaller number of Tommy Canucks given two of them were killed for every one Fritz that died... After two hours and twelve hundred meters from our lines and to the furthest left-hand side of the Ridge, the Pimple fell on April 12th... Germany accepted her loss and retreated over three kilometers... April 9th would forever bear the bloodiest day history would write for Canada's military... But none of us have ever seen the Commanding Officers so elated!... Everyone was thirsty in the frontlines, or drank petrol-tasting water during the battle... and he is buried in a foreign land, in a corner that shall forever remain Canada!*

The Corps commanding officers wrote, *Almost all were citizen soldiers and executed their duties like professionals, as three of the four divisions took their objectives exactly on schedule, by midday on April 9th... The Allies thought we did not stand a chance... It was Canada's day... Canada has earned for herself eternal glory... It is no wonder the Germans couldn't hold us for our artillery work had been terrible, everything smashed to pieces. We had broken their hearts first and there was no fight left in them... As the guns spoke, over the bags they went, men of CB (Cape Breton) sons of NS (Nova Scotia) & NB (New Brunswick) –- FC's (French Canadians) and westerners – all Canucks...So far it was the most decisive, the most spectacular and the most important victory on this front since the Marne and Canada may well be proud of the achievement... The morale of our troops is magnificent. We cannot lose.* A captured German Officer, upon being led behind Canadian lines, was quoted as saying, "This is the beginning of the end!" Germany's Prince Rupprecht penned in his diary, *Is there any sense in continuing this war?* Brigadier-General Alexander E. Ross, who led the 28th North-West, would later remark, "It was Canada from Atlantic to Pacific on Parade! I thought then in those few moments, I witnessed the birth of a nation!" Byng wrote to his wife, *I went over the Pimple yesterday.*

It is a sight: the dead are rather ghastly but a feat of arms that will stand for ever. Poor old Prussian Guard. WHAT a mouthful to swallow being beaten to hell by what they called "Untrained Colonial levies." Currie stated, *The grandest day the Corps has ever seen. A wonderful success. The attack was carried out exactly as planned. The sight was awful and wonderful!*

The Prime Minister in France

To the aristocracy of Ottawa, the only thing more shocking than their men capturing the Ridge was Richardieux being awarded the Empire's highest award for gallantry. The extraordinary letter was received on a common day, as such events seem to happen. Aubrey recognized the Royal seal of the official envelope. *You are commanded by His Majesty the King to proceed to Sandringham on this date of— for the purpose of being invested with the Victoria Cross. You will leave Grand Trunk Central Station at—. You will depart from Halifax on this date of—. Once at the Port of— you will change trains, where you will meet a King's Messenger, and you will proceed from— to— by a Special Coach with the King's Messenger, who will conduct you to his Majesty—*

The letter fell to the floor before an astonished Aubrey had read it in its entirety. Auré had not even mentioned the remarkable feat. As was common, his medal was announced in the papers. Ottawans were shocked. This could not be. "Unutterable nonsense" was the most common reply. The authenticity of the declaration was severely judged by French and English Canadians in the city, but for different reasons. Commendation for the medal required solid support from one's commanding officer, as well a minimum of three witnesses. That four gentlemen could agree with Richardieux was almost beyond reason. Congratulatory letters arrived at Pembina from the Prime Minister and Governor General, an invitation to dine with the former, to shoot on his grounds from the latter.

Mothers, aghast, wrote their sons for explanation. The responses received were a blow to all. Beloved by officers and men[117], the replies read, *His leadership was grand... His beautiful life and character were an inspiration to all his comrades*[118]... *The atmosphere of his life drew us Heavenward*[119]... *He was a prince under fire*[120]... *He would give his dinner to a hungry dog and go without himself*[121]... *He loved chivalry, truth and honour, freedom and courtesy*[122]... *Awarded D.S.O. for his coolness, good judgement, skill and courage*[123]. Major Richardieux, with his delicate sense of honour, had refused to be seen in the presence of a High Command who had his collar turned up. Richardieux was the only soldier his men had ever heard of who did not consume his daily rum. Not even the mothers could claim this of their sons, and all were members of the Women's Christian Temperance Union. He commissioned his pay to the Patriotic Fund. Only at Kellynch's confirmation was this believed. Since Richardieux had been promoted to their leader, their battalion had already been commended on numerous occasions: for promptness in responding to the infantry's call, for excellent shooting, for raids, as well as for providing support fire, ammunition, and encouragement in several locations during

---

[117] A Canadian World War I epitaph
[118] A Canadian World War I epitaph
[119] A Canadian World War I epitaph
[120] A Canadian World War I epitaph
[121] A Canadian World War I epitaph
[122] A Canadian World War I epitaph
[123] A Canadian World War I epitaph

battle. Richardieux refused to withdraw from the prison until his men had left before him, though he was injured more than his men. Mentioned in dispatches for gallant and distinguished conduct in the field[124], Richardieux was praised by his superiors, which his men also explained in letters, *His commanding officer said of him, "He was an example to all ranks"*[125] and *His captain said, "No braver soldier ever led others into battle"*[126]. Richardieux, in perhaps what was the most damning evidence of all, had the honourable mention for valour in a dispatch by Haig himself.

Aubrey went to her weekly Bridge club. English ladies went out of their way to smile and invite her to play. Her husband was greatly complimented and declared a role model to the French. On the way to her carriage, with promises from the other wives to play the following week, she passed a table of French ladies. They whispered in hushed tones over cups of tea, "There goes Mme. Richardieux. Her husband was accorded the Victoria Cross. He's a royalist, you know, a monarchist."

As Aubrey descended the steps of Chateau Laurier, Mr. Harrington was outside. Once he saw Aubrey, he removed himself from his carriage. After giving his hand to help her alight, he shut the door of her carriage.

"Do tell Mr. Richardieux congratulations, and he is most welcome to dine at Rolstern, provided, dear, he explains the story of how he captured his Victoria Cross!"

---

[124] A Canadian World War I epitaph

[125] A Canadian World War I epitaph

[126] A Canadian World War I epitaph

"He has gone on his last commission to that beautiful place called rest[127]," she genuinely smiled in response at her husband's safe return.

Harrington chuckled and answered, "You must be relieved." At Harrington's words, "ta, ta," her carriage drove off. While the carriage drove down the street, working men wore badges of rejection, lest they be harassed. The newest posters were pasted throughout the city's streets. A soldier with his trusted rifle in hand stood before the Red Ensign, the caption reading, "To Victory! The Maple Leaf Forever!"

Loved and only child[128], at least, as of yet, thought his parents, René had toddled from the solarium with a toy ship early one evening after children's hour. Children would spend an hour an evening with their parents in the children's finest attire and best manners. Of the splendid toys depicting the Army, Air Force, and Navy, which his father bought for him in England, René always took to the ships. Although huge for his age, he was a docile, well-mannered little boy and the apple of his father's eye. "Mother's darling[129]" was what Aubrey affectionately called him. Neither his father nor mother had anything to complain of in terms of their child. The nanny never had to discipline René. If the nanny could change one thing about her charge, it was that she wished he would talk more. René was very quiet. With his dark, strong features, and already broad shoulders, René looked quite similar to his father. Aubrey had not realized that gentle giants came made that way. René had green eyes that endearingly reminded

---

[127] A Canadian World War I epitaph
[128] A Canadian World War I epitaph
[129] A Canadian World War I epitaph

his mother of her grandfather, though René's eyes were an emerald green. She missed Emmett every day.

"He's eh handsome little boy, is he not?" Auré said to his wife. For his tone, though, he may as well have said "so he's mine."

Mistresses could have dalliances once securely married, provided they had an heir and a spare. Offspring from infidelities could be raised in their mother's manor, along with the legitimate children of the family.

Wishing for a change of topic from her husband's remark, Aubrey managed to remember from Latin class, "Hoc quoque transibit (This too shall pass)," remarking about conscription.

Auré explained, "Not enough men remain in training camps to account for ze losses, and enlistment is basically at eh stand still. The war claims at least six thousand men eh day. Most would rather not be fed into that."

"Nonsense. Borden was only recently in London for the Imperial War Conference," replied Aubrey, while going over the seating arrangement for the Victoria Cross ball Pembina was to hold in the master's honour. It would be the first true ball in some time.

Auré carried on, "They say he iz not charismatic. One can argue his 'eart is not in it, that he is not eh family man, given the middle-aged Bordens have no children. But the reserved, silver-tongued, Nova Scotia-born Prime Minister is in France now. As an aside from the conference, he is also visiting the wounded who captured Vimy. After seeing what our boyz have gone through, or perhaps we are calling them men now—," he said with a wave of hand to correct himself. "And they deserve that," he conceded in fairness, though without emotion. "After listening to the amputees and hearing their personal stories while sitting at the foot of their hospital beds, seeing their mangled frames 'einously disfigured by trench foot, boils and the like, most of them are young enough to be his own sonz.

Borden will return eh changed man. One cannot possibly be a witness to that and be left unchanged. Perhaps if Borden did not go over there, conscription would not come to pass, or perhapz not this year, but the next or the year afterwards. We will never know. Visiting the boys will change the country more than any conference the British are finally letting us attend, and God knows we 'ave earned it."

In early 1917, Lloyd George created the Imperial War Cabinet. The cabinet included granting the dominions' Prime Ministers a voice in the planning of war and of peace to follow. As stated in the Imperial War Cabinet, Article IX gave reason to believe the British Empire comprised of self-governing nations and colonies. A distinct employ was India. The desire of the cabinet was to see future joint policies created in peacetime and in warfare from governing bodies across the Empire; an unofficial League of Nations came to its foundation.

Aubrey said, "I think the colony is treated just rightly so."

Auré countered, "Similar to his citizenz, Borden solely knows of what's going on over there from the scraps of information he gathers from newspaperz. Surely George and Lloyd George can show him more respect than this."

Aubrey went on, "But Borden is adamant about a volunteer force. He even gave his word to Archbishop Bruschesi."

Auré elucidated, "The effort iz lasting too long. The boys who 'ave been maimed repeatedly and sent back to the front will not be able to carry on much longer. If these same ladz are made to continue, they will be permanently maimed, killed or driven insane."

Aubrey cried, "There must be some other method to allow us to win."

"Vincit Qui Patitur[130]."

"He who endures wins, however—"

"If we are to endure, conscription will 'ave to pass and Canada will see herself torn apart."

Aubrey concurred. Dear friends since girlhood, Rev. Mrs. Tomryn could no longer be near Mme. Desrosiers without dissolving to sobs. Kelly was convalescing from a gunshot wound for what was the third time. He was made to stay in France to return to action upon recovery. Before, Kelly simply would have been invalided to Ottawa to remain. Mrs. Tomryn practically pleaded that Jean-Pierre could take his place. Mme. Desrosiers corrected that Jean-Pierre refused to enlist and she was proud of him. Their sons were the same age.

"But because Borden is now irrevocably behind the soldiers, nothing will stop him from implementing such eh measure. One can safely say nothing really matterz to him at this point but the soldiers who he is in charge of supporting and bringing the country irrevocably behind them, too. And they say conscription is going after Quebec, but it should go after the traitors, shirkers, remittance men, and those damn atheists." He continued in the most irritated tone, "There are even eh few members of parliament who publicly profess atheism." He went on, "Quebec will invariably be dragged into this British problem and will get the short end of it, az usual. This war is bringing out everyone's true nature and ze slackers should be conscripted, like Peter."

"In fairness to males like Peter, this war is turning out to be frightful. It's just not fair."

---

[130] A Canadian World War I epitaph

"Life's not fair, Aubrey. What about the country executing our volunteer soldiers? Their military records are not 'orrible. These lads are not malingers or true deserters. They have usually been too shell-shocked to continue much in battle. Seeing the lad kneeling in the snow, blind folded with his 'ands tied behind 'his back, facing a firing squad... normally the men from his very unit are made to act as the firing squad or they are shot themselves. It is surely 'eartbreaking. The lad volunteered to lay down 'is life for his democracy and his democracy is condemning him to death. Surely, there is no greater disloyalty a country can extend to one of its citizens than that. Often times, the man'z battalion is then made to march past the body as an example in regard to discipline."

Canada would execute 25 of its soldiers: 22 for desertion, 2 on murder charges, and 1 on the act of cowardice. Australia was the only army of the Empire who refused to execute its volunteer soldiers.

"Or what about a returned soldier who is so shell-shocked or wounded he cannot find regular employment. One of the saddest parts about war is what shell-shock doez to a soldier and his family when he returns. To see that man begging on the street for money is truly disheartening after he volunteered to lay down is life for his democracy. These are two of the saddest sights in Canadian history."

Auré ventured on, "Miss 'enrietta says she can hardly be around Peter without wanting to smack him. Am I right to say women only slap men they respect? He wouldn't even return to England to drill with broomsticks in Kitchener's army at the start of ze war. Of our affluent males, most 'ave delightfully gone into the regular army. They could 'ave easily accepted eh commissioned rank and pay. They could have chosen to live in Chateaux like the generals of both mother countries. But they 'ave chosen to fight alongside and partake in the work of the common man in the poor bloody infantry," he finished slowly. "Take Newfoundland, for example. Their high enlistment rate is remarkably out of proportion to their population. Considered by the Empire as even more unworthy than Canada, 'Britain's oldest and most loyal colony' is even more devoted to His Majesty than the dominion is. Ze English are most peculiar this way. Beaumont-Hamel rightfully earned them deathless glory in Empire history. It was said that subsequent to the initial influx of attackers, an incredible serenity befell ze landscape. The regiment's boys became the only Allies discernable to the enemy. They were left by themselves, completely in the open without any Allied protection. They proved perfect markz for all German firearms in that area of the Somme, and the Germans nearly annihilated an entire colony's fighting force.

Eight hundred and one Newfoundlanders confronted the foe that day. Nearly all the regiment fell on British soil before being able to reach No Man's Land. Nor did a Newfoundlander fire a shot. It is believed not eh single German casualty was sustained from the regiment 'olding their section of British lines. It iz surely astounding any of their lads lived through that morning. Of their military, almost half were killed or went missing and almost the other half were wounded. No other military can (or would furthermore) claim such a calamity in Empire history. Apart from their casualties, the survivors, reports state sixty-eight, basically lost all their male relatives of military age in less than thirty-minutes exposure to enemy fire. But every single one of the sixty-eight were at roll call the next day, willing to fight. Of the close-knit regiment, every one of their officers was either killed or wounded so profoundly they could no longer fight — supposedly for the remainder of the duration, which provez they lead solely from the front.

That ancient British island's population iz just under a quarter million and the smallest population of all colonies. The regiment is comprised of mainly native-born sons. Almost every nuclear family in their colony was affected by the carnage of that one 'orrific day's battle. I can't imagine being the Newfoundlanders and receiving those cablez stating what happened.

But their Regiment does not offer excuses, like Peter. They stand and fight and are slaughtered like men, though roughly half at Beaumont 'ad not been around long enough to cast eh ballot in their first election."

After their stance at Beaumont-Hamel, Newfoundland would be the only regiment (800 men) of the British Empire who would be bestowed the title of "Royal" by the King during the war.

Wanting a change of subject again, Aubrey observed, "If this conscription should pass—"

"When, ma chere. And when it does, Peter will be ze last one out of the trenches. And he should be leading colonials, not 'iding behind them."

"You are quite mistaken. He is of the most credited gentlemen in fencing and riding, educated at Eton, then—"

"Then kicked out of Sandhurst for failing 'is exams and for gross insubordination," finished Auré.

"And if he enlists, he will automatically become a commissioned officer. His breed of gentleman would make a model soldier," Aubrey tried to make clear.

Auré ventured to explain, "Any general will concede, and most of our generals are themselves, the mild-mannered man makes the best soldier. Of the Corps' officers, it seems the higher one goes in the ranks, the quieter ones there are. I might add, we, az Canadians, take a lot pride in the enormous fatality rate of our officers. This demonstrates our officers go into battle with their soldiers behind them. A good officer falls in front of the rank and file. Right before eh fray, the ones who pick fights, who brag, who push the smaller ones about are ze last to leave the trenches. The quiet ones, the even-tempered ones, the well-mannered, ordinary citizens-turned-volunteer soldiers are the first to climb over the parapets, to rush eh machine gun solo, to drag an injured man back from No Man's Land. Those farm boys 'o come from sleepy villages and hamlets, with whom you grew up in Saskatchewan, are ze ones who win medals, though basically all our soldiers shy away from them."

Aubrey looked around and attempted to argue her point further and said, "But rules being what they are, with farmers needing to stay back to feed the Empire and Munition factories needing to be manned, etcetera, that really narrows down the pool of those who can serve at the front. And there are still fairly strict medical standards and age restrictions. After all, not everyone is allowed to fight."

"You 'ave reason, Aubrey. Not everyone is allowed to fight. What about the underage? I don't know if anyone gets over that: the underage ones. I don't know what I would do if my fifteen-year-old son went off to war. Anyway, they whimper like puppies in the trenches, but go over the top nonetheless because they somehow think it iz their duty to replace the males who won't fight, males like Peter, who should be conscripted so when they eventually pull the underage back, our numbers won't be depleted. Or those munitionettez who work in such deplorable conditions, at least in England, that the majority will be robbed of 'aving children or of living into old age. But they fight anyway because they think it will help them obtain the vote. Or our precious Bluebirds. Our officers are very vocal that our Bluebirds be granted medals for their bravery, given they are officers, too. However, British officials at first would not do so, given they're women. I would also like to point out our Bluebirds are the only officers of any army 'o are not permitted to carry firearms.

Another point, the Kellynchs are too one of England's most ancient families. When war broke out, Kellynch's father ordered Fitzwilliam to stay in Canada to 'elp spread the effort. Before ze war, Kellynch was here simply expanding the family's business to return to England once his father gave word. To a gentleman in his position, the 'orrors of the trenches are preferable to staying behind. However, Fitzwilliam is doing everything in his power to aid the effort. He is still fighting, although in a round-a-bout way, whereas Peter was thrown out of his family's ancestral 'ome on the grounds of dishonor. That is what a remittance man is — these sons are the black sheep, playboys of noble families who do nothing to make a name for themselves. Remittance men are sent away to the far corners of the Empire to rid their family of the embarrassment and degradation of such a son who 'as chosen to come to naught. Eh gentleman should not be comfotable resting on the laurels of others — specifically, relatives who have given him his leisured world and of his adopted place of residence. Life's not for the faint of heart, Aubrey."

Aubrey retorted, "Well, this obscure colony is more of an embarrassment than all the others to begin with."

Auré replied, "That's why 'is father sent him here; it iz the worst posting of the Empire he could have been banished to."

Borden Announces Conscription

The eighteenth of May dawned with a most tense atmosphere in the capitol. Borden read to an overfilled House of Commons.

"I visited hospitals in Great Britain and France, and everywhere I found our men receiving, so far as I could see, the best of attention. I did not hear a complaint from any man in hospital, except from two who complained to me that the Germans were not fighting fairly because, they both said, 'When the Canadians climbed the Vimy ridge, the Germans did not stand up to them but ran away instead of fighting like men.' I deemed it not only my duty but my very great honor and privilege to utilize every spare moment in seeing our men in the hospitals, and I saw only two men from Vimy ridge who did not smile with great satisfaction when I spoke of their having driven the Germans back. Those men could not smile with their lips by reason of their wounds, but they did smile with their eyes. Let me say to the members of this House and to the people of this country that no man wanting inspiration, determination, or courage as to his duty in this war could go to any better place than the hospitals in which our Canadian boys are found. Their patience, pluck, and cheerfulness are simply wonderful.

There is another thing that should be mentioned, and that is the very, very great kindness of the British people to all our Canadian troops. I have been among them in camps and hospitals and elsewhere, and there was hardly a place I visited where I did not find visitors at the hospitals giving great care and attention to our wounded.

Certain representations have been made to me, and also to the overseas authorities from time to time, that the Canadian troops contracted drinking habits while overseas. I made it my special business to inquire as to that. I inquired of General Turner, General Steele, and of General Child of the War Office, who have to deal with such matters, and I shall place their reports upon the Table afterwards, I shall not stop to read them now. It is enough to say that these reports indicate that such representations are almost absolutely without foundation. The Canadian troops are not addicted to the habit of drunkenness. It was represented to me by General Steele, in whose word I have absolute confidence, that there is less drinking among the Canadian troops than among any other troops in the United Kingdom, and I thoroughly believe that drinking is almost at a minimum."

The Canadian Tommy had acquired quite the repute for drunkenness!

"But a great struggle still lies before us in this war; that is the message I bring back to you from Great Britain and from the front. A great struggle lies before us, and I cannot put that before you more forcibly than by stating that at the commencement of this spring's campaign, Germany put in the field one million more men than she put in the field last spring. The organization of the manpower of that nation has been wonderful. Awful as are the barbarities and methods which she has perpetrated and used, one cannot but admit that the organization of the national life of that country throws into the field absolutely the full power of the nation.

Now, I desire to speak with discretion and moderation in these matters, but I cannot too strongly emphasize my belief that a great effort still lies before the Allied nations if we are going to win this war, and it is absolutely inconceivable to me that we should not win this war. The unsettled political conditions in Russia undoubtedly have handicapped the effort on the eastern front, and thus enabled Germany to make a greater effort on the western front.

Against these considerations, there is the fact that a great kindred and neighboring nation has entered into the war on the Allied side, the United States of America. That important event, which took place during our absence, must exercise a tremendous effect not only upon the issue of this war but upon the future of the world. The fact that citizens of the United States are to fight side by side with the soldiers of our Empire cannot but have a splendid influence on the future of the two nations. Although the relations of the two countries have been good for many years, this notable event must do much to wipe out certain memories, and I know that the Canadian forces at the front will be delighted to fight side by side with those from the great republic to the south.

But although the United States has entered this war, we do not know how long it will be before the tremendous power of that nation can be translated into military effort. It cannot be done in a few weeks; it cannot be done fully in a few months. We know that from our own experience; the British Government know it from their experience, and, therefore, it must not lead to any relaxation of effort on the part of the Empire or the part of any of the Allied nations.

I have no confident hope that the war will end this year. Any conjecture as to the time when it will end is almost valueless."

On the front lines, the "Bon mot (Good word)" was "Berlin or Bust," but it had long since changed to "Blighty or nearer my God to thee." The start of the duration saw troops attend Church every Sunday. The common day soldier was too exhausted to read his Bible or sing before falling asleep, as in the first years of war, though he would keel over into his makeshift funk hole. Carved out of trench walls, a soldier could cover about half his self in the fetal position in the shelter of a funk hole. The lads slept in funkholes. Legs were perpetually stepped on by others going through the trench. Funk holes caving from the rain or shells was endless. The need for soldiers to differentiate between corpses and dozing men was continuous. Over time, dugouts were superiorly adopted to guard against weather and grand bombardments. Scared of being buried alive, as a soldier was buried alive at minimum once every couple months, some shell-shocked troops would not take shelter in dugouts but would choose to stay in the open trenches during shelling. If the officer over them was unkind and did not allow the lad to move to the back of the lines, the lad could count on being at the front for mere weeks before being killed.

"Now, as to our efforts in this war: here, I approach a subject of great gravity and seriousness, and, I hope, with a full sense of the responsibility that devolves upon myself and upon my colleagues, and not only upon us but upon the members of this Parliament and the people of this country. We have four Canadian divisions at the front. For the immediate future, there are sufficient reinforcements."

During battle, privates subsided on paltry minutes of sleep at a time. One hundred consecutive hours saw officers awake through a typical battle. Infantry guns were fired thousands of rounds post-warranty, causing such wear that barrels melted and accuracy became severely impaired.

"But four divisions cannot be maintained without thorough provision for future requirements. If these reinforcements are not supplied, what will be the consequence? The consequence will be that the four divisions will dwindle down to three, the three will dwindle to two, and Canada's efforts, so splendid in this war, can bring himself to consider with toleration or seriousness any suggestion for the relaxation of our efforts.

Hitherto, we have depended upon voluntary enlistment. I myself stated to Parliament that nothing but voluntary enlistment was proposed by the government. But I return to Canada impressed at once with the extreme gravity of the situation, and with a sense of responsibility for our further effort at the most critical period of war. It is apparent to me that the voluntary system will not yield further substantial results. I hoped that it would."

Following the battle of the Somme, replacement troops were scarcely to be found.

"The Government has made every effort within its power, so far as I can judge. If any effective effort to stimulate voluntary recruiting still remains to be made, I should like to know what it is. The people have co-operated with the Government in a most splendid manner along the line of voluntary enlistment. Men and women alike have interested themselves in filling up the ranks of regiments that were organized. Everything possible has been done, it seems to me, in the way of voluntary enlistment.

All citizens are liable to military service for the defense of their country, and I conceive that the battle for Canadian liberty and autonomy is being fought to-day on the plains of France and of Belgium."

Women and some men were crying.

"There are other places besides the soil of a country itself where the battle for its liberties and its institutions can be fought, and I venture to think that, if this war should end in defeat, Canada, in all the years to come, would be under the shadow of German military domination. That is the very lowest at which we can put it. I believe that this fact cannot be gainsaid.

Now, the question arises as to what is our duty. I believe the time has come when the authority of the state should be invoked to provide reinforcements necessary to sustain the gallant men at the front who have held the line for months, who have proved themselves more than a match for the best troops that the enemy could send against them, and who are fighting in France and Belgium so that Canada may live in the future. No one who has not seen the positions which our men have taken, whether at Vimy Ridge, at Courcelette, or elsewhere, can realize the magnitude of the task that is before them, or the splendid courage and resourcefulness which its accomplishment demands. Nor can any one realize the conditions under which war is being carried on."

Shells and bullets were flying every possible way. A message was to be delivered across No Man's Land. Numerous hands went up to volunteer for the task. The two chosen went over the top and were shot instantly upon standing up straight. Another pair of volunteers were asked for. More hands were raised. The next two climbed over the parapet, ran a few yards, and fell in front of their mates. A third set proved necessary. They met the same fate of their previous mates. The fourth time, the officer choked on his tears for want of more runners.

"I bring back to the people of Canada, from these men, a message that they need our help, that they need to be supported, that they need to be sustained, that reinforcements must be sent to them. Thousands of them have made the supreme sacrifice for our liberty and preservation. Common gratitude, apart from all other considerations, should bring the whole force of this nation behind them. I have promised, insofar as I am concerned, that this help shall be given. I should feel myself unworthy of the responsibility devolving upon me if I did not fulfill that pledge. I bring a message from them, yes, a message also from the men in the hospitals, who have come back from the very valley of the shadow of death, many of them maimed for life. I saw one of them who had lost both legs pretty well up to the hip, and he was as bright, as cheerful, as brave, and as confident of the future as any one of the members of this House — a splendid, brave boy. But, is there not some other message? Is there not a call to us from those who have passed beyond the shadow into the light of perfect day, from those who have fallen in France and in Belgium, from those who have died that Canada may live? Is there not a call to us that their sacrifice shall not be in vain?"

Sustaining a five hundred thousand might military was inclined to end in dominion disaster. The drive for Francophone enlistees had come to naught; the government was made to consider its sole recourse.

"I have had to take all these matters into consideration, and I have given them my most earnest attention. I realize that the responsibility is a serious one, but I do not shrink from it. Therefore, it is my duty to announce to the House that early proposals will be made on the part of the Government to provide, by compulsory military enlistment on a selective basis, such reinforcements as may be necessary to maintain the Canadian army to-day in the field as one of the finest fighting units of the Empire. The number of men required will not be less than fifty thousand and will probably be one hundred thousand. These proposals have been formulated in part, and they will be presented to the House with the greatest expedition that circumstances will permit. I hope that when they are submitted, all the members of the House will receive them with a full sense of the greatness of the issue involved in this war, with a deep realization of the sacrifice that we have already made, of the purpose for which it has been made, and with a firm determination on our part that in this great struggle, we will do our duty whatever it may be, to the very end."

Conservatives were overjoyed, and a few Liberals joined in their happiness. Parliament, and soon the country, proved to be rather jolly towards the news. The final commands of officers were often of imploring their men to continue without them before the officers succumbed to their fatal wounds.

Pembina's Ball

"French Canada accounts for twenty-eight percent of Canada's population, though it accounts for four percent of the Canadian Expeditionary Force's population," Hughes stated to the House on a June day.

Furthermore, of Quebec's enlistees, half were English Canadians. Of all French Canadians in uniform, half lived outside Quebec. Spring alone saw 20,000 Canadian casualties overseas. At the same time, spring saw the sole French province give fewer than one hundred sons to the cause. After "God save the King" was sung in the House, members of Parliament set about discussing the new Military Service Agreement bill.

Kellynch was shown into one of Pembina's front rooms. Aubrey had invited him for afternoon tea. He was most relieved to receive her invitation. He had meant to call before but feared rejection. Aubrey beamed. Kellynch gave a most humble apology for past transgressions against her husband. He wished to make amends. Aubrey was most certainly taken aback. Kellynch had come to see Auré, not her. She was hot with anger as she rang for Auré. Her husband had just come from town to sign a medical compensation claim of a returned wounded private. Regulars could not be trusted for such applications without an approved inquiry, usually made by their local Patriotic Fund branch or a committee that held no ties to the soldier. As an officer and a gentleman, Auré had given his word that the fellow was of sound character. The papers were signed in his office at the university, converted from a bathroom into office space due to the cause.

Enlistment for French Canada was governed by affluent English Canada. Kellynch was in charge of the pamphlet, *Pourquoi Je M'enrole* (Why I enlisted). Kellynch wanted Auré to appear in the next issue of the pamphlet.

Kellynch relayed his and Aubrey's conversation to Auré. The apology Kellynch extended to Auré was entirely accepted. Aubrey looked quizzically at her husband after his uncharacteristically gracious behaviour in regard to the effort.

Kellynch removed a newspaper printed a few days prior from his briefcase. Fierce French-Canadian nationalist, politician, and founder of *Le Devoir* newspaper, Henri Bourassa was greatly opposed to Canada's war contribution. In 1914, Bourassa was supportive of Canada's involvement in the war. As time elapsed, however, Bourassa became more and more outspoken against Borden's commitment to soldiers sent overseas, while French-Canadian rights were denied in the dominion. Ardently opposed to conscription, he was the voice for French Canada on the matter and on their position in the war. In response to Bourassa's unyielding anti-imperialistic views, French-Canadian soldier Talbot Papineau wrote an open letter published in the *Montreal Gazette*. Bourassa and Papineau were relatives and came from a very prominent Canadian family. The pair would publicly argue multiple times in letters printed in newspapers across the country.

Papineau expressed, *As I write, French and English Canadians are fighting and dying side by side. Is their sacrifice to go for nothing, or will it not cement a foundation for a true Canadian nation... independent in thought, independent in action, independent even in its political organization — but in spirit united for high international and humane purposes to the two Motherlands of England and France? As a* (French) *minority in a great English-speaking continent... we must rather seek to find points of contact and of common interest than points of friction and separation. We must make certain concessions and certain sacrifices of our distinct individuality if we mean to live on amicable terms with our fellow citizens or if we expect them to make similar concessions to us.*

The following week, Bourassa answered his younger cousin. Comparisons to Belgians, who were made to endure misery by the Germans, and Franco-Ontarians, who were denied rights from Regulation 17, were clearly outlined in Bourassa's response: *To preach Holy War for the "liberties of peoples" overseas, and to oppress the national minorities within Canada is, in our opinion, nothing but odious hypocrisy.*

Most Canadians lauded Papineau, and he instantly became a dominion-wide hero. Previous letters by Papineau stated, *Especially, I want to see Canadian pride based on substantial achievements, and not on the supercilious and fallacious sense of self-satisfaction we have borrowed from*

England. The issue in Canada after the war is going to be between Imperialism and Nationalism... My whole inclination is towards an independent Canada with all the attributes of sovereignty, including its responsibilities.

Kellynch began bravely, "What with our soldiers sacrificing to keep the country together and, pardon my frankness, Major Richardieux, but your most prestigious war record proves not all Frenchmen are, are—" he looked around at loss for words.

"Cowards," Auré nodded simply, as though he conceded. Pembina's master then acknowledged he had read the article.

Aubrey started at Auré's response. She thought to speak for him. *He would not dare do the pamphlet!* Humiliated at Kellynch's rebuff, Aubrey left the room. Once Kellynch and Auré were left together, they automatically switched to speaking French.

As Aubrey walked from the room, Auré said to Kellynch, "Dites leur que je fait mon devoir[131] (Tell them I did my duty)."

The newest edition of the pamphlet, with Auré's picture on the cover and his Victoria Cross story as the featured article, was distributed. He was now a household name from sea to sea. Downtown, Auré received handshakes from Englishmen and forced smiles from wives of men at the front.

Men said, over papers for the next petition at gentleman's clubs, "My son reported Richardieux was a good man on the line... Poor bloke, I heard it said there was only circumstantial evidence for the trial in Regina, for all the scandal it caused... But I must say he's a capitol fellow... Enlisted voluntarily[132] and that's a mark of a gentleman. He can't be all bad."

---

[131]   A Canadian World War I epitaph
[132]   A Canadian World War I epitaph

The president of the Daughters of the Empire reasoned to her staff during the superintending of the next baking bazaar, "His family will not speak to him, on account of his er — rather unfortunate divorce, that is to say, but that does not make him one jot less agreeable. True, generous, brave[133]; he is wonderfully patriotic. Great hearts are glad when it is time to give[134], after all."

"He is acting like an Imperialist: a British Anglicizer... He should return to the 22nd Battalion and support his kinsmen," vocalized cross Frenchmen.

The Richardieux were invited to numerous parties because everyone wanted a Victoria Cross recipient as their guest of honour. It was not until early August that Pembina hosted a ball for the master. Not a Frenchman was present, as all were in a gentleman's agreement to refuse attendance at an event where the guest of honour was a Prussian of Ontario.

The cool evening did not reach the Richardieux's guests for the Victoria Cross ball. The endless candles set a romantic glow in Pembina's ornate hall.

"The time I spent behind enemy lines is of no importance."

"How closely bravery and modesty are entwined[135]," were the conceded murmurs from all around, in response to their host's time in captivity. Auré was now in charming good fellowship with the highest echelon of Ottawa's aristocracy.

While clasping Auré on the back, a laughing Kellynch teased, "Mr. Great Heart, Officer and Gentleman[136]. To what do you object, you Old British Tommy?"

---

[133] A Canadian World War I epitaph
[134] A Canadian World War I epitaph
[135] A Newfoundland World War I epitaph
[136] A Canadian World War I epitaph

A cajoled Auré began, "All of a sudden, the foe had me in his dishonest grasp... The terrain: blasted to the dickens... I asked Our Father every day that my general set over me and His Majesty would find it in their grace to pardon my inability to contribute more to the effort."

Ladies pressed him for details of the palace and the Queen's attire. Gentlemen asked after the state of the city and the King's drink of choice. Auré and Aubrey had stayed with Gran in her city townhouse. Her country estate was offered as a convalescent hospital. Gran had stopped all communication with Aubrey at the onset of Aubrey's engagement. One of Aubrey's uncles had married an American industrialist's daughter years before. Thus far, Gran had refused to meet her daughter-in-law. However, after Auré won the Victoria Cross, Gran actually relented and contacted her granddaughter, to Aubrey's surprise. They were invited to stay with her, provided the divorce not be made known, during their short stay in London. Gran went so far as to ask for a photo of René: the first time she acknowledged her great-grandson.

Aubrey looked across the room to where Auré was encircled. Vimy was being discussed by the lot. She could just hear Auré state from afar, "Well they jolly well ought to have captured her with all the training they received. One of my men wrote me that the lads agreed their objective was basically unassailable, although he went on to pen that enough time was given for them to properly train and the like. They felt confident they could take it. The Ridge was surely to draw attention away from France's campaign in the Champagne area, close to the Aisne River, in the Battle of Arras. Our lads attacked north of the British, who fought close to the town of Arras. The British Forces' objective was to ease the pressure for the French."

Auré disclosed remarkable information about the battle. Aubrey simply did not know from what source he would have learned those details. She had a feeling he had more men who respected him at the front than he let on.

"You know, on the second day of the battle and as the terrain was scaled, the Douai plain's green fields could be viewed on the other side of the Ridge. You have to wonder at how they must have felt when they saw those fields with the battle still raging," added Courtney. Courtney was present at the ball as a guest. Beforehand, Aubrey had never known his proper name. As Auré's batman, since the pair's return from the front, Auré had addressed Pembina's former footman by his Christian name.

Upstairs and downstairs were in an unspoken agreement to partake in the invisible care of estates in exchange for meager wages sent to poverty-stricken families. In the trenches, masters and servants trusted one another with their lives. After proving witness to their master's maiming or death, lower orders were spiteful from their experiences on the front lines and were unwilling to return to life below stairs once discharged from the military.

Kellynch added, "The peak of the Vimy Ridge is actually where one can view the war the most than from any other region in France. One wonders, too, at how the boys felt when they crested the Ridge. And to have been there to see them."

Auré explained, "Another of my men wrote to me about ze formidable success of McNaughton's counterbattery. The vast majority of enemy batteries were found, along with eh few hundred guns which had been put out of commission ahead of ze battle. The foe's firing power had been reduced to near rubble during the fray."

Courtney, who was being treated like an equal at the ball, explained, "In terms of casualites, Medical Officers usually witness a comparison of three to one between light to serious casualties, or "walking" to "stretcher-case," during any given scrap. Although, at Vimy, the comparisons were about equal to each other. The casualties suffered at Vimy often needed more attention and usually endured more prominent, life-alternating, or deadly wounds."

Auré talked to Henrietta so much Aubrey thought he might even ask her to dance! She looked at the two of them conversing pleasantly and thought, *If only he was in love with me!* Aubrey looked to Lawrence and almost resigned herself to the fact that being a mistress was all she would ever have. Aubrey's predicament of her married life reminded her of Jane Austen's *Persuasion*. No one wanted Anne Elliott to marry social outcast Captain Wentworth, though she was in love with him. Auré was akin to Wentworth: he had returned from war with everything to recommend him, ladies falling at his feet, and now he was indifferent to her. Aubrey had her chance to tell Auré she loved him! After all, they were married! Now Aubrey had so many others to contend with!

After all the toasts to the King, to Currie, and to Auré, and after singing "For He's A Jolly Good Fellow," she was alone with her husband. However, his unreadable and reserved demeanor never wavered with her publicly or privately.

Russell Theatre

The servants bowed when their master walked into the room. A smarter husband than Auré could not be found in his Sunday suit. A lover of children and flowers, a good friend and patriotic[137], Kellynch, who actually seemed to get along with Auré and was the closest acquaintance who could pass for a chum, was now a regular guest at Pembina for Sunday brunch.

René was taking his daily walk, which took place precisely at ten in the morning around Pembina's grounds. The Laurentien twins, Joseph and Marie, were with him to-day for a treat. Marie had with her a Bluebird doll. Before the group departed, Joseph was asked by his uncle Auré what he wanted to be when he assented to manhood. "Corps Commander!" was the reply, a position utterly unthinkable for a Canadian had Currie not attained the rank.

Daily fresh flowers along with hot and cold dishes of roast, fowl, pigeon, pheasant, venison, partridge, and hare adorned the table. Their Edwardian brunch was lessened on account of the country-wide war diet.

Kellynch bit the tip of his pipe and explained to Aubrey what he and her husband discussed over the morning. "We went over fundraising events for the Patriotic Fund. Thanks

---

[137]   A Canadian World War I epitaph

to the board members' wives, of course, another enormous amount of jam is being made for those recovering in Ottawa. Auré suggested a billiards tournament at Pembina."

Aubrey was agog. Auré had never been in the billiards room. She was unsure if he even knew where the room was located.

Fitzwilliam then told Aubrey she had good reason to be a proud wife.

Pourquoi Je M'enrole was so successful; the general public wanted to know more about one of Ottawa's star soldiers. *Maclean's* wanted to publish a full story about Auré's Victoria Cross capture, along with his time behind enemy lines.

Auré picked at his Ox tongue.

"It would be most advantageous, Auré," Fitzwilliam continued. He turned to Aubrey and said, "You have a husband who is a stubborn as a Welsh dog." Fitzwilliam finished, "What say you, old stick?"

Auré agreed with Kellynch, half-sighed, and replied, "Of course."

Auré looked resigned. Fitzwilliam beamed. Aubrey was perplexed. She thought, *If he did not want to do the magazine article, would he not say no? Ever since his return, he had been bending at the will of all Anglophones, though he has the most formidable of backbones.* Her husband left abruptly, presumably to change into his afternoon suit.

The *Maclean's* article also stated that Auré thought conscription should be law. He was now a hero from Victoria to Halifax. However, the French were at a loss for words. Such traitorship proved too much for them.

Needing anything to boost the morale of England, and particularly interested due to Auré's past as a Mountie,

Britain's *News of the World* picked up the article and ran the story on their front page. England's colonies, in turn, ran the article of the tall, dark, and dashing Mountie (minus the trial!) who captured a Victoria Cross. A picture of Auré and his beautiful aristocratic wife beside him at the Palace headed the full article. The Richardieux name was now known in every corner of the Empire.

Across from Chateau Laurier and outside Russell Theatre, Aubrey's opera hat was adorned with rosettes, cherries, and lace. Other ladies' hats were of whole birds, stuffed hummingbirds, massive plums, blackberries, and gerberas with ribbon streamers. Even so, the usual wide and elaborate hats to reach past a lady's shoulders were being replaced by smaller, sleeker military-style ones to reflect the trend of the time. The most popular headwear for females was the cloche hat, which was similar to a military helmet.

To every lady's delight, Auré was present, if only for the short time it took to escort his wife to the entrance hall. He would not stay to view the performance. Many ladies blushed to have a Victoria Cross recipient help her alight from her carriage or the ever-more-common automobile.

Peter was conversing with an Ace. Englishmen stood stationary while their wives chattered carelessly. Aubrey knew that the Englishmen present would not leave Auré, lest he be harassed by a Francophone. Nearly all jolly activities had been suspended indefinitely. Solely functions related to the war were socially acceptable. Beethoven, Mozart, and Bach had become banned in music halls. A concert, "To Our Heroes, the Boys in Khaki," was to take place, and, afterwards, a lecture entitled "On Land and Sea, with Our

Veterans." Money was being raised for an orchestra for their Duke of Edinburgh's Own Battalion.

Silk top hats and the new, more plain, low-crowned design were raised in gratitude of service to King and Empire, as Auré doffed his topper left and right in acknowledgment of his time on the front lines while he escorted Aubrey through the gathered assembly. A man greatly beloved[138], he stayed long enough to see Aubrey through the doors; then, amidst much protest, he retired to Pembina for the remainder of the evening.

"Dandy fellows all," Auré and Courtney said in toasting those who were cut down in the early morning of their days. By 1917, almost all originals were gone. Men from the same unit often had a bottle to be opened by the last one or two who remained. Of their old brigade, Auré and Courtney were the only ones left. Their brigade's cognac sat before them.

"A Toronto boy[139] — our mate stated had we not had our rum, the Allies would have crumbled long ago. I suppose no one thought the war would last as long as it has. Died for King and country while keeping line open under shellfire[140]... Billy Bishop garnered the VC last month on June 2nd. He took on an enemy aerodrome near Cambrai and took out three of their aircrafts by himself... Royalty inspected us that day so we were to be in tip-top shape... buried in the motherland... After stand to, I finally hacked off about a foot of my greatcoat to free myself from the two or so cumbersome stones of wallow... It was frightfully chilly, we were dressed as well as could be, and the gunners, or suicide club as they're called,

---

[138] A Canadian World War I epitaph
[139] A Canadian World War I epitaph
[140] A Canadian World War I epitaph

four or five of them to a gun, working with their shirts off it's so hot for them during a scrap... at the start when all anyone thought about was signing up in time... Once the Bluebirds arrived, our officers' quarters immediately felt like our proper residences. Our tents were soon adorned with wild flowers and photos and the like. Women have that effect in wartime... When the 1st Canadian Contingent docked in Plymouth, Kaiser Bill jeered, because thirty ships brought us Canadians, but thirty row boats would return those of us who would make it through. Every fellow in the Corps fancies telling that story," the pair related to one another.

"I say, the Corps is on the way to Lens," Kellynch commented, cradling his cognac in hand. The trio was in Pembina's study one bright summer day for an informal Patriotic Fund meeting. Kellynch added, "When the boys attacked Vimy, Newfoundland was stationed close by, at Monchy-Le-Preux, where they once more fought with distinction. Before they were at Le Tansloy and — what was the second place called? 'Silly-Sally' is the nickname their boys call it — right, Sailly-Saillisel was the place. They too were part of the battle of Arras that started on Easter Sunday, just as Vimy did: Easter Morn[141]. Monchy is a small town, eight kilometers south east of Arras. Their regiment went into action on April 14th. One of their officers said to their commander on the 14th, 'It's a fine morning, Sir.' The commander answered, 'I hope it will be.' They were to capture Shrapnel Trench and Infantry Hill, some thousand yards east of Monchy. To the left of Newfoundland was the British 1st Essex Regiment. However, the creeping barrage

---

[141] A Canadian World War I epitaph for a soldier who died April 9th, 1917, at the battle for Vimy Ridge

that went off at 0530 hours was poorly carried out; it was reportedly far too thin.

The Essex managed to take their objective, though. Shrapnel Trench was empty and Newfoundland overtook it. While the Regiment traversed the long slope of Infantry Hill, numerous were wounded as they met with an enemy barrage. Newfoundland's 'D' Company reached their goal and a lot advanced into a wooded area nearby, though they did not come back out. 'C' Company were right on their target concerning the Hill, although the second wave that was supposed to pass through them, along with the Lewis guns meant to cover them, were wiped out. 'A' Company obtained their goal, a windmill. Then they went on and took Machine Gun Wood. The enemy was forced away. After this, all the Regiment's snipers and scouts were soon knocked out. This happened in the first ninety minutes of the scrap.

The remaining Newfoundlanders were quickly surrounded on three sides of the Bois du Sart and the Bois du Vert by about seven hundred enemy. They were without reinforcements because all the runners had been knocked out, too. Essentially, Headquarters did not know what was happening. At Headquarters, their Lieutenant Colonel ordered one of the officers to go out and reconnoitre the situation. The officer arrived back and reported not a single one of the Regiment's lads was unhurt. As well, up to three hundred enemy soldiers were seen coming towards them less than a quarter mile off. The telephone line to Brigade Headquarters was cut.

The Lieutenant Colonel gathered together all the fellows he could, twenty in all, and they went out to hold off the Germans until reinforcements could come in. The lot dashed down the hill to where the foe was advancing. While they went from ruined dwelling to ruined dwelling in the town, they picked up ammo and guns from the corpses that were spread over the ground. In the southeast area of the town, the Colonel stopped his lot at a certain residence. After he climbed a ladder to reach a hole in one of the walls, he could see the enemy not far away. The foe was climbing into the trench the Regiment had attacked earlier in the morning.

Between that trench and the lot was a hedge, well-banked. The lot dashed over one hundred yards of open ground, in aim of the enemy, and reached the hedge. By this point, nine of our lads were left: two officers and seven others, one of whom was an Essex regular. They opened fire on the Germans and made damnably sure they aimed well, specifically given their limited ammunition. A Newfoundland corporal came to after being hit ninety minutes earlier and dragged himself over to the hedge.

So, there were ten in total who held this line for four hours. They were really rather bright in how they managed the situation; they were careful to take out Fritz' scouts, who went ahead of the German infantry to determine the size of what the enemy was against. Thus, the Germans were left unawares of the Regiment's small party. The Germans thought they were being challenged by a remarkably larger force than what there really was.

In the first few hours, forty enemies fell, of which three quarters of those casualties were caused by their brilliant Colonel alone — Forbes-Robertson, I believe is his name. At about two o'clock in the afternoon, when enemy fire had died down considerably, the Colonel had their sole runner go back and give an update on the situation with an appeal for aid, including that artillery shell Machine Gun Wood that appeared to be an enemy headquarters of sorts, given the nuisance in that area. The message proved delivered. And against orders and under heavy enemy fire, the runner returned to the Colonel to assist further. Some forty-five minutes after the message was received at Headquarters, reinforcements relieved the ten chaps and, simultaneously, artillery started to fire on Machine Gun Wood.

It would be one of the worst battles for the Regiment of the war in terms of fatalities and casualties. More than 160 Newfoundlanders were killed, more than 140 were wounded, and more than 150 were made Prisoners of War. General de Lisle, who commands the British 29th Division, agreed if it weren't for Newfoundland's nine sons and the Essex lad, forty thousand Allies would have been required to recapture Monchy. Work smart before you work hard, eh, old boys? The Regiment is now on its way to the battle of Steenbeek, which is a part of the Third Battle of Ypres."

With his untouched cognac before him, Auré added, "To date, Canada has sent soldiers to nearly every country to see action. We work extensively in England, of course; our Foresters toil in British forests for timber and create Allied airfields for the different air forces. Canadian foot soldierz have been posted to the desertz of Egypt. A Canadian 'ospital ship was on the Mediterranean. Our pilots do train new recruits in America. I believe there are infantry and artillery garrisons in St. Lucia and Bermuda. Mesopotamia played 'ost to some of our engineer units az they worked barges on the Tigris and Euphrates rivers. At ze front, railway battalions, normally working under shellfire, lay and do the maintenance for the majority of the English light railway routes. And one company 'ad to refashion rail bridges in the Yarmuck Valley after they were toppled by Turkish troops in

Palestine. Newfoundland was in Cairo for two weeks before they were sent to Gallipoli."

Kellynch related the news of Tomryn's youngest son, Gavin. In the beauty and strength of early manhood[142], he enlisted shortly after Vimy. After the Vimy Ridge battle, recruitment in Canada increased for a time. "Gavin told his father, 'I am going, my country needs me[143].' The laddie went on to inform Tomryn by that he meant Canada. Of the nine Tomryn children, seven were of military age, including their daughter, who is serving as a VAD in England. Six brothers in all answered the call, one crippled, three killed[144], as of yet. The Canadian Tunneling companies, including Gavin's unit, played a crucial part in Messines in summer. After months of toiling under the Messines ridge, which Germany had in its possession, a number of great big mines were placed directly under the ridge. I believe the number was twenty-five, if I am not mistaken. The 1st and 3rd Canadian Tunneling companies, along with the British and Anzacs, laid them. Almost one million pounds of explosives went off the morning of June 7th. It was the single biggest eruption made by man in history, and it took ten thousand enemy lives. So, it seems mining warfare has ended with Messines."

Auré interrupted, "Tunneling must be eh terrifying war."

Kellynch finished, "The explosion was so loud it was said that Lloyd George himself heard the noise in London. At any rate, Gavin's team had been digging one day when a unit of the enemy came upon them from behind. In their broken English, those Germans explained that some in their unit were trapped. And, by and large, the enemy's English

---

[142]   A Canadian World War I epitaph

[143]   A Canadian World War I epitaph

[144]   A Canadian World War I epitaph

is superior to most Allies' German. We can forgive them for one thing. As it turned out, the enemy's tunnel, God only knows where, had partially collapsed and had blocked some of their unit in a confined area. The good, steady lad and his mates abandoned their sapper roles and joined those Fritz to form a small search team. They dug for hours, how much time Gavin doesn't know, though to no avail. They dug until they could not longer hear the SOS signals. The enemy's tunnel collapsed further, most likely from a shell explosion overhead. The bodies were not found."

Kellynch went on to say that the youngest Englishman, or boy rather, to see action in the trenches was twelve. Auré replied the youngest Canadian in the trenches was twelve as well. Courtney laughed to say that the youngest Canuck to enlist was ten and the eldest eighty.

Even Royalty was known, upon parade inspection, to step up to a very young lad and whisper, "You cheeky boy," wink, then turn away. In recent months, the Canadian public became most vocal about their distaste for the endless butchering, specifically concerning the underage. The fourteen-year-olds of the initial years, after their identities uncovered, were moved to England or stayed on as buglers or drummers. However, overseas still saw grand numbers of fifteen and sixteen-year-olds. Officers did what they could to keep the young ones out of direct fire. Fetching stock for the front lines and the like were what the underage were often made to do. As well, delivering messages usually fell to them, although that was still a remarkably perilous task. Too many letters had been sent across the Atlantic that read, *We had just managed to cut the wire when he was shot. We kept on with my arm around him. I managed to drag him, and we came, clippity-clop, to a clearing station. With tears falling down my cheeks, the ordely looked him over and deemed him too far gone. He would not be saved. The makeshift hospitals and ruddy-worked surgeons were overwhelmed. He shook my hand in farewell. He then calmly went over to a stretch of grass not being used by any of the wounded and laid down.*

Auré had told Aubrey of a new underage in his unit, a Newfoundlander who enlisted with the Canadian army. So excited was the lad to finally find himself on the frontlines, they actually told him to speak quieter while they made their way through the formidable labyrinth that was now the front. Behind the front trenches were nearly fifty kilometers of intertwining support and communication trenches. One of the other officers nicknamed him Labrador; he was akin to a puppy that would not let them be. They told him the name was derogatory.

Once at the fire trenches, Labrador raised his head high enough over the parapet to catch his first glimpse of No Man's Land. Before they could finish shouting to him, he felt the ping of the sniper's bullet and was gone to glory. Who died for his King and country at the tender age of 17[145], Labrador had his identification tags removed by Auré and given to a runner to take back to a superior a few hours after the party's arrival.

Labrador's parents forbade him from enlisting. In turn, he ran away. Because he enlisted under a false name, the military was having a hard time locating his parents to inform them of where his body was interned. Auré told Aubrey that he heard similar stories all the while.

Soldiers wrote, *You can only hope for the best and try to be a parent figure towards the young ones.* At long last, the Canadian Government responded to its people's outrage. A cable was dispatched to London. The Young Soldiers

---

[145] A Canadian World War I epitaph

Battalion was formed for Canadian lads. Those not of age were made to return to Britain. The young ones sang, "When Your Boy Comes Back to You" and "Goodbye Mother Dear," while being taught Boy Scout-like drills after two years of attritional warfare. They were made to stay in England until they turned the newly raised minimum age of nineteen, after which they could return to the front.

The petition, which both Auré and Aubrey signed, was the only one she knew of that all Canadians, French and English, agreed upon.

"We were regular mud larks, were we not?" and "Merci Monsieur, et prenez soin (Thank you, Sir, and do take care)," were said over handshakes. Auré actually laughed as he and Courtney parted ways. Aubrey could count on one hand how many times she had heard him laugh in the years she had known him. Courtney left by the front door. In the old days, such an action could have resulted in dismissal. The only child of aged parents[146], Courtney returned to his native Sudbury to take employment at a bank and to assist his father and mother.

The eldest generation was of the opinion the Empire was descending to Hell with her fall of ethics. Etiquette changed so drastically from the war that elders lamented there were no rules at all anymore. Currie was the only general of the Empire to appear in battle without a mustache. In now bygone moral times, an officer who appeared clean-shaven at St. James would have seen disciplinary action akin to having presented himself without trousers. In the first years of the effort, it was against the law for a soldier to shave his mustache. Soldiers were not permitted to shave their upper lip or they would answer to a colonel. Up to ten days in barracks for showing

---

[146] An underage Canadian World War I epitaph

oneself clean-shaven was standard practice. However, once overseas, officers let their men be.

Mothers were beside themselves over their daughters' behaviour. "Khaki fever" was a pervasive problem. Girls waited until they were young ladies to wear their hair up. Young girls who flirted with men in uniform still had to wear their hair down in braids or pigtails that would swing in the wind. The pet name "flappers" was given to these outrageously forward girls who would go on to set the fashion trend of the following decade. Instead of awaiting the first kiss until their wedding day, young people feigned indifference to bedroom-like situations. Young adults discovered circumstances surrounding the bedroom that were unimaginable at the onset of the effort.

With the entry of the United States into the war, the Yankees were asking their females to help them to victory in the cessation of corsets! Steel was needed to manufacture guns, shells, ships, and any number of other articles. A different sort of undergarment, called the brassiere, was to replace what had been the staple of the female wardrobe for three centuries.

Summer saw the King change the family surname from their longstanding Germanic one to an English one. Streets in England were also renamed. Berlin, Ontario, changed to Kitchener, after the leader. Along with a new name, a new age was being ushered in.

Uneasiness and anxiety were created for the returning soldier who found turmoil in recognizing his dominion. Soldiers were stunned to find women wearing the century's forbidden and illegal trousers. Furthermore, females were employed in their posts! However, this breach of conduct was no longer deemed such because females entering the workforce was now a temporary patriotic and necessary measure to win the war. Hemlines rose steadily. Prices soared to reflect the inflated economy of the endless military machine that was now the Empire. The youngest generation outlandishly thought they had a place in society. The silver ribbon that would soon connect the country in its entirety was well underway. Cavalry, transport mules, sabres, and passenger pigeons clashed with radios, machine guns, motorized vehicles, and aeroplanes.

Hill 70

The enemy watched the approaching supreme army. German Commanding Officers noted, "Canadians, whom the British High Command always employ for the most difficult and costly fighting, advanced with obstinate bravery."

Haig wanted to draw Germany's attention away from the focal operations of the front, mainly from Allied troops surrounding the northern Passchendaele front. To the north of Vimy, by a few kilometers, was the coal-mining town of Lens. The town hosted an important support to Germany by way of rail. Capturing the town would make future English and French battles easier. Currie was made to assault Lens frontally. Following examination of the area, the first objective Currie wanted to take was Hill 70, to the north of Lens, so as to commandeer the highest point of Lens. The reason he gave British High Command to take Hill 70 first was because the enemy would be compelled to counterstrike should the hill be taken. Enemy strongholds would be decimated by artillery and machine guns, and as a repercussion, German defenses in the whole region would become feeble.

The Hill was reminiscent of the Vimy terrain. Vimy had created a map of success and had also given Currie greater leverage in how to approach a fray. Hill 70 would provide the location for a topmost principal moment in dominion history.

The battle would be thought of and led by, almost without exception, Canadian Officers. Formerly, the Canadian military had unfailingly seen action under the wing of the British.

After much combat and instruction in the preceding year, along with extensive preparation, the Corps went into battle at 0425, on August 15th. The show was the first time that Canadians faced mustard gas. The Western Front had scarcely seen a higher level of success as the primary phase of Currie's attack. The initial line fell in less than twenty minutes. Germany's 6th Army then counterattacked with twenty-one set pieces, all of which were withstood by the Corps. In the course of the second part of battle, Currie exhibited faults common to a new Commander-in-Chief. The two set pieces resembled the formidable battles of slaughter of the previous years. The fighting ceased on August 25th. Germany retreated with extreme casualties, some twenty-five thousand. The Corps managed to seize Lens to its western side. Lens in its entirety did not fall to Canada; nonetheless, the capture of Hill 70 showed the Corps to be one of the Allies' greatest chances of victory.

Over 9,000 of the Corps were wounded or went missing, including almost 1,900 deaths. The Hill was, to date, the grandest as well as toughest show of the duration for Canada, second only to Vimy and a major accomplishment for the country. Six Victoria Crosses were bestowed to Canadians. Allied High Command realized that the strategies engaged by Currie at Hill 70 proved to be of a higher calibre of fighting than the previous three years.

Altogether the hardest battle in which the Corps has participated. It was a great and wonderful victory, wrote an elated Currie after his brilliantly devised and executed engagement. *GHQ* (General Headquarters) *regard it as one of the finest performances of the war.* Confidence was never higher as Currie's men agreed larger numbers of enemies would be captured henceforth.

Military Service Agreement

At the doors of Vauréal, the Canadian Service Flag had been altered. Once the Americans entered the war, they produced their "Sons in Service" flag. In turn, Canada reproduced the flag to reflect Canadian heritage. The stitched flag had a white background with red trim and was less than a yard in length. In the centre were maple leaves. Each maple leaf accounted for an immediate relative of the family who was serving overseas. The flag was shown in windows of residences from sea to sea and became enormously popular.

Only one leaf was green (or sometimes blue), which meant one of the Laurentiens was yet alive. A third maple leaf had changed to gold (or red), signifying another son had fallen. Aubrey wondered who had been killed and how the message had not reached her sooner.

Scatter though the people that delight in war[147], "The shell that stilled his true brave heart broke mine[148]," Mme. Laurentien sobbed, once Aubrey was inside Vauréal.

His warfare over, the battle fought, the victory won, but dearly bought[149], Frédéric was gone. His pillbox was hit with a

---

[147] A Canadian World War I epitaph
[148] A Canadian World War I epitaph
[149] A Canadian World War I epitaph

shell. No loved ones stood around him to bid a last farewell[150]. Killed near Lens in his first engagement[151], Frédéric was part of a small group who were manning machine guns in a concrete bunker and who were found dead. The chap sent to give them their meals came upon the lot and found them eerily still, like they were cast out of stone. The stray cat that had terrifyingly wandered into the bunker looking for shelter lay dead in one of the gunners' laps. The cat had no visible wounds. Not a trace or mark of any kind was on them. Their internal organs had ruptured beyond recognition from a shell's reverberation hitting the cement of the pillbox. They had died instantly.

Following Hill 70, the Corps was given respite from action. However, in the dominion, repose could not be found. At the end of August, following arduous strain, the Union Government was formed. Letters between English members of Parliament routinely began with enquiries about each other's soldier sons before stating business. Liberals who were in favour of conscription merged with Borden's conservatives. Conservative Francophones resigned from Borden's party.

In response to conscription of young males, conscription of wealth was urged. Government declared they were justifiably conscripting wealth as well as troops. Aubrey recently lost a servant to Bridge, even though Auré had given her a spending limit on her gambling just before he enlisted. This had not mattered before, but stakes were amounting higher. Aristocrats lived tax-free, though spring saw such public persuasion that the Minister to Finance enacted a bill, the Income Tax War Act, that would bring about the fall of the

---

[150] A Canadian World War I epitaph

[151] A Canadian World War I epitaph

Edwardians. "Blood tax," it was so called by Francophones. Britishers were quick to explain it was a "War upon income tax" and were even quicker to denounce those who opposed contributing to the effort as "dangerous traitors."

Summer saw the temporary income tax measure come to pass. Superfluous servants were let go, hunting rifles and paintings were sold at auction, and peacocks and swans were given away. Regulators of food and fuel ordered preservation and noted that hoarders were to be charged. "Meatless Fridays" and "Fuel-less Sundays" were encouraged.

Police searched for rebels of the Monarchy and Empire. Socialist and extreme groups were outlawed. Government censors surveyed all forms of public media that could be injurious to the war. Newspapers of enemy tongue were banned. Non-compliant editors and publishers were sent to prison.

From sea to sea, war gardens were planted. Auré had the head gardener grow a larger vegetable garden. Aubrey asked why. He explained that Peter could forgo jail with employment at Pembina by working in the garden. The unemployed male faced the "anti-loafing" law of prison time.

Along with a change of Parliament, the Military Service Act was legalized on August 28th. All British provinces were in favour, while Quebec was adamant in denouncement of the bill. For what was the only occasion, apart from Confederation, French members of Parliament stated that Quebec might benefit from leaving. Publicly, Laurier stated the law "has in it the seed of discord and disunion." Bruchesci cited, "The country was facing war between faiths that would result in civil war." Newfoundland also found new government and started drafting their own proper Military Service Agreement.

"They're the reason conscription is law! If they sent more sons to fight their own battles, ours wouldn't have to die!" French and British Canada bellowed at each other.

Not a family in the Empire was unaffected by the duration while, over the summer months, Quebec had enormous demonstrations, protests, rallies, and riots against fighting. Across Quebec, once greeted with tomatoes and rotten eggs, recruiting officers' presence was made known with slanderous jeers and rocks. The militiamen were physically attacked, publicly intimidated, worked at near peril to their lives, and puppets of the miliatiamen were mockingly hanged. Damage, in the thousands of dollars, was done to major shopping districts in the French province. Throngs jeered, "Nous en avons assez de L'Union Jack! (We have had enough of the Union Jack!)" Posters showed Borden's picture, the caption reading, "Author of the odious law and blood tax." Sir Hugh Graham, publisher of *Montreal Star,* printed regularly about Quebec's poor involvement and lack of heart towards his King. Graham's summer home was bombed, though not a person was wounded. *The Gazette*, a Montreal steadfast supporter of conscription, had its windows smashed.

One of Papineau's letters was published in the *London Times*, entitled, "The Soul of Canada." Editor-in-Chief of the *Manitoba Free Press,* John Dafoe wrote in his newspaper, *French Canadians are the only race of white men known to quit. It is certainly not the intention of English Canada to see herself bled white while the Quebec shirker may sidestep her duties.*

Officers could no longer give notice. Newspapers, which the Corps read as well, announced the slacker and traitor were at last made to go over there.

The Corps sons replied, *Canada accomplished splendid victories at the village of Arleux-en-Gohelle. "Must be a special assaulting division"* — *an enemy officer said that about our chaps after we took it. The foe can hardly stomach that we are gaining strength after Vimy and not the opposite of breaking down after such a battle. Fresnoy hamlet was captured, after which the British First Army's Commanding Officer cabled Currie that Canada's original 1ˢᵗ Division was "The pride and wonder of the British Army," and we took Avion Trench as well... Our Father has spared me so far, and I would fancy more than anything right now to see the Canadian Rockies... Although the Westmount slacker ought to be forcibly sent across the pond... I'm infuriated every time I pen a letter explaining what it's like over here while treason is simply allowed back in Canada... Our 5ᵗʰ Division, currently in England, can be disassembled to bring the other divisions' numbers up to strength to cover for those so called "Canadians"— mainly the French who are leading all the cowards, staying behind like the traitors they are... Though, the foe is in hot flight against, and in high opinion of, the advancing victorious army of Canada's gallant sons!*

Major Hill Park

The sun was making its way down over Major Hill Park on a calm, warm day. Loons were in the Ottawa River, which curved around The Hill. The band shell's orchestra played to the park's guests. Across the Atlantic, the Corps, endlessly repairing trenches, sang "The Maple Leaf Forever."

Auré was the most stalwart of men. Sunday was the only day of the week he did not work from dawn until dusk. Despite Auré not permitting a master or servant of Pembina to smile on the Sabbath day, Mrs. Major Richardieux could be seen beaming on the arm of her husband, of the dashing Mountie who captured the Victoria Cross for conspicuous gallantry and devotion to duty on the fields of France and Flanders. Parliament faded in the background while the pair strolled in their Sunday whites.

A different feeling was about Ottawa now. During spring and early summer, the Corps was the toast of the Allied Forces. Because conscription had been enacted, there was a tense impression, as though a harsh sentiment lay about the surface of the country, one Auré said would not go away but would worsen until the war ended.

Nico, Albert, and other little ones were playing at tops. They saw their hero down the gardened pathway. They immediately ran across the way and saluted with posture to win the approval of Currie himself. Victoria Cross recipients were not entitled to a formal salute, though they could be saluted from high opinion. Auré said, with a tone reserved solely for leading his men into battle, "At ease, boys." Only then did they break formation and run and skip about him. Auré seemed almost embarrassed by the endless attention he received from his Victoria Cross status.

A lady was coming towards Auré and Aubrey from the opposite direction. Prior to the effort, females were seen with their purse or small dog. Now they carried their knitting bag. Aubrey glanced at the "Knit or Fight" badge the woman wore as the lady walked past them. Aubrey did not own such a badge. She asked, "I'm confused about our army — that is to say, the Canadians," Aubrey clarified, to distinguish from England's army. "The average Canadian soldier has a grade six education, similar to all Empire armies, England included. I assume roughly the same can be said of France's and Germany's soldiers too. In this regard, all armies are on an equal field.

How do you say — the Corps' numerical strength continues to stay steadfast, even in the face of atrocious casualties. The Diggers, or Australians, aside, the Canadian enlistment rate per capita is the highest of all the Empire's armies, England included. Other Allied enlistment rates have come to a standstill, or at least their enlistment crisis is far worse than it is here."

Auré answered her, "Given Canada is still very young, we are only one or two generations removed from a mainly frontier demographic, az opposed to our European counterparts. One could say the Canadians are better prepared for the living conditions at the front; they're more familiar with farm work, manual labour, and the like. It is also safe to zay that most of our lads have handled a rifle and similar firearms before they enlisted.

Of every ten Canadians, roughly four live close to or below the poverty line. The majority of such families manage to carve out a life with one meal per day. Even so, our diet is by and by superior to many European nations, and our troops generally have eh larger, stronger frame than other armies. Canadian soldiers are also paid one dollar and ten cents per day with additional lodging, uniform, and food provided. Ours are the highest earning Tommies of the British Forces. With the lofty unemployment rate being what it was 'ere when war started, that sort of an income was appealing to a lot of ze lads."

Aubrey replied, "Be that as it may, that is not quite what I am referring to. For instance, German males go through two years of military training, then refresher courses for the next five years. So, when their country goes to war, they literally have millions of trained men to call upon. Canada could not realize anywhere near such numbers if she implemented the same military system because her population is nowhere near the German population. The Canadians barely had an army when war was declared. What militia they had only met on weekends for marches and for chumming around. They rarely practiced shooting during training, besides. Though often times outnumbered, outgunned, and outflanked, Canada has become world-renowned for winning battle after battle and 'the Prussians are said to be the greatest military machine ever assembled,'" she repeated, parrot-like. "I don't understand, in this so-called camping adventure that never seems to end, why don't the Germans simply overtake the Canadians?"

Auré thought for a moment, then cleared his throat. "Napoleon said, in warfare, the importance ratio of morale to physical force is three to one. So, in that way, the boys outnumber the Boche by three to one. Napoleon also said, 'God is on the side of the strongest army.' It is eh common misconception that to conquer in battle, the literal weapons and number of soldiers matter more than anything else. 'owever, 'Altiorem, Citius, Fortior' is not what Napoleon meant either. Right is stronger than might[152] and iz essentially what it comes down to. Mathematically, this seemz impossible, but psychologically, it is correct.

Germany is expertly equipped and trained. Their men understand that when their motherland goes to war, they go with 'er. They are mere cogs that constitute a vast military machine, one of silent passivity and tolerance. They understand this too: that they are simply numberz, that they are disposable. This is perhaps the German army's greatest, if not almost singular, flaw. But this flaw is enough to crack, and can eventually topple an army, even one of millionz.

Other countries, like Italy, are resorting to widespread mutiny and mass execution. This year, 'alf the French army mutinied, and thoze remaining are refuzing orders. Nivelle, France's Commander in Chief, was thrown out, reforms were created, and enough furloughs were given to reinstate some semblance of balance.

One would think that, for the size of the gargantuan Russian army, this military could overthrow any foe on her own. However, peasant Russia, too, is facing pandemic desertion. Their troops are mainly illiterate and poverty-stricken due to their government. They are made to leave their villages, which they have 'ardly left before, never mind their country, to fight for their King, who cares very little for zem. After food shortages and labour strikes, which the

---

[152] A Canadian World War I epitaph

ill-supplied army favoured, they overthrew their monarchy. Tsar Nicholas and his family were shot, 'is daughters finished off with clubs after the shots intended for them ricocheted off the family jewels hidden in their corsets."

Aubrey flushed at so untoward a conversation and in public.

Her husband continued, "Our Mother country did not believe colonials would amount to eh thing. We were just numbers to throw into any battle to distract Germany. Left to our own devices, we have made a different system than our superiors. British soldiers are largely equal to Canadian ones, though Canada is now winning every battle that is thrown at her and morale in the Corps 'as never been higher.

Preparation is everything to the start of eh show. The Corps understands that no paper plan survives first contact with the enemy. Currie remains adamant in creating plans for each show to reduce casualties as much as possible. The lads do not always accept this, but Currie cares for his men and prefers to sacrifice shot and shell before he 'as to sacrifice men. The lads curse him with doing whatever it takes to conciliate British High Command. But, he has maintained his ground with British High Command repeatedly for the sake of our soldiers starting in Ypres, where he commanded the 2nd Infantry Brigade and thwarted eh significant German advance. Alderson thought he was the finest Brigadier in the Corps and elevated him in rank after Ypres. Contrary to what is due to him as a Commander-in-Chief, Currie does not reside in abandoned chateaux's. Like his men's quarters, 'is are behind the front lines, where he reads maps and creates plans on usually less than a handful of hours of sleep each night. Currie often asks for, or more accurately, demands more time to prepare." There was actual pride in Auré's voice as he continued, "If Currie was in the main part of the British Forces, he would be court martialed and stripped of all rank and dignity. But because he is merely safeguarding colonials, his shouts, never before uttered in British militarism history, are frequently permitted. That takes courage.

Canadian leaders 'ave always been against separating the Corps, meaning the transferring of one of our divisions to another section of the British Forces. The Diggers are this way, too, whereas the enemy and the other Allies move their men constantly to whatever part of their mammoth forces needs more men. Our lads almost always stay in the zame company or battalion they enlisted under. Therefore, our lads come to know one another and regard the men they fight alongside with like brothers, like family. For instance, if Philippe was at the front, I'd damn well make sure my body was cut to shreds before his was. But when you are fighting amongst strangers, it is every man for 'imself. This is one of the biggest factors why the Diggers and the Corps will come out of this the two superior armies of either side.

And you 'ave to command respect before you can command men to do anything well. Treat eh man like a gentleman and he will act one. Our officers are taught to be firm but fair. To lead their men like fathers do their sons, like shepherds do their flocks. After eh fray, our Commanders question their men of 'ow they are and wait with blankets and hot drink. How can one not feel loyalty towards officers who make themselves of service to their men? That 'umility would be preposterous in the main British Force. But we do not see that as the weakness they do.

Other Allied armies 'ave and will continue to pave the way for the Canadians to succeed in battle. A number of times, we could not have won the fray we did without other Allied militaries fighting there before us. Az well, the Canadian army is still incredibly reliant on the BEF for stock and logistics. Their staff officers, artillery and additional supporting soldiers enable the Corps to pay closer attention to the actual battles themselves. But, with each battle the Corps wins, our boys see they can fight and perform well. Our senior officers 'ave confidence in the infantry and, in turn, the men believe in themselves and their leaders. Canadian generals treat their men as men and not as numbers. Our regular privates are expected to contribute and offer insight to further the Corps. Each soldier, to the newest recruit, is expected to be innovative and is given eh specific role. In turn, that role gives each soldier identity, which is what happened with Vimy Ridge.

Currie wanted all the troops to see maps of the Vimy Ridge area, which Byng allowed. British High Command thought we 'ad gone irrevocably mad in allowing our regular soldiers to see maps and plans beforehand. Such eh venture had never been seen before in British military history. Before Vimy, maps were reserved for officers or generals because the average Tommy was thought to be too dishonest to be privy to that knowledge. In other words, in the chaos of battle, the regular soldier would always go into any given battle blind, and would figure out the terrain for the first time as he literally went over the top, or be left awaiting orders from an officer who could already have been killed. Before Vimy, the common private was given no role at all, other than to proceed as far as he could and usually on his own. Fighting like this is reminiscent of a pawn in another's man game. This iz similar to Germany's system.

However, the entire Corps was made privy to the maps. Forty thousand maps were given out, roughly one for every two men. The average private was given the same information as his commanding officer. All ranks were acquainted with the battle plan ahead of time. The 'eightened sense of worth was exponential. One of the officers was quoted as saying, 'We had faith in our men and took them entirely into our confidences. We trusted that no one would desert and divulge information to the enemy and no one did.' One hundred thousand Canadians served at Vimy Ridge, and not one account was documented of a soldier who abandoned and betrayed that trust to the enemy. One has to wonder how many countries in history can claim this of their citizens.

Orators shouting for God, King, and Empire will make any gentleman rush off to battle. Those things will get men to the front of any smash. But all of that fades once one climbs over the top. And if that 'ype does not fade, that sense of duty does, once one sees one's friends, brothers, blown to bloody rags.

The battle is won by the men who fall[153], az well as that mutual respect, shown to all ranks, which translates to undying devotion to the officers, coupled with that hope, which in hard times decides everything, and confidence; those traits act as an invisible but protective shield over the Corps. When they go into battle, they fall back on one another, and that gives the lads something worth fighting for. And that's how an army overtakes another several times its size. As long as the Corps stays the way she is, no foe can overtake 'er. Even the formidable German army cannot penetrate our lines.

And it takes courage to enter eh battle where no one thinks you belong — to be laughed at, looked down-upon, treated as vile by the foe. That is warfare. But to be treated that same way by your superiors, then ordered into the feces-laced,

---

[153] A Canadian World War I epitaph

God-forsaken trenches they leave for us, before finishing their battles for them and delivering unto them victory, that is nothing short of, quite frankly, unparalleled character. Don't tell the boys zis, but they deserve the respect they're getting, given that one way an army's worth can be proven is that the enemy respects 'er.

This is the genesis of our nation. Canada is giving back to the Empires, the mother countries who colonized her to show them what she's made of, and she's proving her sterling worth. As our boys are pushing this colony-by-law into nationhood, Borden, who's spear'eading the campaign for the Prime Ministers, will ask the monarchy for greater autonomy amongst the dominions. And the King damn well understands he should grant that or risk losing one of the greatest armies the Empire will ever yield."

Late September 1917

At the Sons of England meeting, roll call of eligible men not in uniform was performed. Similar roll calls were being done from coast to coast. Peter was one of the ones left standing in front of the entire ballroom. The Richardieux were invited as guests because Auré was made an honorary member of the club, given his Victoria Cross status.

The Governor General personally assured Auré that a pardon was in the works, on behalf of the Mounted Force, for the trial he was made to endure. Auré had testified before God, King, and Empire, and the word of a gentleman would not go disbelieved.

Once one of the most hated men of the country, Auré was now among the most admired of the Empire. A circular was making rounds petitioning Auré for a Major General. Just as the Kaiser was Germany's Beast of Berlin, a Welsh-born man who was taught English in school, Lloyd George was Britain's Welsh Wizard, and to French Canada, Auré was the Orangeman of Ottawa.

The sky was grey and overcast. The surrounding terrain was barren of all life form. Like always, it had just rained the night before. The Corps was on a mud track as they marched towards the next battlefield. Birds or wild animals were not to be seen in the dreary, desolate landscape. The continuation of boots hitting dirt and mud was the only sound heard for miles. October saw Newfoundland a part of an overall campaign to take the high ground of an objective. In the opening days of the campaign, the regiment assaulted on the northern front of Ypres in the Battle of Langemark, what the Newfoundlanders called Broembeek. In recent months, the British attempted to take the objective unaccompanied by a creeping barrage. The result was they were slaughtered almost beyond reason. What the British fought through could not be justly articulated. The Anzacs were ordered to depart from the same posting that proved unattainable. The Corps was then ordered to take the objective. After more than two years of trench warfare, the Canadians were unsettled by the demeanor of the Australians that were leaving. The whistling of "Take Me Back to Canada" or the salutation between Allied Armies of "Cheer up! Don't be downhearted!" were scarcely to be heard. The Canadians were being watched because the Germans considered them a force to be reckoned with. The Corps was a distinguished Allied army. What could be worse than anything the Canadians had yet faced? In a muddy corner in northwest Belgium, it would seem as though Hell itself had opened and was releasing its demons.

Preparation for Passchendaele

Passchendaele, or the Third Battle of Ypres, was an engagement no military wanted to undertake. The Somme was confirmed the worst show by the Corps. However, once the Corps moved into their new residence, at the outskirts of the Passchendaele area, paradoxically the longest standing veterans were at an utter loss to describe what they saw before them.

After Germany took control of Belgium at the beginning of the war, the Passchendaele area remained the final region not held by the foe. In the Ypres salient and in close proximity to the flattened Passchendaele village, a ridge was to be taken again. The territory proved immensely important for the Allies and was where many of the initial shows of the war occurred. Level countryside that constituted the battlefield was devastated by the previous year's combats. Along with everything else in the land, the dykes, the irrigation, and the drainage networks had been annihilated. Months prior to the Corps' arrival, rain fell in sheets and had yet to cease.

The landscape had been obliterated beyond comparison. The area proved to be an oceanic view of wallow. The muck was nearly indescribable: six miles of endless, massive shell-holes, predominantly water-burdened.

Currie ordered the reconstruction of Allied lines ahead of battle. Rainfall deluged the area for the length of the Corps' time spent preparing to assault the ridge. From dawn to dusk, soldiers repaired trench walls that caved ceaselessly from the downpour. Cadavers had yet to be removed from pillboxes, one of the only solid articles left in the whole of the area. Legs were continually scratched by rusty barbed wire below the wretched water. The muck was revolting. The wallow devoured men while they slept. It was impossible to traverse through it by any means. The expansive quagmire that was the battlefield required the laying of what the soldiers referred to as duckwalks or bath-mats. The narrow wooden boards were placed to fashion a network of pathways for the Corps to fight their way forward on top of the muck. Duckboards were predominantly laid on the decaying cadavers of thousands of Allies, including Canadian Tommies. Limbs and faces of maggoty, rotting corpses were used for markers. Corpses were some of the only tools at the Corps' hands. The sun's rays caused the cadavers to become bloated and blackened, and they produced gas that would leave a man's respiratory system in ruins. The stench could be smelled miles behind No Man's Land.

Mustard gas would rest quiescent and find concealment in shell-holes and mounds of brick during nighttime. The gas would rise with the sun, causing entire parties of working troops to crumple, unconscious, to the ground. A lad grew disheartened, constantly biding time to examine if he proved gassed. Volumes of gas would stay lively for hours at a time but would stay in the quagmire and water for fortnights.

At the bottom of trenches and shell-holes, frogs abounded, while slugs and horned beetles took over the walls of trenches. Chiefly at nighttime, though at all times, one could hear boots wrested continuously from the wallow over the landscape, a sound that soldiers would recollect the remainder of their lives.

Of the few hard routes in the area, the cadavers of transport horses were shoved to the side to make way for ones who could move stock and supplies. The foe, with the intention of doing away with Allied work animals, drenched and inundated the terrain with gas and shrapnel. Consequently, the legs and hooves of the draught horses were permanently maimed from gas. Lives of horses were calculated by weeks. So frightened were they, horses would eat the reigns, harnesses, and blankets of the others from extreme collywobbles. Severely shaking and tottering, the horses suffered far past what could be put into words.

Sam Brownes were taken off by Officers. To the foe, their smart belts easily distinguished commander from regular. Given the environment, the fray would have no master; each soldier would fight solo. The battle was bitterly resisted by Currie, who guesstimated that of his men, there would be 16,000 casualties. At the beginning of October, Currie told Haig, "Let the Germans have it — keep it — rot in it! Rot in the mud! It isn't worth a drop of blood!" If Currie had been an English General, the defiance he demonstrated most probably would have had him dismissed. Vehemently resisting to go into battle until the poor bloody infantry could be suitably safeguarded by more artillery, Currie appealed for greater time. The petition was rescinded by Haig. As Lloyd George wrote after the Somme, *Whenever the Germans found the Canadian Corps coming into the line, they prepared for the worst.*

Passchendaele

Outnumbered, outgunned, and outflanked, the Canadians took Passchendaele. Nine Victoria Crosses were granted to the Corps. Currie's prediction proved true: there were 16,404 casualties sustained, of which more than 4,000 were deaths. Still facing considerable rains, the divisions alternated attacking the ridge in four separate pushes. The Corps went into action at 0540 hours on October 26th. The second assault transpired on October 30th. On both days, the 3rd and 4th Divisions fought. Hundreds of yards were taken. The 1st and 2nd Divisions then went into action. After the third push, the ridge was in Canadian hands on November 6th. The sections of the elevated ground not captured on the third assault were taken after the fourth drive, the day Passchendaele ended, on November 10th.

Seldom would a man audibly detail Passchendaele to his wife or chaplain for the remainder of his life. Canadian troops penned in their diaries what they were unable to speak. High commendation was given to the bearers for their stamina, perseverance, and valour. At times, bearers were reduced to trudging through waist-high wallow. The bearers faced the difficulty of moving past the stagnant wounded, resembling the dead that the chemical earth quickly joined them with. It was commonplace to see men with fingers chewed off in turmoil during unexplainable pain. Innumerable craters covered with slime prevented the wounded, who crawled in for protection, from surfacing. They were left in agony and drowned among the corpses that inhabited their final resting place.

All armies shared their surroundings with rats. The black and, most of all, the brown rat were despicable creatures. They grew to be as large as cats. They became unbothered and, overtime, plucky to the presence of humans. Outnumbering soldiers by millions, they would devour a defenseless man.

A German General penned, *Unimaginable things had been suffered and performed by the troops, and unimaginable were the demands made upon the nerves of the commanders.*

Canadian medical personnel noted on their charts, *Nearly everyone had been more or less gassed.*

Haig seldomly if at all complimented colonials, but he extended exceptional praise and declared the 72nd advance was, "A feat of arms which would go down in the annals of British history as one of the great achievements of a single unit." Post victory, Haig was shown the landscape. As he sobbed openly, he wept, "My God! Did we actually send men to fight in this?!"

The soldier in the High Command's party replied, "It is worse up along the way, Sir." He paused then said, "Where the fighting took place."

The empire's spirit was never so downhearted as in the aftermath of Passchendaele. For Canada, the show was one more conquest for all that her esprit de corps suffered immeasurably. Currie faced a furious Corps. He responded, "The human body was never called upon to endure more than what was suffered by our men in the trenches."

Tremendous artillery extremely disfigured France's northern countryside. The chalk soil, by way of steel, became overwhelmingly imbued by lime that caused immense shrubbery growth. The botany that grew in the aftermath of conflicts was a symbolic remembrance of battle. Recovering boys, wearing white and blue uniforms complete with red ties, would convalesce out-of-doors in the sunshine. The lads adored resting in the fields, specifically the flowered ones. Outdoor makeshift theatres allowed for breaks from their unvaried days. Drag was a favourite throughout the Corps. France often remarked, throughout the effort, that she had not seen the petal bloom in like ampleness heretofore. The poppy flourished, as scarlet as the maple leaf, unto her sons of Passchendaele[154].

---

[154]   Passchendaele remains Canada's most horrific battle. The poppy is Canada's main symbol of remembrance for veterans. The poppy is described at the end of the Passchendaele chapter to express that Canada remembers its soldiers who have been wounded or killed in action.

Chateau Laurier

"I don't plan on voting; not personally. After all, it's my right as a British subject not to vote," Peter shrugged. At Chateau Laurier, Peter and Aubrey were having tea and walnut cake.

Queen Victoria enjoyed dining at home. Her son preferred to dine publicly. The first grand era of restaurants was ushered into being. Females were banned from bars and could only eat in the upstairs of restaurants.

"I won't either. The day before that mock parliament bit at Winnipeg's Walker theatre, the Premier of Manitoba told those suffragettes himself, 'Take it from me, Ms. McClung; nice women don't want the vote,'" Aubrey quoted agreeably.

Once more, much had changed in the dominion in recent months. Autumn saw Parliament fall into dissolution. The gerrymander that Borden conspired would not be paralleled again in Canadian history. Countrymen, aristocratic and poor, felt superb agreement to defend their country. Which country to defend was causing fault lines that were ever fracturing. To vote Union proved one agreed with the effort, conscription, and the unwavering fight to wrest victory from a foe that now included French Canada. To cast a ballot against Union showed cowardice led by the Kaiser, Laurier, and Bourassa.

By law, soldiers were disallowed to vote during wartime. The newly enacted Military Voters Act gave all men in uniform the vote, including British-born service men.

Those born in enemy countries were denied the vote who had moved to Canada since 1902 and whose mother language, regardless of year of immigration, was of the Austro-Hungarian Empire.

Government made hushed affair permitting Bluebirds to be the first women allowed the federal vote. Solely "Patriotic women" were franchised. Next-of-kin women were given the right because allowing military relatives the vote was morally correct. This amendment concerned all females who had an immediate relative, excluding nurses, fighting overseas. Considerably more English than French females were given the franchise. Quebec Members of Parliament were outraged at females being given the right in the first place. The exceedingly conservative province vocalized complete lack of propriety at the very idea.

Quebec received all scabs imaginable. Much to the dislike of generals, posters changed to *Quebec must not rule of all of Canada, A vote for Laurier is a vote for Bourassa is a vote for the Kaiser,* and *Who would the Kaiser vote for? Liberal or Union? Laurier-Bourassa Reign of Terror,* ran the headline of the *Halifax Herald.*

The front pages of Quebec newspapers were ceaseless with their language and culture being barred from Ontario Schools. With the Infamous Regulation 17 at the forefront, political meetings in Quebec saw more unsettlements, disturbances, and riots than history would write of any other election for the province. Management became well-nigh impossible at city council meetings. Politicians hands became bloodied as they pounded their fists on desks, attempting to control crowds.

Brawls became commonplace. The government responded by outlawing disturbances at political meetings. Widespread public disapproval of the duration saw police dispatched regularly by mayors to dissolve such happenings. Across the province, brutality was habitually found at enlistment assemblies, which were often times hastily made to cease.

In English Canada, soldiers on leave would disallow Liberal candidates to speak at public events. For the initial time since war started, coverage of the effort moved from the front pages. The looming election and conscription were now at the forefront of discussion.

The masses said conscription was largely unnecessary; the 5th Division had been assembled for two years already and could be sent across the Channel. Others stated the unfairness of making those serve who had service members currently fighting. Families who did not have any relations serving should be made to go. Conscripts were made to register the day Passchendaele ended.

The large electric sign mounted atop Chateau Laurier read, "Buy Victory Bonds." The fourth of what had come to be called "Victory" loans was an attestation to honour and patriotism. Bonds were bought in the millions in the dominion. Auré said he would match dollar for dollar what Ottawa raised for the Patriotic Fund during the month of November to let the boys know Ottawa was still thinking of them. Newspapers abounded across the main seating area at Chateau Laurier. The casualties of Passchendaele seemed well-nigh endless. Most present were in discussion of the political landscape. The Lutheran and Catholic vote and the German vote were deeply analyzed by eligible Canadians. The Daughters of the Empire meeting had adjourned. Over the previous year, they had fundraised a Naval ship, a hospital wing, and several motorized ambulances.

The women, lifted by elevator to the main floor, walked past Aubrey and Peter. Chit-chattering amongst themselves, they discussed the weekly meeting: "Resoluteness considered of, firstly, loyalty to King and Queen and Empire. Secondly, of prayer that, 'money, labour, and service be conscripted of every man and woman, so that all may equally do their duty to their King, country and Empire.'" All wore their organization's insignia. Attached to their Daughters of the Empire badge were service bars. A blue bar was worn for a husband, red for a son, and white for a daughter in uniform. Every member had at minimum one bar tied to her badge. A number wore all three and many wore mourning crepe.

Henrietta was pocketing her Card of Honour from the Canadian Field Comforts Commission. She had been commended upon knitting her 100th pair of socks. The Ottawa branch was modeling their latest campaign after Newfoundland's branch. Newfoundland had a drive where six pairs of socks were knit for each son in uniform. Other armies willingly bought the much sought after sock from the Regiment. The Women's Patriotic Association on the island were given awards for their grey knits and took great satisfaction, although maybe with slight exaggeration, in creating the level of excellence for the Empire's military socks.

Owing to the fact that intercourse was largely thought to be a compulsory physical act for males, Canadian High Command made contraceptives legal a number of years into the war. Also allowed were "Maisons des tolerances," or brothels. In red light districts, blue lamp areas were designated to be for officers. Red lamps were for the regulars. Nurses were not permitted in the separate venereal disease hospitals due to the category of the illness.

The military attempted to control the alarmingly high cases of venereal diseases. Docking pay was a minor deterrent for troops who became infected. More grievously, letters to wives of the afflicted soldiers, detailing their husband's sexually contracted condition and therefore unfaithfulness, were also used as means to halt the growing epidemic. Government quickly ended the severe punishment, due to the number of suicides by the recipients of the official documentation.

Aubrey had the envelope in hand. She wondered if she would receive a similar missive. The War Office letter to Mrs. Neville Smith, explaining Mr. Smith's sexually contracted disease, had been mistakenly delivered to Pembina. The Harrington's estate bordered the far edge of Pembina. The late Mr. Smith, a pilot, had been introduced to Henrietta by Hugh when all of them were on leave in England. After Smith's commanding officer's approval of the match, Smith made Henrietta his wife six months after their introduction. She had become his widow immediately after losing Hugh. Aubrey was not unsure Henrietta was sleeping with Auré. *How degrading: he prefers an industrialist's daughter to me*, thought Aubrey. Peter suggested giving Henrietta the letter to show her who was the superior lady.

A smiling Aubrey went over to the group of ladies.

"Killed in action. Beloved daughter of Angus and Mary Maud MacDonald. Brantford[155]—" Henrietta trailed off, speaking to the member next to her as Aubrey came up to them.

---

[155]   A Canadian Nursing Sister World War I epitaph

"Do please excuse me, Mrs. Smith. This letter was brought to Pembina quite mistakenly. Unfortunately, I opened the post, as I did not read the address on the envelope first. Naturally, I thought it addressed to me. I hope you can excuse the misunderstanding. I did not read further than 'Dear Mrs. Smith.'" Tears started falling down Henrietta's cheeks as her husband's last letter, supposed lost, had been found. "May his reward be as great as his sacrifice[156]," offered Aubrey in false condolence. Aubrey would never forget the gratefulness shown in Henrietta's eyes before she turned and hurried away. The sound of Henrietta's wailing from the powder room was reminiscent of a puppy that was stepped on by a thoroughbred at Pembina and left to die a slow, torturous death.

---

[156]   A Canadian World War I epitaph

Raimbault

By far and away one of North America's oldest and loveliest cities, Quebec City was situated on the famed St. Lawrence. City posters showed Germans befouling a Roman Catholic church in favour of conscription, though to no avail. Chateau Frontenac, Notre-Dame Basilica, Rue de Saint Jean and Du Petit-Champlain saw scarcely a male maimed or female in mourning. There were so many men about as well. *How startlingly different from the rest of the country,* thought Aubrey.

Raimbault, Auré's childhood home, was located far from the city and well into the country. Ivy clung to its towering dark red brick. The ornate windows, daunting and numerous, seemed to indicate that their master's secrets were well hidden. The estate did not have the brightness of Pembina but a refined dignity and charm only age can effectuate. Auré's mother could trace her roots to Les Filles du Roi (The King's Daughters). From her ancestor's humble beginnings came textilsts who partnered with merchants who flattered prominent industrialists, one of whose daughters married Lower Canada gentry. His father's side had acquired their fortune through Rupert's Land long ago.

Aubrey came to understand her husband more through his family. Pictures abounded of the large and close-knit family.

Somber mood found the Richardieux at the Vatican. A guard stood on either side of the group. All the daughters were veiled. Out of jealousy, Aubrey noted Mme. Richardieux's veil nearly touched the ground. Auré, Philippe, and Seraphin were in tailcoats. Before reaching adulthood, Auré already stood taller than his father. Another picture was of his parents at the inauguration of Pope Pius X. In later years, a picture showed Seraphin and Philippe at an anniversary for the Chevaliers de Colomb (Knights of Columbus Club). Auré was one of the only gentlemen she knew who did not belong to a social club. In one photo, as captain, Philippe beamed in the center of his rowing team. He led the University of Quebec to championship. Numerous pictures were of the girls or their beautiful mother, from which Auré inherited his features. Many pictures were of vacations in locals around the world or of their favourite resort, Muskoka. Apart from ones of Auré as a child, he was not in any other photos. Aubrey was unsure if that was due to his divorce or from lack of attending functions when a kodak was present.

A warm, sunny afternoon found the nanny and René traipsing in from out of doors. They had come from rolling boiling maple syrup in the snow to make toffee. Once René's layers were unwrapped, Seraphin gifted his grandson a teddy bear. René mistook the stuffed beaver for the wealthy Canadian-born British cabinet minister. Seraphin chuckled at the misunderstanding while his youngest grandchild toddled off with his newfound companion. René immensely enjoyed his time at Raimbault, spoilt as he was. He loved much[157] the physical affection from his French relatives, so startlingly at variance with his English upbringing.

---

[157]   A Canadian World War I epitaph

The Richardieux knew not a single man, and certainly not a woman, in uniform, nor had they lost a servant to the effort. The men in the family spoke relentlessly of conscription. For liberty, truth, and righteousness[158], across all of Quebec, signatures were penned to petitions and meetings opposing conscription were taking place, of which all Auré's male relations were a part. Ill-treatment found the uncommon soldier. Auré said courage was necessary for a Frenchman to enlist. This was said without any pride. In fact, he seemed to take no pride whatsoever in his military service. Auré seemed to be under such stress that he no longer spoke unless spoken to. The muscle he had lost at the front had yet to fully return, though their chef was doing everything he could to reconcile his master's tired physique. Since Auré was now safely returned, one would think he would be in higher spirits. But the alarming rate he had aged during his time away was not rescinding from his frame, though months had passed since his return.

One dark evening over supper was the only time Raimbault acknowledged a conversation of war during their stay. The effort was solely referred to as "England's war." The patriarch of the family stood at regular height and had dark features, as did all his offspring, excepting his two sons, who were considerably taller than him. Conducting business inter-provincially, Seraphin was impeccably bilingual. His accent was nearly as dashing as his son's.

He freely served[159] numerous courses. Seraphin asked, over the fifth dish, "What was that spring battle, again?"

English Canada, in its third year of the effort, had Welsh rabbit as replacement for meat as a main dish for war dinners,

---

[158]   A Canadian World War I epitaph
[159]   A Canadian World War I epitaph

however the protein could hardly pass for meat. Quebec was carrying on as though no war existed, despite the noxious atmosphere in the province from the war.

Auré responded, "Vimy Ridge, Sir."

For Quebec, Vimy Ridge did not mean a great deal, aside from the Van Doos distinguishing themselves at that battle. The province found great pride in taking a stand against the war.

Philippe dined with the family that evening. Philippe shared his time between Quebec City and Montreal. All the members of the Richardieux family could claim great intelligence. Great peace have they which love thy law[160], Philippe was a lawyer and oversaw the legal aspects of the family business. A good son, a good brother, and a good fellow[161], Philippe was a sound gentleman in countenance. Quite tall, though not so tall as his brother, whom he adored from afar, and with dark blue eyes, he had a dashing frame, though not overly so. One could feel his backbone, and yet he had a gentle disposition about him. An ardent lover of military and history, Philippe was extremely versed in the dominion's heritage and current war. He greatly enjoyed discussing dominion history, particularly its military history.

Philippe explained further, "The battle for Vimy Ridge is extraordinarily important not only to our military history but to our country in its entirety. For the first time in Canadian history, all provinces and the territory fought together. Our military will also continue to fight together for the remainder of the duration. Every Canadian should have a working knowledge of Vimy Ridge. Every Canadian should be able to explain the generalities of that show. For they say over the

---

[160] A Canadian World War I epitaph
[161] A Canadian World War I epitaph

three, four days in which that battle took place, our colony became a nation. We took the ridge when no other Allied military was able to do so. In turn, we are starting to think that perhaps Canada is no longer fighting as subordinate to the mother country, but she is fighting at England's side as more of an equal to England in her own right."

Philippe added, "In July, Currie was knighted by the King on the very blasted fields of Vimy he led to liberty and under these big white tents. I assume Currie thought that was better than the ceremony taking place at Buckingham palace.

Father, there is a smart picture of the King, in his regular military uniform, on the Vimy grounds with Currie. It was taken just yards in front of the two. There are a few more officers behind them on this path. They are walking over a duckboard on a narrow tract of earth. On both sides of the tract are endless pools of water and churned-up soil as far as one can see. Currie is just behind the King, who is on a tour of the area. You have to wonder at how proud Currie must have been to show him that."

Seraphin inquired, "Was that the battle where you captured your Victoria Cross?"

"It was at the Somme show." Auré flushed a bit upon answering. He had not been part of that glorious battle. Aubrey thought nothing could again shock her.

"Do you correspond with any of your mates still?"

"The Somme waz devastating to the Corps — she was well-nigh ruined. Most of the chaps who I waz with are now gone."

Seraphin said resignedly, "I understand after Vimy, when it was time to choose a new Corps Commander, London did not confer with the Canadian cabinet whatsoever in the agreement procedure? Parliament was enraged." Seraphin did not understand all war terminology in response to Auré's conversations.

"The Red Baron…"

"Le Petit Rouge, Monsieur," Philippe explained.

"What battle is currently raging?"

Seraphin's youngest son answered, "Passchendaele only ended. Papineau fell."

"Yes, of course." Seraphin understood the name. French Canada saw her promising Talbot fall days after the campaign began.

Philippe continued, "With the war frenzy in 1914, he managed to register with the Princess Pat's. He saw action for a more than a year. He was the one who said the second battle of Ypres was 'the birth pangs of our nationality.' Then he became a staff officer and later moved to the War Office Records at our headquarters in France in acknowledgment of his most likely becoming Prime Minister."

Talbot Papineau was faultlessly bilingual, a scholar, and a brilliant orator and writer. He had been raised in both cultures, being the son of one of Quebec's most famous families and an aristocratic American mother. The unwed, dashing, charismatic, athletic, thirty-four-year-old lawyer had been suited by many to turn Prime Minister.

"However, he felt wrong by not being with his troops, father. He went back to the front and to the Princess Pat's as a company commander. He was conceded rank of acting Major later in summer. At Passchendaele, the regiment spearheaded the assault early the morning of October 30th. He said to another Major, Nevin, with whom Auré is acquainted—"

The elder brother nodded. Auré was uncharacteristically silent during supper. The only time Aubrey would see her husband submissive was in front of Seraphin.

"'You know, Hughie, this is suicide.' His last recorded words. A shell tore him in half as he went over the top. His body was never located."

The *Ottawa Citizen* printed, *Many people who had no personal acquaintance with him regarded him as the one man specifically fitted to lead in the task of reconciling the two races.* England's *Daily Mail* ran a cover story calling him "A lost hero" for Canada.

The family ate in silence for a small while.

Aubrey enquired, "I do not understand the haunting muck of Passchendaele. Everyone talks endlessly of it. It is only muck and this is war. Surely gentlemen can handle mud if riff-raff cannot."

Since he understood the mud better than anyone at the table, Auré answered, "In regard to the wallow, the rules change from the glue-like substance normally found in No Man's Land. The muck at Passchendaele is unlike anything seen before in thickness and adhesiveness. The weather, particularly the rain and winters, are among the most frightful in decades in northern France, coupled with such extraordinary artillery bombardments, which make for a stupendous landscape, quite unseen before. The ghastly, dreadful porridge is so villainous that if one man becomes stuck, four men are required to pull 'im out. It's the most disheartening thing to watch a man trying to free himself from the muck. Only if one sees it can one understand how bad it is. If they struggled in the mud they sunk further and to their deaths. The Passchendaele battle was akin to a different world, where lads and wildlife simply vanished in wallow filled craters large enough to devour residences. Although, the porridge did offer one positive: it greatly reduced the explosive impact of shells, or the shells enfolded in the muck or did not go off at all, saving a great deal of our men as they fought or crawled their way forward, inch by bloody inch."

Philippe added, "It was said nothing could make the Corps ready for what they came upon at Passchendaele. Our longest standing veterans, who have been in France and Belgium since 1915 and came out of that fray, said that if they had the choice of doing that battle again or the war in its entirety to not go through Passchendaele, they would prefer do the war over. The Canadians were at Passchendaele for maybe five weeks. Others who made it out of that battle said no soldier who saw action there could return to the man he was before. Concerning Passchendaele, when reading soldiers letters, to say one is unnerved is nearly a catastrophic understatement. *It feels as though the devil is in the room with one.* For instance, on a summer day, when a lone cloud covers the sun and you are momentarily in darkness: this is what you feel when reading about this battle. It is as though the birds know what is being read and cease singing. Everything about you stops and the room becomes entirely quiet. You feel *too* alone. And this is when they say the devil attacks. You can *feel* the horridness of the battle, as though you are there with the soldiers standing at the start of the Passchendaele fields, looking out at the landscape. But you do not want to see further than that — meaning, the actual battle, because you intuitively know the battle itself would be too horrid to see — and what you feel is so frightening you would not want anyone else to be at the start of those fields with you. One way the nature of the battle can be proven is that none of our soldiers celebrate the incredible victory. That being said, the British Force and the Anzacs made it possible for us to take it; our army could not have captured it without theirs. But all the lads say the same thing: that Passchendaele is their idea of hell. The 22nd said it was an experience they would rather forget, and they took no pride in capturing it.

Another point: Whenever Passchendaele is discussed, the dynamics of the battle, that is to say literally how it was taken, are never explained, unless that is asked for. But concerning all our other battles, especially Vimy, the details are discussed endlessly. It is as though explaining the combat of Passchendaele is an afterthought or seems entirely beside the point when discussing the fray. The only thing spoken of is how bad it was. No one even celebrates that Canada captured it. Have you noticed that, Auré, in regulars' correspondences to their families and officers' testimonies to High Command?"

His brother merely nodded; a silent acknowledgement was all that was necessary.

"I can only read their letters for so long before having to stop and be about others. I have never had this happen to me when reading of our other battles, and I have read a few thousand hours of the dominion's military heritage — that is to say, nearly all of it. One actually has to force oneself to read about Passchendaele, whereas all our other battles are a privilege to read of, no matter how much those frays' casualties affect you. You literally don't want to pick up their letters about Passchendaele because then it starts. It's as though you can hear the moans of the dying and wounded when you have their letters in hand. When you are done reading accounts of the battle, you actually want to leave the room you're in, and leave the documentation in the room too, so as to remove yourself from the situation. I assume this is the same for everyone who reads about Passchendaele. But, I will say this, the fact that our military earned the most Victoria Crosses in our history in the most horrific battle history will write for warfare — that being Passchendaele — speaks to the integrity of Canadian soldiers. Our boys are the pride of the country. A Victoria Cross could never be downplayed, but the Victoria Crosses earned at Passchendaele should be noted for the environment in which they were earned. And, what Haig said about Vancouver's advance at the battle — if that's not praise, I don't know what is."

The record number of Victoria Crosses bestowed to Canada in a single battle would stand a century to follow.

A chill was in the air. All were in favour of a change in topic. Philippe cheerily carried on, "You know, of the seemingly endless facts I've read about our history, I've always remembered the number of Canadian dead at Vimy, down to the single unit. I've never had to write this number down. I assume this goes for every Canadian who researches their history. The week before last, we saw action at Cambrai. Alongside the British, our Cavalry Brigade and Newfoundland, who saw action mainly at Masnières and Marcoing, fought with distinction. It seems every time you read about Newfoundland in action, they fight with distinction," Philippe consented. "The Cambrai smash is considerable to our military history. And Newfoundland will acquire her title of 'Royal' in December. Only twice in Empire history has 'Royal' been granted to a regiment in wartime: once in the 1600's and the other time in the 1880's."

Auré asked his brother, "'ave you seen that picture of Borden and the wounded fellow in 'ospital in France? The wounded is sitting upright in bed speaking to the Prime Minister. Borden is sitting on the edge of the bed. There are a few officers and a bluebird standing close by, given the chap is speaking to the Prime Minister. The tall windows show light streaming in from a charming spring day. The photography itself is lovely. The chap sustained his injuries at Vimy; he is in hospital recovering."

Philippe replied in the affirmative that he had seen the photo.

Auré continued, "It is surely one of the most beautiful photos in Canadian history. Essentially, it is the country saying to the lads 'we see you.' Every Canadian should be able to explain the significance of that picture." Auré went on, "Or that kodak of the lads being evacuated from Vimy? Trucks are driving down this dirt road and the tops are off the trucks. The trucks are loaded with men. Some lads are hanging over the edges of or are sitting on the edge of ze trucks too. All men are of course in uniform and are waving at the camera as they drive down the road in the opposite direction. All of them have one hand raised triumphantly in the air and are smiling, for such is hard to find on the front lines. No Canadian can look at that picture without their 'eart filling with pride and joy."

Aubrey added, "Or the one of Billy Bishop on a landing strip? The photo was taken rather close to twenty-three year old Bishop in his plane. One can only see his slight, toned frame seated in the open cockpit and the immediate plane about him. The field behind him can barely be viewed. He is not wearing equipment, helmet, or goggles, just his uniform. He is looking at the photographer with his blue eyes and a devilish half grin — apparently, he is a flamboyant extrovert — with a light wind in his dark blond hair. What a dazzling shot. That is, to be sure, one of my favorite pictures of the effort."

Auré told Philippe, "There is common appreciation between ze English and French-Canadian units. The French Canadians are deemed to be quite without fear throughout the Corps."

Seraphin knew of one battalion of the Corps in its entirety: The Van Doos.

He tapped his cigar while stating, "The 22nd is the only battalion (1,000 men) whose official language is French in a four-million-man army. That would infuriate anyone. But, of course, the Empire does not understand this, least of all English Canada. And English Canada can't even pronounce the word 'twenty-second' in French properly, so they gave us a bastardized name, whereas the majority of Francophone soldiers are, because they have to be, fluent in English, and they will spend the whole of the duration—"

"Calling us ignorant," Seraphin and both sons finished serenely.

Philippe went on, "The 22nd saw her first engagement at Courcelette in fall of last year. It was one of Canada's finest battles. The Commanding Officer — Auré, you've met him."

"That iz, Lieutenant-Colonel Thomas-Louis Tremblay."

Courcelette would remain one of Canada's most glorious battles.

Philippe turned to their father and said, "Every time the 22nd goes into action, it is not solely a battle, but the honour of French Canada on the line as well. Tremblay is said to take this matter to a very serious degree to ensure his men do justice to French Canada."

Seraphin added, "Given the 22nd is one of the country's finest battalions, that speaks to the valour of French Canadians: they can fight and be the superior soldiers in another man's war."

Philippe explained the 22nd at Courcelette to the table at large. "Really makes one jolly proud. The 20th, 21st, 25th, and 26th were there as well. To start with, the outskirts of Courcelette saw the 2nd and 3rd Divisions advance the morning of September 15th. A creeping barrage was used, though it fell into disarray. She was raised one hundred metres ahead of enemy lines. Therefore, our assaulting first waves became privy to their machine guns. Even so, we were victorious in the attack. A tank aided the 20th and 21st to take the sugar refinery that was a strongpoint on the village's outer edge. The primary trenches of the town were taken soon afterwards.

Then, the 22nd and 25th were ordered from reserves to attack in the evening, at six o'clock. The 26th was with them in buttress. In broad daylight, following only a dainty bombardment and without jumping off starting points, they attacked."

Aubrey interrupted, "Good gracious me, why?!"

"I beg your pardon, Aubrey, once the first lines were captured, Byng had to query the decision of to carry on or to discontinue then and there. He carried onwards. The second phase was, therefore, hurriedly executed," Philippe nodded to her. "Both battalions heartened plump casualties. By bayonet, our lads made the Germans fall back to the heart of Courcelette. Dividing into smaller groupings, the 22nd made for the right of the town. Their aim was to cover that half of the town. The 25th took to the left. They agreed to meet in Courcelette's center. The foe met both battalions, along with defeat, by six-thirty that evening. The assault was carried out in half an hour's time — engagement jolly well done, I say.

Nighttime saw the enemy counterattack four times over. Daybreak found the 22nd's numbers to be two hundred. On September the 17th, the 26th's supply team brought either battalion their only meal in three days' time. They were then made to assault German lines on the outskirts of Courcelette. They staved off numerous counterassaults in order to maintain the village. The fighting went on for three days and three nights. They were encircled by the foe from every possible angle. Nine hundred stood guard the first day. One hundred and eighteen were alive when the smash ended. The

18th relieved the battalions. The Corps won three medals for Courcelette. One went to one of ours, from the 22nd, Captain J. Chabelle. He received the Military Cross medal for taking then defending the village from thirteen counterattacks. Corporal A. Fleming of the 26th won the Military Medal. He guided many who took a strongpoint held in the village. By the end of it, only he and one of his mates were left with breath in their bodies. A VC was awarded to the 49th's Private J. Kerr. Though he had just a rifle for companion, he captured sixty-two enemy and two hundred yards in surplus of trenches. He lived through it; however, all fingers of one hand were blasted away in the process."

The conversation casually changed. Philippe and his father discussed the hockey organization formed in Montreal just days prior. Called the National Hockey League, the founding teams were the Montreal Canadiens, Ottawa Senators, Montreal Wanderers, and the Toronto Arenas.

Philippe said, "The hockey season is to commence days from the election."

Seraphin said contemptuously, "I can scarcely believe Borden is allowing females the enfranchisement. Of course, he was always indifferent to suffragism before the war. I hope I do not live to see Quebec grant the vote provincially. Your mother would never vote anyhow."

Mme. Richardieux nodded in agreement.

Auré said, "The maritimes remain largely indifferent to suffragism. British Columbia extended the vote earlier this year on April 5th. Ontario granted the vote in April as well, on the 12th. One ought to see the movement on the prairies; it is most remarkable, Sir. Premiers are highly praising women's work for ze effort. This coincides with the West's enlistment rate, higher than the rest of the country, with Ontario included in the west."

Hoping to garner approval from her father-in-law, Aubrey added, "And others say it is their right not to vote."

Auré replied without intonation, "Those males should be shown photos of our Bluebirds' funerals. There is something especially woebegone about women who die in battle. Or see what trench foot looks like. To say eh chap loses a few toes would be quite the understatement. A foot becomes so disfigured it is no longer recognizable as a foot. It makes one's stomach turn to look at it. To see a fellow just lying in a hospital bed who has been gassed and the boils or blobs for lack of a better way of describing his wounds, all over him, it makes any woman want to cry just looking at him. It's obvious he's in so much pain. Those Canadians should be shown pictures of our volunteer soldiers being executed. They ought to see what the Medical Corps looked like when they returned from the Mediterranean or be made to aid orderlies with surgery during any given scrap. They should listen to any commanding officer always giving the same command, 'It'll probably be our bloody deaths, boys, but orders are orders.' Or listen to the gurgling cries of your men while they take their last breaths after being poisoned from phosgene gas. One has to dispel so many litres of liquid from rotten lungs before the gurgling starts. Then you hear shells hit your men, while they lie in holes waiting to be rescued, from artillery but from friendly fire that falls mistakenly short of enemy lines in an attempt to cover a rescue team to retrieve them. Or while caught in the open, watch your wounded men, in agonizing pain, turn over to relieve some of the pressure, to have their bodies riddled with bullets by exposing themselves to enemy sights. Or the soldier next to you or your batman have his head hit multiple times with bullets, the last one decapitating him. You are left standing there, covered in his blood, wondering 'ow to pen his wife an explanation of 'is death. Those in the poor bloody infantry are rarely afforded the privilege of a casket. Mass, shallow graves are ze order of the day, where each lad is merely laid on a stretcher and his body wrapped in the flag. At least some are wrapped in the flag. One can argue that leaving eh scrap is the hardest part, given you are made to collect your mates, or what's left of their charred flesh, in sandbags, the bottom half of the sandbag always drenched in blood, to carry them to their final resting place. Ma chere, everything I just said happens to our military regularly. What scrap was it, Philippe?" Auré asked, looking to his brother. "A medical officer saw one of ours, a Canadian, running down a road. Both his feet had been blown off as he ran past the officer in considerable shock on his exposed bones and muscles."

"Ypres," Philippe answered. He continued, "Or that one Canadian at Passchendaele who came upon another Canadian who was lying in delirious pain and in the muck. I don't know how my mates know him, but Gunner Ray LeBrun's exact words were, 'I nearly vomited. His insides were spilling out of his stomach and he was holding himself and trying to push this awful stuff back in. When he saw me he said, 'Finish it for me mate. Put a bullet in me. Go on. I want you to. Finish it!' He had no gun himself. When I did nothing, he started to swear. He cursed and swore at me and kept on shouting even after I turned and ran.'" Philippe continued, "It always suprises me that the severely wounded, often times, can still talk or move and are perfectly coherent."

To remind his sons that the language being used was absurd, given ladies were present, Seraphin interrupted, "That is quite enough."

Auré nodded his apology. "If only those males could spend time at the front, and see what our military goes through, they would not miss another election ze rest of their livez. Lest we forget how great the debt we owe to those who died[162], the tombstone's epitaph of one of my men reads, 'Sacrificed that we hope was for democracy[163].' Another one of my men's reads, 'For God and right, let not a whisper fall that our hero died in vain[164].' In regard to not voting because it is your apparent right not to, mark my words, ma chere, white trash will always say that. That's their motto, embossed on their club napkins, and Peter iz surely their president. Those people are the embarrassment of the country. As eh lady you are taught to listen to a man's point of view. But women think for themselves."

Aubrey replied matter of factly, "Well, Peter says he's not going to apologize for something he didn't do."

Philippe answered her simply, "That surely is a coward's response."

Auré interrupted, "—laughably shallow—"

Philippe went on, "That is indeed a shallow and conceited point of view. That is also incredibly irritating. Irritation implies low quality or a debasing nature. And given the circumstances, that's the definition of cowardice. Don't ask yourself whether you were right, meaning you were right and the other person was wrong. 'Right' should be a synonym for 'integrity' or 'character.' What 'right' should mean to you is 'did you act with integrity?' Can you see how doing nothing under great duress, then giving excuses for or defending neutrality, would tear a country apart, while everyone else is in the trenches? That perspective divides families and causes marriages to end in divorce. Oh, he's allowed to think that.

---

[162] A Canadian World War I epitaph

[163] A Canadian World War I epitaph

[164] A Canadian World War I epitaph

But to act with integrity, he would certainly have to give a superior answer than that."

Seraphin looked to Philippe, who stopped speaking at the acknowledgement. Seraphin went on, "The election will surely see British Canada's dominance fall and, most likely, forever. So, Canada is being ripped apart from the inside and will pay for her nationhood through the slaughter and mud of this war? Well, Quebec will stand steadfast at the side of their 'Old Chief.' Conservatives have scarcely had such high approval."

Late one evening, Seraphin was tending to a church matter. If one could believe so, he was more devout than Auré. The remainders of the household had gone to sleep. Auré and Aubrey were left alone in one of the dining rooms. Auré actually relented and matters other than religion or work were discussed over a midnight meal. "Late Royal North West Mounted Police, Yukon Division[165]," was nearly all Aubrey could get out of Auré as to how he was exonerated in Regina. Auré had known the officer in the Klondike days. Apparently, the man was indebted to her husband because of a hushed scandal owing to gold. After the gold rush, the now-deceased man had risen to a high position in the Mounted Force. He had owed Auré a favour and her husband had used the debt wisely. The affair made Aubrey laugh, and she knew Auré found it amusing, too, though he did not give any indication he did. The pair seemed to be growing quite close to one another recently. She knew he thought her beautiful by the way he looked at her. A few days prior, he took her riding about Raimbault's expansive property to give her greater context of his upbringing. They had ridden on the same horse. *How wonderful if a declaration of love from him would ensue*, Aubrey thought. René was fast asleep, his arms around Lord Beaverbrook.

---

[165] A Canadian World War I epitaph

Halifax

They departed Raimbault after an unexpectedly short stay. Auré insisted Aubrey and their son travel to Halifax. He wanted René to see the wartime ships that the little boy loved. When the change of plans was explained, Aubrey thought her husband wanted to see a mistress and needed his wife elsewhere. Aubrey was taken aback when he announced he was to go with them.

After a few days of travel by train, the young family reached their destination. The dominion's small Navy increased over the course of the duration. It also saw further vessels donated by patriotic Haligonians for the length of the effort. Harbour rules and regulations had been greatly let down due to the effort's massive comings and goings.

"SS Imo," the nanny read the name aloud of the ship closest to René. The pair stood at the guardrails of Pier 6, which overlooked the harbour, on the 6th of December. They waved to the ship. René had a lovely time in the ocean-side city. In fact, his mother had not seen him as happy as in the short week their family had been there.

"To-day thou shalt be with me in paradise[166]," said Aubrey, smiling while she squeezed René in a quick embrace. She was so happy to be with her husband and child on a vacation. *Our*

---

[166]   A Canadian World War I epitaph

only son[167] and what a handsome little boy, thought Aubrey with pride. She had a profound feeling that she should not leave her son but take him with her. "Women's intuition," she chided herself embarrassingly. René was left with the nanny and his parents went to the city's shopping district. The young family would have liked to have rented a yacht but decided to do so when they returned once the war ended.

Belonging to the Netherlands, the SS Imo was late leaving Halifax after neutral examination. She was to sail to New York, then to Belgium for inventory that very morning. A French cargo ship, the SS Mont-Blanc, could be viewed sailing into port. It was bound for France. The ship was consigned with hundreds of tons of wartime explosives, a few thousand tons of picric acid to make shells, tons of gun cotton, and barrels of high-octane fuel. The Mont-Blanc sailed through the harbour and amid miscommunication, it dashed against the Imo. Barrels spilt on board the Mont-Blanc. A fire immediately ensued.

The Mont-Blanc continued into the harbour afire. All of a sudden, a tremendous funnel of smoke billowed into the sky. Seemingly every Haligonian stopped to stare at the tumult. René was the sole thought that came to Aubrey's mind when she saw the smoke. For peace[168] of mind she tried to steel herself that he was enjoying watching the smoke, though she desperately wanted him next to her in that moment. All of a sudden, Aubrey felt the day had stopped being carefree, and all she could think was, *My son, my son[169].* She and Auré were a few streets away from the Pier. To one side of her, firemen were seen running towards the ships. At the same time, a

---

[167] A Canadian World War I epitaph

[168] A Canadian World War I epitaph

[169] A Canadian World War I epitaph

train dispatcher, Vincent Coleman, ran into his office. He hurriedly sent cables to halt all trains bound for Halifax: *Hold up the train. Ammunition ship afire in harbor making for Pier 6 and will explode. Guess this will be my last message. Good-bye, boys.*

Every fibre of Aubrey's being was now screaming, *find René.* Before she could start to make her way through the crowd, a magnanimous blinding light flashed. Aubrey awoke on the ground and to a severe migraine and ringing in her ears. She instinctively reached to her forehead, where she felt pain. Instantly, her hand was covered in blood. Buildings all about her had toppled. Auré's arms were around her as he picked her up. She felt crushed against his chest at his complete disregard of his normal gentleness towards her, given their predicament.

Amidst the pandemonium, gone unnoticed by those around, were Auré's hysterical French cries of, "My son?! My son?!" Then, Aubrey lost consciousness.

The Halifax explosion was the most diabolical man-made explosion in history. Two square miles of Halifax were flattened. The corollary reached hundreds of miles distant to the city. Nine thousand citizens were injured. A handful thousand were left homeless. The same day's evening brought one of the worst blizzards in decades. Every German Haligonian, fourteen in all, was put in prison. Two thousand graves were dug in the aftermath. Coleman was among the buried and was credited with saving the more than seven hundred souls on board the incoming trains, all of which received his last message and were able to stop on the outskirts of the city. The same trains were used to transport the wounded to neighbouring city hospitals and to deliver doctors, Red Cross volunteers, and medical supplies into the city. Forth from the shadows came death with the pitiless syllable "Now,"[170] one of the smallest graves would have been dug for René Richardieux but for his mother's insistence that he return to Pembina to be buried aside his great-grandfather.

---

[170]   A Canadian World War I epitaph

The Khaki Election

The Allies endured a most dreadful year. England suffered one drubbing after another. Amidst the most woeful term of the duration, Canada found solace in her cherished Corps. The country held her "ever-victorious Corps" in immeasurable esteem. Currie penned to Ontario's premier, a Mr. Hearst, *The year 1917 has been a glorious year for the Canadian Corps. We have taken every objective from the enemy we started for and have not had a single reverse... I know that no other Corps has had the same unbroken series of successes.* Canada boasted the top fortified region of the front. Her intention was to preserve Vimy and locale.

Officers were allotted leaves they had not foreseen in order to nurture Union government. The army was un-cheery about waging one battle to attend to another. High-ranking veteran soldiers were given furlough for as much as a month to visit England. Numerous family men obtained permission to return to loved ones. Others were granted passes to care for ill relatives. Many of the men on leave would not don their uniform afresh.

Across the dominion, striation of Liberals and Conservatives all but disappeared. The country had been reduced to Protestant Good Britishers fighting for a colony to achieve autonomy against Roman Catholic Canadiens defending the most abused province of the Empire. Letters to the front, circulars to government, and cries at political rallies voiced the loss of innocence, betrayal of the most sordid election, and abandonment of heritage Canada would know in its history.

I refuse to be like those dastardly English, who would do well to remember that ladies do not lower themselves to such a thing as voting... French Officers do not receive the same amount of dignity and respect as their English counterparts do. Sixty eight Commanding Officers make up the Corps. Solely one is Francophone... English Canada forgot about us far before the effort... Radicals are trying take over French Canada... will stand against conscription "to the death"... The new law is a plebiscite... England is again controlling Ontario, as though the province has reverted back to being Upper Canada... We would prefer to have a civil war than to wage war for His Majesty... In our beloved Quebec, our females are being shamed. They do not want the vote and have too much honour for such a notion; church and government will unite to protect them... Revolution will come first and conscription secondly... Les Canadiens have pulled more than their weight for this wretched war and were dragged into it unfairly... The other side's politicians can't be trusted... should stand in solidarity with their people, not against them... evil... Our families have dealt with too much bloodshed, and the other side can't be made to see reason... Crusade... yellow-backs... They would do well to remember their heritage... Defeat cannot be accepted... What they're doing is treason... Those Roman Catholic priests are surely to blame for leading their people astray... Union government needs to stay in power at all costs... Those slacker Canadiens should do their duty or be told to get out of the country... British Canada will fight to the end... French, foreigner, and shirker are surely synonyms of one another now... German victory is close on our heels... Our dear boys... The King cannot be insulted by his glorious colony refusing conscription... Those with cushy appointments staying behind... Bourassa, Laurier, and Quebec cannot control our Canada... Fighting for the splendid ones overseas will never stop... The old rag cannot be dishonored; conscription needs to come to pass.

The exhausted soldiers, almost all of whom had bronchitis, wrote back letters during the most frigid France in living memory, *Lynching ought to be done to the French!... Conscription is the only issue that counts until the effort ends... Women should obtain the vote, at least the ones serving. They can stand surgery as well as any man and have proven their weight in gold... AND TO THE CANADIANS WHO DO NOT VOTE! THEY'RE WORSE THAN THE FRENCH! COWARDS OF THE EMPIRE! TRAITORS TO OUR DEMOCRACY! A*

BOLDFACED INSULT TO THE WOMEN AND COLOURED MEN WHO ARE DENIED THE VOTE BUT WHO TAKE THOSE GUTLESS, YELLOW, BASTARDS' PLACES ON THE FRONT LINES! AND AN IRREVOCABLE OFFENSE AGAINST THE GALLANT MEN WHO ARE BUTCHERED IN THE GAS-LADEN, MAGGOTY, AND RAT-INFESTED FIELDS OF EUROPE!

Soldiers cast their ballots in informal groups, outside on piles of logs. Officers told their men whom to vote for. Officers also informed troops at large what ridings needed more Union support, after which soldiers allocated their votes to any region they chose to help win ridings. Thousands of soldiers who were not yet legally adults voted. Coloured servicemen, including Indigenous men, were authorized as well. Military votes were sent to England to tally as irreparable damage would be done should the ships convoying the ballots be torpedoed.

December 17th dawned unclouded and crisp from nearly coast-to-coast.

Automobiles became nuisances in cities, and sleighs were used in farming communities amidst the snow.

The *Montreal Star, Montreal Gazette*, and *La Patrie* offices were boarded up and policemen stood at the ready, but little unrest was found.

Five hundred thousand women, registered or not, cast their initial federal ballot. At the polls, females asked for the name of their party leader or who was championing conscription. Some voted how their fallen husbands always had, regardless of who was pro-conscription. Others voted for Borden's party, even if their husband had not previously done so. Daughters were chaperoned by fathers to deter discordance. Nearly nine in ten eligible Canadians and Canadiens, an unheard figure the country had never seen nor would see again, cast their ballot against cowardice.

As the infamy, scandal, betrayal, and endless, fruitless slaughter drew to a close, The Khaki Election crowned what was the worst year history would write for Canada. The Tuesday morning saw the country dash to read the headlines.

The Evader

Upon being informed that he was triumphant, Borden simply departed for his residence. Laurier and his white plume returned to a defeated Quebec. Both sides showed solemnity and lack of merriment in response to the outcome. Union won nine out of ten ridings, excepting Quebec, which voted Liberal almost without exception. Parliament saw two thirds of seats claimed by Unionists. Parliament was reshaped after one third of incumbents retired, historically twice the dominion average from an election. Soldiers voted ninety-one percent in favour of conscription, no matter how they and their fathers voted previously. French Canadian Members of Parliament did not account for Union government, there being but two Catholics.

The two parties retained their typical separate meetings and the holding of the other in contempt. The effort was the sole agreement on which they shared common ground.

England's army ventured to be nudged away to the Channel. The Corps was not in the thick of the mire, yet the dominion was ever aware of justice being wrested from the Empire as they had not yet seen. Daily, Canadians read of disagreeable news about Britain and the "momentousness of the battle." Borden agreed to provide aid in all manner of ways.

The Military Service Act wanted for one hundred thousand, unmarried and childless conscripts. Well-nigh twenty thousand reported for duty. Many months would pass prior to recruits being declared fit for active service. High Command and the government agreed the duration was to last into the next year. Tens of thousands of conscripts would soon be necessary to replace the pummeled Corps. If the duration saw the light of the year hereafter, conscripts would comprise the majority of the Corps. More than nine of ten petitioned conscripts saw release. Appeal committees afforded almost every case.

The 5th Division had been, by and by, disassembled then divided among the other four to reinforce them. Provinces were no longer allowed to exchange alcohol amongst one another or vend independent of their region. The government then halted the assembly of alcohol altogether. To aid with production, a measure was introduced called Daylight Savings Time. Taxes saw elevation. Shocking Aubrey most of all was the abolishment of hereditary titles for Canadian subjects as another move in the direction to create a more independent identity for the country.

Montreal hosted some of the most affluent patriots, though they were the most resented citizens of the province. The city's Patriotic Fund arm did not venture to bring about provocation of its citizens with a fundraising push in the new year. A French (from France!) government-recruiting mission travelled through the French province. Speaking for his people, Bourassa stated the French were "trying to have us offer the kinds of sacrifices for France which France never thought of troubling itself with in the defense of French Canada."

The day before, Germany began the assault on the Seigfriedstellung, or what the Allies called the Hindenburg Line. In her straight, curveless frock-turned-crepe mourning wear, Aubrey sat at her stationary, unable to concentrate. She tried to pray, *Forgive, O Lord, a mother's wish that death had spared her son[171]*, but could not put the words in sequence from grief. "God said, the first born of thy sons shalt though give unto me"[172], a line from Exodus, incessantly came to mind instead. Nearly four torturous months had passed since René had died. At the loss of one's child, a parent became removed from society for six weeks. She could not attend balls or dinners for six months; yet another two months were to be observed until formal mourning ended. Even so, no more parties were occurring as the effort had become a total war.

One of the largest personal amounts to the Halifax relief fund was given by Auré. As of late, the master and wife of Pembina rarely saw one another. His parents' hearts melting with pain[173], René's father and mother were reduced to sleeping on opposite sides of the manor. Aubrey had never known such melancholy. "You will never be forgotten by your loving mother, dear boy[174]," she whispered with the stuffed beaver in her lap. At the Red Cross shelter in Halifax, the biggest shock of her life was in a volunteer sister handing her Lord Beaverbrook. Previously, she had been too stunned to accept the loss of her son, until that hideous moment when the teddy bear was given to her. One of Lord Beaverbrook's ears was missing. The complete backside of his fur was singed.

---

[171]   A Canadian World War I epitaph

[172]   A Canadian World War I epitaph

[173]   A Canadian World War I epitaph

[174]   A Canadian World War I epitaph

At the shelter, all she could think was *Our family circle is broken, our dear boy*[175]. The nanny died in the blast as well. Ever remembered by his loving mother[176], René was thought of at all times. Aubrey glanced at the sole framed picture of René on her desk and thought, *Son of my heart, live for ever. There is no death for you and me*[177]. Aubrey signed the letter to Augusta explaining René's death, *My heart is torn with grief but God knows best*[178]. *Just as we learned to love him, God called him home to Heaven*[179]. *All we had, loved and deeply missed by father and mother*[180].

The Kingstons had not sent condolences or attended the funeral. She knew what they thought anyways: "divine retribution" for marrying someone who was divorced and a Roman Catholic.

Aubrey sat answering letters. Gran had written that Uncle Walter was conscripted. England was conscripting fifty-year-olds. He had recently turned fifty-one and, though a senior, accepted his duty to his King.

The next letter opened came from Regina. *Every noble life leaves a fibre of it interwoven for ever in the work of the world. Ruskin*[181], Mother Augusta quoted one of her favourite poets in condolence to Aubrey about René.

They gave their merry youth away for country and for God[182], penned Mother Augusta of the Agnew boys. Asleep

---

[175] A Canadian World War I epitaph
[176] A Canadian World War I epitaph
[177] A Canadian World War I epitaph
[178] A Canadian World War I epitaph
[179] A Canadian World War I epitaph
[180] A Canadian World War I epitaph
[181] A Canadian World War I epitaph
[182] A Canadian World War I epitaph

with the un-returnable brave[183], Briarch was now gone. Killed near Passchendaele[184], Briarch had been shot re-building the roads before the onslaught of the smash, Mother Augusta confirmed. Hit merely in the high shoulder, he had fallen off the slippery bath-mat he was on and into the mud. A Tommy would lay unconscious in the first minutes after a bullet pierced him. However, at Passchendaele, a gunshot wound proved fatal in basically all cases, due to the wallow. His normally hefty kit must have played a factor in his loss of balance, too, Mother Augusta assumed. To recover his body would have been preposterous amid the porridge. If a lad fell or side-stepped off a duckboard, drowning would instantly occur, unless mates were literally beside him to aid. Mother Augusta surmised that Briarch must have drowned while conscious, given the nature of his wound. Briarch's parents decided his epitaph would read, "Honour thy Father and thy Mother. He did[185]." Rupert's family chose for his epitaph, "Like a soldier fell for King and country on 18th birthday[186]."

More than 1,500 Canadians fell during the preparation of Passchendaele alone from enemy gunners and snipers striking from indisputably every direction, given the Canadians were incredibly easy for the Germans to hit because the Canadians had no cover in the open region. The ridge had afforded a great deal more than 250,000 Empire casualties. Britain rescinded Passchendaele to Germany with no struggle whatsoever in the spring campaign.

On a lighter note, Rupert's bagpipes had been jolly found two years later. They were to return to his mother. Some

---

[183] A Canadian World War I epitaph
[184] A Canadian World War I epitaph
[185] A Canadian World War I epitaph
[186] A Canadian World War I epitaph

small comfort would be taken in their recovery because his body was never found amid the wallow. His parents were unable to visit his grave.

After a shell landed nearby, Rupert was cut to bloody ribbons. Running across No Man's Land, Rupert saw Briarch. The latter was acting as a sniper behind a large oak. Rupert waved and gave a wicked smile. While the salutation was returned, a shell exploded. Rupert was sent sky high; his remains so small they would not be gathered. For a moment, all went quiet about Briarch, who eye-witnessed the event. Bullets fell akin to hail, though momentarily not a single one in the area registered to him. After some time, Briarch gave a small smile where his cousin had last been. Faithful unto death[187], while tears fell down Briarch's cheeks, he turned around and carried on. The polite version was penned to their family. The truth of Rupert's death died with Briarch. He was not able to speak the words aloud.

The 46th, predominantly from Moose Jaw, had the formidable sobriquet throughout the Corps as the "Suicide Battalion." An almost ninety-two percent casualty rate found the 46th in esteem.

Reconciled to spinsterhood, Hortence could not but occasionally find herself in the company of a gentleman caller. She could host amusements, though seldom and in small fashion, if permitted at all. Of course, a matron had to support her. Augusta was frequently her matron friend and did not allow a gentleman to stay until the usual ten o'clock but had the fellow retire far sooner. Hortence could only serve male companions tea, coffee, lemonade, and chocolate, not even cigarettes. Hortence lamented that all honourable men who were her age, twenty-three, were married. Aubrey rolled

---

[187] A Canadian World War I epitaph

her eyes and said aloud, "Oh, I was married at eighteen, even if it was to a Frenchman, and God knows the whole of the Empire hates them, but at least I married! What has she been doing with herself all these years? Hortence is ever irritating! She won't help herself!"

Because Hortence was a spinster, she had taken on a nursing role to give herself something to do at one of the convalescent hospitals in Regina. Aubrey read on. One of the poor convalescents had taken his life. Hortence went on to describe the barbarous act as the most selfish thing a person could do. Aubrey put the letter down. Even Aubrey thought this declaration too far. *Though,* thought she, *What is the difference between a fatally ill patient and a shell-shocked one in the extreme? What a fatal disease does to oneself and one's family is exceptionally hard to bear. The patient is in so much pain they want to die. Are they really choosing to die when, in so much agony, they can no longer bear life after so many years of suffering? Not a soul would dare call this person a coward or selfish or what not. How could anyone be so unfeeling? They say the worst forms of nervous trouble are akin to physical torture. There is often no difference in pain between a fatally ill patient and a tottering one, for all that doctors can monitor the sickness of the former and not the latter. How can she be so exceedingly ignorant and in her position of a nurse?! An abomination! She needs to lose her employment. What — kind of care is she giving those — patients?* Aubrey would not permit the dastardly opinion to be given further voice. The letter was tossed into the fireplace, unfinished. As she walked clear the room, she muttered, "A disgrace to her profession."

In the hall, Aubrey thought she heard a sound. A look was taken down the way. She was unsure, given her hearing was a tilly impaired after Halifax. Every pane of glass in Halifax shattered from the explosion. Mercifully, Auré had been in a shop at the time of the explosion and suffered no great harm, other than scars and minor bruises. There were water spots in the front room. Once she was in the hall, she heard a door shut on the second floor. Perplexed, she wondered if she ought to ascend the grand stairs. *What an odd thought; why would one worry about ascending stairs in one's home?* Mother Augusta came to her, *As soon as one thinks, "that is odd;" that is one's intuition giving the first indication that something is actually wrong.*

Upon reaching the landing of the second floor, she saw that Auré's office light was on. She knocked. An answer did not greet her. In the study, even the mistress of the manor had to ask permission to enter. The door was opened a jot. Jean-Pierre was seated in the master's chair. He was positively wet. Auré was kneeling before Jean-Pierre, who spoke in rapid French.

"I'm dashed sorry. Father only sent word in time after they visited his manor. I am terribly sorry to do this—," Jean-Pierre spluttered. Auré waved him to silence.

Oh, Jean-Pierre was conscripted, that would explain the papers he's holding, thought Aubrey. *His father would naturally order him to apply for exemption.* "We have to get you into Quebec. Do you have relatives there?" Asked Auré.

The answer was no. A footman came to the door and spoke in his mother tongue, "Monsieur (Sir)." Auré turned and looked up at him. For a servant to interrupt a master would have resulted in dismissal in normal times. An understanding seemed to be shared between master and servant. Auré answered him. A master replying to a servant would have been unthinkable. The reply given, in quick French, was to go to the windows. The servant departed.

"However—," Aubrey started to say.

Neither master seemed to listen to her. After a bit of time, the servant returned, though no one noticed until the word "Monsieur" was spoken. In the short silence that ensued, the faint sound of a motorized engine could be heard ascending the drive. "We need to 'ide Jean-Pierre," demanded Auré. "Go to the Virgins' Corridors."

The Virgins' Corridors was where female servants resided.

"Too obvious," before she could stop herself. "And Jean-Pierre will need to change clothes. He will freeze if he stays in those ones."

Out of doors, automobile doors were heard to open. Aubrey suggested that he go downstairs, through the second downstairs service hallway and out the back. Auré argued that ten servants could be there at the very moment. Only one servant would have to speak to a servant at another manor, and the truth would instantly surface through the servant grapevine. Aubrey's boudoir was the decided spot, at the back of her closet.

"Come along, we may yet 'ave enough time to see this through," Auré said. Auré instructed the footman to the master's room to fetch clothes for Jean-Pierre, then to Aubrey's room. One by one, they dispersed to set about their tasks. Aubrey made for her room to see if a servant was along the way. A skivvy carrying laundered cheesecloths was left aghast at her mistress instructing her downstairs to take tea. Aubrey could have bitten her tongue. A more probable task should have been ordered.

Jean-Pierre was shown into her closet to hide amongst the numerous ball gowns. As she crossed the landing of the main staircase and by dreadful luck the Federal agents were at the bottom of the grand stairs in the entryway. A pair of agents were searching for Jean-Pierre. As an ardent pro-conscription Unionist, Lawrence was present along with the agents. Lawrence wanted nothing more than to avenge his son's death by having all the traitors and cowards finally made to do their duty. The small party at the main doors looked up at her. *Dash it!* thought she. *The back staircase should have been taken!*

"I give you my word that the shirker is not present," her husband said in disgust while she descended the stairs. As a gentleman, Lawrence had no choice but to believe Auré. Furthermore, Auré had been with Lawrence's youngest son at the Somme in his final moments. Aubrey balked. Per the Gentleman's code, lying was the most serious offense of all. Lawrence and the agents turned to look at her.

"Please do pardon my wife. The loss of our son has been most difficult for 'er to bear. This is all, quite frankly, too much for her," Auré made quick clarification.

"In the name of God," whispered Lawrence. "I do beg your sincere pardon, Mme. Richardieux. Of course, we shall depart right away. We were only inquiring if you knew the whereabouts of Desrosiers," bowing to Auré an apology.

The trio was partially hidden from view as they went through the colonnade. Rain fell while they passed the bakehouse. A haversack containing bills, food, and some articles, among them a note with Philippe's Montreal address, was strapped to the thoroughbred. Jean-Pierre spluttered that his father would repay Auré, who waived an impatient hand of irrelevancy.

"Now see here!" Jean-Pierre countered, upon being made to stay indebted to Auré.

Then, in an almost pleading voice, Auré spoke, "Jean-Pierre, s'il vous plait (please)."

Jean-Pierre looked from him to Aubrey and back again. "Good God! I would rather go to the front than betray you!"

Auré returned to his usual nature and spoke in rapid French, "As long as you can enter Quebec, you should be safe. If trouble finds you, go to the French police. Be wary of the dominion police flooding in. Stay off the main roads. Avoid public transport. Don't trust an Anglophone—"

"—THIS IS TREASON!" cried Aubrey. Auré brushed her aside.

"God speed," Auré said.

Jean-Pierre bolted from the back of the stables on one of Pembina's magnificent black stallions in a race against time and the setting sun. Her husband let out a long-overdrawn sigh. He spoke French. She doubted he realized the break in habit. "Shall we? We need to return before a servant sees us." He made for the doors.

"How can you remain so calm?!" she spluttered. The conversation had resumed in English.

He replied with his back towards her, "The British army never runs when retreating."

"But Peter was conscripted, exempted, and you called him a traitor!"

"Cowards die many times before their deaths. The valiant taste of death but once," His tone changed to boredom with a Shakespearean quote answer.

"You lied to those agents — if anyone were to know — our reputation." Nothing mattered more to an Edwardian than reputation.

He stopped in a dead halt.

"We — ma chere — we lied to those agentz, and you will not say eh word nor will I, especially to your precious Mr. Lawrence." So he did know about her affairs and did not care! The way he was looking at her dared her to say more. He brushed a lock of hair that had fallen out of her normally immaculate chignon, which took one hour and a servant to create every morning. He made for the manor. The lightning, rain, and wind hitting the gates against the walls returned to her consciousness. But Aubrey stood where she was, rooted to the spot, staring aghast at her husband, whom the country had deemed her prodigal son returned and one of the greatest heroes of the empire, and who was thus revealing himself to be some double agent.

"For whom did you vote?" she asked quietly.

He turned round. "Laurier."

Above the sound of his boots hitting gravel, she thought he muttered the word "bastards." For one wild moment, she thought he might laugh.

Philippe Visits

Aubrey was clutching at the high collar of her nightgown. She wondered if Auré had ever been small. When he was young, his beloved nanny would run her hand through his and Philippe's hair to an instant calming effect. In his later years, one of the only times Auré relaxed was when he lay on top of Aubrey while she rubbed his back. Aubrey made a mental note to do so for him at a later time. When he initially returned from overseas, he slept on the floor. Comfort could not find him in a bed after so much time at the front.

The root of innumerable marriages disintegrating in everything but name, nervous trouble was affecting as many soldiers as gunshot wounds. All armies disclosed in one way or another, "It is as if one is being abused, though from the inside. One can only handle the affliction for so long."

Commencing with shaking of hands or tremors, a contemporary sort of injury was introduced wtih the start of the effort. At first, perplexed doctors described the new wound as physical. It was believed that harm was done to the brain after shock waves were felt from shells erupting. As time elapsed, soldiers far from No Man's Land succumbed to the invisible trauma. By the Somme, the diagnosis was likened to a psychological one. The medical condition composed of two sorts, sick and wounded, of which wounded was thought to be gallant. The term "Shell shock" was banned the previous year. Corps documentation stated the diagnosis as "N.Y.D.N." or "Not Yet Diagnosed Nervous." The Corps referred to the acronym as "Not Yet Dead Nearly."

A statement came from the Canadian Army Medical Corps saying, "Shell shock is a manifestation of childishness and femininity, against which there is no remedy." Frenzied, malingering, and cowardly were names assigned to those thought afflicted with the malady, usually the uneducated man or non-gentleman regular. Other doctors and officers were more kind-hearted. These casualties were often transferred to the rear for bombproof posts.

As an officer, Auré's honourable neurasthenia from war-strain was bothering him. No longer does the helmet press thy brow, oft weary with its surging thoughts of battle[188]; nonetheless, he had awoken screaming bloody murder. Outside his door, there was an unspoken agreement between Aubrey, Llewellyn, and Philippe to keep this night quiet like so many other times.

Llewellyn went to rouse the chef. The small hours saw to any dish provided for Edwardians. Eating never ceased in their leisure world.

After a time, Philippe returned to his own quarters. He could do no more to comfort his brother. Philippe was visiting for a short amount of time, being at Pembina only weeks. Proper vacations were another casualty of the war.

The greatest Ace that the war would acknowledge was accredited with his final kill. Germany's illustrious "The Red Baron," Baron Manfred Albrecht Freiherr von Richtofen, was shot down by the Allies. A part of the Imperial Air

---

[188] A Canadian World War I epitaph

Service, Jagdgeschewader 1 (Fighter Wing I) was stationed at Cappy, a town close to the Somme River. A sunny Sunday in late April, Rittmeister (Cavalry Captain) Richtofen said goodbye in a hug to his German mastiff, Moritz. Richtofen fastened himself into his famed Fokker Dr. 1 triplane. For his former cavalry regiment, he had the plane painted red. The war's most feared flying unit, commanded by one of the most famous German men of the century, set about for British territory.

Atop Vaux-sur-Somme, France, Richtofen's Flying Circus of Albatrosses and the Royal Air Force engaged in a most splendid dogfight. The Red Baron descended quite modestly to the earth in zig-zag fashion. Richtofen shadowed a young, new airman, Canadian Lieutenant Wilfrid "Wop" May. From behind, a veteran Canadian charged Richtofen in aid of his fellow mate. In his single seater, Sopwith Camel, the veteran Canadian plunged considerably, then shot at Richtofen. After, the veteran ascended to dodge the earth. Australian gunners aground opened fire encouragingly. Richtofen continued to chase May. Hit in the torso by a bullet, Richtofen crash-landed in a beet field close to Sailley-le-Sac. Still strapped in his cockpit, Richtofen succumbed to his wounds.

The sensational title of marksman to down Ricthtofen fell to the veteran Canadian, Captain Arthur Roy Brown. Brown would be accorded a bar to his Distinguished Service Cross medal for the brilliant kill. He would not see the Victoria Cross England had sacredly agreed to bestow to the pilot who downed Richtofen.

After recovering Ricthofen's body, the Allies accorded him full military honours and a full Allied military funeral the following day in France. Pallbearers were Allied Airmen. A Royal Air Force member flew above the German Cappy base and let fall a message notifying them of Richtofen's fate. Brown penned the condolence letter to the Prussian aristocratic Richthofen family. The Red Baron's death enormously uplifted the morale of the Allies.

Outside Pembina, the wind whistled in the dark night. A few of the little Laurentiens could be heard running round the upstairs nursery. They were playing with their wooden toy planes SE 5a, which their hero Billy Bishop flew, and Sopwith Camel, the most fancied Allied plane. The Spring Offensive raged on.

"Auré, what are the ages of our younger cousins? Will any of them be called up?" inquired Philippe. Days before, Borden had lowered the minimum age of conscripts to nineteen. In unwonted fashion, Parliament was in secret session. So many of the Laurentiens were gone or still over there that the family could not form a hockey team for the first time in years.

"Not this year, but they will soon if ze war lasts until 1920," Auré trailed off. The war's drudgery had no end in sight. Auré was writing to his commanding officer. The officer had held his rank for months, an audacious length. The officer who informed Aubrey of Auré's transfer had long ere been killed. Philippe took one of Aubrey's knights. He and his sister-in-law were playing chess.

The Treaty of Brest-Litovsk was recently agreed to. Russia had declared Armistice. The Eastern Front no longer existent, Germany's troops transferred west. A massive show was unremitting against the Allies. The foe was desperate to break Allied lines ahead of the untutored American, proudly pet named the "doughboys," debut. Obliteration claimed the British fifth army. The Allies were thrown about in withdraw. The Corps was charmingly unaffected on Vimy territory.

Until war's end, the German army would refuse to attack any territory held by the Canadians.

Nevertheless, Union government, as shaken as the House of Lords, jettisoned every absolution. Old Originals, discharged on a three-month leave, saw government cancel their long-overdue furloughs. Numerous men returned to the dominion against orders, though autumn would see many rejoin their brothers-in-arms. Even so, hardly any soldiers saw their families after voting Union. Cries of duty fulfilled went unheard by government as well.

A pawn moved across the board.

In French, Philippe asked, "How are the French conscripts treated, Auré?"

A rather raucous greeting was shown to Military Service Agreement soldiers. High Command gravely apprised the term "conscript" would see its vocalizer reprimanded. "Conchees" were to be referred to as "drafted men." Some were bullied during training, though once overseas, a soldier could be put in the clink for as long as five days for mistreating a Military Service Agreement troop.

Auré replied in French, "My men say many are frightfully unfriendly to begin with, though once acquainted with regulars they flatter jolly—" A point was grappled for, though not of the chess pieces. The King (anthem of the British Empire) was taken and the match lost — however, off the chess board. Rarely speaking his mother tongue, Auré paused to find the word in French. Unable to do so, he finished the sentence in English, "soldiers."

Philippe said quietly and serenely, "They really have you." The younger brother carried on with a lighter note, "Laval University issued exemption papers for the whole of their student body."

Quebec was sensibly safeguarding all.

Aubrey added, "My dear friend Mr. Edwards was conscripted as well. He too applied for exemption. Ontario is having a terrible time with the matter as well."

Ontario had stringent mandates in deference to her sons in uniform.

Auré interjected, "'is father pulled some strings in London. Apparently, his father 'as not spoken to him since."

Hundreds of repudiated were made to go over there. Refusal meant a court martial and at minimum two years in an army prison. Few would go on to serve their sentence.

Philippe spoke rather angrily, "That Edwards fellow refuses to fight and does not even volunteer in the dominion that has taken him in, and he came here in utter disgrace, I might add. I have met that male on a few occasions. Arrogance is surely the principal trait of the coward. He ought to take my brother's place. Auré has been maimed, a POW and is now—"

Auré interrupted, "'ow much did the Easter Riots cost?"

Philippe assented, "Three hundred thousand dollars in damages. Immediately afterwards, Father ordered that I bring our sisters to Raimbault from Quebec City."

Aubrey said, while pondering her next move, "I could return with you."

Auré informed her she would do nothing of the kind.

While discerning where to place her rook, she said, "Come now, I would like to visit St. Catherine's."

The angry response was, "You are my wife and by law you will obey me."

The pair turned to stare at Auré.

"It iz not safe there and will only worsen az time passes. As for that circus of an election, where Borden let you vote only so that 'e would win—"

Philippe, in an authoritarian tone, told his brother to calm himself. Auré stormed from the room. Aubrey's calm counterattack captured Philippe's queen. Philippe looked at her intently. He played the game[189], but after a while he continued, "Aubrey, anger is a cover for pain. However, the Archbishop spoke to Auré about serving at Father's request. Father also wrote to the Pope about conscription. He was baptized at the Vatican, so he received a reply," her brother-in-law finished quickly. Philippe continued non-committedly, as one does when a certainty must be astutely proven, "Father ordered Auré to resign his enlistment. Surely, for the first time in his life, Auré disobeyed father."

Aubrey asked, "Though why in Heaven's name did he do that?!"

Philippe answered, "A soldier and a man[190], he feels he must. Once a soldier, always a soldier. At any rate, father asked Auré for his word not to go back to the front. Auré was commanded to Raimbault after he re-inlisted."

Aubrey said, resignedly, "So that is why we went to Raimbault." Crestfallenly, she thought he had truly wanted to have a vacation with his family.

"Neither father nor mother have allowed him at Raimbault since his divorce. Did you not find that odd, that he returned for the first time in years? Father told him he was not to go into Quebec City itself because he probably would have faced police harassment and threats to his life from civilians. Father asked him for the last time to resign his enlistment. Auré refused. At that he was told to leave Raimbault. It is surely astounding Father did not disinherit him before. Though the day he did... I have only witnessed father miss Mass once

---

189 A Canadian World War I epitaph
190 A Canadian World War I epitaph

before, when his own father passed. He sat in his study the whole day and did not speak to a soul. We are brothers and comrades, we lie side by side and our faith and our hopes are the same[191], but I had to steal away from the family to come here. Father, though, must know where I am."

Auré acted so capriciously at times that Aubrey felt she would never fully comprehend him. Further hurt over her husband's indifference towards her, Aubrey wanted a change of subject. After much pressing, Philippe explained the Easter riots.

"A Spotter, federal detectives are derogatorily called that, arrested a man in a bowling alley who did not have his papers. If you do not have discharge papers on you publicly, you are sent to jail for a night."

Aubrey nodded to indicate she knew that law.

"Riots were started by a few thousand. The fellow who did not have his certificate was released, but that did not hinder the gathered. A police station was broken into. A number of police officers were beaten. Rocks and blocks of ice were heaved through the streets. A mob also smashed a Military Service Registry. File cabinets were thrown into the snow. English stores had their windows smashed. Then, the military was brought in. On Rue Bagot, forced removal was attempted, but the soldiers met with a hail of rocks. A few mates and I were on Rue Saint Sauveur. Some splintered the glass-light casings of the streetlamps, extinguishing them. In the Lower City, and in the dark and mist, the Ontario Cavalry Regiment raced down the street at full tilt. Soldiers jeered menacingly, 'Come on you French S—s of B—s! We'll trim you!' After that, machine guns were used against the crowds. To hear what was transpiring, one could have mistaken the

---

[191]   A Canadian World War I epitaph

incident for a mass execution. Jails soon found thousands of citizens in them. Tens were wounded. Four unarmed, innocent civilians died. The youngest was fourteen. Quebec will never forgive the government for this."

Philippe Leaves

"Is what is being said actually transpiring on Canadian soil?! How can this be? But this is not what we are fighting for!" expressed members of an incredulous Corps.

A thunderstruck Empire now witnessed the greatest despondency Canada would extend its soldiers. Religious, political, and military heads across Canada pleaded for harmony. Quebec's clergy demanded their people halt the petition of injustice. To countrywide surprise, the order was obeyed.

Canada was tearing herself asunder. The more her prestige grew in the world's eye, the more she was divided against herself. The split between Anglophones and Francophones ever widening, government declared martial law in its two major French cities, Montreal and Quebec City. Military was brought forth to safeguard government and army establishments in both cities. Francophone troops were mandated to stay in barrack due to government mistrust. The handful of thousand soldiers sent from Ontario and the West was remarkable in light of the Corps fancy.

Habeas Corpus was adjourned. Any male who was caught part of the riots was, by Order-in-Council, conscripted. Quebec policemen denied assisting Military Service Agents to impose the new laws. Defaulters, the majority being Francophone, withdrew to forests and made do until war's end. Federal agents scoured the dominion's landscape for evaders. Canada and the United States entered into an agreement that any hidden conscript found south of the border would be made to return or absorbed into the American draft. Tens of thousands of defaulters were in concealment. Early April found more than four thousand evaders apprehended.

For the first time since Confederation, Quebec contemplated divorcing the country. Joseph-Napoléon Francoeur, of the Quebec Legislative Assembly, recited one of the most downhearted speeches to be uttered in Parliament, "If this House is of the opinion that the province of Quebec would be disposed to accept the breaking of the Confederation Pact of 1867 if, in the eyes of the other provinces, it is believed that she is an obstacle to the union, progress, and development of Canada."

The "Francoeur motion" brought about rage and despair in the form of scoundrelly strikes against French Canada respecting conscription, the election, and Regulation 17, among other allies of secession. The Premier of Quebec, Sir Jean-Lomer Gouin, then arose and defended Confederation with a sparkling oration. The House gallantly held steadfast in denouncement of the vote, unescorted by motion. Regardless, both families were unanimous in yelling at the other, "Cowards! Traitors! Murderers!" Canada had never been so at odds with herself as when Louis Riel was executed in 1885. Borden soldiered his young country forward.

Ottawa was experiencing almost uncontrollable dread due to the Spring Offensive. At morning prayer, Auré announced his return to the front. The servants were so upset, they murmured amongst each other. Aubrey always felt comforted by his presence. Obviously, he did not feel the same towards her. She could not bring herself to ask him to stay. She had lost her son and resigned herself to most likely losing her husband, too.

That evening, Auré was in the upstairs library. Beethoven's Sonata No. 31 was playing on the Victrola. A novel was found in his hand. *He allured to brighter worlds and led the way*[192] was a line Aubrey made out from *The Deserted Village*. She was caught unawares at his leisured position. She turned to leave.

Auré said, "Aubrey, you are not getting away that easily. Iz everything alright?"

If he were in love with her, she would burst into tears and sob that every time she looked at him she thought of René, and that she desperately wanted him to stay. The knowledge of him sleeping with others was almost more than she could bear. No, her guard must never be let down.

He carried on resignedly, "Do you ever think of the jewelry I 'ave given you? Your engagement ring perhaps? Dans les moments critiques je disais trois fois, 'Je vous salue, Marie'[193] (In critical moments I would repeat three times, "Hail, Mary") in battle."

Men are such simple creatures. How can he talk of material possessions at a time like this? she thought furiously. She needed to hear that she was loved.

He returned to his tall-backed chair. At feelings unreciprocated, as she left the room, she muttered, "When have you ever helped me through a hard time?" She went to her room to undress without a maid. She wanted to be left

---

[192] A Canadian World War I epitaph
[193] A Canadian World War I epitaph

alone. It took time to take off her silk undergarments and don her matching wrap. Her corset was taken off first. Her six layers of underwear — admired ladies did not wear fewer, and the servants thought silk underwear sinful — were placed to the side. She removed the stockings last.

She had nearly pulled the wrap over her shoulders when Auré spoke, "Aubrey, you may as well let that be." She froze in fright. Then she pulled the wrap completely around her and turned to the closet entryway to face her husband. She wondered how long he had been watching her.

"I think you ought to remember yourself," she said hotly. Even the master needed to ask permission to enter the mistress' boudoir. A move was made to pass him. He gently took her by the arm, though she could feel how strong he was.

Her husband lowered his voice to a whisper in an uncharacteristic break in decorum, "His memory long will live alone in all our hearts[194] but you don't 'ave to be zo brave." He finished speaking by placing his hand around her upper neck and jawline.

She stayed silent, unwilling to look him in the eye, lest her emotions overcome her. He was gone by the time she awoke. *How could one so passionate not be in love? But he must care for me!* she thought, confused by his sleeping with her but not beside her afterwards.

The nonchalant demeanor of her husband gave no indication of the previous evening, when he and Philippe awaited outside for Aubrey.

"Not now but in the coming years, sometime, someday we'll understand[195]," Auré spoke quietly to Philippe about

---

[194]   A Canadian World War I epitaph

[195]   A Canadian World War I epitaph

his and his wife's grief. The brothers had just come from viewing René's grave. Auré remarked that the country was on the verge of civil war and his wife had to go shopping. "The British 'ave gone mad letting their females vote," Auré said in a louder manner as Aubrey approached them.

Aubrey was really going to the city to buy Larrigans as a parting gift for him. Soldiers would often stay in wallow up to the knee or the thigh for as much as forty-eight hours. After certain heavy rainfalls, soldiers could swim to the back of the lines when a trench proved evacuated. The tall moccasin was most favoured for lengthy jaunts in the trenches.

"Or has needles joined ze battle to do volunteer work?" Auré mockingly referenced the wartime dittie. He took her weepers to help her into the automobile. Aubrey's thick white mourning cuffs were made to nab her tears. So lighthearted from the previous evening was she, not a mind was paid to his witticism. The lady's maid was already at the milliners, re-trimming several black mushroom mourning hats with white under-rim. Aubrey would go into the city with them for the errand.

In Ottawa, by and by more residences were displaying signs that read "To let." New dwellings were being designed with electricity in mind and without back stairscases or a below stairs. Attics were constructed solely for storage rather than servant quarters. Consistent for hundreds of years, the average property was being designed differently to accommodate the horseless carriage. Carriages were dismantled and horses sold off. Stables kept motor vehicles or became luxury quest accomodations. Coachmen were given pensions and a cottage on the estate. Stable servants were let go or became mechanics, given aristocrats were above toiling with the mechanisms of their motor cars. Estate holders were compelled to sell their stables and kennels to the now few who could continue to provide the decades-old favourite aristocratic pastime of hunting.

At the train station, the brothers said their adieux.

After they shook hands, Auré said, "Our work must be brought to a satisfactory conclusion or we die in the attempt[196]."

Philippe corrected his brother and said cheerily, "Don't see yourself killed in another man's war."

Auré answered, "Yet remember this, God and our good cause fight upon our side[197]."

Auré had been awaiting her. Under an overcast sky, Auré helped a number of the members of the Daughters of the Empire alight or assist them to their automobiles. He went up to her as she finished relating to another member of their club about a friend of hers, "A gifted surgeon. Killed at the post of duty[198]."

After all her friends departed, Auré addressed her.

"I have eh favor to ask of you, pleaze," Auré began. Henrietta smiled at him. "While I am away, if you could care for Mrs. Richardieux, I would be greatly appreciative."

"Major Richardieux, I cannot stay," Henrietta gave a white lie, wishing to avoid the subject.

"Pleaze, Mrs. Smith."

Such a generous donation from Richardieux was given to the Daughters of the Empire, Henrietta felt she could do nothing but relent.

---

[196] A Canadian World War I epitaph
[197] A Canadian World War I epitaph
[198] A Canadian Army Medical Corps World War I epitaph

"All our beauty and peace and joy we owe to lads like you[199]," she said simply, conceding to his favour.

A grateful Auré bent to kiss her on the cheek to thank her.

From across the courtyard, Aubrey saw him lean over Henrietta. His large frame momentarily obscured Henrietta from view. Aubrey had forgotten the Daughters of the Empire had their office on Bank Street where Auré's automobile sat. She made haste in shopping to return the Larrigans to the automobile before Auré could see the package. Aubrey now understood why Auré had ridden aside the auto to town. Her husband had implied he had business to attend to in the city. Aubrey clasped her hand over her mouth in an attempt to maintain the British stiff upper lip. The final smash. A knife through the flesh would have hurt less. Auré could not love her, such was now obvious. Mistakenly, Aubrey thought she saw her husband actually kiss another female. She could no longer ask him to stay; no, she would never throw herself at a man, her husband least of all, who was unfaithful to her. Since René's death, Aubrey had scarcely thought about Auré's dalliances. Henrietta must have become his official mistress after the Victoria Cross ball. The few horrid crows were the only other witnesses to the intimate scene. They brought Aubrey back to the present moment. They reminded her of something — a scene from *Hamlet*: "The croaking raven doth bellow for revenge." Thoughts raced with all the acquaintances she could go to. Auré seemed indifferent to Lawrence. Then it struck her who could be used. A black-hearted smile crossed her lips. She still wanted him for a lover. It would prove to Auré she did not care about their marriage, either. *I'll let it be known we slept together. Auré will be humiliated. Everyone will howl with laughter. It will*

---

[199] A Canadian World War I epitaph

be Auré's fall from Empire hero. I hope I bear his son. I'll get back at Auré if it is the last thing I do. If it kills me! she avowed. At Aubrey's return to Pembina, one of the footmen was promptly sent to town with an invitation to afternoon tea, the envelope marked Edwards.

Moreuil Wood

Over coffee, crumpets, and custard at Lansdowne, Lady Bird informed Aubrey that her brother had recently seen action. Gabriel and Auré had returned to aid in the Spring Offensive or the Kaiserschlacht.

The Canadian Cavalry Brigade was found to be one of the sole Allied units that was not falling back in the face of the enemy's offensive. To the east of Amiens, Moreuil Wood was a vital railway junction that brought together the English and French militaries. The brigade was trotting through the forested ridge on the foggy morning of March 30th.

General J.E.B. Seely, commander of the brigade, wanted his men to dismount in order to fight throughout the forest. By way of overwhelming guns, the brigade's units were quickly trapped.

One of the three regiments in the Canadian Cavalry Brigade was the C squadron's section of Lord Strathchona's Horse. Commanded by Gordon Muriel Flowerdew, it was the only one not caught by the hail of enemy fire. Flowerdew was a thirty-three-year-old veteran cavalryman, an English-born, British-Columbian rancher. He and his troops were at the northeast of the wood's fringe. Three hundred metres from the squadron lay a gaping area where the foe was clearly visible. Flowerdew cried, "It's a charge, boys! It's a charge!"

Hard on the heels of their commander, his men unsheathed their sabres.

Squadron C galloped onwards to halt enemy reinforcement. Flabbergasted at a mounted unit advancing, the Germans quickly recovered and began using every firearm at their disposal. Brave bugler boy[200], trumpeter Trooper Reginald Longley, was hit and bled out prior to sounding the introductory note for the unit's advance. Moments after the charge began, Trooper Dale had to leap his charger over Longley's corpse. As they galloped across open fields, the cavalry found their sole protection in leaning bent over behind their horse's necks. They carried on while mates slammed to the earth and thoroughbreds crashed into their masters about them. Trooper Dale would explain at a later time that despite the pounding of the hooves, guns, and bombs, the voices of the injured and soon-to-be fatally injured were easily discernable. Flowerdew was gravely wounded in both legs and suffered two bullets wounds to his chest ahead of being able to confront the foe face-to-face, and the commander lost control of his steed. As Flowerdew lay on the ground, he encouraged the brigade onwards while his men rode past him. He cheered, "Carry on, boys! We have won!" Sabres thrust and sliced madly while the squadron attacked astride their chargers in the wooded area. A sole Trooper, Wooster, fought clear the path of the enemy and was able to reach the other side of the wood. In the thick fog and smoke, he was startlingly found to be by himself. Mounted, Wooster made his way to Seely to inform the general that Flowerdew's squadron was completely gone. The report proved overstressed. Of C Squadron, 1 in 3 fell, and a further 15 would become fatal casualties. Plagued by overwhelming numbers and fatigue, the brigade withdrew

---

[200] A Canadian World War I epitaph

afore the tree line. The stalwart drive of C squadron badly affected the Germans, and their plan to take Amiens came to a halt when the second time the remaining squadron charged, the Germans retreated from the area.

Flowerdew was accorded the Victoria Cross, posthumously. He succumbed to his wounds the ensuing day. In her son's place, Flowerdew's mother was gifted the medal by George at Buckingham Palace.

Lieutenant Flowerdew and his seventy-five troopers triumphed over three hundred enemies accompanied by their machine guns and artillery. Moreuil Wood fell to the Canadians, and with the battle, the finality of grand cavalry charges in warfare. C squadron's success elicited great commendation throughout Allied senior ranks. Supreme Allied Commander Marshal Ferdinand Foch of France wrote the Corps was *an army second to none* after visiting the Canadians shortly before. He declared the Canadian Cavalry Brigade "saved the day."

Consumption Fine

Napoleon was quoted as saying, "An army runs on its stomach." Pembina set a resplendent luncheon of numerous courses, much like the Old Days. Auré had returned to the front. Aubrey hosted Lady Bird and Peter, given that her husband was not present to object to their presence. So cross was Aubrey at her husband's return to the front, she did not say goodbye at all. Before Auré left, he had a telephone installed for Aubrey's safety. As the lines were open, she had already listened to any number of other conversations. She had thus far accused numerous military wives of "stepping-out."

Aubrey commented that the Red Baron must have been a high-ranking pilot, given his long career because he killed so many Allies. Whirling the new cocktail in hand, Peter corrected her. Richtofen was actually twenty-five when he died. The latest figure came to Aubrey's mind: some 50,000 Canadians had already been killed in action. She wondered how many more would die by war's end and, in ensuing years, from gas exposure and other battle-like injuries. Peter took a sip of his American drink. He himself was older than Richtofen at the time of Rchtofen's death. For the first time in their kinship, Aubrey glared at Peter as he continued to speak. "Oh so much the better dead," Aubrey heard nurses say. The thought of her fallen chums and of Newfoundland came to mind. The regiment was so devastated at Bailleul during the spring campaign that it had to be pulled from the front lines altogether, until its numbers could be restored well enough to return to action. The regiment was discharged from the 29th Division and stationed in Montreuil at Haig's Headquarters. She was at a loss to defend Peter not being in uniform and no longer cared to. Peter did not even look as dashing as he once did to her. Suddenly, she found him very irksome.

She gave a tired sigh and tried in vain to carry on with the conversation. "What are our underage still doing over there in the fourth year of the cause? At the same time, Longley's mother must have been so proud of her boy. But, how does an officer explain to a mother that her fourteen-year-old son was shot to death? And what were the Germans doing shooting at a bugler? They knew he was underage and not seventeen. You can't mistake a fourteen-year-old boy for a seventeen-year-old young man. But, at the distance the Germans were from the brigade and how close the brigade was to our bugler, he was probably said to be fair game by the Germans.

And, we must give our colonials this — not a lot of mounted units — Allied or foe — have been charging *twice* against machine guns. That's incredibly rare. We could be wrong about the Canadian mettle—"

Over the gravel the sound of tires was heard rather than hooves of the farmers' work horses. Peter's Studebaker was not the only automobile in the drive. The auto was an emblem of conspicuous consumption, and Peter was easily marked war profiteer. He was a traitor to the cause. Automobiles tripled in quantity over the course of the effort. A soldier would not earn enough to purchase an auto if he lived through the duration in its entirety.

Food Management Patrol agents were shown in while Aubrey tended to her favourite sweet, rice pudding. Canadians were rationed by informal gentleman's agreements. Tremendous volumes of food were sent to nourish the Allies and her populace who faced starvation. Coal, flour, sugar, wheat, milk, meat, and beans were all dissuaded and seen as frivolous commodities. The Canadian Food Board, founded in 1917 for the effort, instructed, "Do not serve bread and butter before the first course. People eat them without thought." Posters read, *Back up the Soldiers by substituting fish for meat, vegetables for bread, fruit for pastry, dripping for butter.* Regulations stated meat was allowed for supper only. Yellow sugar was substituted for white. Eggs soared from less than thirty-five cents to one dollar a dozen. Two pounds of sugar had to stretch over ninety meals. Every four pounds of white flour called for at least one relief pound of oatmeal, corn, or whole grain oats. Bread and sugar were rationed in restaurants.

The majority of expenses doubled by way of inflation. Salaries reflected the rise of prices, though soldiers were left with pay that accompanied them to basic training the first year of the war. Hoarders were fined between one hundred to one thousand dollars, sent to jail for as long as three months, or in some cases, both. Few would be made to serve the maximum penalties. Government had not previously, nor would again, have such control over its people.

Aubrey mollified herself from shock and went into the gunroom across the hallway. The federal agents left her with the maximum fine or the equivalent of the average Canadian salary over ten years of employment. For the table's spread, she should have gone to prison. She had an unsettling feeling the sole reason she did not go to jail was due to her husband's status.

Caught for being a hypocrite, the bell of conscience chimed afar. As was their "patriotic duty," Aubrey and Lady Bird had tittle-tattled of many who possessed more than "their fair share." In doing so, they had ruined the reputation of more than one aristocratic family. She wondered who had tattled on her. Worse, the thought she attempted to push clear from her mind altogether was Auré. Her husband had returned to the front not yet fully recovered, and she was acting in such a deprecating fashion.

Peter and Lady Bird could be heard as they moaned about their respective plights. Peter went on to say his father's estate, Chesil, had today the embarrassing matter of fewer than one hundred servants. The estate could no longer host hunting parties due to the implementation of taxes. Duke Edwards once had the Prince of Wales and Randolf Churchill on his grounds for a hunt, where one thousand birds were shot in one day alone. The Saturday-to-Monday had cost Peter's father more than what it cost to run Chesil for an entire year. Lady Bird wailed how some of her jewelry was sold for taxes as well. Something a Bluebird said came to Aubrey's mind again. Henrietta had mentioned to her and Auré, at some fundraiser the three of them had attended, "Of our British dead, the Canadian dear could neither read nor write." They got the flag out for the lad later that evening or the next day, after his broken body was found on a mound of shell casings and placed in hospital, where he died. An Austrian was the soldier who found him, carried the chap on his back, and left him next to an Allied lorry before walking away. Or was that another chap altogether? Aubrey could not remember. Her patience was wearing thin with Peter and Lady Bird. Neither volunteered for the effort in any way. Be that as it may, neither did she.

Peter commented that the high fever he contracted a while ago had yet to subside. He then lamented he could possibly die from the virus. A certain flu had become pervasive in early spring and had so far affected millions in various countries. As well, it was found in military camps on the Western Front to the point where certain battles were delayed. The cold ran its course and the vast majority who were afflicted recuperated.

Aubrey thought, in a terribly cross state, *I contracted my cold from him?! He knew he was sick, and from a virus that could potentially kill me, too. He did not inform me, before we were together, of his malady. How dare he put me in such a position without making his sickness clear!* It was at this hour she knew why she was feeling so under the weather. Her doctor explained that her constant fatigue was due to René.

By now, Aubrey's anger was quite substantial. She thought, in extreme agitation, *Wolves are at my door, and my so-called intimates only care for themselves. They have not even offered to aid in the payment of this ridiculous fine.* She now understood why she had not let Auré see this debasing, slanderous side of her. She respected and admired Auré too much to allow him to view her in such a callous manner.

Aubrey resigned herself to who her kindred friends really were. *It is all rot. Lady Bird is a snob, pure and simple. And Peter is a jolly royal ass. Auré ought to have it out with him, if only he weren't away!* She thought bitterly.

Two servants happened in the gunroom for the daily cleaning task.

"Oh! Madam, I do beg your pardon," exclaimed one of them in fright. Out of fatigue and indifference, asking for silence, she waved at the footmen. An idea came to her. When Aubrey was a little girl and when wolves or other wildlife were on the estate, Emmett would ride out with the groundskeeper to either shoot or hurry the animals off. The servants were handed a rifle each. Once backs were turned, smiles transpired from the two footmen while they went to inform their mistress' guests to leave. Peter's scream was well-nigh equal to Lady Bird's as they scrambled in great haste for the front door.

Llandovery Castle

Spring brought the depletion of numbers to the forefront once more. After the onset of the spring campaign, Borden threw out the exemption of farmers' sons, surely the only males of military age to be exonerated, along with exemptions in all respects, including fatally-ill wives of soldiers. Union Government elucidated that the current campaign was unforseen in the previous year. That being so, it was not a scurvy trick of an election campaign agreement. Citizens would never be so swindled by their government again.

Their sons' exemption certificates obsolete, enraged farmers protested on The Hill. "The forfeiture of agriculture would bring the Empire to her knees!" shouted Farmers. Borden answered that insufficient numbers would surely bring about ruin and downfall of the Channel ports to which agriculture would cease to count. The demonstrators resumed their war work. Augusta wrote that none of the Agnews had yet been conscripted. All were resigned to stay back in order to feed the Empire.

The fall of farm help from the duration created a federal initiative designed by the Canada Food Board, called "Soldiers of the Soil." Young volunteer males, to the extent of thirty thousand, were set about farms from coast to coast to help wartime yield.

The wee Agnews had joined the program to avenge their brothers' deaths. Perpetually in their "SOS" uniforms, they were working towards their three-month bronze service badges. Augusta signed her letter, *The work of righteousness shall be peace*[201].

Well-nigh every prairie son took up his Christian and sacred agreement to the Empire to go once conscripted. Farmers' wives lambasted Government in letters. For faith and liberty[202], their sons were diplomatically over there and concurrently feeding the Empire, while French Canada was slacker incarnate. Quebec accounted for better than double the national average of defaulters.

The onset of war saw the North-West Force close on its character once more. For much of the war, Mounties aided the west where conscripts and riots were concerned. Until the previous year, settlers, all of whom were German, were also monitored over the prairies. The fear of spies and saboteurs had diminished to naught. Government finally permitted squadrons to journey across the Atlantic. Consequently, the Mounted Force was nearing depletion from so many joining the Expeditionary Force. George McKercher, Christine's brother, was to go with one of the two drafts allotted, both of which were Cavalry. The most prestigious police force of the Empire set sail to join the most respected army of the Allies.

Aubrey had come from Vauréal. While she walked back to Pembina, she thought, *My son, I loved you so dearly, my deepest sorrow can never be healed*[203]. *God keep thee, my*

---

[201] A Canadian World War I epitaph

[202] A Canadian World War I epitaph

[203] A Canadian World War I epitaph

son, and rightly bless the life that thou hast laid down[204]. *He wore the white flower of a blameless life*[205], *though,* she tried to comfort herself. Longing to see him, to hear him say mother[206], Aubrey reasoned she would find solace in companionship, though the visit proved she could not yet bear to be near little boys or Thierry with his perpetual crepe armband. "His own words, to fight for freedom[207]," Joseph quoted Nico before he mock-died in front of their aunt Aubrey. The young Laurentiens had been playing at war, the foe against the White Gurkas. German soldiers nicknamed the Canadians so. The Napelenese Gurkas had the superb title of fiercest soldiers on earth.

An idle mind is the devil's workshop. By end of spring, so bored from lack of chums and merriment was Aubrey, she felt constantly irritated, though nothing was the matter. She knew at the front during times of respite, if there was not enough for soldiers to occupy their time, fights ran rampant and depression flourished in armies.

Aubrey's wooden needles were taken up and a pattern set about. The end of the next week saw Ottawa's president of the Daughters of the Empire received at Pembina. Henrietta informed Aubrey her yearly one-dollar membership had been paid in advance in exchange for the donated knit blanket. The two could find nothing to discuss over a spot of tea, so the effort was spoken of.

"Every possible thing was done for our troops but the bedroom," Henrietta said, unabashed, in reference to her time at the front. Peter and Lady Bird never made Aubrey laugh.

---

[204] A Canadian World War I epitaph
[205] A Canadian World War I epitaph
[206] A Canadian World War I epitaph
[207] A Canadian World War I epitaph

The Spring Offensive ended a fortnight prior. The foe was encamped at the Marne and uncomfortably near Paris. Germany's ambition to fell the front ended in dismay. The enemy was left vulnerable, well-nigh defenseless, and on the brink of vanquish. Their troops refused orders but wanted a return to their country to aid their families.

The Allies were exhausted and battered almost beyond repair. The Corps suffered no great casualties, aside from pride, given that almost all land the Corps had arrested, Germany took back that spring.

No news is jolly news, Aubrey comforted herself relentlessly. She could hear Mme. Laurentien, who was fond of saying, "They also serve who stand and wait." She told herself that he was safer away from the very front lines, at least for the time being. But without so much as a telegram from him, her birthday came and went. She burst into tears at the day being unacknowledged by her husband. August saw Borden and all Prime Ministers declare the duration was to drudge on at least a few more horrid years. She could faint. If that were true, Auré, Étienne, and the others would never return.

Newspapers abounded across the large mahogany table. May saw air bombings at Étaples. Defenseless patients, British and Dominion, were the targets. Seven Canadian Bluebirds perished. London papers decried, *This is one of the most diabolical crimes that Germany has committed. Let us hear no more of Germany airmen's chivalry.*

To add to summer's dismay, German U-boat 86 besieged Allied passenger ships. The Canadian *HMHS Llandovery Castle* marked a return passage crossing the Atlantic to England. She had come from emitting several hundred patients to Halifax. The regulation Red Cross markings and lights shining brightly undeniably marked her hospital ship. A terrific eruption occurred near nine thirty the evening of June 27th. The *Llandovery Castle* was torpedoed a few hundred kilometers afar the Irish coast. "Struck and sinking swiftly" was the speedy conclusion onboard the ship. The Bluebirds were in uniform, except for a pair who wore nightgowns. Soon, lifebelts were donned by all. Lifeboats were lowered. The Bluebirds were in Lifeboat No. 5, along with Sgt. Arthur Knight and other crew members. The ropes that held their boat to the ship became caught. Knight broke two axes in an attempt to free the lifeboat, though to no avail.

"We tried to keep ourselves away by using the oars, and soon every one of the latter were broken," stated Knight at a later date.

The boat was set free of the ropes that eventually snapped, though the members of No. 5 were at a loss to row afar their descending ship. Further crewmembers were taken captive aboard the foe's submarine. The enemy was of false opinion that the ship held Air Force Officers and supplies pertaining to the United States. The truth made plain to the enemy, the submarine arose to destroy attestation to its act: machine-gunning persons in the water and dashing against lifeboats were both illegal, according to the Hague Convention.

Knight would thereafter attest that all Bluebirds were "as calm as though on parade... In that whole time, I did not hear a complaint or murmur... there was not a cry for help or any outward evidence of fear."

"Sergeant, do you think there is any hope for us?" Matron Margaret Fraser asked of Knight.

"No," was the answer. Fraser was tossed off the side while the felled Llandovery Castle's whirlpool drew No. 5 under water.

A sole lifeboat, with twenty-four men, including Knight, the lone survivor of his craft, was rescued two days afterwards. The cast about performed by the British Navy recovered strictly bodies. Of the ninety-four Canadians on the ship, 88 perished. All 14 Canadian Bluebirds fell to drowning. A "Call to arms" rocked Canada in reply, a monumental feat itself, considering the country was in the midst of the most political muck and mire she would ever know.

Canada held her nurses in ever-resplendent veneration. When ships were torpedoed or hospitals bombed, sisters would routinely remain at post through evacuation. Solely after all wounded were removed did etiquette of "ladies first" recommence. Canadian doctors attested that sisters exhibited bravery equal to any lad who saw action.

By the fourth year of the duration, Canadian Bluebirds were routinely sent letters penned by British troops imparting they would always be indebted to the goodwill of the Canadian Army Medical Corps. The compassion Canadian medical personnel displayed was at variance with what the English Tommy had ever been acquainted with. By this point in the effort, England regularly couselled Allied armies to treat their casualties at Canadian hospitals.

A bright mid-morning found Aubrey staring at the printed fabric calendar in Pembina's morning room. She pondered how hard Knight must have tried to save the others, specifically because there were nurses with him. She had never heard of someone breaking an axe before, never mind two, and wearing corsets, the Bluebirds did not stand a chance against the whirlpool. Stitched against the coloured fabric were the words, *We'll never let the old flag fall*. Two soldiers held crossed Union Jacks. Dominion Day had just passed, and shortly after that, what would have been René's third birthday. *Could I have but clasped his hand and whispered, my son, farewell*[208]? thought Aubrey in fruitless despair. The Corps was given a prolonged respite with a grand celebration on July 1st. Fifty thousand of the Corps lads partook in a competitions and sports day. Borden and Currie were present. Royal Air Force squadrons flew overhead to safeguard the dignitaries from enemy aircraft bombs. Billy Bishop performed aerial stunts for the crowd. Beer was given to all the fellows in the jollities-filled day of relaxation. The Corps was reposed and merry. As well, given the Corps had not been a part of most of the spring and summer campaigns, its troops were fit to confront open warfare. Aubrey wondered if she would ever see Auré again and supposed divorce would be requested if he did return. She wondered where she would live, at least for the next year, or who would befriend her, given it was the wife who was ostracized after a divorce, no matter what transpired in the marriage.

Aubrey was mulling over the servant issue with Llewellyn. Yet another type-written notice had been given.

"Ouch!" Aubrey's eyes watered involuntarily.

"M'Lady?" inquired Llewellyn, who turned from the window to look towards her.

Aubrey returned the hot tea upon the saucer. Her stomach knotted in guilt. Aubrey could hear Mother Augusta lecturing, "One teaches others how to treat one." Aubrey's tea and, for that matter, all her meals were perpetually room temperature. She always assumed that was because it took

---

[208] A Canadian World War I epitaph

time for the servants to bring her meals through the long corridors and flights of stairs.

For the first year since Emmett's death, Pembina's servants were given the common paid fares to see family for a yearly two-week period. The manor had seen such chaos in recent years. Aubrey declared there was no choice but to reinstate Emmett's method of governing below stairs. A number of servants were on vacation at that moment. Nonetheless, Pembina was understaffed.

It was heard that the Westbrooks sold their Muskoka property for taxes. Calthrop had been in their family for years. Newfangled inventions, such as the electric washing machine and the vacuum, were replacing scores of servants. Even so, many mistresses did not purchase such products, given muddle below stairs mattered not.

"How can this be? Raise her daily ration or give her an easier work load — have her stay!" said Aubrey to Llewellyn, then she coughed harshly. She had had the flu for some time now.

Mistresses offered lovelier uniforms and higher salaries to keep their downstairs as it had always been. Though, workplace unions began to abound. Free time was included in the public sphere. Servant girls spoke about their employment, "The girls who work in factories have freedom. A servant's job is a slimy one because you never 'clock out,' as factory girls do, and then you are not permitted to do a thing you want because your Mistress disagrees with what you think is fun." Employment outside the realm of life below stairs held more integrity and the income was superior. The honour of serving was yielding to antiquity.

"Madam, those days are over," answered Llewellyn.

"Those days" had reigned supreme these thousand years! At the commencement of the duration, most of Pembina's servants who signed up did so for the free trip home after the war, like so many others. She could laugh at the notion. *Ages ago that seemed!* Several of her servants enlisted the first year of the cause. The rest who had left Pembina joined the outside workforce, mainly the clerical sphere, which saw great innovation in recent times from typewriters and the telephone. Following Vimy, she lost a few servants to defend Canada. *Servants of all people, who once knew their place, are demanding rights! Colonials are being heralded as heroes of the Empire! What could possibly happen on the morrow? A man on the moon?! Absurd! That being so, everything of the cause thus far had been absurd,* thought Aubrey.

The manor seemed too quiet now. The silence was hard to bear. She missed the nanny singing those typical war ditties, "Just A Prayer for Her Daddy Over There" or "I Want to Kiss My Daddy Goodnight," before laying René down for his nap. Songs, "The Roses of Picardy" and "Keep the Home Fires Burning," were most attractive across the Empire. "Roses of Picardy" was also sung after the Corps battles. If the battle was exceptionally ghastly, the singer's entire brigade would be in absolute tears by the end of the song. A few of the Corps' favorites were "Farmer's Daughter" or "Mademoiselle from Armentières." Both songs were so crude they could only be sung at the front. A yarn sung in Allied nations was "The Hearts of the World Love Canada."

"Where, oh where are the men of Canada?
Where are those who have gone away?
They are trenching on the fields of Flanders
Bringing honor to us today!

Thanks to the Khaki-clad men of Canada
We're indebted to them always
For the wide, wide world has her eyes on Canada
They are watching her day by day

What has womanhood done for Canada?
They are doing their part today
Sons they have borne they have given gladly
Now they toil for them whilst away
Think, yes! Think of the girls of Canada
Not one minute they waste each day
For they work on farm or in factory
All for those who have gone away

Yes, the hearts of the world love Canada
She's admired the whole world o'er
And those hearts love the men of Canada
For their bravery in this war
And the hearts of the world praise Canada
With her prairies and stately trees
Yes! The hearts of the world love Canada
From the pole to the southern seas
Yes, the seas."

The 8th Of The 8th

A captured German officer was quoted as saying, "The British, they are good soldiers, but the Canadians, they are madmen." Haig reported the Canadians were "really fine disciplined soldiers now and so smart and clean." The majority of British generals agreed the Canadian Corps was one of the Empire's utmost disciplined militaries. A show by cloak-and-dagger was arranged by Foch. The King's truest force, the Corps, was to spearhead the operation. The Corps would lead the Allied assault of all battles the remainder of the duration. Fighting alongside Canadian troops would be the next finest Allied armies, the British Divisions, the 5th and 13th, along with the Anzacs. The Canadians were sent to the Ypres region. Foch then mischievously repurposed the Corps southward to fox the enemy.

Currie chose to forgo the regular precursory artillery bombardment. The English queried their star general on two inducements due to sheer ambition of his design for the coming fray. Since May, Currie had his Corps groomed to face open warfare so as to bring about an end to static fighting. Engineers were adept at exploding stumbling blocks and creating pathways across rivers. Tanks and aeroplanes banded jollily alongside the poor bloody infantry. Artillery worked splendidly with all to free the routes that lay ahead.

Before the secretive show, along with his paybook, each Canadian Tommy was given a note that read, *KEEP YOUR MOUTH SHUT.* The Corps was given the most difficult position of the operation.

The initial day of the campaign was August 8th. "The Eighth of the Eighth" was headed by the Corps' battle cry, "Llandovery Castle." The assault began at 0420 hours and, through thick fog, the lads overtook Marcelcave village. Next came Pieuret Wood, which they had to drive hard for. Afterwards was Wiencourt, where the 26th's band piped in front of their fellows, and then Guillaucourt. Southwards from these locations, the 1st Division captured Hangard Wood, Demuin, Croates Trench, the little village of Caix, as well as bridges. The 3rd Division was given the uttermost perilous objective: taking Amiens-Roye road then reaching the other side of Luce River. Courcelles was taken and then Mézières. Aided with tanks, Hill 102 was captured by Highlanders. Lord Strathcona's Horse and the Royal Canadian Dragoons charged Fresnoy-en-Chaussée, and in Fresnoy, one hundred and twenty-five enemies were made prisoners. Only one aim remained uncaptured on the 8th: Le Quesnel. Four hundred Prisoners of War and forty machine guns were claimed by the 58th. Nine hundred Prisoners of War were taken by the 16th. One of the 16th's bagpipers was instructed by an Officer to play "The Drunken Piper" as their fellows overran machine guns, mortars, and enemy trenches. Eighty machine guns were claimed by the 10th.

The first day of the campaign proved the most championed for the Allied Forces of the duration. They almost succeeded in collapsing the entire German front. The Corps was utterly the source of Commander-in-Chief Ludendorff's statement, "August 8th was the black day of the German Army in the history of the war." The Corps drove thirteen kilometers through enemy territory. Of the Corps' Allies, the Anzacs sliced eleven, the French eight, and the English five. The following day, the Corps sliced a further six kilometers: more than any other army. Canadian casualties were made to wait up to a full day before they received medical treatment, during which time any number bled out from loss of blood or died from shock. In one location, forty rail cars held wounded members of the Corps. Not a soul was available to train them to hospital. The battle for Amiens lasted from August 8th to August 14th. Canada was granted ten Victoria Crosses, along with three thousand further decorations. The Corps was responsible for more than nine thousand prisoners, two hundred guns, one hundred and fifty trench mortars, and seven hundred and fifty machine guns. The enemy retrenched multiple kilometers.

The Canadians took Amiens, after which Ludendorff thought to consider an agreement. The enemy was billowing her flag at full force, undulating in whiteness, rather than bleeding so. Nevertheless, German replacements surged forth, thwarting enemy advancement. Allied guns fell out of distance of striking infantry, causing enormous dismay. The smash became grinding, unsuitable, and toilsome.

Foch ordered the Corps to return to Arras. Byng and Currie were allotted three months to plan Vimy Ridge. Currie was allowed one month to plan Hill 70, and Passchendaele, less than a fortnight. The Canadian military had become a competent and skillful army, necessitating less preparation, over time, before heading into battle. Even so, High Command extended four days to Currie to plot the forthcoming campaign: a battle that was the same grandeur of Vimy. However, the Corps officers had something of a mock-up already written down to aid them for such a battle. A surplus of guns or tanks could not be allotted as they were needed for other armies, though British tanks would aid the Corps. At disadvantage to Canada would be the impossibility of startling the enemy, since days of hard fighting had already ensued. Thus, the foe was entirely aware of the Corps' presence in the area. Nonetheless, Canadian Tommies were rested and in gay spirits. The initial success of the present campaign substantially aided the morale of the troops. The Corps was to attack the grandest exigent she had yet seen of the Western Front. Canada was to execute a matter of exceptional gravity in front of the world for the principal moment in her history.

The whole of Germany's military retreated to its final residence. The Hindenburg Line was the extraordinary cardinal barrier of the German army. The enemy had not constructed a greater secured bastion. Opposite the Canadian front, the Hindenburg Line consisted of thirty kilometers worth of trenches: double the depth along all other Allied fronts.

Behind the Hindenburg line, the infamous Drocourt-Quéant Line, a formidable defensive position, would be the most challenging fray the Corps would see. A German Prisoner of War disclosed to the Canadians who detained him, "The Drocourt-Quéant Line is to be held at all costs." Of the war in its entirety, the grandest set-piece penetration into enemy lines, consisting of nearly the largest number of German soldiers and machine-gunners the Allies would ever face, fell to the Canadians when they pushed through the Drocourt-Quéant Line. The Corps' unexpected conquest of Drocourt-Quéant was superior to that of Vimy. Aided by a British division, the Corps penetrated ten kilometers of the most fortified trench system of the Western front. The smash would remain the grandest set-piece assault the Corps would claim and a masterpiece victory of the British Forces.

Seven Victoria Crosses were awarded to the Corps the day the line fell on September 2nd; the majority were granted to lone troops who assaulted machine-gun nests. More than ten thousand prisoners, more than one hundred and twenty artillery guns, ninety-nine trench mortars, and more than an extraordinary nine hundred and twenty machine guns were taken. *The greatest fighting exploit in the annals of the Canadian nation stands unsurpassed in the entire war,* wrote one British newspaper. Currie was cabled a message from Byng, *smashing of the Quéant-Drocourt Line was the turning point in the campaign.* Currie exclaimed the breaching of the line, "One of the finest feats in our (Canada's) history." By September, the four divisions of the Corps were each being led by a Canadian-born Major-General.

Commanded by Lieutenant-Colonel Bishop, The Canadian Air Force came into foundation in autumn. Although the Canadian Air Force was separate from the Royal Air Force in paper only, Canadian names Billy Bishop, Raymond Collishaw, Donald MacLaren, and Billy Barker were commonplace in every corner of the Empire. Of the twenty-seven grandest ranking Empire aces, ten were Canadian. By war's end, the Red Baron had 80 confirmed kills, France's René Fonck would lead the Allies with 75 kills, and Canada's native-born son, from Owen Sound, Ontario, William Avery Bishop, pet named "Hell's Handmaiden" by the foe, would lead the British Empire with 72 kills.

The enemy was floundering. Her allies were deserting. The possibility of a resolution between the opposing sides had vanished. The Allies were driving all quarters and progressing on all fronts. Advancements made were measured in kilometers and not yards.

Aubrey's trifle summer cough persisted to an autumn cold. She had a consistent headache and burning of the eyes. She had a nosebleed that did not quite cease. When she began to bleed from the ears, she had Musgrove check her. Along with her lack of appetite was a loss of stones. No longer able to wear her wedding bands, she toiled with them while Musgrove asked for other symptoms. He explained that he, as well as numerous associates of his, had been treating patients for a specific harsh cold these previous weeks. The first death only recently occurred in Quebec City.

While she fiddled with the engagement ring, she noticed an engraving. There was an inscription carved on the inside band. She was uncertain if her translation of the words was correct and, given his medical background, she asked Musgrove if he knew the meaning. Musgrove furrowed his brow in puzzlement. He answered, "You are correct, Mrs. Richardieux. The inscription is definitely Latin. Latin is the most romantic language, because the words are dead. That is to say, the meaning of the words can never change or alter, much like the inscription itself. It reads: *Ever Thine, Ever Mine, Ever Ours*, Beethoven's words to his immortal beloved, whose name was tragically lost to history. When I ascend to Heaven, I shall like to know her name, along with many other questions I would have answered." Musgrove's last words were laced with venom and fury from informing so many of his young patients that they were due to take the Last Rights. The virus was mainly attacking the young and able of a shattered Canada.

Something to live for! Auré did love her! Somehow, Aubrey had never realized this. As though a light shone brightly in her eyes, everything became startlingly clear about their marriage. She thought, *In Regina, he took me to socials regularly, and he does not even like socializing. He must have done so because it made me happy. Perhaps, at some point, he had wanted to tell me he loved me.* The Mounted ball, the night he enlisted, the day he left for the front, and the Red Cross fundraiser ball immediately came to mind. *He must have always took my indifference for simply that! Indifference! Had I known he loved me, I never would have been unfaithful! How could I not have known?! Auré must have felt so hurt from having to socialize with Lawrence! How could I have hurt him so? Auré did everything he could to keep Peter away from me because he knew all along Peter was not a good person! How could I have done what I did with Peter?!*

Emmett always said what a man needed to hear from his wife, more than anything, was that she was proud of him. Had Auré ever heard so much? Oh! What she would give to have him back. What if he did not love her anymore? After everything he had been made to endure in their marriage, his love certainly seemed to have changed to disinterest. Perhaps a letter to him might be sent and everything could be laid bare. But the probability of him surviving grew smaller each passing day.

The Minister of Militia, Sydney Mewburn, gave reason to believe one hundred and twenty thousand more conscripts were required. Married men, ages twenty to thirty-four, would be made to answer the call. French Canadians accounted for less than one in four conscripts, a glaring vexation to the other side. Solely following the toughest push, and a favourable result made clear in a battle, did Military Service Agreement men see action.

Alas! What links of love that morn has war's rude hand asunder torn[209], Aubrey thought in regard to her husband. Surely, he would be killed. Nearly all her male companions had been. The current campaign was so profound; that he had lasted this length of time was remarkable. She wondered if there was anything left worth fighting for at all. She vowed Lawrence would never set foot on Pembina henceforth. Never again would she attend an event with Lawrence present, if Auré wanted that. Perhaps they could forgive one another for all the affairs and start anew.

She had ruined the reputation of almost every aristocratic family in the city. What little ties he had to his family he severed completely to fight. She thought, *There must be something for Auré to return to, other than a ruined reputation — all because of my callous nature — and an — empty manor.* She could possibly perish from her malady before he even returned. A person could be gone hours after contracting the flu. *Atonement must be made!*

From Amiens to Arras, which was a trench system, the Corps was well-nigh fractured. The yet-unfinished Canal du Nord was the next objective and would be the second hardest show for the Corps over the course of the war. "Very furthest we can go," was what Ludendorff said of the Canal. It held the Hindenburg Line together in its entirety. Currie wanted to assault the area: a stronghold the Allies had not previously considered to assault. The proposal was so dauntless and bold, Haig had to abrogate the Army Commander to allow

---

[209] A Canadian World War I epitaph

Currie to carry on. Currie's four divisions alone would face twelve enemy divisions and thirteen machine-gun companies.

Byng visited Currie himself in the days before the battle. Byng asked of his former protégé, "Old man, do you think you can do it?" Currie agreed he could.

Lieutenant-General Currie penned in his diary, *Granted our fellows are in the right mood for a scrap, and all the devils in hell cannot stay them.*

At the end of September, the Corps was funneled through a two thousand six-hundred-yard dry section of the Canal. Should the enemy catch them as they went through the dry section, the lads, with the most seasoned veterans in the lead, would be annihilated. After the initial phase of the assault, they were to spread out over ten thousand yards to overtake the position. The front in its entirety was assaulted in the largest unaccompanied day attack of the duration. Aided by the British, the Hindenburg Line was handsomely shattered. The breaking of the spine of the Hindenburg Line was another major grievance for the foe, as it provided war material and reserves to the whole of the region.

Without federal government, relief organizations, doctors or nurses — most of whom were over there — in September, the expeditious dilemma of Influenza had Ottawa Mayor Fisher send out word to the civilians of his city, "They are not dying because we do not know about them. We know where they are, but we have nobody to send. Knitting socks for soldiers is very useful work, but we are now asking the women of Ottawa to get into the trenches themselves."

All capable women were called on to aid. Fifteen hundred responded. The depleted police force also assisted by hauling and chopping wood for fires. All churches, schools, theatres, and concert halls, along with the University and all settings of "public gathering," were ordered to close. Stores were made to close by three or four in the afternoon. By mid-month, Ottawa saw thousands of patients.

Aubrey knew not how to run a convalescent hospital, but she did know someone who could. Few households owned a telephone, though perhaps he did. She rung for the operator. All lines were still. No one took her call: too many telephone employees were ill. Formal calling required an ornate frock. She donned trousers. She had never seen the streets of Ottawa so deserted. Citizens were not allowed to meet in groupings of a handful or more. Shaking hands had become illegal. Streetcars were treated daily with disinfectant. None were manned anyhow. The conductors were all down with the flu.

So many Service Flags hung in windows. Seemingly countless had red or gold leaves. Posters featured a sinking Allied ship and a descending enemy submarine. A solider held an unconscious Bluebird in the waters. The man's fist shook in the air. The life buoy the man clung to read, *Llandovery Castle*. The caption stated, *Victory Bonds will help stop this.*

A sole Dominion Officer halted her. She was embarrassed to be seen in the presence of a man with either of her legs on each side of her thoroughbred. By the end of the decade, ladies were permitted to ride the same as their cavalier counterparts.

Through his surgical mask he exclaimed, "Madam, you cannot be here! Where is your lady's maid? Make haste!" A lone ambulance siren was heard in the background. She rode onwards to Sandy Hill. The peeling of church bells indicated yet another funeral. The practice would stop for the duration of the virus due to the sheer volume of deaths in the city.

Once at his residence, because she did not have a footman or a lady's maid with her, Aubrey did something she was not certain she had done prior. She knocked on the front door. An upper housemaid, who had replaced the footmen, answered. An incredulous Kellynch met her in the front parlour. Kellynch agreed to help her turn Pembina into a convalescent hospital.

Pembina's tennis courts were converted first. Their pristine lawn was no more. Blood and surgical tools upon her silver trays, which had been in her family for generations, lay commonplace. Protective masks were worn by all on the grounds. From workers being sick, they had to wait for trains to transport the wounded. Then, they came by the multitudes.

After four years of attrition, the war had turned to one of locomotion. Every sector of the front saw the enemy army falling back. The enemy of ever-advantage was losing morale, on the verge of collapse, and defending a starving Germany from British blockade. The Corps claimed one stunning victory after another by taking Bourlon village, Bourlon Wood, which looked down on Canal du Nord. Then the Corps captured the villages of Rallencourt and Sailly, Cambrai, a crucial railway network and management area, and Canal de la Sensée. Canadian Tommies penned, *The devil himself cannot stop us!... One cannot stay in place or be shot dead, but going forward one will assuradely be cut to ribbons... Take down all the Frtizie's possible but others in the Corps are showing restraint and treating our prisoners with due care... My chance to defend Canada!* The Corps was capturing so many prisoners, guns, strongholds, and villages that the Allies styled the One Hundred Days campaign of the war as "Canada's Hundred Days." In response, "The Last Post" trumpeted relentlessly. The thrashed Corps saw one hundred sons fall per day.

Influenza

The Royal Newfoundland Regiment was stationed in the Flanders region to the east of Ypres. They were to maintain a railway line in Ledeghem. Remarkably, they covered five kilometers and along the way took five hundred prisoners, ninety-four machine guns, and eight guns, with four of the guns belonging to a single platoon (28 men). Under cover of thick fog, the regiment advanced towards German lines the morning of October 14th. The Germans were sliced from their position by Newfoundland's B Company, including the platoon that took the four machine guns. The company took a total of three pillboxes from German hands. The morning went on, the fog thinned, and, consequently, B Company was left exposed to enemy sights. The Newfoundlanders had to cross a creek, two yards in depth, called the Wulfdambeek. They made their way through the creek. Casualties began to mount. The foe had a complete view of the regiment. Nearly one thousand yards after the Wulfdambeek, shelling caused the company's advance to become hampered. The company's artillery was too far behind them. The number of wounded grew still. Led by the platoon's commander, a band along with a Lewis gun group attempted to outflank the foe. When the gunners could go no further, the section commander and one of his soldiers volunteered to advance further, just the two of them and a Lewis gun. The pair went on in small rushes in the face of heavy enemy fire. Three hundred yards from their objective, the enemy battery, the pair's ammunition was gone.

Privy to the predicament of the two Allies, the Germans brought forth reinforcements. The soldier volunteered once more to return to his unit, one hundred yards behind the pair's present location, to retrieve more ammunition. He did so entirely in the face of heavy enemy fire. The section commander and the soldier were now the only two left unwounded of the band. The two then successfully drove the enemy to farm structures close by. From the soldier's actions, his platoon was able to push towards the Germans, and secondly, his platoon did not suffer further casualties. The platoon took a further eight prisoners, four machine guns, and later another field gun. The soldier, who enlisted at fifteen years of age, from Middle Arm, White Bay, would be bestowed the Victoria Cross and would also be accorded Le Croix de Guerre (France's highest medal of honour and the equivalent of the Victoria Cross) along with a gold star.

There were fifty deaths per day in Ottawa from Influenza. Across the country, patients were put on plywood and cinderblocks to keep off corridor floors of overcrowded hospitals. Gymnasiums were turned into secondary hospitals. Auditoriums changed to temporary morgues. Undertakers' supply of coffins completely diminished. Funeral parlours ceased announcing death tolls to newspapers when numbers became almost innumerable. Christian burials were overlooked. Mass ones became commonplace.

Pembina's first floor was now converted. Musgrove was given his own room on the estate. He was at Pembina so often that he simply stayed indefinitely. Musgrove was so exhausted he slept in his day suit and wore the same attire for days in a row.

The most downtrodden year of the war saw expenses in the dominion and fatalities on the front lines take to the air. Aubrey knew not what to tell the chef to make for her charges for the coming festivities. Turkeys for Thanksgiving were in short supply. She could not stomach a thing, besides, from feeling so sickly. So tired was she from the virus, most of the time it was a struggle simply to stay awake the whole day.

She had come from instructing servants to utilize more old shirts, handkerchiefs, and cotton for the convalescents, due to regular hospital supplies having become almost obsolete in the city. In the main hallway, Aubrey beckoned a remaining footman to stand erect. Likewise, from coast to coast, Pembina's volunteer force for the sick was toiling nearly to the extremity of human endurance.

Aubrey went to her stationary, ever fatigued. *Can't forget that parting kiss that sealed your love for me*[210], she repeated quietly when no one was near. A poor sleeper, she solely slept undisturbed in Auré's arms. But now, she woke constantly from fever and night sweats, or worse, dreams of René. She thought endlessly, *He is at home and safe in Heaven*[211] as well as *May angels guard your grave is the wish of parent's heart, my boy*[212], she thought to try to calm herself. But she would look around at the darkness, yearn for Auré, and the words *Gone. There is no other. Mother*[213] would repeat endlessly in her mind. She would become overwhelmed with missing René and burst into tears.

---

[210]   A Canadian World War I epitaph
[211]   A Canadian World War I epitaph
[212]   A Canadian World War I epitaph
[213]   A Canadian World War I epitaph

Blankets lay across her, but no amount could now warm her. She was writing to the heartsblood of a lad who fought with the Little Black Devils (90th Winnipeg Rifles). Hands tanned and freckly, she enclosed a lock of his hair into the addressed envelope. The sniper had been recovering nicely from his war injuries but had contracted the virus and died a few days prior at Pembina. Many of the Corps' injured succumbed to Influenza in one of the major Canadian hubs for convalescents. Had the wounded survived the virus, they simply would have returned to their families. Since the lad was from a village outside Winnipeg, she was reminded of the city and three of its sons. At Pozières during the Somme, and after all his mates were killed or had become casualties, Lance Corporal Leo Clarke of the 2nd Battalion found himself solo in a trench against twenty-two enemies, of which two were officers. "Nobby," Clarke's nickname, disposed of all rifles, grenades, and bayonets about him. Hand-to-hand combat then ensued. His revolver was twice spent of all cartridges, after which Clarke seized and spent German rifles until they were emptied. An officer then plunged a bayonet into Clarke's leg beneath the knee. Considerably wounded, a wrestling match ensued between Leo and the officer. Clarke was able to successfully bayonet the officer with the officer's proper weapon.

Twenty-one Germans were killed. The remaining one was made prisoner. Afterwards, at Regina Trench, a shell explosion buried Clarke alive. Charlie Clarke, Leo's brother, was close by when the explosion happened. Charlie did what he could to find his brother. When Charlie removed enough earth to uncover him, Leo called out, "I knew you'd find me, Charlie!" His spine broken, twenty-three-year-old Leo was rendered paralyzed and had grave internal wounds.

Under medical care, he died a week later, on October 19th, and precisely five weeks following his stance in the trenches. Unknowing of his Victoria Cross, declared by British High Command the day he died, Clarke would be granted the medal posthumously. Clarke lived in Winnipeg, where he was neighbour to Sergeant Major Frederick Hall and Lieutenant Robert Shankland. Both had been awarded the Victoria Cross as well. All of them lived on the same road: Pine Street. The street was distinguished throughout the entire world, as three Victoria Cross recipients lived there simultaneously. The record would stand a century to follow.

Étienne had written that her husband had been conceded the rank of General. The position was principally refused, as Auré felt unjust leaving his men. After a time, though, he was ordered to take the position. Numerous generals had fallen from the desire to truly lead their men. After time, generals were forbidden to join any fray, the knowledge they boasted being too notable to perish.

Mother Augusta had written recently. Aubrey was surprised the letter was delivered at all because the post was affected by the virus. Sacred Heart had turned into a makeshift hospital, like countless other institutions across the country. Mother Augusta was of the opinion that at least a few patients were starving, but no milk could be delivered. The ones who brought milk were bedridden with the flu.

Across the prairies, not a soul was permitted to enter or leave their village or town. In Saskatchewan, entire towns were quarantined. If one tried to leave their town, they would face arrest. To cough, sneeze, or spit in public resulted in a fifty-dollar fine. Masks were mandatory.

After shrapnel had partially blinded George McKercher, he had been invalided to Regina. Along with an honourable discharge, he brought back the virus. His wife and two small children became infected. Soldiers who survived the war returned to kill their own families. Mother Augusta supposed he had lost hope after he lost them. Aubrey would miss George. She had curled and danced the tango with him any number of times.

Christine became a nurse's aid out of tribute to her deceased loved ones. Such was common for women in her position. She had stayed on at Sacred Heart to help the doctors. She succumbed to the flu after contracting it in the hospital. Mother Augusta had spoken to Mrs. McKercher about the pain of losing all her children and grandchildren within weeks.

Aubrey did not finish the letter. She heard stories similar to Mother Augusta's all the while. The most recent letter from Lawrence would go unreturned as well. *O soul of my soul, I shall meet thee again*[214], Aubrey thought of Auré, while she wrote letters to the families of those who died under her care.

Kellynch, in a rare moment of spare time, sat with a newspaper across from Aubrey. It was documented at the Canal du Nord, Canadian battalions had three to six hundred regulars who brought down thirty to forty machine guns by themselves. At the Somme, two or three machine guns decimated the equivalent number of troops. The Corps fought against ten to twenty times the typical predicament in prior engagements and, although with high casualties, was victorious. Also, Canadian forces were in Minsk and Archangel to aid the "Whites" against the "Reds" of Russia's opposing armies. Canadians were, too, in Siberia, fighting alongside the British and anti-Bolshevism.

---

[214] A Canadian World War I epitaph

Henrietta had also taken up permanent residence at Pembina to aid in running the hospital. Henrietta's knitting lay near Kellynch. The remaining servants were too overwhelmed to consider the now trifling task of tidying a knitting bag. The commonplace knitting bag had two cross-stitched soldiers, each holding a Union Jack. Beneath the soldiers read the motto, *Knit and do your best.* Henrietta fought in one fray and then another. Nurses who returned from over there faced no respite but entered the trenches of a different sort.

Kellynch sat reading page eleven. Though Influenza killed tens of millions more than the war, it was found in the back pages of papers because the war took centre stage to all.

A consoling Fitzwilliam said softly, "They say the war could end soon." Bulgaria declared its agreement at the end of September. On October 18th and 19th, the Corps freed some sixty villages and towns. Their eleven-kilometer advance on the 19th would be the furthest sliced by the Corps over the war. "They say," was the most exploited term of the duration, and the departed value of these words was marked at the passing of the second year. The dominion was chary to concede the end might be in sight.

"Curst greed of gold, what crimes thy tyrant power has caused[215]!" Aubrey quoted Virgil. Possibly, her husband could return. He was stationed north of the Somme River. The next day, Musgrove successfully persuaded Aubrey to stay in bed. The Allies were perpetuating their strongholds into fall.

---

[215] A Canadian World War I epitaph

The Battle

Musgrove looked upon Aubrey's sickbed in the now lone wing left unconverted. The virus had fled! The end of October saw the worst of the epidemic in decline. But Aubrey did not feel in finer spirits. She was weaker. Influenza often debilitated only to leave the patient altogether. Pneumonia would then normally ensue by attack of the respiratory system, the result of which was that the person would drown in their own fluids.

The call of the Empire had come to her finest men. It was as though it was her judgement day. It was as though it was his zero hour[216]. Peter sat, head bowed, cowering across from Aubrey's emaciated frame. His cowardice was paralleled only by her wrath.

"I forgive you," Aubrey said unexpectedly, in an act of exemplary gallantry.

The whistle blew[217]. Every corner of the seven seas saw armies amassing of the two Powers: God and Satan.

"Spread out and on the alert!" came the former Archangel's[218] order to his serpentine subjects. The Angels

---

[216] In WWI, the term *Zero Hour* referred to the literal time when a battle started

[217] In WWI, a whistle was often blown by an officer at the start of a battle to inform soldiers they were to leave the trenches

[218] In Christian tradition, Archangels are the most powerful Angels who lead all other Angels

emerged to confront their fallen, erstwhile commander, the devil.[219]

"What shall come of you?" sliced Peter, the speculative subversive, in self-harrowing fashion.

"My time on earth is over and that is fine," Aubrey calmly said, to the consequence of a terrific din on Peter's emotions.

It was as though Peter was shot through the heart at her graciousness.

"Do you not wish revenge? That Auré may seek rightful retribution?" Peter thrust at the now ex-regular to bloody her back into fighting on the evil one's side.

"His happiness matters more than that to me — to have him hurt further by the knowledge of my unfaithfulness." At Aubrey's valour, the big guns seemed to open up and Peter's resolve was thereby decimated.

Peter began to weep.

"Thus are the fortunes of warfare, Peter, but are we downhearted? No!" came the dupes of the devil.

However, the excitement was intense. The bonds of narcissism and the chains of pride, vanity, and conceit fell wayside. Peter the betrayer[220] was left with only one thing: his conscience. The full weight of his sins took hold of him, mind and soul. The searing knowledge of the consequences of his transgressions became all-consuming. The gnashing of teeth had begun[221].

---

[219] In Christian tradition, the devil was created by God as an Archangel before he rebelled and was cast out of Heaven

[220] In the Christian Gospels, Peter, the apostle, betrayed Jesus three times before Jesus' death

[221] In the Christian Gospels, hell is described as a place where there is weeping and gnashing of teeth. *Gnashing of teeth* means remorse

"No! Look what I've done to her! I've killed her! How could I have done this to another?! Take me instead, God! I deserve to die!" he roared.

The skirl of the bagpipes was heard afar the Old World as Aubrey quelled, "Promise me something?"

"Anything!" Peter shouted, desperate to make amends, to somehow right this terrible, tragic wrong.

"Never let Auré know of you and I being together."

Peter was rather deaf from shell shock. He stared at the floor in dereliction of duty. A moment's scruple ensued. To and fro, to and fro rang the artillery duel of the two Powers. The frontal seven-trumpet charge[222] of the Angels drowned the ghastly ordnance of the foe.

"We are well-beaten, he hath went west[223]!" though before cowardly retreat, Lucifer diabolically, infernally hissed, *"When we get you back, we'll sift you like wheat!"*

But conviction and integrity were stronger, for the lad now belonged to the Grand Cause. Leaning heavily on the barrage of his psyche[224], Peter set his jaw.

"I — I agree," he said in his deep voice while he looked her in the eye.

"May I have your word?"

"Yes," came the serene reply.

---

[222] In the Bible, the number seven is a number signifying completeness. Trumpets are instruments of celebration, praise, and victory, especially that the heavens are powerfully proclaiming the victory of God

[223] In World War I, the term *went west* referred to a soldier who was killed in action

[224] *Psyche* is Latin for *soul*

The piping alarums from the Immortal Salient[225] of Peter's countrymen to return to the colors resonated with, "As a — gentleman?" Aubrey asked while she struggled for breath, as blood had entered her lungs.

"Upon my honor as a gentleman, I give you my word," he said quietly, lest she be disturbed, that she may lie upon her deathbed peacefully. Peter looked calm on the outside, but on the inside, he was screaming, *No. I would rather hang myself than live with this remorse, this all-consuming guilt, another day of life. Auré is the only one from whom I could seek repentance, the only one who could abate this pain, and he must never know. Away could I scurry, for the aristocracy is dying out, our world is ending, too many gentlemen are buried on the fields of Europe — I've done nothing for the effort. But to hang myself would be cowardly, for a gentleman remains one when no other is at present, and I'll remain one until my dying breath. Bong sang ne peut mentir[226]* (A noble nature cannot play false), *for when faced with adversity, a man of character looks unto himself and these Canadians. Who I've always looked down upon. Who no one thought belonged in a war of gentlemen. The Germans and Allies alike aggrieved the Canadians the most appalling treatment and, in the hell of the Western Front, they've forged their colony into nationhood. The shock troops of the Allied forces. The enemy himself will not attack the Canadians – if this doesn't speak to a country's integrity.*

Auré can never know, must never suspect this. I'll, I'll return to England — and face father. He'll be disgusted with me. I've done nothing with my time here. I'll have him

---

[225] *Salient* means *a bulge in the line of a battlefield.* The *Immortal Salient* refers to the notorious or horrific battlefields of World War I

[226] A Canadian World War I epitaph

bequeath my inheritance to our convalescent hospital so I may pay my debt to these colonials and my own servants who fought for me.

Auré must return to Our Fair Dominion to say goodbye to her. But no man is allowed to leave the front. I could petition to take his place. Surely father could have me exchanged in time — the least I could do for Aubrey and Auré — this way I can avenge my brother's deaths and father, for once, would be proud of me. I'll lead my men from the front, single-handedly, and should I perish — I'd rather die a gentleman than live a coward. Because she forgives me, I could never betray her!

From Aubrey's forgiveness, Peter was sent to a fate worse than death to him: sent to his personal hell, forever bound to obscurity and to indentured servitude to someone who did not respect him, his father. His fate was sealed; Peter would return to his Rome[227], head of his church[228], to spearhead the reformation of his people[229], and shackled and chained to his gentleman's agreement. Peter would remain a gentleman until the end of his days.

---

[227] It is traditionally believed that after Jesus' death and resurrection, Peter went to live in Rome

[228] Peter became the first leader of the Catholic church, or the first Pope

[229] Peter acted as a disciple of Christ, initiating the spread of Christianity in the western world

The Beast of Berlin

Canadian Major Billy Barker was flying from France en route to England one autumn day. The morning on the last of a ten-day roving commission saw him atop Le Fôret de Mormal (Mormal Forest). After shots were fired from Barker, an enemy reconnaissance aircraft fell apart mid-air. A Fokker biplane proceeded to strike the Canadian in the same moments. Alhough he was wounded in the right thigh, Barker attacked and came away the victor. He then found dismay a-flock of Iron Crosses. Barker's grey eyes could not be deceived. He was in the company of sixty enemy aircrafts! Fifteen Fokker D. VII's promptly broke formation to down a solo Barker.

The Sopwith Snipe that Barker commandeered was promptly peppered with shot and shell. His five-foot ten-inch frame suffered numerous affronts, including a serious wound in the left thigh. Yet so, he downed two enemies by way of a spin. From blood privation, he fainted. Consequently, his aeroplane fell to gravity. He awoke mid-air to be confronted by a second formation. However, Barker downed an enemy once more. After his left elbow was almost entirely shot off, he fainted a second time. While still in air, he came to and downed another enemy. From extreme wounds and exhaustion, he tumbled into and out of awareness. He then dived from a third formation in order to reach Allied territory, though he met with a fourth formation. Charging steadfastly, he dismantled the last formation. He was credited with four kills in total, three of which perished in flames. His overall kills were brought to a dashing fifty. He crash-landed behind Allied lines.

Barker would recover and obtain letters of adulation from George, George's son, the Prince of Wales, and Borden. The most marvellous hullabaloo Air Cavalry would see over the duration saw Barker endowed the Victoria Cross. Also, by war's end, Barker would be granted the Distinguished Flying Cross, the Military Cross with two bars added to the medal, the Distinguished Service Order medal with a bar added to it as well, and be mentioned in dispatches for gallantry three times. From other Allied countries, Barker would be awarded two Silver Medals for Military Valour from Italy (Italy's second highest medal of honour), and Le Croix de Guerre. Canada had the supreme distinction of her native-born son, from Dauphin, Manitoba, William George Barker, claim the title of the most highly decorated soldier history would write for the British Empire. The record would stand a century to follow.

Aubrey thought he was Michel, he had aged so when he walked into her bedroom one evening. Through much tribulation at rest from all his labours[230], Étienne had been granted leave. He was the only Old Guard or 1ˢᵗ Division she knew to have survived four years indebted to His Majesty's Services, as shown by the number of chevrons on his sleeves.

Generals agreed that if not in a bombproof setting, it was essentially impossible to survive the entire theatre of war. After Frédéric's death, since Étienne was the last remaining

---

[230] A Canadian World War I epitaph

brother of his family serving, he was moved from his position as a gunner to a bombproof position in the rear. Student and soldier of Christ[231], over the course of the war, Étienne was sent to hospital nearly twenty times: for gas exposure, gunshot, and shrapnel wounds. Aubrey was too weak to write and needed his assistance. He was a brave soldier and true friend[232]; Étienne was immune to writing last letters for others.

The letter addressed to Auré was finished. Left with Étienne, as well, were instructions that she be buried next to Emmett and on the other side of René, so that her son would be surrounded by family. He then ran a hand over Aubrey's hair and kissed her forehead. "Goodnight, beloved[233]," he said gently. He silently left the room.

At the start of November, the Corps captured Mont Houy, a sixty-metre high hill, then heavily defended Valenciennes, the last major occupied French city where the Canadians were outnumbered three to one but took 1,800 prisoners. The Corps then freed minor villages. The Corps members were staying with, and were waited on nearly hand and foot, by civilians in their residences and no longer in dugouts. Monetary payment was continually and crossly refused. What was demanded of the Canadians were to accept offers of coffee, alcohol, and physical affection from their grateful hosts. The soldiers worked hard to maintain the Corps in a glorious light. A common catchword was "Hustle the Hun!" and Canadian rations were largely handed to the boys and girls of the inhabitants. On crowded French roads, the liberators

---

[231] A Canadian World War I epitaph

[232] A Canadian World War I epitaph

[233] A Canadian World War I epitaph

were cheered onwards. The foe, in tenacious retreat, saw the Corps push towards that emblematic city.

There is something sublime in calm endurance[234]. Outside Aubrey's room, Musgrove confided to Fitzwilliam and Henrietta that he was shocked beyond all reason that Aubrey was lasting as long as she was.

Henrietta exclaimed, "But how can this be, doctor? The original ones to contract the illness had some sort of immunity to the second phase of the virus. How can she be dying?"

Musgrove replied, "The majority did receive an immunity, but not all."

The trio then discussed the forced resignation of Ludendorff the week before, on October 26th, and that Turkey and Austria had signed their respective agreements. Newfoundland sliced hard to cross the River Lys and then pushed to come to the river Scheldt. Then, on October 26th as well, Newfoundland was ordered out of the front lines and given a respite in billets. The Regiment's war was over.

In Ottawa, every electrical light had been wired jointly to spread word of the coming end. To-day saw all electrical lights blink twice. The abdication of Keiser Wilhelm II had occurred on November 9th. Blackberry syrup was used for toasts. Champagne, a favourite of the Edwardians, had long ago faded from their diet. Ottawa's streets saw people congregate to celebrate the fall of Germany's House of Hohenzollern.

Lights were set to blink four times to assert the establishment of peace. Ottawans found themselves glancing at electrical lights many times each passing day. At Pembina, the declaration was presumed to be announced the very day, yet the announcement did not happen.

---

[234] A Canadian World War I epitaph

The Armistice

Auré looked out the window at the lovely, calm winter day. The sun was setting in a cloudless, brilliant blue sky that gave the appearance of a deceptively warm day. The temperature was really somewhere just below zero degrees. A sparkling layer of snow covered the landscape to a stunning consequence. *What did she always say about such days? A perfect day for falling in love?* he thought. He took one last look out the window and closed the door. He shut out the last rays of sunlight, along with the last rays of her future and the light of his life. He leaned his forearm against the door and rested his forehead to his arm. A sigh was heaved. Unable to protect his wife, he was finally a man defeated.

High Commands were making their way through the forest towards the boxcar. He turned his sable silver beard[235] to look at her. Lying on her deathbed, characteristerically British in her quiet way, it was obvious that Aubrey's end had come. No longer a lady, her complexion had turned blackened-blue. Black and white people were hardly distinguishable by

---

[235] In Shakespeare's *Hamlet* Act I, Scene II, Hamlet is told by Horatio that he saw the ghost of Hamlet's late father, the former King of Denmark. The ghost's beard was sable silver. The reference to *sable silver* means *the status of the deceased ruler*

doctors. The afflicted became extremely darkened from lack of oxygen.

Auré removed from his breast pocket his last letter, penned in Latin and in the trenches on the eve of his first battle. He then laid down his general's jacket, along with his armour, at the foot of their bed. The early morn saw affirmation dispatched to Ottawa. Church bells, factory whistles, fire station gongs, sirens, horns, bugles, and tins responded in kind. Civilians quickly changed into daywear and made haste to the city's downtown. The grandest parade the capitol would ever see was under way.

Without knowing if he was being heard, without a trace of pride, without a hint of French, the sole time his voice was to flow ardently, Auré began to read aloud,

"My dearest Aubrey,

Neither a letter or a poem can adequately convey how deeply I am in love with you, though I am most gratefully compelled to pen these trifle lines. Should our marriage cease where it is now and should I be denied the honour of growing old with you, I wish that you may fall asleep safe in the knowledge of my love for you.

If love ever found itself at first sight, it was with you and I. That charming afternoon by the creek when I saw the most beautiful woman I have to this day ever seen, I instantly knew in my heart we were meant for one another.

I moved to Regina to be with you, so that no other might hinder the beginning of our marriage. I learned English solely that I may speak with you. These recent years have been the most joyful of life to me. I thank Our Loving Heavenly Father every day for giving me you and our René for the short time He granted us our son. Of all stations in life, I am most proud to call myself husband to you and father to René.

As the battle for Canadian sovereinty raged on over the plains of our forefathers, I felt compelled to aid our gallant kinsmen by fighting alongside them, in my small part, for our country's greatest undertaking. For this reason, I enlisted and fought for the two of you. My love of country is only surpassed by the love I feel towards you and is the only justice that compels me to fight in battle during the most grievous of times. In my darkest hour, I think of you, my darling[236].

Because you estranged yourself from your family in marrying me, I had to ensure you and René would be taken care of, lest something should happen to me in battle. I knew you married me because you have always wished to remain in Ottawa and not return to England, and I could give you that. I tried to create a better environment to leave behind for you than what I had made for myself at the commencement of the war. My actions were effectuated solely for your sake."

Her breathing became regular.

"At the same time, I have tried to be the man your father was not. I like to think my fighting for you on the front lines has healed the hole in your heart left by him, as he did not fight for you when you were a little girl. I know what a tremendous impact that has had on your happiness over the course of your life. I only ever wanted you to feel safe and whole in my embrace. I have always been faithful to you, here on the front lines as well. Do please excuse my numerous shortcomings and the myriad of ways I have hurt or have failed to protect you and my foolish pride at not explaining all of this sooner. I would not want to go through life with anyone but you. Should I perish, I consider my short life blessed that I had the privilege of our marriage. And as the sun is setting

---

[236] A Canadian World War I epitaph

(on the British Empire[237]), I leave the words of a great poet simply to be whispered if ever you need to know how I feel,

'Never misjudge the faithful heart of your beloved, for our love will remain,

Ever thine,

Ever mine,

Ever ours,'

Your unfailing loving husband,

Auré."

He placed the letter on the nightstand beside Aubrey's wedding bands and the charred Lord Beaverbrook. Auré took her limp hand in both of his and said, "Now I'm left wondering why you're still fighting this."

Vocal cords ravaged by Influenza, though in perfect French, Aubrey said, "I had to say goodbye. That was a beautiful letter, Auré. Thank you for writing that," as tears fell down her cheeks.

The small hours saw Belgium's Havré village fall to the Canadians. At the same time, a statement arrived at Corps headquarters. An agreement had been reached between the Entente and Central Armies. The agreement would come into effect in mere hours' time. Runners dashed over a few tens of battlefield kilometers to give word of the immediate end. The task yet befell Currie to apprehend, alas, the Allies' final objective.

The husband asked, "What of Peter? Did he ever hurt you?"

---

[237] *The sun never sets on the British Empire* was one of the British Empire's most common expressions. During the Edwardian era, England owned twenty-five percent of the world's land, and, because of this, it was always daylight in a part of the world that England owned

O valiant heart[238], the devoted swallowed hard to clear the blood from her throat. Aubrey explained she let Peter get away by saying the repatriate had returned to England to honour a gentleman's agreement.

Desperate to comfort his wife, to offer some solace if not from the sheer strength of his loving arms before she left their world, he questioned, "Are you frightened to die?"

Hail to the steadfast soul, hail to the spirit which dared[239], the answer was "No."

The reassuring reply was, "You do not need to be brave. This is our time to be honest with one another."

"I'm not frightened to die. I don't live in fear. I will do this — serenely," Aubrey said, gasping for breath amid the humble reply. If the general had ever looked at another with admiration and respect, it was then.

And faith and hope and love shall greet the morning light[240]; while the sun rose, a Highlander pipe band led their men over the cobblestone. The most revered army of the war had the high distinction of parading into Mons and setting her free. Emaciated Belgiums were overcome with gratitude towards their liberators. Endless and great physical affection, tears of felicity, and presents, namely flowers, blessings, sweet biscuits, hidden wine, and inexpensive ribbon were gifted to exhausted though jubilant members of the Canadian Expeditionary Force.

The lights blinked the final time.

"What shall be of me without you?"

---

[238] A Canadian World War I epitaph

[239] A Canadian World War I epitaph

[240] A Canadian World War I epitaph

The Mighty British Lion sounded her final great roar unto her most inconsequential colony, as the wife spoke to her husband for the last time, "I will always be with you."

He kissed her on the cheek and said, "Goodnight beloved, never goodbye[241]. Love and remembrance last forever[242]." Auré held Aubrey in his arms where she took her last sigh.

She was leaving, England was leaving, with no daughters of hers to accord the beauty that defined her and her predecessors, she was taking with her the last golden age, the last age of elegance, and the last great House of Saxe-Coburg Gotha in the line of Windsor.

He, like his colony, had gotten off to battle with a fierce duty to defend her, to protect her, out of loyalty to her. He had returned battle-hardened, scarred with blood on his hands, and death clung to his heart. But he had returned victorious and in command of her respect. With their final conversation, so too was the passing of the torch of thy Grand Old Empire unto a colony that had risen to nationhood.

As Canada stepped out of the shadows of the Empires and took her place in the sun, her loyalties to France and to England she would forevermore carry with her. That Canada should remember her sons, who gave of themselves as they marched off to warfare and in selfless death brought their descendants nationhood of a debt that cannot be repaid.

The war-torn nations were bound to one another in the burying of their sons, a generation of soldiers lost to history who fought with gallantry for the Empires, with chivalry toward the enemy, and who, in laying down their lives, let fall the last age of gentlemen in the culmination of a Great War.

---

[241] A Canadian World War I epitaph

[242] A Canadian World War I epitaph

1919

The war ended the previous year. The last-recognized British Empire soldier to die in battle fell two minutes before the Armistice. The soldier was Canada's, a twenty-five-year-old fiancé, Private George Lawrence Price from Nova Scotia of the 28th, who was shot through the heart by a sniper east of Mons and died in the arms of a comrade. Buglers tooted the cessation of shot and shell. Soldiers were heartsore or downhearted. Further troops were simply tickled to death. Some were wary that all battles had ceased and kept fighting.

Ottawa saw more than twice the people who were at the declaration of war pour onto its streets to celebrate that the war was over. Not a soul lauded the Allies.

George and the Queen catered a private luncheon to the man who was largely believed to be the finest General of the Allied Forces, Sir Arthur Currie.

Vimy Ridge stayed under British command and Germany did not endeavour to recover the region the remainder of the duration. From Vimy Ridge until the end of the war, the Canadian military did not lose one battle. Haig admitted that Canada had become a minor, though sovereign, ally to England. That not one soldier perished from starvation was a monumental milestone in Empire history.

Usually, the Canadian soldier spent two years, and at most five years, overseas. Those who suffered due to gas were made to stay in Europe for further care. Distraught over the effort and desperate to be reunited with loved ones, troops often lied about injuries. In the future, untrue testimony would haunt soldiers when their health benefits and veteran pensions were denied over supposed clean bills of health from wartime physicians' declarations.

Canadian soldiers stayed on as an army of occupation until 1919 by the Rhine river. By fall, almost the entire Corps had returned. Countless parades, dinners, speeches, and other celebrations were showered on the Old Boys.

Much had changed in the colony the soldiers left. In June, the Paris Peace Conference, The Treaty of Versailles, affirming the war to be over, came into effect. Canada's signature, autonomous from Great Britain's, was penned to the declaration. Thus, from Canada's war effort, the dominion was granted nationhood status. Borden was given membership to the Councils of the Empire and represented Canada as independent from Britain in the League of Nations.

Laurier died of a stroke in February. September saw the Prince of Wales lay the cornerstone for the Peace Tower.

Along with the returning soldiers came the Spanish Flu. The government did everything in its power to halt the epidemic. Surpassing all educational services and quarantines, the virus traversed the country in a week. Entire communities disappeared. The Indigenous and Inuit Peoples endured the worst. Labrador saw one third of its citizens die and half the Inuit. Prince Edward Island isolated itself from the rest of the country. Fifty thousand Canadians were gone in mere weeks. The average life expectancy fell to the late thirties from the early fifties.

Nicolas heard his parents discussing Okak, Labrador, when they thought he was not present. Almost all two hundred and sixty residents succumbed to the flu. The mere tens who did live attempted to save the corpses from the starving sled dogs before escaping. Thankfully, his family was spared. One in six Canadians had been infected by the flu. More than four hundred Ottawans died. The countrywide crisis led to the creation of the Federal Department of Health.

The patriot's blood's the seed of freedom's tree[243]. It was an ugly winter day in Vauréal's oak grove. At peace after war[244], the Laurentiens were privately commemorating the first anniversary of the Armistice. Those who lived and those who died, they were one in noble pride[245]; Michel and Étienne were quietly discussing numbers with one another. Currie had disclosed to Borden a detail about the dreadful spring campaign that happened the year before: "Sir Douglas Haig himself told me that in the dark days of last spring, the one comforting thought that he had was that he still had the Canadian Corps intact, and that he should never regard himself as beaten until that Corps was put into battle." Auré was standing with Michel and Étienne in silence, his new normal.

"Six hundred and twenty thousand in uniform... Four hundred and twenty-five thousand overseas... One hundred and seventy-two thousand wounded... More than three thousand, eight hundred were Prisoners of War... Eight thousand, eight hundred served in the Royal Navy... Twenty thousand underage fought. More than two thousand, two hundred were killed in battle. The fifteen and sixteen-year olds

---

[243] A Canadian World War I epitaph

[244] A Canadian World War I epitaph

[245] A Canadian World War I epitaph

who fell in the line of duty numbered nearly one hundred... Three thousand, one hundred and forty-one nursing sisters volunteered. Two thousand eight hundred and forty-five overseas. Fifty-three Bluebirds laid down their lives... Four thousand or one in three Aboriginal men, who were able to fight, served. Aboriginal Canadians were amongst the most admired snipers in France and in Belgium. Francis Pegahmagabow, an Ojibwa man from Perry Sound Band, Ontario, was awarded the Military Medal as well as two bars. Pegahmagabow was the highest decorated Indigenous soldier of the war... One in four Canadian males of military age were in uniform... One in seven Canadians were killed in the various operations of warfare... One in ten Canadians had been in uniform... One in five Newfoundlanders were in uniform. Newfoundland had more than six thousand two hundred sons and daughters serve in its Regiment. More than one in five Newfoundlanders in uniform were killed in action. Two thousand five hundred were casualties or Prisoners of War. One hundred and seventy-nine sailors perished at sea. Thirteen hundred and five found their final resting place overseas... Seventy Victoria Crosses were awarded to the Corps. One Victoria Cross was awarded to Newfoundland, garnered by seventeen-year old Private Thomas Ricketts. Ricketts would remain the youngest living Victoria Cross recipient soldier in history... The death toll: sixty thousand Union Jacks were buried around her Canadian sons as faithful British subjects were laid to rest under their King's flag... The Western Front had not moved more than forty kilometers in either direction from the commencement of the duration."

The young nation of eight million offered exceptional assistance to the Allies. But the extraordinary achievements Canada accomplished and obstacles overcome were not done in solidarity. Centuries of tolerance between the two families came to the vanguard of stupendousness, not to be seen again.

Conscription concluded solely by the Armistice. Forty thousand conscripts went to England. Twenty-five thousand were sent to France. Conscripted men made critical contributions to the Corps' successes in the last year of the war, and at the same time, the conscription crisis had almost caused civil war. The country had never nor would see again the brink of such a calamity.

The grand pride of Quebec, the 22nd Battalion, fought with distinction in all operations of war the battalion had seen action in. Over the duration, the 22nd's strength was reinforced in surplus of ten additional times. In 1921, the battalion would be bestowed the title of "Royal" by George after its accomplishments in the war.

Federal soldiers remained in Montreal until 1919, and the effects of the 1917 election would disfigure politics and the veil of solidarity between the two families for years to follow.

Mme. Laurentien was wearing black except for her white collar. Older females often wore second mourning until death. The strict Victorian mourning traditions had lessened considerably as a result of the war. However, the majority of Edwardians retained their old customs.

'Tis only those that have loved & lost can realize the bitter cost[246].

"Words fail our loss to tell[247]," Mme. Laurentien said quietly, as tears fell down her cheeks to Fr.—. "Beneath this stone in soft repose is laid a mother's dearest pride[248]," she finished as Fr.— pulled her towards him.

---

[246] A Canadian World War I epitaph

[247] A Canadian World War I epitaph

[248] A Canadian World War I epitaph

"Greater love hath no man than he lay down his life for his brother[249]," he replied. He tried to comfort her in an embrace.

"Our baby boy[250] has given us great joy, though," she smiled faintly while wiping tears away. She was holding the hand of Toulouse, a primary school-aged boy they adopted, orphaned by Tuberculosis. Thousands of children were left without parents after the flu. Many families took in orphans and raised them as their own.

She went on the explain the loveliest way to mend a broken heart was to give away what one wished one had. After burying three sons in as many years, for the first time since they lost Pierre, because the family adopted Toulouse, she felt like the sun would shine tomorrow.

O mother of sorrow, for the love of this son[251], Mme. Laurentien would shortly receive three Silver Crosses, informally called the medal that no mother wanted. Only mothers who made the "Supreme sacrifice in the name of righteousness" were granted comparable "Undying Glory." Attached to the purple ribbon, carved on the silver was a Maltese Christian cross, along with a crown and maple leaf. This was a uniquely Canadian honour, an emblem signifying the country was a crucial component to the Allied triumph and equal to other countries in the Empire.

He wrought his country lasting good[252]; Étienne had been granted the Military Cross and the Distinguished Service Order. The measure of life is not its span but the use made of it[253]; Auré had been given his wife's various medals, awarded to her posthumously, for services rendered during

---

[249] A Canadian World War I epitaph
[250] A Canadian World War I epitaph
[251] A Canadian World War I epitaph
[252] A Canadian World War I epitaph
[253] A Canadian World War I epitaph

the epidemic. The purple ribbon with the Lion and "For Valor" was pinned to Nicolas' chest. Auré had disposed of his Victoria Cross to Nicolas.

The daughters were all present. Pierrette had been given permission to leave the convent to attend the ceremony. Not all the Laurentien daughters were yet married. Given so many young men died during active service, many girls would never go on to marry.

The servants stood behind the family. After centuries of estates demanding one hundred servants, the same properties needed less than fifty after the war. Vauréal now employed mere tens of servants.

Those who desired to live went out to death[254]. Nicolas looked to the graves of his brothers. *Unis dans la mort comme ils l'étaient dans la vie*[255] (United in death as they were in life), he thought. Nicolas knew he was fortunate; many families lost more than three immediate relatives from the effort and Influenza. The three marble tombstones sat upon empty graves. Young men, ye have overcome the wicked one[256]; Canada's sons were laid to rest in Empire war graves overseas. A large maple leaf was carved at the top of each tombstone. The youngest of three brothers who gave their lives for humanity[257], Pierre was buried underneath the largest oak along with his brothers. Their epitaphs were in Latin. Pierre's epitaph read, *Sleep on, my brave young hero son, beneath your laurels so bravely won. Mum*[258]. Just a high-school boy, but a real man[259], Pierre had a second

---

[254] A Canadian World War I epitaph

[255] A Canadian World War I epitaph

[256] A Canadian World War I epitaph

[257] A Newfoundland World War I epitaph

[258] A Canadian World War I epitaph

[259] A Canadian World War I epitaph

inscription that read, *Age Fifteen*. On either side of Pierre were his brothers. Sorrow vanquished, labour ended, Jordan passed[260], Frédéric's epitaph stated, *Like Moses' bush he mounted higher, flourished unconsumed by fire*[261]. He was killed when he was twenty-six years old, the average age of a Canadian soldier. He saved others, himself he could not save[262]; Jean-Baptiste's inscription read, *He died to save another*[263]. He perished at Ancre Heights during the Somme and was one of 18,000 Canadians with no known grave.

Death is swallowed up in victory, memoria in aeterna[264] (Latin for "In everlasting memory"); epitaphs for Canada's Glorious Dead in France, Belgium, England, and at home were of, *Nothing left but beautiful memories, his loving wife and baby... Write upon his grave, he died that Britain might endure... A son of England—from Canada, given to the Empire... He responded to the mother country's call... Who died for King and country... A Canadian boy who gave his life for the Empire and freedom... Britannia, guard well in peace our loved one's resting place... One of the many Canadian Indians who died for the Empire... Via Sacra. Of such are empires made... Beloved daughter & sister who answered the call of country and honor... For love of the Empire he lives in the freedom he died to save... For King and country thus he fell, a tyrant's arrogance to quell... He died for England. It is well... Duty nobly done for King and Motherland... For King and country. Pour la patrie* (For the homeland)... *She fell facing Britain's foe... For England, Home and Duty... Our only boy is sleeping in Flanders fields where poppies blow...*

---

260   A Canadian World War I epitaph
261   A Canadian World War I epitaph
262   A Canadian World War I epitaph
263   A Canadian World War I epitaph
264   A Canadian World War I epitaph

One of Canada's gifts to the Empire, a life... Au Roi et au Patrie un fils du Canada a noblemen tout donné (To King and Country a son of Canada has nobly given all)... *Indian—Tribe 6 Nations. Died for honour of Empire... British Columbia Indian. Died for King and country... England called, who is for liberty? Who for right? I stood forth... She did her duty for King and country... Killed in action doing his duty like a British soldier... Our boy, England's man... In loving memory of our beloved sons who died for King and Country... For the Glory of the Grand Old Flag... For his country's sake... Mortuus est pro Canada* (Latin for "He died for Canada")... *He is not dead whose memory still is living within a nation's heart... O Dieu, prenez ma vie pour votre gloire et celle de Canada-Francais* (O God, take my life for your glory and the glory of French-Canada)... *An Indian. To his country's call doing his duty. That is all... One of Canada's best... A gallant soldier under his own and adopted flag... He gave his word & died for home & country... For Canada he served... Beloved only son, gone home with his uniform on and his duty done... He died fighting for the country he loved so much... I lie here, mother, but victory is ours... Far from his Canadian home our soldier boy is sleeping... Spirit in Heaven, Body in France, Memory in Canada... He died for Canada and the Empire... 'Tis the mark of a nation's hero... Died at Vimy Ridge... Over him now the red poppies grow, nodding a lullaby of rest to our dear boy... He fought the foes of Canada and died on a battle-field... Our lad is a hero, Great Canada's pride. For glory he died... Honour the memory of Canada's bravest and best... He shall have dominion from sea to sea... For Canada... A French Canadian's love of mother and Canada... Vive le Canada* (Long Live Canada)... *He died to help the maple leaf to live... A gallant Canadian who gave his life for his country... Beloved son, proud Canadian... The brave rest in a nation's love and never die... This corner of a foreign field shall be forever Canada... Tomorrow will be Canada's day... The Maple Leaf Forever... O Canada, He stood on guard for thee... In years to come when time is olden, Canada's dream shall be of them.*

Lines from Lieutenant-Colonel physician John McCrae's "In Flanders Fields" were impressed upon all Empire war graves.

Michel opened the ceremony by stating, "Que ton sacrifice et nos prières t'ouvrent les portes du ciel. La famille[265] (May your sacrifice and our prayers open the gates of Heaven to you. The family)."

After the final blessing was given, Bijou stepped forward. "That Canada has become a nation in her own right, there is an on-going discussion for a new flag. The Prime Minister would like a new flag to represent the country's new identity. Many say that since Canada fought under the Union Jack, the country should remain steadfast to England. The debate is causing quite a stir, though it has nonetheless garnered some two thousand entries. One flag in contention is blue, red, and white. There is a bar on either side and a tri-maple leaf in the center.

However, there is another in consideration. The poem I wrote for this one is entitled, 'The Red and White Flag.'" The gathered stood in stoic resignation. Bijou drew breath,

"Representing peace, equality, and character
What Canadians are fighting for
What this young man died for
His casket was draped with the red and white flag

---

[265] A Canadian World War I epitaph

The maple leaf rested atop
The blocks wrapped around either side of the casket
This Canadian flag
Was chaperoning one of her son's home
Duty bound to accompany this man across the Atlantic
The flag will ensure the soldier is seen
On the long journey in place of his family
For she carries with herself the weight of the nation
The flag draped over the casket
Embraced the soldier with the debt of all Canadians
And all others in countries who this peacekeeper
paid the ultimate sacrifice to free
Ambassador to thy nation
The flag will be presented to his mother in
condolence of servitude of the soldier's homeland
Guarding this lifeless body
The soldier is laid to rest
With the respect of the nation
Like a torch holding an eternal flame
Symbolized in thy flag"

Bijou then read Binyon's "For the Fallen." "At the going down of the sun and in the morning—," but Nicolas was not paying mind. He was looking up at his uncle. Ottawa and Regina named parks and buildings after Auré for his Victoria Cross status. Nicolas did not need to be told that Auré was perpetually smoking and in alcoholic spirits. Such was obvious from his appearance. His normally broad shoulders now looked almost monstrous in their discrepancy. People stopped going to church twice on Sundays due to the war. What worried Nicolas most was his uncle had stopped attending church altogether. A widower wore mourning for at least one year and joined society three months after the death. His uncle had been well taken care of after the war and the epidemic from those who his wife had aided. However, after a short time, Auré had become a recluse. Nicolas was reminded of a ghost when he looked at Auré, given his unnaturally white pallor. When one visited Pembina, one spoke solely to Llewellyn. Étienne would wake the household with his nightmares. Nicolas wondered if Auré did too. At least Étienne had his family to comfort him. There was a fecklessness, almost abhorrence, among the returned men. Auré was no exception. He was moving away. He gave no indication to where he was to go. He rarely spoke to the Laurentiens anymore, declining all regular invitations to dine. Michel could not ask him where he was moving to, as the gentleman's code did not permit Michel to ask such questions. A gentleman should honour another's privacy. Even so, Nicolas desperately wanted to know.

After the last post was played, the family and servants started for the manor. Nicolas stood looking at Auré while he walked by. During the war, numerous strikes and riots, notably the Winnipeg General Strike, prompted speculation that revolution could follow. These problems reached crisis proportions the last year of the war. Government responded by way of a federal police organization. In 1920, the Dominion Police would disband and become part of the Royal North-West Mounted Force. The King would change the name to the Royal Canadian Mounted Police.

Nicolas wanted to cheer Auré and said loud enough only for Auré to hear, as the others walked around the pair, "You'll always be my captain."

Auré turned back and ran a hand through Nicolas' hair and, trying to comfort him, said, "The brave never die, being deathless they but change their country's arms for more, their country's heart[266]." Auré then made for the manor alone. The image of his fallen red knight would give Nicolas nightmares the rest of his childhood. In saluting the army, Auré removed his top hat, and as gracefully as a dancing master, made a final dashing bow to the Armed Forces and retired with full military honours.

---

[266] A Canadian World War I epitaph

Alberta

The late 1920's

The Saturday weather was just below zero degrees. The clear blue sky belonged to a beautiful winter day. The iconic sound of steel hitting ice, that felt like home to a Canadian, was heard repeatedly in the background. The puck had been dropped at four in the afternoon. There were two hours of daylight to play.

With his skates laced over his shoulder and hockey stick in hand, Nicolas set out for the local rink. He was to meet the rest of his platoon. After walking nearly a mile, he found the rink. Nicolas sat down on the bench, next to the other sole seated player.

"Welcome to Canmore," said the man, who introduced himself as Allan Tipperney. He was average height with a slim, toned frame, and dark brown eyes. Tipperney was taking a short drink during a pause in the game. The other players were still on the ice.

"Thank you. It's quite the view," Nicolas returned.

Nestled at the bottom of the majestic Rocky Mounties, Canmore, Alberta was a sight to behold. The lone bald eagle that soared high overhead could scarcely be seen.

A considerably tall player, stationary and leaning over, was catcalling to another on the rink, making his teammates laugh.

Tipperney tossed Nicolas a jersey, which he put on. The jersey's name read, *Humboldt.* His number was thirty.

"We'll formally introduce you to all the guys once the game is over. But for now, I'll give you the run down. The goalie to the left is one of the best shots in the province. The man playing forward was the rookie until you showed up. The right wingman is second in command. And that man—," he paused.

The tall player had stood up and was skating towards them.

"That man is the captain. A war hero from back east, although he doesn't like to talk about it," Tipperney said.

Nicolas looked over and became thunderstruck.

The captain came to a stop in front of the sideboard. In his skates, he stood towering, about seven feet tall. He wore a plaid shirt that was undulating in the light wind against his broad shoulders and tanned frame.

"You made it. How lovely it is to see you again. A spitting image of Pierre. Your brothers would have been proud."

Once Nicolas recovered from shock, the pair shook hands.

"How was Depot?" asked Auré.

"I graduated at the top of my class. Passed all the tests with flying colours, except for the height one. Almost failed it."

The pair laughed. The family, the war, Canmore, and each other's ranks were briefly discussed. Auré began skating backwards. His hockey stick, held in either hand, rested across his large thighs.

"Lace up Nico, and welcome to the Force," he said in his signature commanding tone. Before Auré turned, he gave a slight nod of acknowledgement at the incredulous expression Nicolas wore.

"He's married to—" Tipperney explained further.

"He's married!" Nicolas shouted. He turned to stare at Tipperney.

The game carried on.

"To a lady named Henrietta. She's from back east too. They have twin girls, both as blond and as blue eyed as their mother. One of them carries his first wife's name. The other is named for—"

Nicolas resumed looking at Auré.

"The story concerning his first wife is rather remarkable."

Nicolas did not bother to stop Tipperney to say he already knew the story.

"The last year of the war, his wife became ill. As soon as he found out how sick she was, he left the front. We've never even seen him leave the office early. The sole thing that surpsasses his work ethic is how religious he is. He must have loved her. His wife was sick for months. She was bedridden for weeks. She died just hours after he came home. They said she waited for him."

There was a break away. All the players charged the puck.

"Apparently, they had quite the love affair," Tipperney finished.

"One for the ages," was the muttered response.

Nicolas stared incredulously as Auré skated down the rink. Then Nicolas broke into a smile while he watched his captain. His fallen red knight had mounted.

Someone took a shot on the net. The goalie deflected the puck off to the side. The puck hit the sideboards and was sent down the opposing end. Auré and his mates dug their skates into the ice and raised their hockey sticks in the air as they all turned sharply and tore off down the rink after the puck.

Acknowledgements

All officer's quotes are exactly the officer's testimonies and are denoted by italics or quotation marks

Books

Berton, Pierre. *Vimy.* Anchor Canada, 1986.

Bieler, Philippe. *Onward Dear Boys: A Family Memoir of the Great War.* McGill-Queen's University Press, 2014.

Bird, Will R. *And We Go On:* A Memoir of the Great War. McGill-Queen's University Press, 2014.

Brown, Malcolm and Shirley Seaton. *Christmas Truce.* Pan Macmillan, 2014.

Clint, Mabel. *Our Bit: Memories of War Service by a Canadian Nursing Sister.* Barwick Ltd, 1934.

Cook, Tim. *At the Sharp End: Canadians Fighting the Great War, 1914-1916.* Volume One. Penguin Books Ltd, 2007.

Cook, Tim. *Shock Troops: Canadians Fighting the Great War, 1917-1918.* Volume Two. Penguin Books Ltd, 2008.

Cook, Tim. *Vimy: The Battle and The Legend.* Penguin Random House Canada, 2017.

Douglas, Tom. *Valour at Vimy Ridge.* Formac Publishing Company Limited, 2017.

Dutil, Patrice and David MacKenzie. *Embattled Nation: Canada's Wartime Election of 1917.* Dundurn, 2017.

Glassford, Sarah and Amy Shaw. *A Sisterhood of Suffering and Service: Women and Girls of Canada and Newfoundland During the First World War.* UBC Press, 2012.

Granatstein, J.L. *The Greatest Victory: Canada's Hundred Days, 1918.* Oxford University Press, 2014.

Granatstein, J.L. *Hell's Corner: An Illustrated History of Canada's Great War, 1914-1918.* Douglas & McIntyre Ltd., 2004.

Jankowski, Paul. *Verdun: The Longest Battle of the Great War.* Oxford University Press, 2016.

Leach, Norman. *Passchendaele: Canada's Triumph and Tragedy on the Fields of Flanders.* Coteau Books, 2008.

McGeer, Eric. *Canada's Dream Shall Be of Them: Canadian Epitaphs of the Great War.* Uniform Press, 2017.

Overy, Richard. *World War I: The Definitive Visual History from Sarajevo to Versailles.* Penguin Random House, 2014.

Morton, Desmond. *Fight or Pay: Soldiers' Families in the Great War.* UBC Press, 2004.

Morton, Desmond. *When Your Number's Up: The Canadian Soldier in the First World War.* Penguin Random House Canada, 1993.

Reid, Mark Collin, editor. *Canada's Great War Album.* *HarperCollins* Publishers, 2014.

Toman, Cynthia. *Sister Soldiers of the Great War: The Nurses of the Canadian Army* Medical Corps. UBC Press, 2016.

Webb, Jonathan. *Canada's Wars: An Illustrated History.* Scholastic Canada, 2010.

Wilson, J. Brent. *A Family of Brothers: Soldiers of the 26th New Brunswick Battalion in the Great War.* Goose Lane Edition, 2018.

Websites

"46th Canadian Infantry Battalion, CEF," *The Encyclopedia of Saskatchewan.* https://esask.uregina.ca/entry/46th_canadian_infantry_battalion_cef.jsp.

"A Battalion Apart: Tales of the Princess Patricia's Canadian Light Infantry and the Ric-A-Dam-Doo," CBC.ca https://www.cbc.ca/edmonton/interactive/princess-pats/.

"The Battle at Vimy Ridge," *The Vimy Foundation.* https://www.vimyfoundation.ca/learn/vimy-ridge/.

"Canada and the First World War," *Canadian War Museum.* https://www.warmuseum.ca/firstworldwar.

Canada's History. https://www.canadahistory.ca.

The Canadian Encyclopedia. https://www.thecanadianencyclopedia.ca/en.

Canadian Great War Project http://www.canadiangreatwarproject.com.

Canadian Soldiers. https://www.canadiansoldiers.com/.

Dictionary of Canadian Biography. http://www.biographi.ca.

Edwardian Promenade. http://www.edwardianpromenade.com.

Government of Canada. https://www.canada.ca.

The Great War: 1914-1918.

https://ww1.canada.com.

The Great War: 1914-1918.
http://www.greatwar.co.uk.

Historica Canada.
https://www.historicacanada.ca.

"History," *Camerons.ca*.
http://www.camerons.ca/history/.

"Le Canada, A People's History," CBC.ca.
https://www.cbc.ca/history/
EPISCONTENTSE1EP12CH2PA3LE.html.

Legion Magazine.
https://legionmagazine.com/en/.

Library and Archives Canada.
https://www.bac-lac.gc.ca.

The Loyal Edmonton Regiment Military Museum.
https://www.lermuseum.org.

Newfoundland & Labrador in the First World War.
https://www.heritage.nf.ca/first-world-war/index.php.

Princess Patricia's Canadian Light Infantry.
https://ppcli.com.

RCMP Heritage Centre.
https://rcmphc.com.

The Royal Newfoundland Regiment Advisory Council.
http://www.rnfldr.ca/history.aspx.

Saint John Free Public Library.
http://saintjohnlibrary.com.

Seaforth Highlanders.
https://www.seaforthhighlanders.ca/.

Veterans Affairs Canada.
https://www.veterans.gc.ca/eng/remembrance/history/
first-world-war.

"Who's Who: Sir Robert Borden," FirstWorldWar.com.
https://www.firstworldwar.com/bio/borden.htm

Made in the USA
Monee, IL
15 June 2021

71343410R00246